PETER LAWS is an ordained Baptist minister with a taste for the macabre. He writes a monthly column in the *Fortean Times* and also hosts a popular podcast and YouTube show which reviews thriller and horror films from a theological perspective. He lives with his family in Bedfordshire.

peterlaws.co.uk   @revpeterlaws

By Peter Laws

THE MATT HUNTER SERIES
Purged
Unleashed

UNLEASHED

PETER LAWS

Allison & Busby Limited
12 Fitzroy Mews
London W1T 6DW
allisonandbusby.com

First published in Great Britain by Allison & Busby in 2017.

A CIP catalogue record for this book is available from
the British Library.

First Edition

ISBN 978-0-7490-2088-0

Typeset in 11.25/16.25 pt Sabon by
Allison & Busby Ltd.

The paper used for this Allison & Busby publication
has been produced from trees that have been legally sourced
from well-managed and credibly certified forests.

Printed and bound by
CPI Group (UK) Ltd, Croydon, CR0 4YY

Look, Mam . . . it's me!
This book is dedicated to you, with loving thanks for the life and
work that has become mine, only because of you.

'For our struggle is not against flesh and blood, but against the rulers, against the authorities, against the powers of this dark world and against the spiritual forces of evil in the heavenly realms.'

Ephesians 6:12

PART ONE

APOPHENIA

PROLOGUE

The rabbit crawls out of its grave again.
Soil and stone crumbling in its paws.
Twitching, sniffing, seeing light.
Sees more than you ever could.

Rabbit moves from grass to road.
Looking up, and hearing rain.
Mud and wet things on its fur.
Sliding through the waving wood.

People see and hide their smiles.
Some try hard to scratch its belly.
Stays away the best it can.
Makes its way from stone to sand.

Past the grass, and through the trunks.
Rabbit hears her giggling.

Whispers weave, ears prick up.
Rabbit sniffs the air for blood.

Through the tree it settles, staring.
Swinging, swinging she looks out.
She can't see the shadow smiling.
Meant to crawl . . . it's learnt to walk.

Even though the night's way off,
Rabbit waits, and likes the sound.
That she makes upon the ground.
Hind legs slowing, turning round.

Pretty.

CHAPTER ONE

Jo Finch sat in her old primary school, chewing her nails, surrounded by twenty-one other parents. Each of them was painfully folded into a midget school chair with their legs forced under impossibly low desks. The other parents looked sharp and important. Many had taken time off work for this, so a lot wore suits. Jo noticed a lot of the women wore knee-length leather boots that had really decent stitching. They were absolutely *not* from Primark, put it that way. While Jo, on the other hand, sat there glowing in the brightest yellow fleece that ever fell from the sun. With matching leggings too.

God.

She felt like a naked Homer Simpson. A walking buttercup, lighting up chins. Her boss at the Merry Poppins Cleaning Company may well have been one of her best mates, but Kassy West was never the type to confuse friendship with favours. She'd given Jo exactly ninety minutes off work for this school tour. There had been no time to change.

It occurred to her that perhaps she didn't need a tour of this school anyway, since she knew every inch of it. Each turn of the corridor, each crack in the concrete playground. A couple of decades ago *she* was the little pigtailed firework running around here, in cheap clothes even then. But while the shape of the place hadn't changed, the vibe of it *really* had. Even the big green radiators were gone. The ones that looked like they'd fallen from an Industrial Revolution steam train. They'd been replaced by some sleek-looking white boxes with a constant red light, blinking on the corner. Good luck melting Crayola on *them*, Jo thought. Then she shivered. Come September next year her daughter Seren would be five, which meant the government had their legal claim on her each weekday. She'd be all by herself in this familiar, unfamiliar place.

The only thing that looked the same colour as the old days was the floor. She rubbed the tip of her trainers against it. Yeah, the hexagonal wood *was* the same. The light caught the historic scratches and scrapes. Maybe there were even a few scuffs from her own little buckled shoes when she sat in this exact part of the classroom, back in 1993. It should have felt like a million years ago. Only it didn't. It didn't at all.

Something throbbed in her gut so she pressed her hand against the yellow.

Her boyfriend Lee sat next to her, smelling of engine oil. She winked at him but he didn't wink back. He was too busy scrolling through his phone, checking to see if the job lot of premium golf tees he'd invested in were selling. They'd met on Tinder three months ago, where he'd described himself as 'an entrepreneur trapped in a mechanic's body'. As he thumbed through the listing, he had his usual business face on. The panicky bite of the lip, his skin white enough to vomit. The *constant* sniffing. Turns out it takes aeons to shift ten thousand of those tees, even if they *were* made of top-grade African Blackwood from Senegal.

She glanced at the huge windows which were covered in crepe paper pumpkins and black cats cut from card. She looked through the skinny legs of a badly scissored witch and gazed across the school field. The roof of the preschool was just about visible over the hedges. Seren was in there *right* now. Four and a half and already living her own life, for one morning a week. Doing stuff Jo couldn't see – which felt great and horrible, all at the same time. Mostly horrible, though. Her hands were probably covered in orange and black paint; her shoes would be filling with sand. Prepping her princess outfit for Halloween, maybe. She'd be doing what kids ought to be doing, *playing* with stuff, because Seren *loved* to play. Jo looked back at the walls of the classroom. Unlike the windows, they had hardly any pictures up at all. They'd stuck maths problems up instead. One of them said 24 minus 16.

24 minus 16? Sheesh.

Even *she* had to work that out on her fingers. She felt that flutter again. Seren could barely count how many feet were stuck on the end of her legs, which brought a quick little thought, like a needle prick to the heart. Perhaps this would be the place her daughter's life would start to fail. Her first step into the loser camp, like her mother.

Jo blinked and looked in front of them, where a gorgeous woman, fresh from the Amazon, rested her head on her husband's shoulder. He was wearing a killer suit and a pricey-looking watch. Really James Bond-y. He kissed the woman on the top of her shiny hair, like they were at the opera or something. She'd bet that family could do 24 minus 16 in six different languages. Bet they shot long division and history questions at their kids all the time. Over every dinner (up at the table) instead of on the couch laughing hard at *SpongeBob SquarePants* and eating nuggets. Like her and Seren did most nights.

Lee was picking his nose, as if being in the back row put him in some sort of invisibility bubble. She nudged him hard and slipped him a tissue under the desk.

'Ta,' he smiled.

He had beautiful teeth. She'd thought that the moment they'd ordered their first Meat Feast in Pizza Hut on that first date. When he smiled as they brought it out and slung it in front of him, she'd thought wow. He cleans his teeth *really* well. He's hygienic.

She jumped when the classroom door suddenly rattled open and swung wide on its hinge.

'Showtime.' Lee slipped his phone away.

The head teacher swooped in, riding a whoosh of air, with a hefty mane of permed white hair that bounced as she moved. She sprang up and down on the balls of her bright-red prostitute boots like she might blast off into the ceiling at any moment. She was clapping her hands repeatedly, eyes wide. A seal on ecstasy.

Lee whispered, 'Someone throw that woman a fish.'

Jo sniggered.

'Hellooooooo Class! I'm Mrs Walmsley and I'm delighted to welcome you to Menham Lower School.' She was wearing a blue knitted shawl over her shoulders, covered in red butterflies. *So many bracelets, jangling.* 'Mums and dads! Carers and guardians! It's a privilege and a pleasure to see you all here at our Open Day. I hope that you'll feel as much a part of Menham Lower as your children will. Unless you send them to Newker School, of course, in which case . . . good luck . . .' She pushed her hip out and slapped herself playfully on the hand. 'Better not say that, or *I'll* get put on the naughty step.'

Lee's jaw clicked open.

Jo however, smiled. Because this woman reminded her of a CBeebies presenter and despite the eye-rolls and tuts from the other parents, she thought that was a *good* thing.

Walmsley nodded to a young girl in the corner who wheeled a

table over with a sandbox on top. 'This is Lauren, everybody. One of our teaching assistants. Say hi, Lauren.'

Lauren didn't speak. She half-smiled. She looked about twelve, but was probably twenty.

Walmsley waved her hand across the sandbox like it was a prize fridge on a gameshow. 'Here at Menham Lower we understand the function of fun, the energy of education and the unapologetic priority of play.'

Jo felt her breath flow out. *Maybe this is going to be okay.*

'Your children can *read* about velociraptors in a textbook. Other schools do that. But it's quite another thing when they become a palaeontologist themselves . . . and feel the past in their precious little hands . . .' She turned to her assistant Lauren, who was staring up at the skylight, oblivious. She cleared her throat and fed the line again, only louder. 'And feel it in their *precious little hands*!'

Lauren jerked like she'd been hit by a cattle prod then she plunged her hand into the sand, scrabbling around for a few awkward seconds. She pulled something out. Walmsley leant forward, eyes wide with manic excitement. The look that primary school teachers and serial killers have. 'Oh my goodness, Lauren, what *do* you have there? Is that what I *think* it is?'

When she finally spoke her voice was stilted. Mechanical and monotone. Like someone had just pulled a cord in her back to make her talk. 'Mrs Walmsley. It *is* what you think it is. Look . . . an amazing diplodocus.'

'A diplodocus! Wow!' Then in a sharp whisper, through teeth, 'Hold it higher, Lauren.'

Walmsley quickly pushed the sandbox aside and motioned for the adults to stand. 'And with that . . . let the tour commence.'

Seats scraped back and everyone went to stand. For one jumpy second Jo thought her backside was trapped in the chair. That she'd have to do the entire tour bent double, with a red plastic seat wedged onto her bright yellow arse. But Lee grabbed her hand and helped her shimmy free. She glanced back through the window, at Seren's preschool one last time.

'Come on, you,' Lee said, sliding an arm around her shoulders. 'Seren's going to love it here.'

She smiled at him, at the way he squeezed her.

The tour was lengthy but excellent. The school was clean and well looked after. The lottery grant had clearly bought some decent paint. When *she* was a pupil here, back in the day, the place looked more like a concentration camp, with a few Rugrats posters for emotional balance.

Best of all, though, the pupils looked happy. Really content. They were amazingly polite too. All in uniform. Grey skirts and trousers. Bright-red jumpers with white shirt collars sticking out. She could picture Seren wearing that. The two of them on that first morning next September. The morning that was racing toward her like an out-of-control Tube train. Her in her yellow cleaner's uniform, Seren in her red school uniform and the little lunchbox they'd especially buy for her first day. Which was the first day for both of them, she knew that. The new stage.

Jo had this naive hope that she'd keep her sobbing in until *after* she'd dropped Seren off. She didn't want to freak the kid out. She'd save her implosion for the car, but she'd drive round the block away from the school. Up by the ambulance station. She'd already picked the spot.

Throughout the tour Jo was doing what every other parent was doing. Mentally painting her child into each classroom, into each corridor. In the toilets Walmsley discussed the importance of hygiene, but Jo was too busy seeing Seren standing at those Lilliput taps. Were they too high? They looked it. She imagined Seren washing her tiny hands after the plastic frog on the wall had vomited handwash onto them. In the classrooms she'd see Seren sitting at a desk, scrawling a picture of Mummy or Peppa Pig, or more often than not, their little rabbit Six. She hoped the kids got plenty of chances to draw here.

Now and again she'd see the other parents catching each other's eye to share a very particular blow of breath. The sort of gear change sound that signalled to them all that the first stage of their kid's life was truly swinging shut. For ever.

The melancholy was multilayered too. Because Jo had no other kids. Doctors said she couldn't have any more, since Seren's arrival nearly killed her. So every time Walmsley opened her mouth and pointed to some wallchart, it gave Jo that prickly panic she sometimes got at night. When she wondered what the hell she was going to do with her life once the State took over the childcare. Merry Poppins Cleaning full time, with *her* back? She'd rather adopt a Brazilian street child.

Could she do that, actually?

It was in the playground that Jo stopped seeing Seren.

Instead, Jo saw her five-year-old self trying to hopscotch across the exact same cement that stood here today. Stumbling like an idiot, because all the Finch family members were about as coordinated as a kite in a tornado. She remembered other kids laughing at her. Calling her 'lanky legs' . . . oh, to be called 'lanky' again when these days she was more globe shaped. But then one clear image came, chiselled into her memory. It swam to the surface and made things so much better.

Of her and the three girls she miraculously fell in with, six months into this primary school. Girls she *still* hung out with, even today. *The* gang. *Her* gang. The best set of friends you could possibly get. Right now she pictured them all, walking the playground of her memory. Her now boss, Kassy West. Steph Ellis, who was a supply teacher at this school, nowadays. How crazy was that? Steph teaching music in classes she learnt to play the recorder in. Steph was a cool woman. Jo loved Steph a lot. And then there was good old Rachel Wasson who nobody ever saw any more since she moved away, but who she thought of often.

She pictured herself and those girls, back as kids in uniform here. *Strutting*, even at six and seven. Owning it, like they would own it all the way through their teens. Flipping a finger at the chumps on the side saying, *ha! We're kind of a big thing.*

Then walking alongside them, she suddenly saw little Holly Wasson. Flickering in the background like a projected image from a faulty bulb.

She felt suddenly cold. Had the sensation of small blunt fingers touching the small of her back and reaching up. She blinked the image away.

Lee caught her staring. 'Jo?'

'Do you think Seren will make friends?'

'She'll have to, won't she?'

Wrong answer. She glared at him.

He coughed. 'I mean, of course she'll make friends. *You* did, didn't you?'

'Best ones ever.' She noticed the parents had started heading to the music block. 'Steph's working today. She says her kids are going to play us some Halloween songs on the kazoo.'

He gave an exaggerated gasp, 'You know, I have *always* dreamt I'd hear that in my life. Come on.'

She smiled as he laced his hands into hers. Then they hurried across the playground, laughing.

They were the last ones into the music block.

It was a decent size. Probably three times bigger than the other classrooms. Yamaha keyboards sat in a row by the wall. A huge blue Ikea crate was filled with tambourines, shakers, and that odd, hollow, cylinder thing you scraped with a stick that nobody *ever* sees again once they hit secondary school. The room was filled with rows of wooden benches in front of a small, temporary stage. A set of curtains was currently closed, splashed with glitter stars and sequins. A murmur came from behind them, which sounded like excited children. One of the parents budged up to let Jo and Lee squeeze on the end.

'Fab school, isn't it?' a mother said. She smelt very rich.

Jo nodded, but she didn't smile. Because she had just noticed that something was wrong.

Lauren, the teaching assistant, was struggling with a cupboard door, while Mrs Walmsley hurried around the class, looking like she'd lost something, or rather lost *someone*.

'Where's Steph?' Lee leaned into Jo. 'Thought you said she was the MC for this?'

Jo looked around, fingers tapping. 'She's supposed to be.'

Just then, she noticed Walmsley's face shift. She'd stopped looking for Steph and was now looking puzzled at the wall behind them. Jo twisted to see what the big deal was. It was a wall filled with a kids picture display. Creatures that had featured in classical music, it seemed. 'Flight of the Bumblebee', 'Peter and the Wolf', that sort of stuff. Only they were all upside down. Every one of them. Even the banner above them had been flipped. Jo turned her head on its side to read it.

Music of the Animals.

She ran her eyes across the manic hand-drawn streaks of foxes, cows, goats then she saw a scrawl of an angry black crayon animal.

A hare.

She stiffened and looked away. Thought of Holly again.

Relax. Breathe.

'What's wrong?' Lee's voice.

'Nothing,' she shook her head and turned back. 'Nervous about Seren.'

Walmsley was back now, pulling at the cupboard door and

shaking her head. Then she whispered into Lauren's ear, who nodded and hurried out of the classroom.

'Alright, folks. There'll be just a teeny-tiny delay. We can't seem to get into the music cupboard to grab the kazoos.' She turned to the curtain. 'And you can't play "Monster Mash" on a kazoo without . . . a kazoo. Can you kids?'

Voices spoke in unison from behind the curtain. 'No, Mrs Walmsley.' It was either cute or creepy, depending on what mood you were in. The latter, Jo decided.

'Lauren's just gone to find our music teacher, Mrs Ellis. So please, make yourself comfortable. And in just a few moments we'll hear some wonderful music from some wonderful children.'

'Your mate is *so* in the shit,' Lee whispered.

'Shhhh.' She looked over at the corridor, hoping to see Steph trotting toward the door. But Lauren was already coming back. Alone. She pushed through the doors, panting, and held up the key.

Walmsley beamed. 'Stop the clock! Kazoo's are coming.'

The invisible kids cheered into the curtain.

Where the hell is she? Jo checked her phone for a message. Nothing.

'Maybe she's ill?' Lee said. 'Or her *kid's* ill, maybe?'

Jo didn't speak. She was too busy watching Lauren walk to the store cupboard door. Then even before the key was fully in the lock, Jo stood up because something was prickling her skin and telling her to move.

'Er . . . what are you doing?' Lee whispered.

She took a step forward. A few of the parents looked up at her, frowning. *Where's the bright fat yellow one off to? Is she doing the clown dance at this show? Is that why she's dressed like a moron?*

'Jo?' Lee grabbed the corner of her fleece. Embarrassed. 'Sit down.'

'Something's wrong.'

Another step.

Then another, pushing herself though the confused parents. She moved toward the two teachers who now had their backs to the crowd. They were reaching for the cupboard handle. She wasn't exactly sure why she was moving, only that she was and that she ought to. She also knew not to look at the wall behind her, where all those upturned animal eyes were watching her.

Could she hear them? Snuffling, snarling, sniffing?

Especially the hare.

She had a sudden flicker of memory. Her and the girls again. Teenagers now and as tight a gang as ever. Laughing by Kelsey Pond in the park. Rating the boys in their class out of ten and chucking pebbles in the water. Counting the ripples while Holly stood looking at them through the branches of the big tree. Wanting to play. Always wanting that.

Then the memory vanished because an animal was growling loudly. And this time it was real.

It was just as the door swung open. The parents behind her had probably assumed the sound was just a creaky hinge. But she knew straight away that it was a living, breathing creature.

Then there was another noise that drowned the growl out.

Mrs Walmsley screamed.

Jo's first thought was, *Wow. That's really high-pitched.* How *crazy* that sounded, given where they were. You go into a primary school and you kind of expect to hear kids screaming now and again. But not the teachers. Never the teachers. Walmsley sounded like a mad woman in a tower, wailing at the sea. But then it didn't really matter any more, because lots of people were screaming now, scrambling over each other in a bundle of floundering limbs. Benches scraped and toppled over. Some flew for the exit. Selfish gits.

While the more heroic ones leapt toward the stage to grab the children behind the curtain. The kids were squealing and crying themselves now, spilling out of the gaps to see what was making the grown-ups roar.

In the commotion it seemed like Jo was the only one in the room who was rushing *toward* the opening cupboard door. The only one who got a good look at poor Lauren, who was now stumbling backwards from it in a mad, skittish dance. Her arms and fingers grasped at the air as she fell backwards from the growling thing.

Jo saw it, just then.

Just as the skinny calf of Lauren's leg slammed into the front bench. Just as Lauren buckled and started to drop to the floor with a gasp. When her head dropped down like a tonne weight and replacing it was a huge black shape that lurched out from the cupboard. It sprang up on Lauren's chest and the stage exploded with kids screaming. *So* much noise.

And there it was, pinning Lauren to the bench.

A huge black animal, that Jo thought might not be an animal at all, but some sort of man who might spring up on its hind legs at any moment. But no, it was an animal. In fact, it was a dog. A dog that she knew. It was Steph Ellis's Labrador, Samson. Growling at first and squinting a lot, like it had only just discovered light. At one point it looked up at the ceiling, and the fluorescent strip lights picked up its muzzle, caked with blood. Blood that looked dry. The side of its stomach was pulsing in and out as it panted frantically. Then it was startled by a scream and it jerked its head down to find the source. It nuzzled into Lauren's neck, digging it's teeth in so it could dig the sound out. Jo saw fresh, thin-looking blood squirting across the floor.

Oh, God. That girl.

Jo lurched forward to help, but quickly felt a heavy hand grab her shoulder to yank her back. It was Lee and a few of the other parents. The guy in the suit and his maths whizz wife. They were gripping small metal chairs in their hands, hunched over like gorillas. Lauren yelled out for help in a muffled, underwater voice and within seconds the growling stopped. Instead the classroom was filled with horrible thuds and wet squelches as Lee and the other parents hammered the crazed dog into oblivion. Lauren cowered and sobbed silently, under them. Her little frame jerked with the blows as the dog finally slid off. Parents frantically tried to close the curtains. Others tried to cover the kids' eyes, but they only had so many hands. Plenty saw. There was lots of future therapy being birthed here.

Jo wanted to help. She really did.

In her head she could vividly see herself dropping to the floor to grab Lauren's hand, which now shook like it was electrified. And with her free hand, Jo would pull out her Samsung and dial for help, and try hard not to slip in Lauren's blood. But she couldn't do any of this noble stuff since she couldn't move. Because there was something in Samson's dying eyes that was flooding Jo's bloodstream with cement. The way he looked at her, even as he crumpled next to Lauren's glistening black shirt. As he heaved out dying gasps as the guy in the suit pummelled his head. She thought she saw Lee put up a hand in front of the man, 'That's enough, mate. Bugger's dead as a doorknob.' Only it came out really slow, in a long, drawn-out drone.

Deeeaaaaaadassssaaaaadoooooooorrknobbbb.

Jo still couldn't move. Because she kept staring at the way Samson's eyes rolled backward into his head, toward the cupboard behind him, as if he wanted to show her something in his final seconds.

She wondered just then if this entire sixty seconds of insanity was simply to present her with what he had done. You know, like cats do after they've killed a baby pigeon? How they drop it at your feet and say . . . *this is for you.*

She kept thinking the same thought, over and over. You have to call Kassy. And Rachel. Yes, even Rachel. You have to call Rachel Wasson and get her back home. You have to *make* her come back. You have to gather the girls, and she wondered if that was a message from the dog too.

Gather them.

She followed the dog's insane, dying gaze and looked at the storeroom door, now open. The basket of kazoos lay strewn across the floor, swimming in blood. The light wasn't on, but even from here, Jo could see the dim shape of her friend Steph Ellis in a shadow. The frizz of her blonde, natural curl was obvious. Her head was cocked to the side, wet-looking. She looked like a life-sized puppet with the strings cut. Her legs and arms folded at weird, jaunty angles. And like a puppet, her wide eyes stared out with pupils turned to painted wood. Her throat looked totally black and Jo thought, why would that be?

Why do you think, you idiot? Why do you think?

Then Jo heard another scream, weaving with the rest. Her own.

CHAPTER TWO

Professor Matt Hunter stood in the long, bone-white corridor of the Arts and Humanities block, drumming his fingers on the hardback book in his hand. He was completely alone, unless you counted the series of life-sized statues that lined the corridor. A master's level student had sculpted them all out of chrome and was exhibiting the entire clan this month. Most of them were dictators and megalomaniacs, peppered with an occasional talent show judge. The student should probably get high marks for technique, but low marks for subtlety.

He'd been hovering out here for five minutes now, and in that time Matt had discovered that Stalin had the biggest face. This was handy. He leant towards it and checked his reflection in the curve of Stalin's cheek, stooping because Matt was just over six foot, but Stalin must have been five-four, tops. He swept his fringe into place. His blue silk tie looked as straight as it could possibly get, but he tugged at it anyway. Was having the top button fastened *too* formal? Too Stalin-like?

He unhooked it and saw a Vegas lounge singer staring back.

He opted for somewhere in between. He tightened the tie, left the button loose. That'd do.

The double doors to the Charles Fox lecture hall were right in front of him. Beyond them, he could hear the murmur of people inside. But the rumbling voices were already dying away and the sound moved into a single muffled drone. It was the publisher's voice, Beth. She was giving some long-winded introduction. A list of his achievements, such as they were. A checklist of qualifications, a spattering of awards and prizes. He noticed they'd left out his finest moment to date. Building an original arcade Pac-Man cabinet from scratch last autumn in his garage. Took him months, that did, but Beth skipped it.

This felt awkward out here. Twitchy-feet, pursed-lips awkward.

He'd specifically asked to be allowed to sit in the front row along with everybody else so he could just hop up when it was his time to speak. He'd lectured at this uni for what . . . three years? Never once had he done this lurk-at-the-door, drum roll thing. But Beth worked for the marketing arm of the publishers and she'd insisted that tonight was *Not. A. Lecture!* It was a full-on 'look-at-me' event for which they'd shipped in stage lights and a backdrop. Canapés had been ordered, she had stressed this. He needed to make an entrance. Some newspapers had turned up, including some tabloids. Impact was required. *Think Ted Talks*, Beth kept saying. Over and over. *Think Ted Talks.*

So he stared at the doors and waited for his call. He was dangerously tempted to push the 'look-at-me' button to the max and run into the hall with his arms in the air, squealing like a contestant on *The Price is Right*. Maybe he'd cartwheel up to the lectern and crash right into it. Spin round and finger pistol everybody in his Vegas suit and shout, *Sssssup dogs!* That'd make an impact. That'd be memorable.

A chrome-Hitler, standing a few dictators down, shot Matt a fixed pointed finger and told him to calm down. Told him to breathe.

Matt looked down at what was in his hands. The reason tonight was different to any other.

The book.

The cover image was of a child's hand, holding a brush and painting a smiling face on a rock. The title above it read '*In Our Image: The Gods We Tend to Invent* by Matt Hunter'.

The first time he'd held this bad boy in his hands was a month back. Standing in his dressing gown early one Wednesday, belly full of pancakes and gawping at the box the postman was handing over. Back then he'd skidded on socks across the kitchen tiles and ripped that package apart. Ravished the damn thing. Flung polystyrene snow in giddy fountains around the breakfast bar as Wren and the kids rushed in behind him. He'd said two words in response. Looking at it now, the exact same phrase fluttered out over his breath.

'Holy shit,' he said. His first ever book. And not even an academic tome destined for student satchels and annual eBay cycles. No, this was being pitched as 'popular sociology'. This was aimed at the masses. It'd be sitting in Waterstones alongside footballers' biographies and erotic shenanigans.

He was about to laugh, but the sound quickly fizzled in his throat. Beth's muffled voice had changed its tone. It was growing into that compère crescendo, cranking higher and higher, roughly in line with the beating of his heart. A boxing announcer, setting up the first round. He literally jumped when the double doors opened a crack, the furry seal parting like lips. One of his students popped his face through the gap, a black fringe flopping over his eye. 'Professor?'

'Flynn. Hi.'

'You're on,' then a smile. 'There's quite a crowd in here.' His face was sucked back into the door.

Matt stiffened and looked at his watch, alone for the final few seconds. A tick of memory made him check that the bottom button of his jacket was unfastened. Wren had told him this was the way of sophistication. He stooped and caught a final glimpse of the silver Stalin and had a sudden vivid picture in his mind. Of this same art student next year building an igloo from all the unsold copies of the icy Matt Hunter books that nobody ended up buying.

Focus.

He pushed through the doors and locked down the side hatches of his brain.

He could hear Wren's voice in his head saying, *just enjoy it, okay?*

The lights hit him and it made him squint. At least he was professional enough not to cover his eyes and cower like a frightened deer. Beth was on the front row. She gave him a sharp, solid but noticeably unsmiling thumbs up.

Think Ted Talks; Think Ted Talks.

It wasn't the biggest lecture hall in the world, but he could tell that it was pretty much full.

He hoped they'd remembered his water. He needed water. Like a hefty gulp from a bucket, *right* now.

He trotted up the stairs and the room filled with applause. Not the usual golf clap stuff from his classes. This sounded more like water rushing. He chose not to cartwheel, there were no arm flails, but he was sure his feet felt springier than they normally did. Then as he finally touched the podium his nerves did what they usually did. They dutifully slid back into the shadows and slinked off backstage. Replacing them, he felt a welcome shot of adrenalin kicking in. A goofy sense of fun.

A picture of his book suddenly flipped up on the huge screen

30

behind him. '*In Our Image: The Gods We Tend to Invent* by Professor Matt Hunter'. He heard himself saying it again, 'Holy shit.' He was ninety-seven per cent sure that it was in his head and not out loud, but everybody laughed so he reversed those odds. Then he opened the book and the clapping rippled down from applause, to the familiar seal flapping, to silence. He saw Wren and his seven-year-old-daughter Amelia beaming up at him. Even his oldest, Lucy, looked semi-engaged. Quite the feat.

Remember this, Matt, his brain said. *Log this moment.*

Then he smiled at everybody and said, 'Hi. It's good to be here.' He remembered thinking he sounded incredibly posh. A little too academic. But he ignored it.

He looked down, gently folded the spine open and started to read.

'Don't be fooled by my business card,' Matt read. 'I am *not* a doctor. Yes, I have a doctorate. Yes, the letters "D" and "r" are machine-etched into a plastic plaque on my office door, but obviously I'm not a *doctor* doctor. I study human *belief* not human biology (though in the coming pages you'll be surprised at how often these two disciplines slide into one another). But seriously . . . if you slice straight through the knuckle of your little finger in a drunken lawnmower accident, I can pretty much guarantee you won't be calling the good Dr Hunter to sort it out.'

A few chuckles came from the crowd.

'Now on the other hand, if you see the blood squirting from your hand and you want to ponder its deeper meaning, then I'm your man. If you want me to chart Christianity's obsession with blood symbology, for example, or explain why some naked Aborigines cover themselves in blood before they hit the dance floor, then by all means give me a call.'

31

His daughter Lucy laughed loudly at that, with her little Jack Russell yelp. He smirked.

'But no . . . I'm not a proper doctor. And yet the journey you and I are about to take is, in many ways, a doctor's journey. You see, I'm here to make a diagnosis for millions of people. And that, reader, includes you. Those fingers that turn and swipe these pages right now? They are attached to a body that is suffering from a bona-fide affliction. You'll struggle to find medicine for it. There's no quick cure. And . . . I'm afraid your test results are back, and I'm going to have to tell you straight. You are suffering from a disease known as . . . drum roll please . . . apophenia.

'Okay, so it's not the most well known of ailments. You've probably never seen a disease-of-the-week TV movie about it. Yet millions across the world have a terminal case of it. If you don't recognise the name, then you'll certainly be familiar with the symptoms because apophenia describes humanity's relentless insistence on reading patterns and meaning into random data. We do it all the time, every single day, but this is more than just spotting a face in an upturned plug socket. Or seeing Pac-Man every time you pull out the pizza slice that is closest to your right hand. That's pareidolia, by the way. When we see the simple *appearance* of patterns. That's not such a problem. I've made my peace with pareidolia. Yet for millions, pareidolia quickly develops into full-blown apophenia, when you start reading deeper, cosmic significance into those patterns.

'Imagine this scenario, if you will.

'It's Thursday night. You're excitedly heading off on a date with a new connection, but the car breaks down on the way to the restaurant. It's just "one of those things", you say, and you call the lady to apologise. You rearrange for the next night. Friday comes, you drive to the restaurant, but a storm floods the road. You're embarrassed, you're apologetic, you try it one more time. On Saturday night you reverse off your drive when a drunk ice-cream van driver veers into the back of you and totally writes your car off. As the car spins, you can hear the guy's stereo playing. Elvis is singing "Sheeeee's the Devil in Disguise".

'You call the girl, you talk about it, but by now she decides to write the relationship off. Because despite these events being total accidents, she thinks you're the most unreliable fella in the world. Even if it wasn't your fault, you obviously invite bad luck. While you, on the other hand, happily agree not to proceed. Because you're wondering if the universe is trying to tell you something, i.e. stay the hell away from that devil woman. She's cursed.

'But the fact is, there's no cosmic force at work in this scenario. You're neither lucky nor unlucky. You're just experiencing the randomness of the universe.

'Only our brain cannot handle that interpretation because it isn't comfortable with chaos. Instead, we've evolved into pattern-making machines. We read deep meaning into any old stuff.'

He paused for a moment to take a sip of water, the gulp making a little but embarrassing squelch across the microphone. Which is when he saw the woman a few rows back, in a black jacket. Her big collar was sticking up like Count Duckula. She had a tiny laptop open in front of her, small enough for an Ewok. She tapped at it with thin fingers. In the glow of the screen Matt could see her eyes which rolled up to meet his . . . she was *glaring* at him.

He cleared his throat. She glared some more. He went on.

'Sometimes this pattern making is good for us,' he said, 'We hear a growl in the woods at night and our brain says it's probably time to leave. Now maybe there's nothing to actually fear at all (perhaps it's your wife's gut rumbling) but that little horror narrative that plays in our head has probably saved our ancestors from a lot of hungry panthers. Yet the thing about apophenia is that we can't seem to switch it off. We're obsessed with the idea that essentially random events have some sort of huge, *cosmic* meaning. We see the Devil's face in the billowing dust from 9/11, and shudder. We find the perfect parking space at the supermarket and thank God for the blessing.

'The conspiracy theorist, the alien abductee, the religious fundamentalist, the talent show contestant. They all swim regularly in the murky pools of apophenia. And let's be honest . . . my fellow atheists do it too. We argue God can't exist because the Crusades were "evil" or that systematic child abuse is "wrong", as if such concepts reflected a fixed framework *outside* of ourselves. But even our sense of morality springs from little more than the current consensus of the human tribe. Even those morals could change, if a society willed it.'

He'd been scanning the crowd, trying to catch every eye. Something a lecturer friend had always taught him to do, but he found his gaze falling on the woman again. She was pressing her lips together and shaking her head with disgust. She looked down at the little laptop and tapped something out.

'Knowing there are no frameworks or designs beyond ourselves can bring a sense of liberation to some, despair to others or shoulder-shrugging indifference to the rest. But if life is meaningless, does it mean that our *inventions* of meaning don't matter? Not by a long shot. Let's melt when we watch our children sleep, why not? Let's marvel at the sheer space inside an atom. Great. And let's make laws that reflect our commonly agreed morality. Fine.

'But let's accept that you and I are little more than machines of instinct that must eat, sleep and reproduce, and that our insistence on meta-narratives, be they religious or secular, are literally just

34

that. They're big old stories that help us sleep at night. Yet what wonderful stories they can be . . .'

The woman tutted. A quick suck of the tongue from the roof of her mouth to make a sound loud enough for people to notice. *Pop*. Matt shrugged, smiled at her and carried on.

'I may not be a *doctor* doctor, but I have a very real prognosis. The human race has a severe case of apophenia. We think we are part of a plan, but we're not. We can ignore that. We can let it freak us out. We can even let it throw us into a maelstrom of loneliness and despair. But I have another suggestion. Why don't we let that knowledge spur us on to do something truly brave and wonderfully human?

'Let us learn to find the inherent beauty of an essentially incoherent universe. It will take training. Your brain won't like it. But your life will love you for it.

'Perhaps then we won't assume the bad news at the doctor's shows that a deity is displeased with us. We might not trample on our fellow workers because we think the world "owes" us a promotion. We might come to accept that life is just a thing that happens. Perhaps Ray Bradbury's Martians said it best, when they urged us humans to stop fussing and simply "derive pleasure from the gift of pure being."'

She tapped some more, chewing the inside of her mouth and chuckling to herself. Head in a constant shake from left to right.

'In the pages that follow I do not propose that we destroy the gods or liquidise the so-called supernatural realm. How can we, when statistics tell us that transcendent faith continues to grow across the globe? My suggestion is rather more simple than that. Let us study believers with enthusiasm, let us reflect on them, let us even learn from them, and yes . . . let's put a stop to the truly crazy ones. But let us accept that we, like them, are believers too, in frameworks that may not really be there. And let us recognise that the gods, the ghosts, the fates, the angels, the rights, the wrongs, the so-called order in the universe are little more than symptoms of our chronic case of apophenia. The gods are everything we're not, that tell us everything we are. They aren't our creators, they're our reflections. They are *us*. They are psychological and social helpers, made lovingly and comprehensively . . . in our image.'

Matt swallowed. He looked up and folded the book softly over, leaning back from the microphone. 'Er . . . that's it,' he said. 'Prologue.'

The lecture hall crackled into applause and the main lights came up a little. He ran his eyes up the crowd. The Charles Fox lecture room had a steep slope of tiered seating, so he could see all the stacked rows of faces staring at him, flapping their hands together. His students filled a sizeable chunk of the fold-down chairs. They'd all sat together, like a tribe. He saw many matching hipster beards and man-buns. He'd had a good crop this year, some proper deep thinkers with a surprisingly low quota of religious fundamentalists giving him hassle this term.

There were other lecturers from the uni, scattered midway back. Some applauded more vigorously than others. More than a few were checking their watch to see when the free booze was getting wheeled out.

But the ones he really wanted to see were sitting on the front row. Lined up like the proverbial eager beavers. His seven-year-old Amelia was jabbing a finger at her bright-pink kids' camera. She'd promised to film the evening for him, even though the publishers had a professional cameraman brought in especially. She caught his eye and stuck up a thumb. 'Got it!' she mouthed. Looking proud and part of it all.

His eldest, Lucy, wasn't clapping, but she was looking around the room at everybody else doing it. She seemed really quite surprised at the enthusiasm. And Wren . . . his wife. She was holding up a glass of champagne that she'd snagged from somewhere. She raised it in his direction and winked at him, tucking a lock of red hair behind her ear.

I'm proud of you, she mouthed slowly. Then took a gulp.

Beth from the publishers suddenly sprang up onstage and grabbed the lectern. The applause died down.

'Thank you so much for attending this reading tonight. *In Our Image: The Gods We Tend to Invent* is out in shops and online tomorrow but of course you can buy copies here tonight. And don't forget to catch Professor Hunter here tomorrow at twelve, at the Haddon Charity lunch. He'll be sharing some more from the book and signing again. But for now . . . we'd like to open it up to the floor. So . . . do we have any questions?'

It wasn't hard to spot where the press were sitting. A clump of hands shot up, all in the same two rows, and the highest belonged to the pissed-off woman with the big collar and tiny laptop.

Now the lights were up he saw that the jacket she was wearing was black leather, and she had a leopard skin scarf, tied round her throat, crazy tight. 'Chloe, go ahead.'

'Thanks . . . Chloe Reynolds, *Daily Mail* . . .' She sprang to her feet and held up a gizmo that looked more like a taser than a recorder. Its red light was flashing. 'Professor. I understand your book was originally aimed at academic circles?'

He smiled. 'My usual crowd, yes.'

'Yet your publishers urged you to widen the audience. In fact, they sped up the release of this and greatly increased the marketing budget in the last few months. Why the manic rush to get this book out?'

'Well . . . clearly it's an amazing piece of work . . .'

A few titters from the audience. A snort laugh from Amelia. But eyes of stone from Chloe.

'But speaking more seriously,' Matt said. 'Each day science is demystifying the universe so you'd expect belief in gods and the supernatural to diminish, but it isn't. On a global scale it's actually *growing*. And the divisions between faith groups are expanding too. We're seeing dangerous chasms open up. Frankly, it's a crucial and volatile time in our religious, cultural history which I—'

'But that's not why they've bumped your book up is it? The book's *subject* is a side reason.'

He frowned. 'Actually the book's subject is kind of the whole poin—'

'No. They're printing more copies of your book because of *you*.'

He waited. 'I'm sorry, I don't follow.'

'Your own personal profile. It's risen since the summer. The Hobbs Hill serial killer, I mean.' She pushed her recorder forwards. He noticed many of the faces in the room moving in the same direction. Heads zooming in for a close-up. 'Your stepdaughter was almost his final victim but you managed to talk him down. You were instrumental in tracking down the killer. Do you reflect on that case in your book?'

He shot a quick look at his family. Wren was reaching over and grabbing Lucy's hand. Lucy shrugged and gave an *it's fine, really* smile. Even from here he could see how forced it was. Her mouth was a crooked line. He leant into the mic. 'I don't think this is relev—'

'Your stepdaughter's name's Lucy, isn't it? And her real father's currently in prison for domestic—'

'Whoah, whoah, let me stop you right there, Chloe.' He put up his hand and looked hard at her. 'If your readers are expecting a true crime book then they'll be disappointed. I briefly mention the Hobbs Hill case but this is a sociological study into the nature—'

'So you don't think he was wrong, then?'

'Pardon?'

More people leant forward.

'His drowning multiple women and nearly your wife's daughter. From what you've just shared with us, you'd say that was a morally *neutral* act? Correct?'

He looked across at Beth. He assumed she'd be ticked off by the distraction of all this. But her expression was quite the opposite. She was smiling, with a curled finger tapping against her chin. If she had a moustache, she may have twiddled it. She nodded at him, to answer, so he did.

'Now listen. What happened in Hobbs Hill was utterly wrong. Vile in fact.' He was gripping the lectern, which felt way too presidential. He folded his hands on the book in front of him instead. 'But when I say something is wrong I'm obviously speaking from an agreed standard that's been bred into my DNA after millions of years of evolution. Morality is the air I breathe, but—'

'*But?* When it comes to murder there's a *but*?'

'If the gods don't exist then morality can only come from social consensus. Theoretically there could be a planet filled with people where the majority of them rejoice in murder. "Evil" would be "Good" for them. Now *my* brain couldn't handle that system and on that planet *I'd* be the psychopath. But without some sort of deity I can only say it's wrong by my standards. I can't appeal to some fixed framework beyond humanity. Apophenia tells us a system is there, but it's not.'

'So morality is relative?' Chloe cocked her head to the side. 'That's a dangerous attitude, don't you think?'

'Not at all. I'm not advocating murder and I'm certainly not saying we *need* God to be moral, either. I'm just saying we *choose* our morals . . . that argument is just basic, GCSE philosophy, Chloe.'

He really didn't mean that as a cheap put-down, he was just making a point. But some of his students chuckled at that and he watched her bristle.

'And your wife's ex-husband? Lucy's real dad. Was his domestic violence just a—?'

'That's enough.' He put a palm up.

'And is it morally okay for a writer to jump on the Hobbs Hill murder buzz to shift more books?'

'*Oh, come off it.*' He stepped out from the lectern. 'You guys did a six-page spread on the Hobb—'

Beth sprang onto the stage, so fast she might as well have teleported. He could see Wren in the front row, teeth clenched. Lucy was scrolling through her phone. Beth, the consummate publicist shut it all down with one, straightforward sentence.

'Aaaand . . . next question.'

A hand shot up.

'Yes?'

'Reece Farn, *Daily Star*. What about ghosts . . . don't you think they might exist?'

Twenty minutes later and the questions were done.

Everybody spilt back out in the foyer, mingling with each other and taking selfies with the shiny dictators. The first thing he did was ignore all that and find Lucy, to see if she was okay. He nodded and smiled as he politely pushed through the crowd, until he found her by the big window, looking out onto the fountains near the lawns. Wren was by her side.

He caught Wren's eye and she leant in to kiss him. 'Good job tonight.'

'Hmmm,' he shrugged, then spoke to Lucy's reflection. 'Listen, I'm really sorry the reporter brought all that up,' he said. 'Are you okay?'

She shrugged again. ''Course I am.'

'Because if you'd like us to head off home, then I can grab the car.'

'Relax. It's not as big a deal as you think, you know.' She was chewing the corner of her mouth. 'Aren't you supposed to be mingling?'

He clocked her reflected eyes. That flicker of the lashes that said, don't go there, please.

So he looked at Wren and they both slowly nodded. They had this unspoken agreement, after all. Lucy saved all talk on Hobbs Hill, and her real dad, for the counsellor the police had now provided. She didn't want to bring any of that stuff home, though ignoring it all made him jittery. Especially on the occasional nights when Lucy had the nightmares. When he'd hear her go into the bathroom and turn on the taps just to cover the sound of her crying. Wren would be fast asleep snoring, but he'd stand by his door in his pyjamas waiting. To see if she might call out for someone. She never did.

'Anyway, this is a party and I'm sixteen so' – Lucy whirled away from the window – 'can I have some champagne?'

Wren laughed. 'One glass.'

He laughed too, and spotted Amelia walking over with a floppy paper plate, full of mini-doughnuts. 'And don't give alcohol to your sister.'

Wren kissed him again. 'Now go and schmooze, you big schmoozer.'

Prosecco started fizzing into glasses. Canapés that smelt odd came drifting out. Beth handed out flyers for the charity lunch tomorrow, while Matt sat at a glass table and signed books. Throughout the evening the PA guy played sickly smooth jazz that Matt hadn't requested. At one point, he was *sure* it was a Kenny G album. Evidence perhaps that the gods really did exist after all, and were casting down prophetic banality on his efforts to deny them.

He signed forty-four books, not that he was counting. Actually, he *was* counting. Sometimes wondering if without Hobbs Hill he really might have sold only fourteen books.

We want to bring publication forward Matt. Just to tie in with the news profile. Nothing crass . . . just getting your message out to more—

He put that from his mind.

When he'd scrawled enough of his name, (with a little smiley face that he couldn't resist) Beth tugged him by the elbow so he could mingle with 'key people'. Some magazines were interested in him writing articles. At one point, someone from *The Sun* asked to take his photograph. He tried a wide, friendly smile but hadn't realised that chrome-Hitler was right behind him. Thankfully, laser-eyed Beth did. She swooped in and whisked him and the photographer up the corridor. She stood him next to something less incendiary for the shot. A tall, fake pot plant.

'That's better,' she said.

It was fun, actually. The chatting, the mingling, the sight of people with his book under their arm. He kept an eye out for Chloe from the *Mail*, just to clarify his argument, but she was *long* gone. Her mind was clearly made up about him. He could picture her right now, sitting in the Starbucks down the road, hunched over a MacBook and Frappuccino. Feverishly typing up how morals were now 'off the curriculum' in 'Britain's Once-great Academic Institutions'. That Matt Hunter couldn't even bring himself to say things were 'evil' and 'wrong'.

But the best part, as corny as it sounded, was the drive home. When he sat in the passenger seat, still tipsy and giggling, finishing off a plastic glass of Prosecco, while Wren drove. Randomly, the theme to the Muppets came on the radio and Amelia and Lucy insisted they keep it on. It was when all four of them joined in singing, '*It's time to start the music*' like a pack of deranged, goggle-eyed Kermits . . . *that* was the most profound moment of all tonight. London passing by the windows, his book in his hand, the wonderful belly laughs from Amelia, and the actual bona-fide giggle from Lucy. A sound he hadn't really heard since the spring. The glances from Wren that said, *you look fit in a suit*.

Life felt good and balanced and *right* that night.

The only part that turned sour was when Wren finally pulled the car into the drive of their new house.

CHAPTER THREE

Sometimes when a cat knows it's going to die, its frightened little body pushes out this gunky gel through the follicles. It's pretty weird. Turns the coat into a matted, gooey mess. It doesn't happen every time but it does happen, now and again. It gives off this smell too, which is impossible to categorise. Not pleasant, not unpleasant.

Rachel Wasson wasn't a vet or biologist. She hadn't the first clue as to why this slime stuff comes out, or what it's made of. But when she was twelve years old her black and white cat Pob died during a bone-dry August in 2001. After six days of secreting this gel stuff, Pob stretched across the kitchen lino and he started twitching. Paws grasping at phantom mice, fur soaked in this *stuff*.

Mum was out at the chemist that morning, panic-buying roll-on deodorant because her short experiment with aerosols was leaving her pits red raw. But Rachel's nine-year-old sister was home. But then, Holly Wasson was *always* at home. Up in her room, drawing pictures of dogs and cats and birds, as she often did back then.

Though by the time November came around, she'd draw nothing but rabbits and hares.

Rachel called her down so she could come and see Pob die. After some timid padding down the stairs Holly stood there in the doorway, chewing the nail on her crooked little finger.

'I suppose,' Rachel had said, 'we should sit with him.'

Holly tilted her head and nodded. They sat together on the lino.

Every now and again, as the years ambled by, Rachel Wasson would dream of this moment. The two sisters kneeling down on the glistening floor. Rachel's blonde ponytail was pulled headache tight (to Mum's specification). She remembered how it dangled like a ship's rope over her shoulder, the weight tugging her head down to the floor, toward Pob's quivering chin. And as she put an ear to his tiny breaths the only thing she could think of was how similar death was to birth. That Pob must be remembering what it was like to be born. To be pushed out of the mother cat, thick with new-life goo. Maybe a cat's hormones can't tell the difference between the start of life and the end of it.

'Do you think it hurts?' Rachel had whispered to Holly as Pob's eyes grew wide, then back to slits. Wide again. Then slits. Hinting at either animal transcendence or basic agony.

Holly didn't answer, but she did clench her knuckled hands in prayer. She said 'Dear Jesus . . .' Then lifted her hand about a foot above the dying cat. Waving it like a magician about to levitate his assistant. '. . . stop the pain.'

The gloopy belly rose one last time, higher than before, then something happened that Rachel never, ever forgot. The belly slunk back to a final, frozen stop.

Dead.

A drop of water splashed off the lino and Rachel realised it was a tear falling from her eye. Her chin started to go, but Holly slipped a hand into hers. 'It's okay, Rach,' she said and touched her chest.

'He's still with us. The angels are with him. Don't you feel it?'

Rachel remembered pulling her hand away. Not keen on touching the fingers that had just prayed Pob into oblivion. And so they both folded their hands back onto their knees. They both cried together for maybe twenty minutes. Then Mum came home with her big hair bounding. A Boots carrier bag dangled from her teeth as she unbolted the back door. When she spotted the furry lump on the floor she dropped to her knees between them both. Swooping the girls together with her long thin arms saying something like, 'Don't you fret, girls. The mice in heaven are fast. Pob'll have plenty to do, *plenty* to do.'

They say, don't they, that one of the top reasons to buy a kid a pet is so that it will die. That a dog, or cat or Syrian Dwarf hamster gasping its last will ease a child into the reality of our morbid world. What they don't always mention is that those first experiences can define a kid's view of death for the rest of their lives.

Because ever since that kitchen morning, Rachel tended to think of gooey fur when she heard about people dying. Like the subject of death clicked a little switch in her nasal cavity and released the strange scent of endings. The following year, her PE teacher got himself snapped in half on holiday, in a bike crash in Cardiff. Rachel could smell Pob in the assembly that morning, as the head, Mrs Dixon, clawed the podium and announced the news. Just before her voice went all wobbly and strange and the head of geography took over.

Or when that young guy on her sound engineering course at uni died of sudden death syndrome. It was during freshers' week and she'd smelt Pob then, too. Especially during those drunken, ill-advised, midnight treks her friends had pulled her on, through the supposedly haunted corridor where he'd been found (half in bed, half out, todger dangling, so 'the legend' said). Then there was the intern at her first recording studio job. Brain cancer. Her grandma, her first boss. Stroke and stroke.

But of course, the worst time was the bad week, the horrendous week. Only a few months after Pob's death when a teenage Rachel woke from sleep in her old house and the entire place had *reeked* of him. When all the police arrived. When the neighbours gathered on the pavement outside. The week she became one of 'the Barley Street girls'.

Yeah, there'd been a lot of opportunities to smell that gooey fur over the years. A dull sniff at all those funerals. In her weaker moments, lying in bed at night, she'd think the reason she could still smell Pob was because he actually *was* still here. Just like Holly said he'd be. That through all these years, he was still following her into the bathroom like a long decaying spectre, slinking his invisible, matted fur around her legs whenever she stepped out of the shower.

But she knew better.

This was just how memories worked. The brain got branded with the senses. Mental associations ticked even after many years had passed and now she was almost thirty. As she got older she noticed she was smelling that cat less. Thinking of *that house* less.

Which was why it felt so odd to smell Pob tonight, here in a Yorkshire hotel.

It was strong enough to wake her at just around midnight. Pulled from an ocean dream into an unfamiliar room, with a creaky bed with a swollen mattress she was convinced she'd fall out of. Pob's smell and the memories that came with it (of Holly . . . of the old house) were so pungent that Rachel sprang quickly out of the bed and nearly tripped on her suitcase on her way to the bathroom. She took a swig of mouthwash to see if the smell would go, even though she knew it was just her silly brain making her smell it.

She fumbled with her glasses and slipped them on. She drank a glass of water and went back to the main bedroom window to let some air in. As she popped the window she caught a reflection of herself in her *I-bought-them-because-they're-ironic* Hello Kitty pyjamas. Her short black hair with the floppy fringe was sticking up in a pillow-prompted Mohican. *Through* herself she could see the Yorkshire moors outside. They still had wet-looking mist creeping over their curves. A bit like *Hound of the Baskervilles* country, this. There are animals on these hills.

You aren't going to sleep for hours, Rach. Might as well do something else.

She perched on the end of the creaking bed and popped open her aluminium flight case. She checked that the batteries for her microphones and recorders were fully charged. She'd spent the day out on these moors, recording the wind for a sound effects library she was contracting for. She sat on the bed and listened to today's work for five minutes through a pair of headphones that cost as much money as her first car. She really was impressed with the stereo separation on today's work. The client was going to be pleased.

But the dead cat smell quickly devoured the air, and after a while the recorded wind in her ears started sounding too much like distant moans coming from deep in the cracks of the moors. She switched it off, pulled the headphones off and neatly packed the whole thing away.

She turned on the TV instead. Ate a complimentary packet of three custard creams while watching *BBC News* repeating the same stories every twenty minutes. Then when she was really bored with that, she did the last thing she could think of. She switched her phone on for the first time that day. In an ideal world, she wouldn't even have one of these things. She envied the 1950s folk. She liked unhooking from the world. She had no interest in social media. Taking moody filtered shots of tonight's pizza? No thanks. Plus, if she was honest, she despised talking on the phone. Hated the pressure of the ringtone, which always sounded like a social alarm clock going off telling her to get ready for articulation and professionalism. She wasn't that bad face-to-face, but phones had a weird habit of lobotomising her.

The phone had no interest in her hang-ups. It buzzed with a voicemail and she had one of those mad, early morning thoughts. The type that had no basis in reality, but only in emotion. That maybe it was Debbie. Her first and only 'proper' long-term girlfriend who she'd met after uni. The one she'd actually fallen in love with. Maybe this would be her calling to say she'd been dumb to leave. That she'd finally admitted she'd been brainwashed into turning her back on her sexuality, because she'd joined a church that told her to drop girls like they were hot (from the fires of hell).

But it wasn't Debbie. 'Course it wasn't.

She tapped on the screen and didn't recognise the number. Maybe it was someone from the company, checking she'd grabbed the sounds, or a recorded message that she might have been mis-sold PPI Insurance. She hoped it was that. Something innocuous.

It was around then that the smell of Pob flooded the room so intensely that she had to walk to the window to open it as wide as possible. It really is weird the way the mind works, in the deepest ditch of the night. Conjuring smells that aren't there. Or are *probably* not there.

She gazed out at the rolling black hills, took a breath and spoke to her reflection.

Grow up, Rachel.

She clicked the message on. It was ironic, because what she heard made her feel the exact opposite of grown up. She heard a voice that raced through the phone line in a tone that instantly sucked a decade and a half from her life.

'Rach? Rachel Wasson . . .'

Her jaw dropped at the message.

'It's me, Jo Finch. I got your number from your mum. Erm . . . listen, you've got to get back to Menham as soon as you can. No excuses this time because . . .' A sniffle into the

49

phone, a gulping in of air for the next part. *'Steph's dead.'*

Rachel put her hand on the window sill, surprised at how dreamlike this felt. Maybe it *was* a dream. Maybe she'd turn round and spot herself dribbling into the pillow of that hefty, concave bed, waiting to roll off. But then the voice came again, and she knew she was awake.

'So for once, Rach, you call me back. Anytime. Wake me up if you have to.'

The phone clicked off and Rachel stared at it for a long moment. The first thing she thought was, *oh, look. The smells gone.* And it had. Pob's scent had vanished as quickly as it came. But then it *would* be gone, she thought. Because her trusty little messenger of death had delivered his latest portent and was slinking back to his ghostly basket. Until next time.

It took her half an hour and a tiny bottle of gin from the mini bar before she called Jo back. And since this was the first time they'd spoken in years, she rehearsed what she'd say. She actually wrote it down on a Post-it note. She'd planned to start with, 'Hi, it's Rachel. Sorry it's after midnight but you did say call straight away. And I'm sorry for not phoning in years.' But as soon as she said 'Hi, it's Rachel,' Jo gasped and then crumbled into quiet sobs on the other end of the line. Rachel sat there listening to the whimpering for a few seconds, then she asked the real question that had been wriggling through her mind for the past thirty minutes.

'How did she die?'

And through the sniffing, all Jo could say was, 'It's come back. I think it's come back for us.'

CHAPTER FOUR

Wren pulled the car into the new Hunter Family Homestead, which was a cosmic leap away from the ASBO central townhouse they'd only just moved away from. No longer did coming home mean locking up the car under the gaze of abusive, crotch-grabbing hoodies. No longer did Matt have to partake in the morning bin bag ritual of trudging across a lawn filled with discarded beer cans, condoms and Ginster's bloody pasties wrappers, fuzzed with morning dew.

Their old house had been bought up as a buy-to-let and he had occasional pangs of guilt for the students the landlord planned to pack in there. He kept telling himself that students like nightclubs and love cheap kebabs. Who knows, maybe they find regular local knifings of anthropological interest. He tried not to think about that.

They'd stumbled across this Edwardian semi on Rightmove one night. Scrolled onto the less expensive parts of Chesham, Buckinghamshire. It was an estate prone to manure smells from the farms and surprisingly frequent power cuts but he'd take cow shit and occasional darkness over amphetamine-fuelled gangs any day of the week.

The place was thirty per cent smaller than the last house but it was four hundred per cent more homely. Plus it was just a nine minute and fifty-three-second bike ride from the Tube station for work.

They'd lived here for four weeks.

As they pulled in he spotted the really ironic part. They now lived a brick throw from an old Anglican church, lit with a yellowed floodlight. For years now he'd rejected the church and his own, ancient ordination, and now he stared at one every time he brushed his teeth. But, so what? So what if the bell ringing and congregational singing sometimes filtered out the TV, or woke them up whenever he and Wren attempted a *really* lazy Sunday. There was a funny quirk in it being close. The presence of church, so near.

Standing here tonight, feeling the late breeze come up over the hill as he looked up at their new house, he was even tipsy enough to ignore that little voice of panic that sometimes said, 'BIG *mortgage this, isn't it? Been a bit* AMBITIOUS, *haven't you?*'

Then he'd drop-kick that thought with another: this place is perfect.

Amelia, his youngest, was the one that shifted the mood, bless her. She was sitting in the back seat with her tiny chin buried into her chest. He saw her staring up at her new bedroom window.

Matt popped the door. 'Out you get, Midget. It's light years past your bedtime.'

'I want to sleep with you and Mummy tonight.'

Wren crouched by the car. Her voice soft. 'Amelia. We've been through this.'

'I won't snore.' She looked at Matt. 'Daddy? What do you think? Can I stay with you two?'

'You have a room,' he tapped a finger at himself, 'with an amazing paint job, remember?'

She tried to smile but her eyes were on her bedroom, which always made her voice uneven. 'Then I want my light on. The main one. And I want it on all night.'

'Amelia you're seven—'

'*All* night. And the door open.'

Kids are manipulative, so the magazines said. Masters at it, in fact. But then this *was* a new place and a new room. That kind of stuff freaked kids out, didn't it? Change. Weren't certain little kids identical to certain little pensioners that way? They break out in a heat rash if their routines get messed up.

He and Wren looked at each other, then nodded, way too tired for the hassle. So they granted each other the permission to give in . . . *again*. Supernanny would be slapping her forehead right now.

'Okay, just cos it's a late night, you can have your big light on,' Wren said.

Amelia finally (and slowly) slipped out of the car.

'But this isn't going to be every night, okay?'

Amelia nodded, 'I know.'

They headed inside and kicked off their shoes. He crunched a kiss into the crown of Amelia's head and then he watched Wren tug her upstairs. She trudged up slowly, her little hand gripping the white-painted banister, white-knuckle tight.

'Night, Midget,' he called up. 'I love you.'

'Night, Daddy.' Her voice sounded quiet. Younger.

The humanity chips in his brain started laying on the guilt for not letting her share their room tonight, but the parent-survival sector smacked it down. There was nothing in the shadows of her room. Nothing 'watching her' like she'd announced over breakfast this morning. The room wasn't haunted. As cruel as it felt, she'd just have to get used to the change. What was the alternative: sleep with him and Wren for the next few months? Or years? Was that good parenting for a seven-year-old? Helpful prep for the world? Nope.

Still felt crap doing it, though.

He turned to Lucy who was peeling off her jacket. He wanted to see how she was, but she clipped it shut with two quick words. 'Night, then.'

He smiled at her. 'Thank you for coming tonight.'

'There were more people than I expected.' She headed for the stairs. 'Oh . . . and your phone's ringing.'

He turned and noticed his iPhone was vibrating on the side table, starting to revolve in a slow circle as the glass surface buzzed. He grabbed it and looked down. He expected it might be Beth, telling him to wear a better tie for tomorrow's charity lunch. But when he held up the phone he was surprised.

DS Larry Forbes was calling.

Matt sank into the lounge sofa, sensing that the alcohol in his system had reached the calming, nanny stage.

Lie down, it said to him. *Rest those eyes, time to sleep and dreeeeam.*

He rubbed a knuckle into his eye and tapped on Accept Call under Larry's profile picture. In the shot Larry wore a floppy Mexican hat that Wren had insisted on them all wearing at a recent barbecue here.

Matt lay back on the sofa. 'Hey, hombre . . . you know it's almost midnight . . .'

'Yeah, sorry about that,' Larry's voice had a slight Geordie lilt, an old echo of his Durham upbringing. It seemed to come out clearer late at night. 'I just didn't want to disturb you at your colouring book party. How did it go? I really would have been there if I could have.'

'It was pretty great, actually. I signed a lot of autographs. I'm pretty much a superstar DJ or something.' Matt thought of the hairy, fat pensioner who took the first signed copy, which prompted a tipsy laugh. 'Sort of.'

'And there was free food, I take it? Free booze?'

'Prosecco.'

He sighed through the phone. 'Shite.'

'Larry . . .' Matt started giggling, 'must you always resort to the language of the billiard parlour?'

'And you saved me one of your books?'

'I thought your priest said you shouldn't read it. Aren't I a bad influe—'

'Matt,' his voice dropped a tone. Business mode engaged. 'What are you doing in the morning?'

He curled his feet up onto the sofa, gazed up into his new ceiling and spotted a crack in the plaster he'd not seen before. Crud. 'I haven't anything official till the afternoon.'

'Have you ever heard of Menham, South London?'

'I've heard of the second. Not the first.'

'It's a town along the Victoria line. It's in my patch. In fact, I used to work there as an officer, back in the day. My first patrol job when I moved down south.'

'So what's the problem?'

'Probably only need you for an hour. Maybe two, tops.'

'Need me for what?'

'We've got a body . . .'

'M-hmm . . .' He squinted at the crack in the plaster. Damn. That better not be an old water stain because the pipes in this—he blinked. 'Sorry. Did you say a body?'

'Yes . . . and we've got other stuff. Weird stuff.' Larry waited. 'Your type of stuff.'

Matt breathed into the phone. 'I see.'

'Kind of scratching our heads here, to be honest . . . I'd have waited till the morning but I thought you might get snapped up on some publicity thing. So can you make it?'

Matt yawned. He considered falling asleep right there. 'Text me where and when.'

'Perfect. I'll send you it now. Goodni—'

'Hang on. Who's the victim?'

'A thirty-year-old primary teacher. She left one son and a husband.'

'Oh,' Matt sighed. 'And her name?'

'Stephanie Ellis.'

Matt nodded. 'I'll see you tomorrow, then.'

'Brilliant, thanks,' he said. 'And I hope this doesn't put a dampener on your night.'

The phone went silent and Matt lay back as the sofa wriggled its teddy bear arms around him.

The time has come, alcohol said. To drift and rest and drift again.

He thought about a Pop-Tart. That'd be perfect right now. An uncooked Pop-Tart with no plate, just a strip of kitchen roll. But his eyes were already closing and the projectionist in his brain had started formulating a detailed, new attraction for tonight's main show. An unwelcome dream of chrome dictators piling up pyramids of corpses called Stephanie, while he looked on and signed books with a crayon in his fist.

CHAPTER FIVE

Your next station stop . . . Menham . . . Menham . . . Please mind the gap.

Matt looked up from the book he was reading on the Raelian movement. He was speaking at a conference next month on pseudo-religious groups. These guys claimed ancient aliens had started the human race, Battlestar Galactica-style. Pretty wild, but technically no more nutty than all the other god theories out there. He slipped his bookmark in his page (a Starbucks receipt) and dropped it into the zip compartment of his bag.

The free-flowing drinks last night had thankfully not ended in much of a hangover but he still felt dehydrated. He kept swigging his bottled water as he stepped off the train. Glugging it down like a baby lamb with milk.

He'd never been here, to Menham. But there were murals on the walls that were presumably supposed to give a good first impression. They depicted life in the industrial 'old days' here, but oddly, the people in the pictures had fish heads. Chimney sweeps, men in overalls, industrialists on trains, scientists with clipboards. They all had bug-eyed fish heads. It was like something from a Bosch painting. He assumed the artist was showing that Menham had maritime links, being close-ish to the Thames. Or perhaps the great sea god Cthulhu used to hang out here, and turned all the locals into amphibians. He'd have to ask.

Either way, Menham Station had a single-hatch newsagent selling something he hadn't seen in years. Caramac. He bought one and greedily snapped bits off with his teeth as he headed up the steps to swish his Oyster card.

The street was flooded with autumn sun as he stepped out. Enough to make him squint, but not enough to warm him much. He saw a run of shops with Halloween stuff in the windows, including a huge mask of Frankenstein's monster leering from a charity shop window, and a cafe that was belching out dubstep music. His nostrils flooded with the smells of exhaust fumes and chip fat. Locals wandered by chatting, with reasonably human-looking heads. It looked a lot more peaceful over the road where a large park stretched out behind the old iron railings. He watched the empty trees sway gently in the breeze, their dead, brown leaves dancing at the base of the trunk, like they were trying to climb back up and recapture their glory days.

The sudden blast of a car horn snapped him out of it.

Larry's black Mazda loomed up on the kerb and almost crushed Matt's toes into jam. He stepped back and the window slid down.

'Gee whizz . . .' Larry leant his head out, the swoop of his grey fringe flapping in the breeze. 'Is it *really* you? . . . The *actual* one? Can you autograph this for me?'

'Sorry, but I don't sign old people's body parts. . .' He trailed off when he saw what Larry was actually dangling out of the window. A copy of the *Daily Mail*. It was folded back to show a picture of Matt looking at his most mean and gormless last night. One of those off guard shots the paparazzi do, of celebs halfway out of taxis, gussets showing, looking hammered. He recognised the moment. When he was pushing through the crowd, looking for Lucy. His expression looked furious.

He hopped in the car and tossed his bag in the back seat, noticing Larry's little cross and rosary curled in the cup holder between them. He nodded to the newspaper. 'Give me that thing.'

'Congratulations. You made the heady heights of page thirty-six.' Larry pulled away from the kerb, chuckling in that high-pitched bird sound he often made. 'Or should I say the *bottom right-hand corner* of thirty-six.'

Matt folded the paper back and read out the headline. '*Hobbs Hill Professor Says Murder's Not Evil.*' He let out a long, lip-flapping breath. Then he read it through quickly. It was exactly the type of angle he expected. Alarmist, knee-jerk, hypocritical, and worse . . . annoyingly well written.

'It says here I'm dangerous and . . .' he ran a finger down the paper, 'part of the subversive assault on traditional British values, which frankly I kind of like. Maybe I should put that on my business cards.'

'Do that and they'll burn you at the stake,' Larry laughed but then his smile faded. 'Anyway, you better turn to page four.'

'Ack, don't tell me. One-star book review?' Matt started flicking the pages.

'The victim. The case I need your input on.'

'Oh . . .' He slid the pages back with his thumb, like a bank-teller counting money. Then he hit page four and let it open.

TERROR IN THE CLASSROOM

He saw a large picture of a school playground with police cars and two ambulances. Crowds of adults and children were huddled outside looking distraught. In amongst the text was a little shot of a living Stephanie Ellis, beaming up from the page. Her blonde hair sprang from her head in big, frizzy curls. She had Sideshow Bob hair – that was Matt's first thought. Just over her shoulder he could see a seaside pier. A holiday shot. She was all bright-eyed with sea and arcades and ice cream dripping. The face of a teenager who happened to be in her thirties. Lots of teeth and lots of freckles. And beneath her, black ink pressed against white paper declaring her:

DEAD

Matt quickly read it through.

Apparently 'a much-loved teacher', Mrs Ellis had recently 'not been herself'. She'd been acting distant and confused at work. It never actually said the word 'depression', but there was a strong *nudge-nudge-wink-wink* vibe that she was going through something like it. At 3 a.m. yesterday morning, she'd taken her dog on its lead and had come into school for some unknown reason. She'd opened up, tapped in the alarm code, and let herself into her own classroom. Used her own key. Then she'd hidden herself and her dog in a store cupboard.

Turned out the dog didn't like 'such bizarre behaviour' and so it had turned on her. The words THROAT TORN OPEN were in capitals. He read phrases like: '*A freak accident*'; '*a terrifying experience*'; '*a tragic loss of a wonderful mother*'. Parents had killed the dog when it leapt out at an open day. A staff member was injured but stable.

There was a side panel too. An opinion piece that said: *The Killers in Our Homes – When Will Britain Take Dangerous Dogs Seriously?*

Matt looked up. 'This was an animal attack?'

'Yep.' Larry flicked an indicator. 'You look confused.'

60

'Sorry, but I assumed you called me on a murder. You think I can help with this?'

'I'm hoping you can.' Larry said it quietly, then he pulled the car into a street with a large school field running alongside it, filled with quivering grass. Up on a slight hill, Matt saw the brown bricks of a building. The place from the paper. A large purple sign stood near the gates saying *Menham Lower School – Wilkommen, Bienvenue, Welcome!* The school logo was a string of children, cut like streamers from paper. Permanently joined at the hands.

As they drew closer he spotted a small crowd of people hovering outside the school gate. Some of their faces floated in the steam from coffee, in styrofoam cups. One or two had those folding camping chairs, the sort you pop open.

'Who's that? Just gawkers?'

'They've had a few of those since they closed the school yesterday,' Larry said. 'But this lot are different. They're from Menham Evangelical Church.'

Larry had stopped the car at the closed gate, engine still running, and pressed a button on his radio. The car filled with a hissing squelch. 'He's here. Come and open the gate.'

As they waited, Matt leant toward the window. He counted six men out there on the pavement. Some were touching the faded green metal railings. A few had their eyes closed, lips moving silently. 'They're praying.'

'Been doing that since this morning.'

'Was Steph Ellis part of their church?'

'Nope. They just do a lot of prayer walking in Menham. They're known for it. They have a little club that strolls around town. They ask God to bless it. Saw them bless a Burger King once. Hands on the window and everything. No harm, I suppose.'

'I guess that depends on what they're praying for . . .'

'They're part of an ex-prisoners programme at the church,

61

which seems to be working. They call it the Phoenix Club.'

'Sounds like a Harry Potter fan site.'

'The reoffending rate's pretty impressive.'

'Right . . .'

'Hey, whatever makes my job easier works for—' Larry spotted Matt buzz his window down. 'Er . . . what are you doing?'

'Morning,' Matt called out, waving at the men.

They turned their heads.

'How are the prayers going?'

A skinny, tall man stood amongst them, with a checked shirt and a bald head. He smiled and said, 'They're going very, very well, thank you.'

A policewoman was at the gate. She was jangling a key in the lock and pushing it back. It creaked louder than an oil rig collapsing.

'And may I ask what you're praying for, exactly?'

Another man stepped forward. This one had glasses and a perfectly manicured goatee. His voice projected much further than the tall, bald guy. It was a preacher's voice. Matt could tell that tone at a hundred thousand paces. 'We're praying for protection, for the town,' the man announced. 'We're keeping the bad things away.'

'Well,' Larry leant over to call out, 'we appreciate all the help we can get.'

'Then why not join us?' the goatee said. He sounded American.

The squealing gate finally came to a stop.

'Got to get on,' Larry shook his head. 'Thanks, though.'

The car pushed forward into the school and Matt noticed the men turn back to the gates. Except the American, who pushed out a huge palm as they moved past. Aimed it directly at Matt so he might pray as the car drifted by.

Matt smiled at him as the window buzzed up, but he turned

away. 'They never ask permission, these folk. They just stick out a mitt and zap you with a prayer. Like they think they're Iron Man.'

Larry parked the car at a skewed angle, directly on the playground, so when Matt stepped out he put both feet straight into a hopscotch grid.

'Two seconds.' Larry wandered over to the policewoman. They muttered to each other, probably just getting a general update. Matt hung back and watched the Phoenix club who were now back to their wobbly head prayers. Funnily enough, he'd done one of these himself once. Back when he was a church minister he and about six pensioners had shuffled up and down the high street, praying blessings on the community. Seemed like a good idea at the time. Something he'd been recommended to try at a clergy conference. The idea was to ask God to prosper the businesses, bless families, encourage local people. The sort of stuff nobody tends to argue with. But half the pensioners (some of them lovely and earnest) kept closing their eyes outside the curry house, praying for the Muslims to leave the country. Loudly.

There were complaints. He hadn't done another.

He was about to turn when he noticed another figure on the far side of the street.

Another man. But different.

He was standing in an alleyway, just under a street lamp. An older bloke with a black, curly beard. Matt's literal first thought was that he looked like the male model from that old *Joy of Sex* book. The one with the pencilled sex drawings he'd often flicked through in the library when he was a teenager. This man looked like that. All wiry and bristly, with a 70s tweed jacket with elbow patches and some baggy-looking brown cords.

He was standing still, looking at the school. But then occasionally 70s sex man would glance down to jot things on a piece of paper. Local reporter, maybe? Friendly neighbourhood street perv?

Then one of the prayer team spotted the bearded man, and shouted something that sounded odd and sharp on the morning air. The tall guy shouted, 'Get away from here, you witch!' The bearded man took a step back and trudged off into the alleyway.

Matt frowned and took a step forward.

By then Larry was back and already tugging at his elbow. 'Come on. Chop-chop.'

'Did you see that?'

'There're some odd locals around here. Let's get on.'

They reached a set of double doors and Matt noticed a bright-purple plastic rack, which was presumably for the kids' scooters. It made him think of Amelia. Of last weekend when he and she took turns on her scooter, bombing down a hill near their new house. A hill that was way too steep but one that made them laugh like maniacs and hug each other at the end.

'Oh . . .' Larry touched the doors and paused. 'You're alright with blood, yeah?'

CHAPTER SIX

You could smell it in the air. That hanging, metallic odour. The tang of iron. It was impossible to miss the sight of it too, splashed near a small kids' stage, on a wooden floor of the music room.

'Watch your step,' Larry said as they padded around the dark brown, flaking circle. They were both wearing elasticated blue overshoes wrapped around their own, looking like genie slippers. A couple of MC Hammer backing dancers, that's what he and Larry were.

Matt looked down at the dried pool of blood. 'I'm confused. The newspaper said she died in the store cupboard.'

'She did, but the dog came rushing out when they opened the door. This is as far as it got. Some of the parents managed to stove its head in with a few chairs.'

'Community spirit is alive and well . . .' He crouched down and saw wisps of fine, thin, black fur sprouting from the thick, sticky floor. 'Is all this blood from the dog?'

'It's a mixture. A lot came from the teaching assistant, Lauren

Berkley,' Larry said. 'It tugged a chunk from her shoulder and bit a piece of it clean off. Thankfully it caught inside her shirt. Doctors managed to pull it out and stitch it back on.'

Matt felt the Caramac turn suddenly acidic in his gut. 'That's the storeroom, I take it? Where the body was?'

'Correct. And don't worry too much if you step on some of this blood. The testing's all done. Cleaners are going to blitz the place once you're done, anyway.'

The trail of reddish-brown paw prints led from the pool on the floor to the gap under the storeroom door. He could see wild and chaotic streaks in it, where the dog's claws had frantically scraped and scampered.

The door had a sign saying *Music Cupboard*. It had some hand-drawn pictures in the corners. Guitars, bongo-drums, keyboards and a microphone. The images were too good and too meticulous for primary school level, so he knew the kids hadn't done this. He wondered if Stephanie Ellis had drawn these herself. Pictured her with her big hair, sitting at home at her kitchen table late on a weekday. Sipping red wine with that big smile of hers. Taking great care, with pursed lips and multiple felt tips, to hand-draw all those tiny musical notes that floated on the waves from each instrument.

Larry went for the handle and pulled it back. Matt felt his chest tighten at the stench.

'So . . . this is why I called you.'

Abattoir.

That was the word that came to mind once the door creaked back.

It looked like an abattoir with huge arches of blood sprayed up the back wall. A nauseous-looking pool soaked the far corner, thick enough to look black. *She died there*, he thought, as he stared at the corner. She died *right* there. Scattered among the blood were golden kazoos that had fallen from the shelves. They were sticky with it, tilted on their sides, like shipwrecks trapped in a thick sea.

'Jesus.' Matt cupped a hand over his nose and mouth.

'I'll get you a mask.'

He shook his head. 'I'm fine. There's just . . . so *much* of it.'

'That's cos the dog clipped right through her jugular. She'd have bled out in under a minute but obviously she . . . well, she thrashed about a bit.' He pointed one of his stubby fingers up at the wall. One long jet had even reached the white tiles of the ceiling.

'And you're absolutely sure it was just a dog that did this? There were no other wounds on her?'

'It looks like it's just the dog, but I'm waiting for confirmation on that.' Larry patted the phone in his pocket. 'Till then, I'm keeping an open mind.'

'This animal . . .' Matt finally took his hand away from his mouth. Forcing himself into small shallow breaths. 'The paper said it was her own pet? Sounds rather unusual.'

'Oh, it's rare but dogs do attack their owners. Put them under enough stress and they turn wild, but then . . . I guess that's the same of humans, too.' Larry sniffed. 'Mrs Phillips wasn't quite herself anyway, but hiding out in here seems to have sent the dog for a loop.'

Matt paused for a moment and took in one of the taller arches of blood. 'What do you think she was hiding from?'

'Life, maybe? The head teacher says she'd had a brief bout with depression last year. Maybe it came back.'

He paused for a second and thought of a fellow minister back in the day who woke up one Sunday morning and couldn't get out of bed for church. He literally couldn't shift his legs with the stress of it all.

'But . . .' Larry caught Matt's eye, 'if she was actually scared of something else . . . then I thought maybe you could tell me what it was.'

Matt shrugged. 'And how on earth would I work that out?'

'By reminding me what the hell those are . . .'

He blinked. Followed Larry's gaze.

He turned, 180 degrees, and looked at the back of the storeroom door. The inside of it was plastered with sheets of A4 papers, hastily stuck with gaffer tape. The ones at the bottom were thoroughly splashed with blood.

'According to the staff, these sheets weren't there before,' Larry said. 'So it looks like she put them up, before she locked herself in. I recognise them but I need you to tell me exactly what they mean.'

Matt walked toward them slowly, the plastic of his overshoes crinkling against the curves of dried blood. He tilted his head, frowning at the symbols carefully drawn in black biro. Each page had about twenty symbols each, all of them the same. There were six pages that he could see. 'That . . .' Matt pointed a finger at the sheets, 'is really very odd.'

'I'm sure I've seen these before somewhere.'

'In a church probably.'

'So they aren't Satanic?'

Matt laughed and shook his head. He pointed at one of them: a letter *P* with a *T* across its stem. 'This is called a Staurogram or a Tau-Rho. It's from ancient Greece. It's a combination of their word Tau – that's the T-shape – and Rho – that's the bit that looks like a P.'

'Yeah, but what does it mean?'

'It's an alternative symbol for the cross. The early church used it. It's not that common, but you do see it in a fair few chur—' he stopped talking.

'What?' Larry said.

Matt dropped lower. Became a dwarf at the bottom of the door. He grabbed one of the shelves to steady himself. 'Wow.'

'Wow, *what?*'

He tapped a finger toward the paper, being careful not to actually touch it. 'Can you see the animal picture?' The sheet was sodden with dried blood.

'Yes. We thought it might be a swan.'

'It's not. It's a pelican. I haven't seen one of these in years.' Matt gazed at the scrawled animal. The wings were hunched up over its chicks as it fed them with long slivers of pink meat, which dangled from its beak. 'There's a legend . . .' he said to Larry, but with his eyes fixed on the bird. 'There's a legend . . . during a time of ancient famine, a mother pelican got desperate to feed her young. There was nothing left to feed them so she used her beak to tear open her own flesh. She fed the meat to her young, so they'd live. She let them drink her blood too.'

'Well, that's messed up.'

'So says the Catholic?' Matt looked up at him. 'Larry, the Christian church picked up on this legend and applied the symbol to Jesus. They said *he* was like this mother, giving his flesh and blood, so that his children could live, and be restored.'

'Ah, right. When you put it that way it's not that bad—'

'Actually the Christian gospel is still pretty twisted . . . pretty dark . . .' Matt said. 'Anyway. This pelican symbol's cropped up in Dante, in Shakespeare and it was especially popular in medieval times. Pilgrims sometimes wore a badge with it on, with rubies for the blood.'

'And today?'

He screwed up his face. Shook his head, 'You *occasionally* see it in churches, though not that often. I'm pretty sure some Cathedrals have a golden lectern depicting this . . .' Matt said. 'Anyway, it's a sign of Jesus's provision and protection. I wouldn't say it's that well known.'

Larry rubbed his chin for a moment and turned back so he could watch the corner of gore. He had his fingers hooked on the back of his neck. Matt noticed Larry did that a lot when he was thinking.

He pushed himself back up and heard his knees grinding. 'So she locked herself in . . .' Matt leant toward the door, 'with just a latch?'

'Yes. Obviously the dog couldn't work it so he was trapped and flipped out.'

'But up until the attack, *she* could have easily left.'

He nodded. 'They keep iPads in here for music work so they tend to lock it with a key from the outside. But there's a latch on the inside that'll open it up. It's there in case kids get shut in and need to get out.'

'So . . . she closed it with the latch on . . .' He caught Larry's eyes. 'Hiding from someone outside? In the classroom maybe?'

Larry said nothing, just walked toward the door and pushed it open, gesturing for Matt to follow. 'Speaking of animals.'

It felt good to get out of the metallic, cloying air of that butchers room. He followed Larry across the class, stepping wide over the pool of dog blood that he suspected would never, *ever* come out of that wood.

They reached the back of the classroom.

'And *this* is the other thing,' Larry said. 'Why would she do this?'

The wall was covered with children's pictures, but now they were closer he could see there was something wrong with them.

'They're upside down,' Matt said.

'All of them.'

Matt hinged himself at the hip and tilted his head so he could see them the right way up. They showed animals from music, songs and symphonies, scrawled in crayon. No pelicans, that he could see. He could see the rips and tears in the corner of the pictures, where someone had pulled them from the wall and stapled them back up again. Blood started rushing to his head.

'Did you fingerprint the stapler?'

Frank Sinatra replied, singing *Fly me to the moon and let me play among the stars . . . .*

He turned back upright and saw Larry scrabbling for his mobile.

'Give me a sec.' *Let me know what life is like on Ju—* 'Hello? This is Forbes.' He wandered over to the window to answer.

Matt waited, perched on the edge of the kids' tables while he scanned the strange pictures. Stick people and animals, paraded across the wall on their heads. Pointed ears shot down like legs while legs sprouted upward like pointed ears.

The smell of blood was still there, making his nostrils twitch.

Larry stood at the window for a minute. Nodded a few times, then he said, 'Thanks,' and dropped his hand in his pocket. He clapped his hands together. 'Well . . . I'm sorry for wasting your time, Matt.'

'Huh?'

'Pathologist just got back. He's confirmed the cause of death. Mrs Ellis died from a deep dog bite to the side of her throat. Nothing more.'

'But you suspected there might be something else? Another wound maybe?'

'I was keeping an open mind. But there aren't any other unusual prints in there either. It's her hand on the stapler. Her hand on the door latch. Looks like the papers are right. We've got a troubled woman, doing a few nutty things before shutting herself in a cupboard.'

'And the symbols?'

He shrugged. 'You said they were for protection. Maybe she Googled them.'

'She'd have to Google pretty deep to get the pelican symbol. Even the Tau-Rho . . .' Matt looked back at the storeroom and clicked a finger. 'CCTV!'

Larry smiled, and the smile turned into a tiny chuckle. 'I do admire your enthusiasm but they don't have cameras in the classrooms. It's a child safety risk. There's a few cameras at the gates and one that covers the playground.'

'And?'

'They recorded Mrs Ellis and her dog rocking up here at about three in the morning, yesterday. She was alone. It's the last image of her alive. Next time anybody saw her was yesterday at the open day.' Larry looked down at his fingernails.

Matt stood up from the desk. 'So that's it? You're just moving on?'

'Not quite. Now I go and tell the husband that he was right all along. His wife was killed by an unstable dog.'

'Does *he* have an alibi?'

'You sound like Columbo.'

'Does he?'

'Yes,' Larry nodded. 'They have a seven-year-old son. The kid was having a lot of bad dreams lately so they let him stay in their room. He was there last night. Slept next to the dad till the morning.'

Matt thought of Amelia again, scared of her room, and he saw him and Wren dressed in prissy Victorian-era outfits refusing to let her sleep in their bed, and forcing her to sleep in hers, instead. Compassion? What's that? The child *must* learn.

He blew out a whistling, guilty breath. 'I want to come.'

'Pardon?'

'Let me come with you. I can ask him about the symbols. Find out where she learnt them from.'

'Don't you have to get back?'

He checked his watch. 'I've got ages.'

Larry shrugged. 'But you let me do the talking, right?'

'Right.'

'Right.' He paused for a second, then he shrugged and they headed out together, Matt taking one last look at the room and the blood pools in it. Outside, an officer with gloves helped them peel off the MC Hammer shoes, now caked with drying blood, and he greedily sucked in fresh air as they crossed the playground to reach the car.

Larry gave the nod to the policewoman. 'Cleaners can start.'

Just before Matt got in the car he glanced up at the building and noticed the CCTV camera, watching them all with its never-closing eye. Then he looked over at the gates to find the church clan. He thought he might toddle over there, just to dig a little deeper, but they were gone. In fact, the entire street outside of the school looked totally empty and desolate. No moving cars, no locals walking. The only movement was a cold breeze, which blew the leaves in a twirling dance along the pavement.

CHAPTER SEVEN

The front door creaked open. Behind it was a woman in her sixties. Steph Ellis's mother. Tiny she was, with a bunched-up little face and hunched shoulders. A Jim Henson puppet of a woman who didn't smile when the door opened. But then, losing a daughter tends to take that body function away for a while.

'Hello again, Evelyn,' Larry said.

She stared at him. *Through* him.

'I'd like a quick word with your son-in-law, please.'

She closed her eyes and nodded. Old lips pursed, tight and pale.

'And this is a colleague, Matthew Hunter.'

Larry had dropped the Professor bit. Wisely, Matt thought. No point in flagging up that this woman's dead daughter was becoming something of a theological exhibit. It didn't matter, anyway. Evelyn had exactly *zero* interest in Matt. She shuffled back on slippered feet and let them through as she stared at the wall.

The hall had laminate flooring in pine effect with black and white flowery wallpaper. A large, glass, fairy-tale mirror hung on the wall with a silver, gilded frame. He'd seen this look in the Next catalogue. Seemed to be the thing at the moment. The only clutter he could see was from a small boy's action figures that were lined up at the bottom of the stairs. He could smell dog in the air too, which was the first time he realised that the four-legged murderer happened to live in this house too.

'Where is he?' Larry asked.

Evelyn cleared her throat, which made a tiny bit of food pop onto her lip. Something white. 'Greg's in the conservatory and he's been there most of the day.' She looked at their legs. 'Take your shoes off.'

They kicked them off and slid them into a neat row.

As they headed through the lounge to the conservatory, Matt wasn't quite sure what he expected. Perhaps a red-eyed widower rocking in a rattan chair, surrounded by tear-wet wedding albums. But as they walked into the bright, glass-filled room he saw Mr Ellis with his son. If he was remembering the article correctly the kids name was Josh Ellis, the seven-year-old that Larry said was having the nightmares. They were leaning over a table about a metre and a half square, both of them with fine little brushes, flicking dust from the rooftops of a spectacular village scene made from Lego.

Okay, this *was* an investigation and these two *had* just lost a mum and wife. But this was Lego.

'Wow.' Matt walked closer. 'That's incredible!'

Greg looked up and smiled. 'It's Innsbruck.'

'That's in Austria,' the boy said. 'In Europe.'

'I *see* . . . well, you've done an amazing job. It's really spectacular.' Matt went to crouch. 'Sheesh . . . may I?'

Greg nodded.

Matt dropped a little so he could look over the rooftops. He always did this with models. He got low so he could look *through* them rather than down at them. Seemed cooler that way. There were little mountains in the distance made of grey bricks, with white bricks at the top for snow. They'd made cobbled streets from different shades. The cows even had tiny bells hanging from their necks. A full diorama and seriously impressive.

'This must have taken days,' Larry said, immediately demonstrating his Lego incompetence.

'Try months.' Greg nodded to a neat pile of small, transparent plastic crates. Each of them was filled with different-coloured bricks. There were postcards stuck to them too, as a guide. Cut-outs of ski-chalets and hotels. A bar of Milka chocolate sat on the side, half-eaten.

'We went on holiday here last year,' Josh said. 'Me and mummy have been building this ever since. She says it'll win competitions . . .'

Matt waited. 'Well I'd vote for it in a shot. It's superb.'

Josh smiled. 'Me and Daddy are going to finish it, now Mummy can't. Aren't we?'

Greg wanted to speak. He even cracked a big smile, but it was so false that it half faded instantly. He just stared into the plastic village square for a second and dropped his head quickly to his chest. Josh seemed to understand exactly what was happening because he quickly looked away and started brushing a tiny skier. For a few seconds all Matt could hear was the swish of the brush, the ticking of the radiator, the whimpering of the widower.

Greg wiped his eye with his thumb, quickly as if nobody might notice, then he slid his arm around the boy and kissed him square on his head. Holding the lips there for a few tender moments, whispering into his hair, 'Now how about you go and watch TV for a minute. Grab some more chocolate from Nana. You deserve some chocolate.'

Josh nodded and handed the little brush back to his dad. He passed through Larry and Matt but paused at the door. 'Daddy?'

They all stood silently, looking at him.

'Yes?'

'Be careful with the roof tiles on the cafe. Mummy says they always slide off.'

Greg put up a thumb as Josh turned to go but he seemed to look at his dad for a long moment, not wanting to let him out of his sight. Like if he was to look away and turn back, there'd be another empty space in his house.

'Go ahead, son,' Greg said, with a softness that could break the heart. 'Then we'll fix up the cable cars next.'

Josh nodded then left. He signalled to Matt to close the doors.

'Grab a seat,' he said. 'Would you blokes like a drink?'

'We're good, thanks,' Larry said, as he and Matt sank onto a wicker sofa. It creaked under them, like twisting rope. 'Greg, I just wanted to pop round to confirm the cause of death.'

A pause. Long enough to hear children in another garden outside, laughing. 'Go on.'

'It was just as you thought, a dog bite. Nothing more, nothing less.'

There were two little brushes that were still in Greg's hand. Matt noticed the knuckles around them gradually turning white. Greg turned to the window, sucked in a breath then flung the brushes away as hard as he could. They bounced off glass with a sharp little crackle and skitted across the floor. He stared at his shoes in silence.

Matt went to speak to Greg's back, to express his condolences but Larry caught his eye and shook his head.

Just wait. Give him a sec.

'She had the same sort of Labrador when she was a kid,' Greg said, finally. 'I never wanted one but she said a family needs a dog. That it'd be good protection.' He shook his head at the psychotic irony of that statement.

'Protection from what?' Matt said.

'Burglars, I guess,' he turned halfway back. 'We argued about getting it. But she fell in love with him. She said Samson always knew how she was feeling.' That last bit made him laugh, bitterly, then he turned full around, with a slow, calm voice. 'I wish those parents hadn't killed it, you know. Because I'd much rather have dragged it into my back garden myself. I'd have really liked to have torn that dog's tongue out.' He finally sank into one of the chairs. 'I'd have liked that a lot.'

Silence, then the neighbour's kids laughed again outside.

'And it had never shown aggression before?' Larry said.

'Do they *ever*?' Greg said. 'Watch the news. These dog owners always say they'd never hurt a fly and let them play with their babies until it rips their—' He stopped himself. 'Anyway. They're time bombs, waiting to go off. All of them . . .' he looked at Matt. 'I don't know you.'

'I'm Matt Hunter.'

'You're a policeman?'

'No. I'm—'

'The symbols I mentioned,' Larry said. 'They looked religious to me and that's Matt's area.'

'So *are* they?' Greg said. 'Religious, I mean?'

'Yes. They're Christian signs of protection. Fairly unusual ones. Was your wife a believer?'

Greg shook his head. 'Protection from what?'

Matt shrugged. 'Evil. The Devil. Was Mrs Ellis scared of anything you'd describe in that way? Did she mention any—'

'Nothing at all.'

Larry waited. 'Some of the other staff at the school. They said Mrs Ellis was—'

'Dammit . . .' Greg slammed a hand on the arm of the chair. Dust particles burst like fireworks, and somehow the sound must have thrown pressure across the room, because a little Lego woman fell over with a click. 'Stop with the Mrs Ellis stuff . . . just call her Steph.'

'Sorry. Of course. Her school colleagues said Steph was distant lately. That she wasn't quite herself. Perhaps another bout of depression?'

He shook his head. 'She had a bit of stress. School's got OFSTED coming up. Nothing major.'

OFSTED? Better sort that blood-soaked floor out pronto.

'And if you don't mind me asking . . .' Matt said. 'Were things okay at home? Was she—'

'Things were fine!' Greg snapped, and he looked at Larry. 'He's talking like she killed herself or something.'

'I'm sorry, I didn't mean—'

'She was *fine*. She had as much stress as anybody else. Sometimes she couldn't sleep so maybe she went to school to do some work. She liked working on the kids' displays. She was . . . arty.'

'At three in the morning?' Matt said.

Larry caught Matt's eye and gave him a tiny shake of the head. *Stop asking questions.*

It was too late. Greg was leaning forward on his chair, pissed off.

'*Yes*, at three in the morning. Why not? She was kind of whacky when she wanted to be and that's one of the reasons I loved her . . .' He paused for a moment. Gazed at the Lego village, at a tiny little car with a family in it: a Dad, a Mum and a little boy pulling up to a hotel. He stared at it. 'I dunno, maybe she was knackered and fell asleep in the cupboard and Samson just flipped, but listen . . . she wasn't crazy. She wasn't *troubled*. Life was okay for her. Work was good. She had great friends here. In fact . . .' he ran a hand across his chin, 'in fact she was getting together with a bunch of old girlfriends this afternoon. They were going to have a picnic in the park and she wrote that on the calendar *that* night. So don't go thinking she was making plans to top herself. And she hardly did it by setting a dog on herself, did she?' He finally stopped, and caught some breath.

'Mr Ellis,' Matt said, 'I'm sorry.'

'Please . . . just call me Greg, okay?' He waited for a long moment then looked up, his face apologetic. 'Do you want to know the last thing she said to me? Before we went to sleep that night?'

They both nodded.

'Me and her let Josh in our bed because he's been having bad dreams. He fell asleep between us and me and her just talked. Just before she drifted off, she took my hand and . . .' He stopped. His chin started to twitch. His chest rose in tiny little jerks. 'She kissed me on the head and said . . . I was . . . that I was the best thing that ever happened to her. And that was the last thing she ever said to me.'

'Greg?' Matt said, and the children outside immediately stopped laughing. 'What happened in the morning?'

'Well, I get up for work at six and I always tiptoe out of there so I don't wake her. I don't put lights on. Josh was next to me, I know that. But I didn't even notice she wasn't there when I left the house . . . Josh says when he woke up he thought we'd both just gone to work. So he just spent all day on the model . . .'

'He stayed at home all day?' Larry asked. 'He didn't go to school?'

'It's too far to walk, so he just sat here confused all day, waiting for his mum to . . .' Greg looked down at his hands. They were trembling.

Larry turned to Matt. 'Give us a second, okay?'

'Okay,' Matt stood and headed for the lounge. The conservatory and mini-Innsbruck began filling with the sounds of deep, bitter tears. Just as he went for the door that led to the lounge, he saw something that startled him.

A tiny hand vanished from the glass.

CHAPTER EIGHT

Bless him.

Josh had rushed to the sofa and thrown himself on it, eyes fixed on the Scooby Doo cartoon that was playing on the TV. He was acting like he'd been watching this the entire time, and not lurking, listening to the grown-ups.

Matt walked up and quietly sat next to him. 'Oh, I've seen this one,' he nodded at the screen. 'It's the one when they meet that guy who's made of fire.'

Josh nodded. 'Actually it's electricity. He's about 10,000 volts.'

'Zoinks . . . that's a lot.'

'Yeah, he can melt through snow and gates and doors and stuff.'

'That's probably pretty handy . . . I guess.'

They watched the screen for a while. Shaggy and Scooby were tiptoeing through a factory, looking for food. Both were wearing earmuffs. He let it play out for a few moments. 'I guess you heard us talking then?'

He was silent.

'Would you like to talk about it? About your mum?'

Josh reached for the remote control and tapped the volume down a few notches. The funky bass lines of the cartoon soundtrack sank into the background. 'He's wrong, you know.'

'Who is?'

'Daddy.'

Matt looked back at the conservatory. Maybe he should wait until Larry came back—

'She *was* scared.'

Matt turned on the sofa. 'Of what?'

Josh had blonde hair, curled into a tuft at the front. The collar of a white shirt poked out from under his jumper. Smart-looking. As well organised and pruned as the house itself. As ordered as the coloured stacks of Lego bricks. 'Daddy goes away sometimes.'

'With work?'

Josh shook his head. 'With friends, I think. Sometimes he stays over.'

'I see.'

'On the nights he isn't here, Mummy freaks out a bit . . . like last week.'

'What happened last week?'

'He wasn't home again so she woke me up in the middle of the night. She said we had to hide.' Josh stared at the TV. The 10,000-volt monster thing was stomping through a corridor, enraged. 'She'd pulled all of her dresses out of the cupboard. Then she got me and Samson and said we all had to climb in. We shut the door and hid.'

'Was Samson okay with that?'

Josh nodded, like it was an odd question. 'He was fine. He just cuddled up.'

'Do you know who she was hiding from?'

He finally turned to him. 'She was hiding from the bad thing.'

A pause. 'What's the bad thing?'

'She wouldn't say. She said she kept seeing it in town. Said the bad thing tried to talk to her once, in the park.'

'It can speak?'

He nodded.

'So the bad thing was a person, then?'

'No, I don't think so,' he shrugged. 'She just said the bad thing came back to Menham and that it was in our garden that night and she didn't want it to know anybody was home. That *we* were home. So we hid in the cupboard.'

Matt looked back at the conservatory. Larry had his hand on Greg's quaking shoulders. 'Did anybody else know about the bad thing?'

'She said her friends had seen it. A really long time ago.'

'Which friends?'

'Dunno,' he shook his head. 'She said I didn't have to be scared but I was because . . . well, because *she* was. She was shaking . . . like this.' He held out thin, pale hands and trembled them.

'So . . .' Matt said. 'Did you stay in the cupboard for long?'

'About an hour. Then she started to cry and she kept saying she was sorry. I slept with her that night, and did it for the rest of the week.'

'What about your nightmares, I heard you—'

'I didn't have any nightmares. I just didn't think I should leave her alone.'

He caught his eye and smiled at him. 'You're a brave, decent kid.'

'Thank you.' Josh seemed like he might cry. 'That's nice.'

'And last night was your dad next to you all night?'

'I think so, yeah. He snores anyway, so I heard that a lot.'

Matt laughed, 'And what about that night your mum hid you in the cupboard. Did *you* see this person? This thing?'

''Course not.'

'I see. Perhaps it was in her imagi—'

'But I heard it . . . I think.'

Matt glanced back at the conservatory. Larry was tugging his jacket into place. They were starting to stand up.

'Or rather, I heard its friend.'

'It has a friend?'

'Mummy says it does.'

'So what did you hear?'

'I heard singing.'

'Like a person?'

'Like a little girl . . .'

Matt leant in, 'Is this little girl the bad thing?'

The door to the conservatory rattled open.

'U-uh,' he shook his head. 'Mum says the little girl *brings* the bad thing. That's how it works.'

Larry started coming through, still talking.

Josh quickly leant in to Matt and grabbed his hand. The kids palm was clammy and very warm. He whispered, 'So you'll find them for me, won't you? The girl . . . and the thing . . . And you'll kill them both dead . . . for what they did? Shoot them or something. Set them on fire?'

Before he could say anything Greg came up behind them. He grabbed the remote control. 'Best not watch this stuff, eh Josh?'

The TV clicked off, and the raging fiery monster vanished from the screen.

'It's alright,' Josh nodded to Matt. 'We've both seen this one before.'

They headed back to the hallway where the mum was waiting by the door, rearranging ornaments on a side table while she bit her lip hard. The thought crossed Matt's mind that Steph Ellis was more delusional than anybody had realised, what with the singing thing in her garden. But the thought sounded hollow in his head

84

and he wondered what Josh may have actually heard, in the lowest caverns of night. He could have easily slipped into a dream, he supposed. Matt wanted to ask Steph's mum a few questions too, but Larry had already made it clear it was better just to give them all some space.

It was as he leant against the wall to tug on his shoe that he first saw the calendar. It was hanging by the telephone. A few of the entries jumped out, because they were in red ink.

October 3rd: Sharing Assembly
October 12th: Derry Farm Trip (Josh take wellies!)
October 21st: Greg DENTIST!

But it was today's date that made him deliberately dawdle, while lacing up his shoe.

October 29th: Steph. Picnic with the Girls. Menham Park.
Gazebo. 12:30pm

Interesting.

He felt a hand on his shoulder and almost jumped. He turned to see Greg standing there. 'Look . . . I'm sorry if I was a bit harsh. I know you're just doing your job.'

Matt stood. 'Don't apologise.'

'I just don't like it when people say she was crazy. She wasn't crazy.'

'Understood . . . and Greg,' Matt took his hand, 'I am so sorry that you're going through this.'

It was a very strange thing to say. It sounded like you were apologising for somebody's tragedy, even though you didn't cause it. But there was something powerful and universal in that bundle of words. Just one of the rituals humans have.

Greg nodded, and smiled. 'I appreciate that.'

The mum clicked the door open and before they left Matt turned to see if Josh was going to join them in the hall. But he was still in the lounge, unseen. Matt called out a goodbye, and he heard a faint response back.

'*Bye.*'

He and Larry didn't talk as they walked down the path. Stepping out from the clouds of grief has a tendency to do that. In fact, they didn't talk much, even as the car jerked into reverse as Larry backed off the kerb outside. While they waited for a break in the congested road Matt took a final look at Steph's house. He noticed a wheely bin stuffed with rubbish, including what looked like Halloween decorations of skeletons and witches. Clearly such images were no longer wanted in this house. He glanced from window to window, pausing at the upstairs bedroom. Maybe it was the parents' room. Maybe it was the kid's. But he could just about see a faint shape standing there. A child's shape. He couldn't be sure but it must have been Josh standing behind the net curtains, watching him leave. It just looked skinnier than he was. Smaller.

Then with a surge of the engine, they headed off onto the street, and he started breathing normally again.

Larry lurched the car up by a kerb outside Menham Station, engine still running.

'Like I said,' Larry looked at him. 'Hope I didn't waste your morning.'

Matt turned in his seat. 'So you're not going to dig any deeper? Or speak to these friends of hers?'

Larry smiled. 'Matt. I have *lots* of cases. Some of which have an actual murder victim.'

'And how do you know this isn't one of them? What if the kid's right and she was being followed by something?'

'Some*thing*?'

'Sorry . . . someone. She said she saw a figure in the garden.'

'Look . . . the symbols had me a bit jumpy. I was thinking some cult thing maybe and you're just up the road, but the pathology report is beyond doubt, Matt. It's a canine attack.' He waited for a moment. 'Of course, I'll keep an eye out on this, but at least for now I think we're done here, evidence-wise . . . you look disappointed.'

'Just feel for the kid. And the dad,' Matt shrugged. 'It's intriguing, that's all.'

'Well, these things are rarely boring.' He reached over and shook Matt's hand. 'Thanks for coming out. I'm glad I've got you on hand.'

'Just send me a cheque.'

'Funny,' Larry nodded at the clock on the dash. 'At least you'll be back in time for this charity lunch thing.'

'Oh, that.'

'Are you guest of honour?'

'Ha! Hardly. It's just a uni thing. Each year they gather up any faculty who've written books this year. Then we sell signed copies at inflated prices to raise money for the building. This year they want to build a curling metal slide from the top floor to the bottom.'

Larry curled his lip. '*Why*?'

'It's an art thing that gets students from lecture to lecture quicker . . . that's assuming if they can get *me* off it, of course.' Matt stopped suddenly and reached into his bag. He pulled out a copy of *In Our Image* and passed it to Larry. 'Before I forget. One incredible book, as promised. Just don't tell Father Michael.'

Larry quickly reached into his pocket and pulled out his wallet.

'Don't you dare. It's a freebie.'

'Nah . . . take it.' He handed over a £20 note. 'For the slide. For the kiddies.'

Matt laughed and popped the door. 'You *will* let me know if anything develops?'

'Of course. Thanks, again.'

He pushed the door shut and watched Larry pull away. He gave a toot of his horn, then eased back into the Menham slipstream and was gone. Matt waited for a minute. Maybe he could grab a quick coffee to take on the train with him. He could catch up on his reading for the Raelian movement thing and find out why they loved the Swastika so much. But that's when his mind drifted, because the entire time he'd been considering it, he'd been staring across the street. At those spindly trees he'd seen earlier. They were swaying again, over the metal railings, and he saw the grass that swooped up beyond them, and the winding path lined with lamp posts and litter bins. He could just about make out the roof of something near to a large pond in the distance. A gazebo.

'Menham Park,' he whispered, then glanced down at his watch. 12:07. He should probably get going to make this uni dinner thing on time.

It took him about three seconds to decide.

CHAPTER NINE

Home town.

Weird phrase, that. Sort of reminded her of those brands you burn into cattle so the farmer knows which shed that particular animal belongs in: 17b or S6. Something like that. And even if it was a hard-working, industrial, resourceful cow, who managed to scale the farmer's fence at night, who managed to steal a car and drive to Eastern Europe so they could start a new life as a bartender . . . even then it'd *still* have that flap of mutilated skin somewhere near its backside with its shed number on it.

Rachel Wasson had loved Menham growing up. Like really *loved* it. It was the centre of her world, with a decent school and cracking friends. Best of all, it was just a Tube ride from the South Bank. She'd spent countless hours there with her dad seeing old Hitchcock films at the BFI. But things happen. Situations change. And by the time her dad was dead it was just her and her mum and her sister at 29 Barley Street.

Which, let's face it, seemed to be what the house preferred. She'd often thought that, back when it all happened. And she'd thought that many times since, actually. That the house had only ever wanted *girls* there. Until her beloved Menham became sufficiently polluted to make her want to run away from it very, very fast, the first chance she got.

There were a few other girls at school who also wanted to escape Menham. They told her that her best bet was to marry rich. A footballer, maybe. A businessman. These girls were so repellently old school and Disney-warped that they made Rachel both furious *and* depressed. So she got out of Menham on her own. She studied for her A Levels like her life depended on it. She got a job working at Brodie's shampoo factory behind Menham Fire Station. Slamming plastic tops on bottles until the raw centre of her palm was nigh-on arthritic because Dad was dead and her increasingly strange mum was skint, so she was flying solo. She passed her exams, bought the car that shampoo built and wheel-spinned out of Menham at warp speed to Exeter Uni. She studied sound engineering there. Got her geek on, but for an actual purpose this time. Found herself, cut her hair short, blagged her way into the audio industry by getting some work experience at a sound library up in Manchester. Which led to an actual, real-life job at the end of it. She'd become that ultrarare breed of creatives. One who got paid for it.

Detail. That's what Rachel Wasson was known for in the shrinking sound effects industry. Detail and authenticity. Like how a watermelon sounded utterly different to a pumpkin when you drop it on the floor. Such detail was excessive and pointless according to some, but it was going down well with her firm, and with the growing number of radio and TV producers who regularly used her massive library of sounds.

But despite the budding career and the Manchester flat, and despite her presence on a completely different electoral roll, there was a branded bit of her body, lurking somewhere under her new, consciously retro clothes. A label that said: property of Menham, South London.

Home town, she thought, as she pulled her little Fiat off the roundabout and through Roulette Street. That was the name she and the girls always gave to the road that led to the level crossing. Once through, she knew she was now truly moving through the cold, lizard flow of Menham's bloodstream.

She passed by Menham Comprehensive and noticed something. They'd demolished the old sixth-form block. *Twats!* The brown, corrugated block where she'd studied her way out of Menham was now a stoopid all-weather pitch. The space where it used to be made her instantly angry, like the town had swallowed up one of her most sacred buildings.

But then she spotted the Sports Block, and for the first time since she left the Yorkshire hotel she smiled. A sharp, vivid image of her and the girls popped into her head. Sitting up there with Steph, Kassy and Jo, customising their uniforms with tiny tweaks. Forming trends that would race across the school the next day. Of all those boys who kept wandering past them, gawping at their curves like preprogrammed lab mice. Mostly those boys were looking at Kassy West, of course, who was such a force in school that even the teachers kind of worshipped her. The way she glided into rooms, swooping her fingers through her blonde mane, like a frickin goddess. The way she'd answer the teachers back with such harshness, it was a wonder she was never expelled. The way she treated the boys like crap. Kassy would stand in a dinner queue, posing as if there was a TV camera somewhere. One that only *she* knew about. She'd have this patented tilt of the head that said Kassy West didn't give a shit about anything. Which drew you to her, ironically. Like cats do. Who treat you like dirt yet have this twisted way of earning your admiration.

Whenever Kassy sat with Rachel and the rest of the girls, they all looked like the cover of a cool Blondie album. Whenever Kassy *wasn't* there, they became Bewitched. But the point was Kassy was *always* there, because the girls were *always* together. Which made *all* of them strong. That was the part that Rachel missed. That she missed very much, actually.

Steph Ellis the neat freak with a blond afro, always on another planet, but piss-your-pants funny. Jo Finch, the flappy dumb one who couldn't even spell the word 'spell' yet would sit up with you and stroke your hand for hours, listening to you cry about how crap your parents could be. And Rachel, the funky alternative one, the only one who ever had the guts to stand up to Kassy's ranting.

She felt a weird sense of disorientation, regression, even. Driving past that school. Felt that familiar, deep desire to be with those girls again. To be in *that* collective at *that* particular time. To be what they all once were. Then the weird yet familiar switcheroo happened, where the thought of being back in that group wasn't a fun prospect at all. It was frightening. Disgusting, even.

One of them was dead.

Poor old Steph.

Statistically speaking she always knew this day would come. It hits anyone who moves away from home. It's almost cliché. Chris Rea could write a song about it. 'Driving Home for Funerals'. The retreat we all do for the aftermath and funeral of old best friends. People who had barely been acquaintances for the latest third of your life, and yet are moulded into your neural pathways deeper than anybody you will ever meet again.

She swung her car into the Pay and Display at Menham Park, knowing her old house on Barley Street overlooked this entire area. But of course, she flat out refused to turn and actually look at her street. She'd have to process this entire Menham experience in chunks. The town and the girls first – that was intense enough. Then Mum and *the house* would come after.

She shivered. Was that the smell of her old dead cat Pob on the air? Were his dead ears twitching up in the dusty rooms of that old house behind her? Were dead eyes rolling left in dry skull sockets, delighted to see her car pull in? Was Pob purring and slinking through the trees and the soil, purring in his own way, saying, welcome Rachel . . . welcome back to the house of death?

Her hand was trembling.

She kept facing forward and power-walked toward the gazebo, for this insane picnic Jo had said they were having. With the Hodges of all people. Something she would never have attended under normal circumstance until a dead friend finally shook her out of her selfish fear. She was holding a packed lunch in her hand, which made her feel so pathetic and childlike that she felt like throwing it in the bin so she could just chew on her own heavy breath instead.

She passed the playground that *still* had the same old metal swings and roundabout. They hadn't even replaced the hideous metal rocking horse that used to terrify her as a kid. The one with the flaring nostrils. The one that wanted to crush children's hands and turn them into Eton Mess. The only thing they'd added was a set of warped mirrors, the type you'd get in an amusement park. She caught sight of herself in the most normal one, and flattened the sides of her green cord jacket down. She grabbed her floppy black fringe and slapped her hipster quiff back to its usual position. But as she logged that snapshot of herself in the mirror, she saw a stereotype. The artsy, creative girl, with the MacBook Pro and a frequently updated blog. And she could almost smell the pretentious vinyl scent on her fingertips from the album collection she'd been building back in her flat. Of David Bowie and the Beatles and other bands that she was really trying to get into. And the funky analogue watch with the Japanese anime character, that seemed to suddenly tick loudly like a social bomb on her wrist.

Seeing the reflection slowed her to a stop.

Her persona, her look, fitted into the jazz cafe orbit of the BBC Media Village in Manchester. The Clark Kent nerd glasses, which looked so great on her, seemed now like a sad attempt at transparency. Like this was an obvious declaration that she was a lesbian, since nobody in Menham would even know that she was. But she'd been in Menham for what, twelve minutes? And already her home town was denying her a chance to dress how she wanted and be who she wanted to be. She was dreading Kassy rocking up, looking as catalogue as ever, no doubt. Frowning at how Rachel looked these days. But that's not what really got to her, deep in her gut. What really got to her was gazing at herself while some kids laughed on the swings and others ran past kicking up bits of damp woodchip over her shoes. They kept running past the mirror, back and forth, so that her reflection shimmered in and out. Saying . . .

In this town, Rachel, you are the girl from the weird family. The scary family. You are from the family who will only ever be defined by the death house. Because actually, that's what your little cow brand says, no matter how much you hide it. It doesn't even say Menham down there, does it? It says something else. It says: this is the sister of the famous Holly Wasson. This is a Barley Street girl.

'Rachel?'

She froze, unsure of where the voice had come from. When she turned she saw an overweight woman standing by a revolving roundabout. And it was the once rake-thin Jo Finch, who was now huge, standing in a grey blouse and black baggy culottes.

'Jo?'

Jo flung her massive arms open and hipster Rach 2.0 was wiped instantly off the earth. Her crap disguise sizzled into the air under the cold sun. Now, once again, she was a fifteen-year-old Fugees fan with one of her *bezzy mates eva* clumping along the path with her arms wide, bingo wings swaying. Smelling of Avon perfume with a strong hint of ghost cat, crushing her in an unashamed, weeping hug, with words that just might unravel everything that had happened in the last fifteen years of her life.

'You're home, Rach. You're finally home.'

CHAPTER TEN

Matt was fully aware that Steph Ellis was dead. Which meant her girlfriends may not turn up for their little gazebo park date at all. Dog-fuelled death wasn't usually followed by *let's have a picnic*. But if they *did* come, to talk about it maybe, to cry about it, then Matt wasn't sure how he'd play it at all. Would he just sidle up to a bunch of grieving women, a complete stranger, and start asking about singing little girls and bad things?

All this pondering vanished in a pop as soon as he saw the painted wooden gazebo.

Standing inside it, slipping a satchel from his shoulder, was 70s *Joy of Sex Man*. The guy he'd seen lurking outside Menham Primary School earlier this morning. This time, however, he wasn't alone. A woman was with him, leaning her elbows on the wooden panel of the gazebo. She was looking out at a morbidly obese oak tree nearby, pointing at it and talking. At first, Matt thought she might be one of Steph's school friends, someone who'd turned up early to the meeting, until he realised her bobbed hair was actually bone-white, not bleached blonde. The closer he got, the more he knew she was probably in her sixties, just like the bearded guy who she turned to kiss for a moment. Planted her mouth deep into all that wiry, brown face hair.

He trotted down the hill toward them as they settled themselves onto the wooden benches that lined the inside panels of the gazebo. They pulled out a flask and white camping mugs. Beardy man was shaking the last morsel from a sweetener dispenser into his drink, and was doing it with such focus and precision that he failed to notice Matt approach. The woman, though, she caught his eye. In fact, she spotted him from *way* back. She said nothing to the beard next to her, gave no indication. Just watched Matt cross the grass and step around the overflowing bin with its merry troupe of dancing flies. Her gaze was constant and quiet as he ducked under the huge swoop of the oak tree whose thickest branch reached up to the gazebo like a fat witch's finger.

Close now, he could see her denim jacket had embroidered flowers on it and it covered a long, flowing black skirt underneath. Art teacher. That was his first thought. An old, probably pretty in her time, art teacher, who wasn't afraid to stare.

Matt reached the steps and held up his hand. 'Hi.'

The man looked up and instantly stopped rattling the sweetener out. His beard perked up into a huge shopping-centre-Santa smile. He nudged the woman. 'Well, would you *look* at that.' He sounded Welsh.

'Sorry to interrupt you,' Matt waited at the bottom of the steps. 'But I think I saw you up at the school earlier. At Menham Primary?'

He nodded and set the cup down. 'And I saw *you*. In fact, I saw you go right on inside, Professor Hunter.'

'Yes, I was helping out with—' Matt's eyebrow went up a notch at the mention of his name. 'We've met before?'

97

'Oh, you and me go *way* back.'

Matt clenched his teeth, 'I'm terribly sorry, I don't remember.'

He grabbed his satchel and swished the zip open, then he pulled something out. The corner of the newspaper. It was the *Mail*. 'Joyce and I first met you this morning, over our Coco-Pops.'

'Ah.' Matt smiled. 'That thing's following me around today.'

The man nodded, and neatly folded it back into his bag. 'It was a silly little article, really. But we did order your book off the back of it. The elves at Amazon are digging it out as we speak.'

'Then I like you already.'

He chortled a little. 'Well it looks fascinating, and actually . . . you could say we've got similar interests . . .' The man stopped talking and suddenly frowned at Matt who was still standing on the bottom step. 'But don't stand down there like a pop bottle, son. Come on up and have an Earl Grey.'

He stepped up to them and was reminded of his tallness, because his was the only head to waft through the threads of spider silk that swooped between the wooden beams. They stretched all the way from the tree branch to the gazebo roof. His forehead broke the web in two and the sticky fibres fluttered down.

'Urgh.' Matt wiped the gluey strands out of his hair. 'I've been slimed.'

'Yup,' the man nodded. 'Right on the noggin.'

Matt smiled at the word 'noggin'. It was impossible not to. He put the clean hand out to shake. 'And you are?'

'Name's Bob Hodges. And this is my wife, Joyce.'

Joyce, who hadn't spoken yet, took his hand and held it for longer than people normally do. She leant into him and Matt saw her nostrils, and the tiny white hairs in them, quiver. She was smelling him. She quietly gazed into his eyes for a full ten seconds. Long enough for Matt to make an awkward joke.

'Please tell me there's not a spider in my eye,' he said.

She laughed, then put her other hand across the top of his so that both were wrapped around it. Her fingers were dry and crackled. A lizard's skin, but very warm. She suddenly let the hands go and smiled. 'Well, aren't *you* interesting?'

And aren't you kooky?

'And do you smoke, Matt?'

'Er . . .' he shook his head, '. . . does a cigar at Christmas count?'

'No,' she looked at his chest. 'I thought I could smell smoke on you.'

'I reckon that's the Earl Grey . . . or my cheap deodorant.' Matt sniffed the air then took a seat, while Joyce wrinkled her nose and shook her head, frowning. 'So, Bob . . . you were at the school earlier, making notes. May I ask why?'

'I was just trying to get to the bottom of what happened to our client yesterday.'

'Client?' Matt took the cup Bob was handing over. 'Do you mean Steph Ellis?'

'I do. We've known her for nigh on fifteen years. Joyce and I used to be science teachers at her secondary school. We taught Steph and her friends way back around 2000 – you know . . .' he did finger quotes, 'in ye olden days.'

Joyce crossed her legs, and patted her skirt flat against her knee. 'But she came to see us last week. And that time it was in our . . . current capacity.' She also sounded Welsh, but not quite as broad as Bob.

'Which is?'

Bob pursed his lips before speaking. 'We're demonologists, Matt.'

The words dangled in the air, swinging back and forth, and the couple just sat in the breezy silence, waiting to see how Matt would respond.

'Ever met one of our kind before?' Joyce said.

Matt pushed his lips forward, instantly thinking of Milo

Simonetti, a young guy from Swindon who he'd debated at uni last year. Milo worked on the deli counter in Tesco by day, and drove out demons by night. Matt had given the kid every chance, and been super polite on stage, but Milo had made it so easy for the crowd to mock him. Shouting 'Harry Potter is a Spiritual Terrorist!' was perhaps his finest misfire, and Matt could still hear the giggles and hoots from the atheist crowd as Matt dismantled the kids worldview. A hundred students shouted 'Expelliarmus!' and 'Wingardium Leviosa!', as Milo slumped off stage, amid screeches of laughter. He'd felt like a bit of a dick after that, but was kind of vindicated when Milo got arrested the following month. He'd misdiagnosed a doctor's receptionist as being possessed by the Egyptian demon Ammit. Naturally this freaked her out. So much so that she tried to jump off a viaduct, until a doctor called to confirm that her demonic episodes were just good old-fashioned epilepsy.

'The demon business,' Matt said, 'is a very dangerous game.'

Bob nodded slowly, missing the point. 'It most certainly is, but we're fighting the good fight.' He pumped the air with his fist.

Joyce leaned forward. 'We study all elements of the paranormal. Not just demons. We do angels and spirits. Hauntings, possessions, psychic phenomena. I'm a medium myself.'

Oooo, the temptation to ask if Bob was an extra large.

'And on the demon side ... are you connected with the churches?'

She laughed at that. 'Sadly most denominations tend to either ignore this stuff ... or condemn it outright. We find that Christians prefer to avoid the supernatural. '

'Which is ruddy ironic, if you ask us,' Bob said.

'I see.' Matt looked down at his tea. 'So is there a lot of call for demonologists around here?'

'We're getting more and more requests these days,' he said. 'You'd be amazed.'

All the while, Joyce was looking at Matt intently, or rather, she now seemed to be looking *around* him. Just over his shoulder. Just above his head. Eyeing up the silk spider strands that were probably waving in the breeze from his hair.

'Now, I'm more the nuts and bolts end,' Bob said. 'I take readings and make notes. I record any activity. I log and chart it, because Matthew, I have to be honest with you . . . I'm a sucker for a spreadsheet.'

Joyce's eyes finally flicked from around Matt, *to* Matt. 'He's been known to measure the cut of his sandwiches . . . with a ruler.' She laughed gently through her fingers.

'Whereas my better half here,' he placed a palm softly on her shoulder, and squeezed, '*she's* the engine. She's the medium. She connects with the ether and sifts the good – the restless souls, the dead just wanting to get peace – and the bad. The negative spirits itching to screw everybody up. Light and dark, basically. That's our business.'

'And there's a *lot* of dark out there,' Joyce said. 'Bob's building a database on metaphysical hotspots in London. He's working on a smartphone app. We're thinking of calling it Spirit Advisor.'

'Though we might still go for Spoogle,' Bob's eyes flashed. 'You know . . . like it's a spooky version of—'

Matt snorted a laugh right into his tea, and it splashed up his nostrils, because according to his students the word spoogle meant something much more racy. Ah, the beautiful English language. He spluttered out a quick apology, 'I'm sorry.' He wiped his lip with the back of his hand, still smiling. 'I like Spirit Advisor. Sounds more classy.'

'Don't apologise. I know we sound a little odd, but we've been doing this for years,' Bob went on. 'We've had a few articles published in journals. Got a couple of books up on Amazon. So you see we *do* have similar lines of work.'

101

'Apart from one tiny fact . . .' He smiled, awkwardly. 'I don't actually believe in the supernatural.'

'But it's still your bread and butter, isn't it? It's still what fills your mind each day. You know . . . the strange stuff . . . the gods and monsters.'

Joyce leant forward a little. 'And it *is* the strange things that grab you, Matt. I can tell that. In fact, it's been the case even back when you were a little boy, hasn't it? It's very, very clear from your eyes.'

'M-hmm,' Matt said, in almost a groan.

'So you see, you are very similar to us.'

Matt waited for a moment, then he checked his watch. 'So . . . Steph Ellis. Why did she come to you?'

'Because she was terrified,' Bob said. 'She was connected with an old case we worked on, back when we were still teachers. Only she felt those forces were opening back up again. And Joyce happens to think she's right.'

Matt noticed Joyce had reached up to her neck. She pulled out a chain with what looked like an Egyptian ankh dangling on the end. She turned it gently in her fingers.

'What case?'

Joyce stopped turning the chain. 'The Barley Street Poltergeist.'

Another expectant silence.

'Sorry, but I haven't heard of that one.'

'I suppose it's not one of the famous cases. It was hardly an Enfield or a Borley, plus it only lasted a week. But it *was* powerful,' Bob said. 'Plus . . . and here's the *best* bit, Matt . . . it's only a hop, skip and a jump from where you're sitting right now.'

Matt sat straighter. Started to look around.

'Number 29 Barley Street . . .' Bob's voice switched to pantomime as he wiggled wizard fingers to point. 'It's *right behind you*.'

Matt followed Bob's gaze and twisted himself round. The

gnarled, knuckled finger of the oak tree stretched toward the gazebo. Not far from it was a small lake, with a happy family of swans gliding across the surface, in single file. And beyond that was a long stretch of grass where a few guys were practising their rugby throw. It was at the far end that he could see a set of iron railings and a neat row of tall, thin trees. The windows from a long row of Victorian terraced houses peeped through the dead, empty branches.

'Right there?'

'*Right* there,' Bob nodded. 'The one with the green door.'

He could see it, very clearly, though it hardly looked like Amityville. Just a Victorian terrace, with one of those protruding bay windows he quite liked. The type of sill you'd sit up on and read comics in when you were a kid. Even from here he could tell that the grass in the front lawn looked like it hadn't been cut in aeons.

'A lady called Mary Wasson still lives there but the incident we're talking about happened in 2001,' Bob said. 'Back then Mary lived there with her two daughters. Just after Halloween, in the first week of November of that year, they started reporting anomalous phenomena in the house. Taps came on at full pelt in the middle of the night. Strange rattles and bangs were heard as they slept. The youngest girl was nine at the time . . . her name was Holly Wasson. One morning she woke with claw marks on her back and legs.'

'Claws?' Matt set his cup down. 'Did they have pets?'

'They did. A cat called Pob . . . but it had a very good alibi,' Bob grinned. 'It had died a few months before. Besides, these marks were much larger than a cat or dog. It was heady stuff, Matt. Very frightening. The local papers reported it as a poltergeist, which is certainly how it's *known* as, but . . .'

'But?'

'That was just a symptom. Barley Street was much more

than a poltergeist. Much more than just a mischievous spirit.'

'It was an infestation,' Joyce said.

Matt finally took his eyes off the house and turned back round. 'You mean a demon?'

'We think so,' she said. 'Or at least an extremely negative spectral energy. One with, I believe, a distinct personality. Something that could manifest itself . . .' She dropped her eyes to the floor. 'One that was very destructive and very, very old.'

He looked at them both and at how earnestly they sat there, wringing their hands, looking pained. At one point Bob reached over and gave Joyce a reassuring pat on the knee. It was the sort of thing old couples do, when they recall a difficult trip to the doctor's. A part of him was tempted to guffaw at them, just like that. To say: listen to yourselves! You're in your sixties. You should know better, look at the way you're building all this up. The necklace-clutching high drama of it. But he didn't say anything like that, and frankly he didn't want to. For a start, maybe they'd given those symbols to Steph. The Tau-Rho and the pelican. So offending them might make them clam up from tying up that particular loose end. But more than that, he kind of liked them both. Annoyingly they had a way about them. A kindness.

Matt leaned forward, elbows on knees. 'But how's this old Wasson case linked with Steph Ellis?'

That seemed to make Bob a little giddy, 'Oh, I *am* glad that you're interested. Someone of your calibre.'

'Hey, I'm just a teacher. Just like you guys. So . . . about Steph?'

'Steph was very good friends with Mary's daughter, back then. Not Holly, but the older one, Rachel Wasson. There was a little troupe of girls in those days. As thick as thieves. And how's *this* for kismet . . .' Bob pointed a finger at Matt. '*Guess* who's going to be walking up those gazebo steps . . .' He checked his watch. 'Any. Minute. Now?'

Matt feigned ignorance. 'Who?'

'All of them. Rachel Wasson. Jo Finch. Kassy West. The whole clan. I think that together we're all going to get to the bottom of what might have *really* killed Steph.'

He wanted to put both hands around his mouth and shout *psychopathic Labrador* really loud . . . but instead Matt opened his hands in a sort of *who'd-a-thunk-it* gesture. 'They're coming here? Well, fancy that. Hey, I know we've just met but would you mind if I stuck around? Professional interest, you understand.'

Bob started nodding eagerly, but Joyce raised a hand.

'Why were *you* at the school?' She tilted her head. 'What on earth did they find up there to have to call a religion professor in?'

He could see her eyes flashing, the eager chew of the bottom lip. Like he was about to admit that yes, of course, the police had naturally found hoof prints in the blood. Or ectoplasm clogging the wounds.

'I'm not at liberty to say. But it was just a favour for a friend, and from the looks of it, this was nothing more than a tragic animal attack.'

Her shoulders sunk and she shook her head slowly. 'I beg to differ about that.'

He was about to reply, but now Bob was up on his feet, clapping his hands together. He started waving someone frantically over. 'And here they are. Right on time.' He turned to Matt, with a sharp little flare of apophenia. 'Amazing timing that you happened to be passing through just now. Maybe the spirits are guiding this. Bringing you into it.'

Matt turned to see some figures up on the hill, near to where he'd been earlier. A hefty woman was navigating her way down the slope. Behind her, a young woman was standing on the brow of the hill, as if she was deciding whether to follow or not. She wore thick trendy glasses and short dark hair. Dressed in a blazer, like many of the students he taught. She seemed to be shielding her eyes from the sun, though it wasn't particularly bright now. If anything, it was clouding over.

Matt waited with the Hodges as the figures approached. The terraced roofs of Barley Street were visible through the swaying tree branches. Number 29 sat there, looking mundane. No bats flying from the chimney. It was as they got closer that Bob turned to Joyce.

'Look at how grown up Rachel is . . .' Bob said quietly. 'She's changed her hair but . . . dear me . . . doesn't she look like Holly? Doesn't she *walk* like her?'

'It's her first time back in a decade,' Joyce nodded. 'Must be awful for her.'

'Holly Wasson . . .' Matt said. 'That's the younger sister?'

'That's right.'

'Is she coming too?'

For the first time, Bob took his eyes off Rachel. 'I'm afraid that Holly Wasson never made it through the infestation.'

'What does that mean?'

'I mean that the week of activity was too much for her. It wore her down until she couldn't come out from it. But then that's precisely what these entities do. They grind people down until they break. Pain is sport to them. Despair is what they worship.'

'The demon in the house . . .' Joyce said quietly, 'it always did focus on little Holly . . .'

'It was poor Rachel that found her.' Bob nodded toward the girl in the glasses, coming closer. 'Her sister had hung herself in her bedroom. She used the cord from her stereo and dropped off the sill just like—'

Scratch, scratch.

Matt looked up quickly. They all did.

Something was scampering across the roof of the gazebo, an animal. He ran his eyes across the wood and sensed Joyce clutch

106

her jacket across herself. But then he quickly knew what it was. It was the long branch of the tree scraping the roof in the low breeze.

That was all.

Just a tree, stroking them softly with its fingernails.

It felt colder.

'Can you imagine,' Bob said, sadly, 'to be for ever nine years old?'

Bob reached out for Joyce's hand and squeezed it. Then he took a deep breath, let go and headed down the steps toward the two women, so he could greet them. It was then that the spider finally appeared. A small one, scuttling out from Matt's fringe. It tickled his forehead and slid down a silk rope to dangle directly in front of his eye. He raked it away with his hand and flung it to the floor, hoping there weren't any more little wriggling things hiding up in his hair, waiting for their cue.

He looked across the two girls' heads at Barley Street.

And Barley Street looked right back at him.

CHAPTER ELEVEN

What rabbit's wanting most of all, is for you to ask a question.
To walk beside its burrow and to lean your head right in.
Branches spring out of the dirt, fingering the heart that hurts,
weaving up into your skirt to trickle down the chin.

Questions could be anything, so choose whatever, shallow, deep.
Throw your voice into the hole, as veins of nature start to creep.
Once your head is framed with soil, twigs and branches at your cheek,
You can call your question out, cos rabbit's ready now to speak,

yet

Warrens are colossal things, they run for ever, underground.
Most folk think they're ten foot in but warrens go far deeper down,
carrying your question round. Comets tumbling with no sound.

So wait a while and rabbit comes, from the dark to sing its song.
Answers dripping from its lips. Answers that you hope are wrong.

CHAPTER TWELVE

There was a lot of hugging. Tears were shed.

Both expressions came mostly from the big woman, who was called Jo Finch. She was a twenty-nine-year-old local cleaner who was quick to tell everybody that she'd been present at the school yesterday. She kept making the point that she'd seen more gore than anybody else had. This wasn't to brag. It was a purging. It was group therapy. She'd watched Steph's dog go 'swivel-eyed crazy'. She'd seen it 'chomp' into the teaching assistant. She'd seen 'jets of blood'. But it was obvious what moment had frightened her worst of all. Because in the telling of it her eyes had a horrid gothic throb about them, and her skin vanished, so that the white of her skull could shine through. It was when she'd seen little Josh's mum Steph Ellis, her body sitting in the sticky puddles on the floor. Her palms had been open. Her body 'all twisted and bent'.

She described that sight as 'something out of hell', which at first sounded a little dramatic to Matt, until he remembered how high the blood had sprayed. Steph's eyes had been open, apparently.

Staring up at the top corner of the room. And what felt to her like the final insult. 'Last thing she saw was a ceiling tile. Not her son, Josh. Not her husband, Greg. Just a fluorescent bloody light and a piece of polystyrene.' As she shivered and sobbed through it, it was impossible not to keep thinking of his own mother, slashed and stabbed at the hands of a schizo, one sunny Sunday afternoon. And how he had thought an incredibly similar thing when he had found her. That his mum's last image was a plate of Sunday's dinner. That shop-bought food was pressed into her face as she breathed her last gasps into . . . into fucking *gravy*.

Never leaves you, that stuff. That mocking, indignity stuff. It wriggles into the nightmare cortex of your brain and makes a sturdy hole.

He blinked. Joyce's hand was on his shoulder, squeezing it. Not speaking, just smiling softly at him and sniffing his pain.

He zoned back in, embarrassed. Joyce let go. They all sat.

The bottom line of all this was that Jo Finch was thoroughly traumatised by it all and she hugged Joyce a fair bit, but mostly . . . *mostly* she kept turning to the hipster-looking one, Rachel Wasson. She'd clamp those arms around Rachel like the breeze might whisk her up at any minute. Carry her right across the park and over the hill.

Rachel Wasson, by contrast, didn't cry.

She just stood there being polite and quiet, responding to hugs but never offering them. She answered polite catch-up questions from Bob because apparently she was the only one of the girls to have moved away. How's things? (*I'm doing great thanks, really, really great*); where are you living now? (*I'm up in Manchester, got a little flat*) and what are you doing with your life? (*I work in sound*). Whatever the heck that meant. Through it all he noticed something that he wasn't sure anybody else had. Though Joyce may have. She seemed to notice everything.

Rachel scratched her wrist, a *lot*.

She'd shove her fingers right up the sleeve of her jacket and scrape it repeatedly, like she wasn't even aware she was doing it. Maybe she had eczema, but he doubted it. Something told him this was psychology, not dermatology. A nervous, repeated twinge. And who could blame her? She said it was her first time back in Menham in a decade.

He noticed how she was yet to turn round and look at the place. At her sister's bedroom window.

He caught her face and the curve of her profile and wondered how those features must have contorted on the morning they witnessed Holly swinging. He wondered what tiny mocking details haunted *her*?

For ever nine, Matt thought, and immediately pictured his own little girl, Amelia, as a bizarre whisper in his mind said . . . or for ever seven.

Don't you dare, he thought, and ordered his brain to scrap the image of her climbing a table with a cord in *her* hand. The subconscious could be a cruel little factory sometimes, making its desperate connections.

Bob introduced Matt to everybody as a 'fellow researcher', then added he was from a London university, with an interest in the paranormal. 'He'll be an asset in this,' Bob said.

It was after ten minutes of catching up, peppered with the groans of *poor, poor Steph* from Jo, that they finally settled down onto the benches. Bob pulled a cool bag out filled with sandwiches. He offered some to Matt and he took a bite of chicken tikka, knowing that he was risking being late for the charity event, back at the uni. He took another chomp and thought: *what the hell am I doing here?*

But then Joyce looked at the two girls and said, 'Let's talk about the bad thing. Let's talk about the black rabbit.'

'The *what?*' he said, and then he knew exactly why he was here. A little boy had asked him to kill the bad thing that had stalked his mum after all. And besides . . .

It's the strange stuff that grabs you, Matt. It's the gods . . . and the monsters.

The word 'rabbit' did something to Rachel Wasson. She stiffened on the bench next to him. The creak of the wood sounded like each nodule of her spine was locking into place. She even stopped scraping her wrist, which was just as well. Any more and she'd be filing shards off bone.

'I thought Kassy was coming?' she suddenly said. A stall.

Jo nodded. 'Since when was Kassy West ever on time?'

'Since never.' Rachel smiled as if welcoming the feel of it on her face. Then she glanced at Joyce, who was eyeing her and her mouth became a line again. 'I don't like talking about this. You *do* know that.'

'But the deeper we bury these entities, the more they root.'

Nice fusion of pop psychology and whacked-out demonism there, Matt thought.

Joyce leant over and gave her hand a squeeze. Cracked skin against smooth white. 'Matt knows about the poltergeist, and about Holly.'

'Oh . . . okay.' She looked away from him. Embarrassed.

'So what I really need you to tell him about is the manifestation,' Joyce said. 'Can you tell him what you and your friends saw?'

She said nothing for a moment. Sucked her lips in a little and caught Jo's nervous gaze.

Matt turned to her. 'You don't *have* to talk about this. Must be intense enough being back here.'

She smiled at him for that. She held his gaze too, but then the colour in her face faded just as quickly as the sun was dimming in the sky. She looked down at her tennis shoes. They were grey Adidas with bright-yellow laces. Matt's oldest daughter, Lucy, had a pair like that. 'Just so you know . . . I'm not sure what to make of this but . . .' She swallowed and nodded. 'But it was the first week of November, 2001. The poltergeist had been rattling in our house for six days by then, so it was almost done. Bob and Joyce had already started coming over to study it.' She looked at the couple. 'You always brought us something. Piles of chocolate, magazines, books. Me and Holly liked that part. You coming.'

'It was our great pleasure,' Bob said.

'Anyway, this was the night before my sister . . . the night before Holly died. Me and the girls were drinking cider with some boys in the park, but I was freezing and wanted my bigger jacket. I didn't want to go home by myself but the boys wouldn't come with me. They were scared.'

'Of your house?' he asked.

'Yeah . . . my house was kind of a thing in the local paper by then and it turns out people think poltergeists are contagious. Like a ghost's going to jump from you onto them.' She looked at her palm. Traced a line in it. 'Kassy was having too much fun getting the boys worked up, so she stayed with them. But Steph and Jo came with me, even though they were scared.' Rachel looked over at Jo and smiled at her. 'We were walking up my path and I think it was *you* who saw it first.'

Jo nodded.

'You sort of yelped and said, "what the hell is that?" And me and Steph looked up and we all saw this . . .' Rachel laughed nervously at the absurdity of it. 'This shape up on the roof, over Holly's room.'

'*Right* over the top of it,' Jo said. 'Crouching, like it was trying to climb down and get in.'

'It was dark, and hard to make out but . . . we could tell it was big. And it was really skinny. Then as soon as we saw it, it sort of turned its head.'

'It was some sort of beast,' Jo whispered.

A breeze rattled the skeleton tree. Everybody went silent for a moment to hear it.

'Or perhaps it was a trick of the light?' Matt said. 'Or somebody up there? A prank?'

'No, no. The shape was all wrong,' Rachel said. 'Its legs, were . . .'

'They were like hind legs, and its head didn't look right. It looked like . . .' Jo stared toward Barley Street 'like some sort of rabbit.'

'*Or a hare*,' Rachel whispered and immediately started scratching again. 'I always think of it as a really, really tall hare. Standing up.' She pulled her jacket across her, tight, then caught Matt's eye. His crappy attempt at a poker face. 'Look, I know it sounds insane but it really didn't look like a man *or* an animal. It was more like . . . like both. And when it saw us it sort of swivelled its head and went to stand. Right up on its hind legs like a person would. And I swear it was as tall as you are . . . and that's when we ran. We ran all the way back to the park to find the others, and none of us dared look back.'

'Did Holly see it?' Matt said. 'You said it was over her room.'

'I should have stayed,' Rachel pressed one hand into the other. 'I should have called the police right then. But this thing scared me so I sat in the park and drank cider instead. Got drunk enough so I could face going home. And when I finally did, the rabbit was gone. I popped my head in on Holly, just to make sure she was okay but she was fast asleep. She looked normal. Next morning, though . . .' She slowed for a second and blew out one of those breaths pregnant women do. Made an 'o' shape with her lips. 'Next morning she didn't get up for breakfast. Mum sent

115

me up to get her and that's when I found her. She'd hung herself, sometime in the night.'

Jo was already on her feet. She hurried over to Rachel and slid her arm around her shoulders, pulling her in. The bench that he and Rachel shared creaked suddenly and dangerously loud. Still, Rachel didn't cry.

Of course he understood the feeling of walking in on something like that but he didn't say he understood because he knew how annoying it was when people say that. Because they don't. Our agonies are pretty much bespoke, after all, and Rachel's was a particularly vile flavour. All he said was, 'Rachel. What a terrible experience.' He put a hand on hers, even though he barely knew her. He had a flash of his old self. The church pastor, comforting the bereaved in the pews of his church, who all look haunted, in their own way.

The gravity of the conversation had dropped the group to silence now. Instead, they heard the sounds of the park. The guys who were playing rugby on the grass suddenly roared as they charged against one another. Matt turned to watch them and saw Barley Street leaning through the spindly trees. Looking oddly closer than it had before. Like it had picked up its petticoat and shimmied a little nearer for the fun.

'So what did the police say about this figure you saw?'

'What I expected. That we were drunk. That we must have been imagining it,' she shrugged. 'Who knows . . . maybe they were right.'

'*What?*' Jo's mouth dropped on a hinge. 'How can you say that? You know what we saw.'

'*Do* I?'

'Careful Rachel . . .' Joyce shook her head. 'Don't let the passing years make you cynical. That figure was the manifestation of the negative force that was terrorising your house. I felt it back then and frankly . . .' She touched her chest with her palm. 'Frankly . . . I've started to feel it ag—'

'*Aww, not that wascally wabbit again!*'

Every head turned quickly, and at the end of their gaze was a woman. She was striding up the steps of the gazebo in a cloud of perfume, with advert-rich blonde hair bouncing as she came. Her face was attractive but was so thick with make-up she had that false, uncanny look. A Japanese android crossed with a John Lewis counter girl. Tap a fingertip on that cheek and you'd leave a hole.

'Kassy, you're late,' Bob said.

She ignored him and stared at Rachel. 'Well, wow-fooking-wee . . . it's Rachel Wasson. Rarer than a Sasquatch.'

CHAPTER THIRTEEN

Rachel nodded. 'Kassy.'

'And who's this?' She clicked a fingernail in Matt's direction. 'Boyfriend?'

After all the tension he was surprised to hear Rachel laugh out loud. The sound of it shattered the gloom from seconds ago. She went to stand. 'I've only just *met* him, idiot.'

'Yeah, right. And erm . . . the French exchange student look . . .' Kassy looked her up and down. 'How's that working for you?'

'Clearly not as popular as the German Drag Queen.'

He heard Kassy snort a laugh. Rachel grinned.

'You two,' Jo slammed a hand on the wood. 'This *isn't* the time.'

But of course it *was* the time. In fact, it was the precise time. Because Matt saw Rachel and Kassy share a look and an awkward smile. The glance from Rachel that said, *I've got to breathe a little and the mockery of old friends might just provide it.*

Kassy plonked herself on the bench and started sucking on one of those vapour pipes. A ghost cloud quickly framed her head. 'Please . . . carry on. You were just on about the wabbit.'

'Actually,' Matt looked over at Bob and Joyce. 'You mentioned that Steph came to speak to you recently. To consult you.'

'That's right.'

'Can you tell us why?'

Joyce pressed her fingers together, and arched them into a temple. 'She wanted to talk about the entity.'

Rachel looked up. 'Why, after all these years, would she—'

'Because she saw it again,' Joyce said. 'Recently.'

Rachel breathed, slowly. 'When?'

'This month.'

The girls shared a look, and Rachel said. 'Where?'

'Once in her garden. Once by this old tree . . .' She nodded to the oak. Everybody turned to it. 'Don't worry, it's not there right now, I can tell. But mostly it was near your house on Barley Street. Enough to make her a very frightened girl. Steph wanted you all to meet with Bob and me so we could work out what to do about this. And look . . . here you all are.'

Rachel, Kassy and Jo glanced at each other again.

'Sadly, Steph can't be with us today, like she'd hoped,' Joyce said.

Kassy spoke through her cloud, 'Noooo shit.'

Bob tutted and wiped his hands off one another, like there was dust on them. 'Folks, the bottom line is there's unpleasant forces at work in Steph's death. Evil ones that ought to be sent on their way.'

'*What* forces?' Matt asked, getting kind of annoyed now. 'You do know that Steph was killed by her dog?'

'Yes . . . but demons can enter anything they like.'

'Really? Can they?' Kassy laughed. 'Like a table? Like a Samsung phone charger? How about a Sky box, cos mine won't record *Songs of Praise* for some reason? Which is pretty satanic behaviour, if you ask me.'

Matt went to laugh but held it back. He plucked at his lip instead.

'Don't be daft. Clearly, I mean a malignant entity can enter an animal or a human.' Bob raised a finger. 'Like when the Devil entered the serpent in the Bible.'

'That's myth, Bob,' Matt said. 'It's fable.'

Kassy raised her vape stick. 'Hear, hear.'

'Ah, but the only reason you *say* that is because you haven't seen the things *we* have,' Bob said. 'Evil exists . . . *spectral* evil. And it's rare I admit, but sometimes it can enter living things and make them do what they do not want to do. And yes, it can even make strange, poltergeist activity happen in a home.'

'Like what happened at my house,' Rachel said.

'Precisely. And how else do you explain that *and* the creature on your roof?' Bob swiped a hand across his beard. 'See . . . Joyce and I suspect this demonic force may have tormented Steph in her last days. We don't know why, but it clearly did. Then when it finally wanted to take her life, it took possession of her dog and killed her.'

Everybody looked at Bob. Even the tree shut up rustling for a second.

'You're not serious,' Matt said.

'What else accounts for the data?'

'Haaaang on. You mean like a puppet?' Kassy held up a hand. She flapped it like a mouth. 'Like a Satanic frickin' Kermit? That's actually hilarious.'

'Kassy!' Jo hissed. 'Shush.'

Rachel said nothing. Just pressed her glasses slowly back up the ridge of her nose.

Matt raised a hand. 'And how exactly might this spirit be *sent on its way?*'

'I strongly believe we need to ask Holly Wasson that,' Joyce said. 'She's the key to understanding all of this.'

'And what gives you that impression?'

'Because I've heard her calling out.'

Rachel flicked her gaze at Joyce. 'She calls to you?'

'Not to me . . .' Joyce shook her head and pointed. 'To *you*, Rachel. She calls to you.'

He saw her shrink. Right there on the bench. Her shoulders, her body, her face, shrivelled. Like she thought she could will herself smaller and be harder to see. A vampire in the sun, crumbling to dust. Jo, Kassy and Rachel kept looking at each other. Even Kassy went quiet.

'I hear her asking for you. Shouting out your name sometimes . . .' Joyce looked across at Barley Street, and tilted her head. 'Rachel, she's doing that *right* now.'

Silence.

He'd been present in a Watford hotel's function room once where he'd watched a tangerine-coloured spiritualist called Devon Blake stride the stage and contact the dead, on behalf of the giddy, weepy punters. They were perched on banqueting chairs, debit cards a little emptier than when they'd first walked in. He'd been researching the event for his book and had found it to be a red-hot buffet of apophenia. Blake would mention random facts that could literally apply to anybody, while people in the crowd took them as A-grade phantom revelation.

I sense that someone here tonight has lost a man to cancer.

Half the room started pulling out the hankies and nodded sagely, whispering, 'He's amazing.'

And he distinctly remembered logging the reaction of people who heard that their loved ones were reaching out from beyond. They'd often dissolve into tears. But they'd be happy tears or big sniffly thank-you sobs to think that the lost were still out there. Still caring. Still reaching out.

He watched Rachel, with the hint of Holly's spirit in the air, but she didn't look happy at all. She had turned to stone.

121

He broke the silence with a question. 'And how do you propose asking Holly?' *You do know she isn't checking her Twitter much these days?*

The word he'd expected was coming was finally said, though it still felt wonky and ridiculous when it came out.

'A seance,' Joyce said, 'at Barley Street. *That's* where Holly's heartache is . . . and that's where the evil spirit manifested to the girls. I feel like the barriers are going to be thinnest there, so all we do is ask her. Then we might find out what killed Steph once and for all . . . and more to the point, what this poisoned spirit actually wants. Heck, we don't even know if this rabbit is Holly's enemy—'

'Or her friend,' Rachel said quietly.

'*Exactly*. Or pretending to be. We need to ask her.'

There was no more hiding it and he knew it was unprofessional, but he couldn't help it, because he was watching a grieving girl get programmed with nonsense from the same people who probably programmed Steph Ellis to hide in a cupboard.

He let out a long, lip-flapping breath.

A mental image instantly popped into Matt's head. Of DS Larry Forbes in his police car, driving somewhere in London right now because he'd *known* that this case wasn't going anywhere. He'd sensed this was little more than a weird accident. Instead, Larry would be tracking down real-life killers right now, with bona fide murder victims. Here was Matt, thinking he might just have an instinct for amateur detective work. Turned out that all he had was a fully working radar for screwball weirdos. What else was new?

He felt embarrassed. He checked his watch.

'When would you want to do this . . . seance?' Rachel asked Bob.

'Joyce just needs time to prepare and meditate. We were thinking tomorrow night – 8 p.m.?'

Rachel looked off into the park, pondering all of this, so Matt asked the obvious next question.

'And who's paying for this?'

Bob frowned. '*Paying?*'

'If these guys agree to a seance, doesn't that make them your clients? Like Steph was? Shouldn't you tell them how much you charge?'

Joyce gave a low chuckle under her breath but Bob looked at Matt with a sad shrug of disappointment. 'There *is* no charge. Just fuel us with tea and biscuits and we'll be fine.' He looked hard at Rachel. 'So you'll ask your mum if we can do it.' Not a question. Not a request. This was more like a Jedi mind trick.

She stared at the floor.

'Rachel,' Matt said. 'You know you don't have to—'

'I'll ask her,' she said to Bob.

'Excellent.' His beard swooped up into a scratchy-looking smile. 'And Matt . . . I really think you should join us. Come and see things you've never seen before.'

Matt's phone buzzed like wasps in his pocket. A welcome moment.

'Sorry folks. Two seconds . . .' He pulled it out: Beth from the publishers. Her name pulsed on the screen like a prodding finger. He clicked on her text message.

Where are you? Other speakers arriving. Call me!

'Everything alright?' Bob said.

'I'm going to have to head off.'

'Busy man. But I hope you can join us for the seance tomorrow night,' Bob said. 'You'd be more than welcome.'

'Thanks . . . but I've got a lot on.'

'Ah, the book and everything.'

He nodded.

'Then why not come and write about Joyce and I?' Bob stuck his bristly chin out. 'We'd gladly give you interviews about our work.'

'I'll bear that in mind.' He shook Bob's hand while the girls started talking together. 'It was good to meet you. And thanks for the tea.'

'Wait . . . take this.' Bob reached into his bag and pulled out a plastic box file. 'It's information on the Wasson case. I reckon you'll find it interesting.'

Matt whistled when he saw the tape, nestled amongst the folded papers. 'Wow, Bob. VHS?'

'You *do* have a player, don't you?'

He thought of the loft of his new house. The endless stacks of cardboard boxes thrown up there when they moved in last month. He nodded. 'I can dig one out.'

'Good. Then take it.'

He shrugged and took it, looking at Joyce. Keeping his voice down so the girls wouldn't hear, he said, 'Quick question. When Steph came to you, did you give her anything? Maybe something to protect herself?'

'That's an interesting question,' Joyce said.

'Well, did you?'

'I gave her a cross,' Joyce said. 'On a necklace.'

'Anything else? Any other symbols?'

'Just the standard cross.' She frowned and made no mention of the Tau-Rho or the pelican symbol. She took his hand in hers again and spoke much louder, so the others would hear. The girls got the message and stopped talking. Joyce had the floor. 'You know, Matthew. It's often said that we mustn't open our minds so much that our brains fall out.'

'Wise words.'

'But equally, if we close our mind too much, the brain struggles to breathe. It will regress into something less than it could be.' She squeezed his hands. 'So when you go home, when you see your family, when you fall asleep tonight and ponder Holly Wasson and the topics we've discussed, would you consider a question for me?'

He glanced down at the phone in his hand. 'I've really got to go.'

'What if there *are* such things? Would you at least consider that?'

'Will do.' He turned to Kassy, Jo and Rachel. 'Good to meet you all and I really am sorry about your friend.' He glanced at Rachel. 'And about Holly.'

She nodded slowly and he saw her gaze shift from his shoulder to beyond him, so that it was finally fixed on Barley Street. He was pretty sure this was the first time she'd looked directly at the house since he'd seen her. He saw her face flicker again, a child, staring up at the worst sight of her life. Her lips the same colour as her skin.

'And Rachel?' he called back.

'Mmm?' She stared at the house.

'Sometimes there *aren't* such things. Okay? Sometimes there are just sad events and us getting through them. But you know, eventually . . . we do get through them.'

She pursed her lips and pulled her eyes from the house. She smiled at him and mouthed the words, 'Thank you.'

He ducked under the tree as its branch started up a fresh session of roof scratching and as he crossed the field he noticed that the swans were being incredibly noisy, over on the pond. He realised he'd never heard a swan crying out before. They were freaking out for some reason and it sounded like metal scraping metal.

He hurried across the grass toward the train station, not once looking back at the gazebo, though he did look down at the box full of crazy in his hands. He had the silly idea that if he was to look up again, Barley Street would be closer than ever now. Breaking through the trees and muscling in. But when he looked at it, it was where it always had been, with only one difference. The curtains of the upstairs bedroom, Holly's room, were now open, and the window was open too, so that the white material fluttered and slapped through the gap like the hem of a dress. Around him, as the swans wailed, that same wind raced to him, and caused a dance of brittle leaves to scurry up his legs.

CHAPTER FOURTEEN

Rachel stood on the cracked pavement and looked up at the infamous house of mystery, rabbits and death.

29 Barley Street.

The house where she'd seen her first ever Disney movie. Where she'd eaten her first ever toasted sandwich. Where she'd first had a dream about girls. Where she'd seen her first corpse.

It was pushing 5 p.m., so the sun had finally started to plunge behind the high rises, over near the bypass. Now the sky had turned almost purple. It made the house look bruised.

She'd spent the last few hours with the girls, on Menham high street, sitting in what used to be a cafe called Citrone's. They made ice-cream floats back when Rachel was a kid but now it was a Costa Coffee. But then wasn't everywhere? Without the Hodges there, talk of spooks was thankfully kept to a minimum. So they chatted about each other, about work, and life and relationships. Rachel kept things vague about her own love life, not that she was ashamed of her sexuality. Only this Menham reunion was complex and mind melting enough without bringing *that* in the frame. Jo had cried. At one point Kassy had laid into Rachel for never coming home and never being in contact. *What sort of friend does that?* she'd asked. Rachel didn't give a response because she didn't have one. A crappy friend, she guessed. A selfish one.

Thankfully toward that last hour, they'd laughed. Somehow, they'd laughed a lot.

But when Jo offered to let Rachel stay at her and her boyfriend's place, she knew she had to say no. Because Barley Street was calling her. Or rather, her mother was. From deep inside its empty rooms, from along its cold, quiet hall. Her mother was in there with the spiders and the dust, and she needed to talk to her about this seance.

It's not like this would be the first time she and Mum had spoken since she left. They'd talked on the phone now and again (though the term 'talk' was wildly ambitious). She'd even managed to get Mum to visit her in Manchester a couple of times. That equated to lots of silence and mental finger drumming in restaurants. One of the few things Mum *did* say, though, was: 'I wish you'd come back sometimes. Come back to the house.'

Now Rachel was actually *in* Menham, so how could she not? Besides, there was a seance to organise.

Breathe.

The professor's words kept playing on a loop, in the tannoy of her head: *Sometimes there are just sad events and us getting through them.*

The front door was painted with the exact same flaking green as she remembered. With four glass squares in the top, stained with 50s sunbeams firing over a hill. Behind the glass, she could see the same old net curtain with tiny tears in it. She'd been pushing fifteen when Holly had died here, and Rachel had managed to stomach living – and the worst part *sleeping* – here for a few more years.

But once the studying and saving was complete, she escaped. She pictured herself just over a decade ago, on this exact same path, eighteen years old and loading up the car with a duvet and crates of CDs, rolled-up posters and a cheap microwave. She'd even cut the grass that morning without being asked, and had given her mum an awkward, almost hover-hug on these steps and she remembered looking up at Holly's window for one last time. That painful but bright moment when she assumed she would never, ever return to this place. In the younger days when you genuinely think you can outrun your memory.

Yet here she was, with her gaze doing that familiar slow crawl up the tatty-looking brickwork to the grimy glass of Holly's room. And what she saw there made her gasp hard. So sharply in fact, that she actually stumbled backwards in a sudden flash of vertigo.

Holly was at the window, looking down.

The corners of the house stretched and twisted as the figure upstairs leant toward the glass. Then she heard that familiar, banshee creak of the windowpane opening. The *eeeeeeeek* wail she'd always hated, but Holly said she liked because it sounded like a seagull. As the metal creaked and squealed a face leant out that wasn't Holly after all, but was Holly's creator. A strange woman's head who said, 'Are you going to stand outside for ever?'

'Hi, Mum.' Rachel caught her breath and looked back up. 'I'm sorry to just drop in on you like—'

'I've made lasagne,' Mary said, close to monotone. 'There'll be plenty for you.'

'Oh . . . right.'

'So, come in.'

Rachel shifted her rucksack. 'I don't have a key any more.'

Mary looked confused at that. 'But it's open. And when you wash your hands, you get right up to the elbow, remember? *Right* up.'

'I remember,' Rachel said, and the window upstairs screeched shut. Only this time Rachel didn't hear metal. She heard rubber and plastic and copper wire. The twist of a power cable, pulled tight with a pendulous weight.

You can do this, she said to herself, *it's just sad events and us getting through them.*

She even visualised a team of guys from work high-fiving her like they do in TV. Telling her she'd smash this and be fine. But in reality, Rachel knew she could cry on this path, right now. She could turn away and rush toward her car and never, ever come back here. But that felt like a very immature thing to do. And what had this last ten or so years of burying been, if not an immature attempt at dealing with that horrible week? Judging by her nightmares and dead cat smells, that method wasn't working. Time to try the adult approach.

She wouldn't cry. She'd go in. She'd wash her hands, and her forearms and elbows and be a grown-up.

So she stepped toward the door, to find it really was open.

In fact, now it was gaping wide, eager to let her in.

'You're letting the cold in,' Mum mumbled, as she trotted down the staircase.

CHAPTER FIFTEEN

Matt shuffled on all fours across the wooden panels of his new loft, so that the kneecaps of his jeans dragged channels through the dust. His daughter Amelia had wanted to come up here too. Insisted, in fact. This was a new house, and she wanted to scope out every room (as long as it wasn't her own). He got the impression that she was spying out alternative bedrooms. She crawled directly behind him.

'Do *not* fart,' she said. 'I'll get it right in my face if you—'

'Release?' he faked the sound of one against his palm. Something loud and wince-inducing. She squealed and her hand slapped the back of his thigh, hard. 'Ow.'

She giggled.

So did he.

They shuffled on.

There was no light bulb up here so he'd have to rig one up some day. Just another little Saturday job to add to the expanding list of DIY. So they could see up here Amelia had fished out two head

131

torches. An old Christmas gift from one of Wren's aunts. One was shaped like a monkey's head and the other, a tiger's. Both with torch bulbs for eyes, threaded through a stretchy Velcro strap. She'd opted for the tiger. He moved his head like a robot, and the monkey's eyes blazed its sentry beams across the piles of cardboard boxes.

'It's like that bit in Indiana Jones.' He turned back to her. 'You remember that massive storehouse?'

'Nope.' She squinted from his beams. 'What's VHS anyway?'

'Ah . . . well . . . let me tell you the tale . . .' He filled her in on the wonders of magnetic tape, and the ancient war with Betamax, while he dragged boxes out filled with CDs and tapes. At one point, he found an old Donkey Kong game he'd had as a kid. One of those old Nintendo flipper things, with two screens. 'That's coming down.' He slipped it into his back pocket for later. It'd be perfect for downtime between lectures. During, even.

He finally found the Akai video cassette recorder (now with Video Plus!) sitting under a pile of stuff he'd taped from TV. *The Day the Earth Stood Still, Jason and the Argonauts*. A few TV shows.

Amelia read the spine of a tape. 'What on earth is *Airwolf*?'

He grabbed it. 'TV Gold, is what *that* is.'

He shimmied the player out, fished out the remote control and coiled up the dusty SCART lead that was still hanging from the back, then he and Amelia headed back toward the ladders. She spotted a stuffed turtle she'd bought last year from the Sea Life Centre in Birmingham. With a little baby teddy, tucked in a pouch. She grabbed it from the box. '*There* it is!'

She went to move off, smiling.

'Amelia?'

'Yup?'

'How's the room situation going?'

She slowed down. 'What do you mean?'

'I mean, will you be turning the light off tonight?'

Neither of them were looking at each other properly. If they did, they'd blind each other with the head torches. So he was looking at her arms when she pulled the turtle a little tighter toward her. She spoke in her I'm-being-reasonable tone. Her negotiation voice. 'Maybe in a month. How about that?'

'And this feeling you get in your room. What's causing it, exactly?'

She shrugged. 'Maybe it's a ghost. I bet a lot of people have died in this house.'

'Not necessarily.'

'Er . . . it's over a hundred years old. I checked. So I bet someone died here. Maybe even in my room. Maybe in *yours*.'

She was possibly right, not that it mattered. 'But have you got enough evidence to make you scared? Do you *see* anything? Like proper people and shapes? Do you hear them?'

'Nah. It's just a shadow. It doesn't say anything.'

'Perhaps that's because it's *just* a shadow.'

'Hmmm,' she started to pick something from her nose. 'It's usually when I'm about to fall asleep.'

'Interesting . . .' he said. 'Then here's your new word for today . . . ready?'

'Yep.'

He ran a hand across the air. 'Hypnagogia.'

She looked at him, puzzled. 'Huh?'

'When the human brain's about to fall asleep it starts making dreams even before you've fully nodded off. When you're half in and out of sleep, it's hard to tell the difference between a shadow, and what your brain is making that shadow into. Happens to lots of people. That's why so many people see ghosts at their bed . . . cos they're dreaming, essentially.'

A whisper in his head: *Only those girls weren't asleep when they*

133

saw that rabbit man on the roof, were they? They were wiiiiiiiiiide awake.

She said nothing. Just listened.

'I appreciate that you're scared and unsettled. We've all had a rough few months, and remember we can always talk about that, whenever you want.' It was a veiled reference to what happened in Hobbs Hill. The real spectre that he suspected was hanging over both Amelia and Lucy. They'd tried to keep her away from the news reports of her sister almost being murdered up there, but she wasn't an idiot. Amelia had Google written into her DNA. He looked at her for a few moments. 'But I don't think you have to worry about ghosts, okay Midget?'

She said nothing. The beam didn't move. She was biting her lip. Was she shivering? He thought of Josh Ellis, building his mother's Lego.

Crumble time.

'But if you want your bedroom light on . . .' he said. 'Then you *have* the light on. No worries.'

He saw her shoulders relax, and then her tiger beam moved again and fell on the video player.

'So what's on that video thing you brought home, anyway? A film?'

Yes. It's a new flick called *The Holly Wasson Interviews*. That's what it said on the spine of the tape Bob had handed over, anyway. But to Amelia he just said, 'It's a work thing and it'd be boring, I bet.'

She nodded. 'Then grab that Airfox thing as well, and we'll try that sometime.'

'*Airwolf*,' he beamed at her, and grabbed the tape. 'You won't regret it.'

He headed down the ladder first, so he could be there with his arms open in case she slipped. Outside he noticed that the sun had sunk, and he could see droplets of rain falling from the dark sky and slapping against the pane. For some reason, it made him think of that big old oak tree, out there in Menham Park. Getting wet and swaying in the wind, scraping the wood of that gazebo.

'Er . . . you two?' Wren appeared at the bottom of the steps. 'It's time she started winding down for bed.'

'Okay, Mummy,' she called out from the hole in the ceiling.

She started to climb down, and it was just as her foot left the ladder and sank into the carpet that he heard his mobile phone ringing. It was the theme music to *Murder She Wrote*.

Which meant Larry was calling.

'Larry,' Matt closed his bedroom door and peeled off the Velcro monkey torch. It left the scar outline of a primate's face on his forehead. He tapped one of the bedside lamps on and it threw his shadow up the wall. He lay back onto the bed with the video player and Bob's box of delights next to him. 'Did you get my message?'

'About your little picnic in the park, with Steph Ellis's friends?' Larry said. 'I did.'

'And those two ghost hunters . . . sorry, how crass of me. I mean those demonologists.'

'The Hodges . . . yes. I'm aware of them. And you're saying you reckon there's not much to this thing about Steph being followed before her death?'

'Not really. Looks like the Hodges have been filling her head with supernatural ideas. Demon rabbits and whatnot. I suspect Joyce may have even passed on the pelican symbol, even though she *says* she didn't. Bottom line is, I guess this is why you get paid the big bucks cos you were right. Seems like it's just a crazy dog story, after all.'

Larry said nothing.

'You still there?'

'U-huh.'

'So . . . why'd you call me?'

'Erm . . . .well, you got me thinking this morning. When you asked about the CCTV, and if anybody had seen Steph and her dog arrive at the school that night . . .'

'You said only one camera picked them up.'

'That's right. The playground one.'

'But you've found another?' He felt his eyebrow spring up.

'No . . . but this afternoon, I did have a little wander round the back of the school. There's an old people's home there, called Sapphire House. Their garden backs onto the Menham Primary.'

'They have CCTV?'

'Shut up about CCTV . . . you're obsessed.'

He laughed. 'Go ahead.'

'I chatted to the warden there. Seems like one of the residents can't sleep at night, so she often sits in the lounge and watches TV. She was up two nights ago. The night Steph was actually killed. Right around the same time, too. She says it was 2 a.m. because she'd just started watching a rerun of *Dallas* on ITV 3, and that's when it's on. I checked.'

'What did she see?'

'She saw a dog, looking at her through the glass window.'

Matt glanced at the windowpane. The night was throwing bigger drops of rain now, and they trickled down the glass in jerky rivers.

'And get this . . . it was dark, and the security lights had tapped off again. But she insists that the dog had blood all over it. All over its mouth and right down its front.'

Matt frowned. 'Hang on a sec. Steph's dog was black. How could she see blood in that sort of light?'

'Because this dog was white.'

Matt pushed himself up from the bed, with his elbow. He sat on the edge. 'Really?'

'Really. And she said this one was very skinny, with its ribs

136

showing. She said its eyes looked a bit mad and it was licking blood off its lips while it watched her. Scared the shit out of her.'

'A *different* dog?'

'Yep, and it kept watching her till she heard someone calling it away. Then she says it just turned and loped off into the bushes.'

'*Who* called it?'

'She didn't see.'

'Then what was the voice like. A man, a woman?'

'Well, this is where it gets a little spooky. She said it sounded like a little kid was singing . . . a girl. Some sort of nursery rhyme, she said. Said it was the sweetest singing you ever heard . . .' Larry sniffed. 'Which'd scare the crap out of *me* at that time of night, never mind a pensioner. Anyway, she went to bed and locked her door. She didn't tell anybody because she thought people would say she was going doolally, or getting dementia. When she finally read about Steph in the paper she told the warden about the dog straight away.'

Matt was sitting on Wren's side of the bed, staring out of the window and the old church next to their house. 'So . . . we're saying there was a *second* dog that might have killed Steph?'

'That's right, which means it's possible that the only reason Steph's dog went wild when the doors finally opened again, was because it was trying to protect her.'

'You said Steph's dog definitely had her blood on its mouth.'

'It did. But maybe it was trying to nudge her awake or something. It's a theory, anyway. But basically, we have another dog.'

Matt pondered it. 'Then how did that one get out of the cupboard?'

'Maybe whoever was singing, let it out . . .'

The rain had started drumming against the window now. Fast enough to obliterate any trickles that were trying to race gravity to the bottom of the pane. None of them made it.

137

'How believable is this old lady?'

'I just met with her, Matt. She has no history of dementia. She wasn't asleep. I reckon she saw what she saw. Which means, if there really is a second dog then things are a bit more complicated.'

'No shit.' Matt looked down at the video player and at the Holly Wasson bumper pack Bob had given him. He shook his head. 'So who else could have been there?'

'I suppose the Hodges would say *what* else was there?'

'You need to find out *who* it was.'

'M-hmmm . . . anyway. I just thought you'd like to know.'

'Thanks.' Matt nodded. 'And thanks for a thoroughly odd day.'

'My pleasure.'

'So what are you up to now?'

He laughed. 'Now don't shoot me but me and the wife are off to church. Our priest's doing a talk on the Biblical Principles of Marital Romance.'

'Whoah, easy tiger— ' Matt flicked his gaze toward the door. He could hear a girl sobbing.

'Matt?'

'Sorry, Larry. Gotta go.' He stood up.

He said goodbye and tapped the phone off. He opened the door a tiny crack and noted the ridiculous expectation he had, that he might see Holly Wasson standing there on his landing, coiled cord in hand. Instead, he pushed the door back and just leant against the doorframe, sighing. Not with frustration, but sadness. He listened to Amelia and Wren in the bathroom. Wren was speaking with her most soothing, gentle tone because their youngest was tearfully refusing to go in her room. Telling her mum that she hated this house, that she hated her room and that a house was only a home if it felt safe.

CHAPTER SIXTEEN

Mary Wasson clinked a plate full of runny lasagne onto the dining-room table. 'Oh, it's a terrible business,' she said, in that vacant, slightly metallic voice she had these days.

Rachel looked down at the food and wondered if Mum was referring to Steph's death or what was for dinner. The meal was so full of deep-red tomato purée that it looked like a placenta sitting there, with a few lumps of half-red garlic bread seeping into it. She slowly pressed a fork into the grey-looking meat and each prong slid through.

'Killed by her own dog. That's very *strange*.' Mum's face was gaunt, and around it her black hair still hung long, but it was extremely thin-looking. It used to shine, that hair. Shine and bounce. She'd curl it up just to nip to the library or even for that jazzercise class she used to rave about. She'd prep herself so she'd feel like a dancer in the wall-to-wall mirrors. People used to comment on her hair because every happy strand would join forces with the others, linking arms to make a thick, rich mane that even Kassy said was decent.

But Holly's death had ruined even that.

Suicide is like a gas. It lingers in the air and cannot be wafted away. It hangs there invisibly, seeping through the cracks of the house that hosted it, so that it fills every room and every person. And it filled Mum's hair. In the weeks that followed the hanging, those strands no longer stood together. They weren't on speaking terms any more. Each of them became a separate, thin, spider strand, dangling from the dome of Mum's scalp, the curve of which could be clearly visible when the light was right.

Like now. She could see the white glistening arc of Mum's scalp now, shining through a once lush, but now devastated, forest of thin, dead trees.

Rachel once heard her mum being described as a weather girl. Which on one level sounded like a sexist insult until later when she realised she'd like that said to *her*. But now the weather girl was a grim, lonely chambermaid of a woman whose busy fingers would often scratch behind the thin arch of her ears. Rachel saw dandruff flutter onto the table almost every time she did that.

'Steph's in a better place now,' Mum said.

Rachel nodded, though she wasn't even sure if she believed it. 'Yeah.'

Mum pressed a fork through the slit in her thin lips and with a start Rachel heard it clink hard against her teeth. Then Mum took a sip from her mug, which had clear liquid in it. Vodka.

She also had a new cat called Finlay, who kept trotting in now and again to stare at them both. Especially at Rachel, as if Finlay could smell that old imposter cat Pob, hovering around her.

Mum still loved animals. All around the dining room those cheap and dated pictures of creatures still hung, in thin frames. Tigers and wolves, bears and birds looked out. But behind mum, on a shelf, was something new. Standing there were at least a hundred tiny penguins made of porcelain. Some with little hats on, some with skis tucked under their wings. It was a huge collection that she'd cramped together to one side so she could leave space for future additions.

'Spectacular set of penguins,' Rachel said.

Mum ignored her completely.

She scooped up a little of the meat, seeing the juice dripping through the metal slits and thinking that this looked like the stuff that spurted out of hedgehogs on country roads. She took a quick breath to swallow it.

Mary set her fork down and turned her head slowly towards Rachel. 'Do you know what *I* think?'

She looked up, puzzled – was she supposed to guess? She shrugged instead.

'I think you belong *here*.'

There was no warmth in it, no sense of sadness or hope.

'Mum, we've been through—'

'You . . .' She lifted her arm and pointed directly at her, then she gazed across the walls, at the floor, then finally up to the ceiling. 'You belong to this house.'

Rachel waited and pondered the words. 'Can't you hear how odd that sounds?'

'Truth sometimes *is* odd. You should be back here.'

'But I couldn't, could I? I could never live—'

'Don't say never . . .' Mary pushed a finger toward her own lips, which glistened with juice from the meat. For the first time she looked like she had emotion in her eyes. A sort of twitchy sadness.

'I'm sorry, Mum, but it's not going to happen, but you could always visit me in—'

'Shhhhhhhhhh.' She put both hands back on the table by each side of her plate, fingers arched like a spider.

'It's not that I don't . . .' Rachel felt her tongue pushing the back of her teeth to form an 'L' sound, but she trailed off from

141

saying 'love' and did something else instead. She started to reach her hand across the table, sliding the wrist along. The one that was raw from scratching. She reached her fingertips toward Mum's hand. There was a distinct slowness to it, a cautiousness and Mum stared down at the approaching touch with something like confusion. The impending experience of physical contact. 'I do love you, Mum, but—'

She yanked her hand away from Rachel just before they made contact and she pushed her chair back with a crack. She swigged the last dregs of vodka from her mug and looked over at what looked like a bottle of grape juice on top of the fridge. 'I *suppose* you'll want a drink now.' Like thirst was a crime of utter selfishness.

Rachel pulled her own hand back instantly; a futile attempt to suggest it had never been reaching out in the first place. Her cheeks flushed with embarrassment.

Mum stood on her tiptoes, trying to grab the grape juice that was just out of her reach.

Sad events . . . get through . . .

Rachel swallowed, then quickly stood up. She moved towards the fridge. 'Let me help, Mum.'

'You don't know where anything is.'

She reached up for the grape juice. 'I'll just grab—'

'*You don't know where anything is!*' She grabbed the bottle.

Rachel got the message. She moved back to the table and sat back in her place, staring at the tablecloth, at her fingernails, at anywhere but her mum's eyes, which were also avoiding hers. There was that horrible buzz of emotional electricity in the air, which she was tempted to break with a joke, like she often did as a kid. *I say, I say, I say, what's brown and sticky, Mum?*

But she sat there and listened to the air crackle instead.

The bottle of grape juice looked years, maybe even decades out of date, which prompted a wild thought as Mum sloshed liquid into two grimy glasses. She's going to poison me with this stuff. She's going to trap me in this house and store me with those penguins in the space she left on the shelf.

Mary stumbled a little as she set the drinks on the table. 'A toast, then.'

Rachel slowly took her glass and felt a shift in her own facial muscles, a resignation because this was a familiar thing. She knew what was coming.

'To Stephanie . . .' Mum's eyes rolled up to the ceiling and she pushed her glass up towards it, all the way, until her elbow locked. *Click*. 'And to our little Holly. May they both find peace. And may they come and see us whenever they want.'

Swig.

And this is why I stay away.

They drank and ate, knives clinking and clattering, loud and noticeable in the silence. Every now and again Mum's new cat would wander under the table and press itself against her shins, slinking itself around her like a snake. All the while she tried throwing conversations over, only to see them fizzle out like crap matches. Bored, she glanced around the room and saw a local paper curling off the edge of a side table. The headline: *Masturbating Man Flees School Gates!*

Sheesh. Being back in Menham really was a riot.

Suddenly Mum plonked two satsumas in the middle of the table, which turned out to be dessert. Her heart sank.

It was a ground-shaking, call-Sky-News shock when Mum finally said something that wasn't about Holly or this town. An actual question about her daughter's actual life. 'I suppose you still work in that horrible big building? The one with the glass?'

'No,' Rachel sighed. 'Remember I called you a couple of months ago?'

Actually it was four months ago, Rachel realised. She knew that because she remembered standing in her flat that night, building up to the call, pacing the room like Rocky Balboa prepping for a big finale fight.

'I said I was moving to a new company? That I'd be recording sound full-time?'

'Oh.' She lazily grabbed a satsuma and started to sink her sharp nails into it.

'I've started that now and I'm getting more and more work.'

'Well . . .' she said, with a horribly dismissive wave of the hand, 'there's a hell of a lot more to life than money, and you really ought to know that by now.'

There were various things that pissed Rachel off. Like how Debbie used to load the dishwasher in a constantly 'illogical' way, like how the guy in the flat above her still kept his alarm on at weekends, like how her boss could never keep eye contact with her, whenever they talked in a corridor. She knew her anger was coming because she'd suck her bottom lip in under her teeth, so much that the lip pretty much disappeared.

She noticed that she was doing exactly that, right now, and once the breath was in, it came flowing out in a voice three notches louder than before.

'Actually, Mum, there *is* more to life.' She snapped it out loudly. Pushed back her chair.

Mum sucked a sliver of orange from her thumb. She took her time over it.

'There's my new flat. There's my *new* friends. My new *life*.'

Mum's thumb dug deep into the peel again. A jet of acid leapt into three bubbles on the table. She looked down at it.

'And my hair. I've got a completely different haircut and you haven't even mentioned it. You haven't even said my glasses don't suit me, because I *know* you think they don't.'

Mum blinked slowly and looked up at Rachel's head. 'Do you have a boyfriend yet?'

'Jesus Christ . . .' The words popped like a bubble, and it made her pause for a second. 'You barely even know me.' She looked down at her lap. 'And you say you want me here but whenever I call you, you barely say a word and whenever you visit me I know you're hating it because it somehow doesn't count unless you see me in this house, and whenever you look at me—'

A sudden bumping sound came from upstairs.

Mum looked up.

'Are you listening to me?'

'Did you just hear that?' A smile started to form. One side of the mouth twitching up.

Finally, Rachel stood, tossing her napkin on the table. Her face had switched from anger to exasperation, heartbreak even, and for a second she saw her reflection in the horrible thick mirror that hung from the rusting chain. She could see the flash of that little girl who'd lived here for all those years, and for a second she couldn't tell if it was her reflection looking back, or if it was Holly, hiding in the mirror. Ready to climb out and throttle her, while Mum held her down.

Mum went to stand. 'I think it came from Holly's room.'

'And *there* you have it!' Rachel clapped her hands together once. 'We can see it now. You're not interested in anything that ever happens in my life because that's all post-Holly, isn't it, Mum? That's all invisible. And nothing even *exists* post-Holly. Does it? Nothing even *exists*.' Rachel stopped to catch her breath and suddenly looked at her surroundings, disorientated. Like she'd fallen asleep in one place and woken up in another.

Mum set her satsuma neatly on the table, then she rose from her chair.

'Oh, come on. You *cannot* just walk out. You need to listen to—'

She cut herself off when she saw Mum not walking away from her, but towards her. She leant near to an astonished Rachel and put a hand gently around the back of her head, just like she used to. Like when she was little and terrified of making the Brownie promise, or when Kassy had said something horrible enough to cut. Or when she'd found herself feeling lonely and different and she couldn't figure out why. The weather girl would swoop into her bedroom and without saying a word she'd slide her hand around the back of her head and hold her into that wonderful hair that smelt like how a ten-year-old girl thought Paris catwalks would smell. And things would feel brighter.

It felt like electricity, when those fingers touched her scalp again now.

Mum pulled her close and kissed her softly on the forehead, lingering with her lips of orange zest and cold meat. Rachel felt her shoulders crunch into some sort of submission, the slow bubbling up from whichever part of the brain programmes tears. But Mum let her go as quickly as the affection began. Hair all thin again, she turned and walked through the open kitchen door, looking at the ceiling as she went. 'I *did* hear something.'

Rachel stood for a moment in the kitchen, with her eyes closed in the silence. The ghost of her mum's fingers still caressing the back of her head. Then she walked silently into the hallway and saw that Mum was now sitting at the very top step of the staircase, her hands folded neatly in her lap. A child patiently waiting for a friend to come running round the corner.

Rachel wiped a tear from her cheek, with the palm of her hand. When she called up, her voice was quiet. 'Mum?'

'I heard something.'

'You must have imagined it.'

'I've been hearing it more and more, lately.' Mum smiled and turned to look down the stairs. 'Come on up, love.'

Rachel's body locked into place.

'Come up the stairs,' she said, smiling. 'Come up the stairs, and sit with your mummy.'

Somewhere in her head, she could hear the echo of herself saying, 'Let's just go back in the kitchen. Tell me all the penguin's names.' But she was already grabbing the banister with an outstretched hand. Then with less hesitation than she expected, she started to walk up, with a growing succession of floorboard creaks. Mum's eyes were fixed on something on the landing.

'And you'll sleep here tonight, won't you? Your old bed's there.'

Be brave, she thought. *You are almost thirty, Rachel. You can do this.*

Work through.

She nodded. 'I'll stay the night.'

She neared the top and followed Mum's gaze, looking through the banisters. The landing had four doors. Her old room, Mum's room, the bathroom and Holly's room at the end. And it was Holly's that looked completely different than the rest. Enough to make Rachel let out a tiny little gasp.

Every inch of the door was taped with photographs. There were maybe a hundred Holly Wassons staring out. Some were colour, but most were photocopies and repeats of the same shot. Overlapping and obscuring each other, some were even upside down, with more underneath in a weird, chaotic tapestry. Rachel couldn't see her reflection but she knew her own skin was turning pale. Her eyes shifted from picture to picture as her back pressed more and more against the wall, and the window that opened into Menham now presented her with pitch-black night.

'It's okay, love,' she said. 'There's nothing to be scared of.'

'Mum?' Rachel said. Her voice tiny now.

Mum didn't look at her, in fact neither of them took an eye from Holly's door, but at least she answered. 'Yes?'

'Do you ever think it might help, if you moved somewhere else?'

When Mum spoke it was strangely melodic. 'Oh, I'll never, ever leave this house, Rachel. Not in a million, million, billion years.' Then she reached out and clasped her hand around her daughter's wrist. 'It's not just you who belongs here . . . *I* do too.'

CHAPTER SEVENTEEN

Rabbit knows it's 2 a.m. Doesn't need a fancy watch.
Rabbit senses time as if the ticks are on its heart.
Slides along the pavement and pushes through the fence.
Cracking back the wood, splinters raking through its fur.

House looks dark and sleepy, quiet shadows build a
ladder in.
Rabbit slips inside the garden. Very quiet, delicate.
Other creatures hear it coming,
Rabbit has so many friends.
Insect, mammal, branch and soil.
Grease the way with blood and oil cos

Lights are on and look, she's in there!
Later on she'll fall asleep.
Rabbit may just kiss her gently,
Just before he starts to leap.

Across her body, round her ankles.
Up and in and roundabout.
Paw and tail and fur becoming.
All that she could do without.

CHAPTER EIGHTEEN

Matt's home office was in a shed. Not a shovels, wheelbarrows and cobwebs type of deal, but one of those posh jobs. Halfway between a small chalet and a summer house. The estate agent had been positively orgasmic over it, and to be fair, so had Matt. It was dry and insulated with a radiator that ran off the main house gas feed. Wooden floor too. Plus, it had these cool little downlighters, wedged into the ceiling beams. The last guy who lived here was a photographer, so he'd had these lights fitted to show off his arty prints on the wall.

Matt had only put one picture up so far. A huge, framed poster Wren had bought him for his thirtieth. The UK quad poster of one of his favourite vintage movies, *The Time Machine*.

So it was a proper man cave, only less cavey and more like a brightly lit, Ikea customer service room. Which wasn't a problem. He'd loved this space in the daylight, but when he first saw it at night, he wanted to marry it. He called it 'The Cabin' and insisted everybody in the Hunter family do the same. A name plaque was currently on order, through eBay.

He looked at The Cabin now, as he headed across the garden, VHS player tucked under one arm and The Holly Wasson Season One Box Set under the other. Freshly cut keys dangled from his mouth and he tensed when some of the still sharp metal rattled against the bottom row of his teeth. He stepped up onto the decking and hitched all the gear onto his hip as he fumbled with the patio door.

When it swung open there were no shed sounds. No *Mary Celeste* creak. No cobwebs springing into his face either, and no dull sniff of mould. Just a smooth swish of the brushed trim and a clean, bright room, smelling of pine. Square boxes packed with books were stacked in the corner, Minecraft-style, next to two new bookcases that were currently empty. Except for one, he'd noticed. Wren must have been in here because she'd put his own book up there, shop-display-style, open at the spine.

It was nicely warm in there and his little Simpsons beer fridge was plugged in. Dutifully chilling some Newcastle Brown.

Holy shit, life was good. Which was saying something, after the horrendous summer they'd had.

He sank at his desk, flipped open his laptop and tapped a Philip Glass album on. Wren always said his music sounded like a car alarm going off, but he found the repetitive, classical strings and rhythms helped him concentrate. Got him in the thinking zone. He wrote most of his book to *Koyaanisqatsi*. Yeah, Matt was down with the kids.

He wrote another apology email to the publishers. Apologising again for missing most of the fundraiser today. He fired it off and shrugged, not that bothered.

He still had the leads to connect the VHS to his laptop, after he transferred their wedding video a few years back. He rigged it together, slipped the Holly tape in. Then sat back in his captain's chair and popped a beer.

He didn't press play just yet.

Instead he started pulling out the other papers that Bob had given him. Each was in its own plastic sleeve, numbered with a sticker saying 'Barley' on it.

He leant over and clicked the desk lamp on, spotting his reflection looking back at him from the glass patio doors. His head hovered in the garden. They weren't really overlooked here, so there was no need to shut the blinds. It felt kind of freeing being able to look up now and again at swaying flowers and bushes, or back at the house and kitchen window. He could see Wren in there now, tinkering with a white cardboard model for a building she was designing. But mostly, tonight, he saw the black void of his garden, with his face staring back.

He shrugged, opened up the file and pulled out an A4 sheet, which said Barley Street #1. It was a meticulous list of each example of paranormal activity in the house.

Matt ran his finger down a few.

Saturday, November 3rd 17:30 (approx.). House key strangely missing (again) – see Thursday, Nov 1st, 12 p.m.

'Strangely missing . . .' Matt muttered into his beer. 'Call the exorcist! Someone's lost a key!'

He read on.

Saturday, November 3rd, 21:25 (approx.) MW (code for Mary Wasson, according to the side panel) heard cracking glass from kitchen. Milk missing from fridge. Bottle found in cupboard with top smashed off. Glass shards missing.

He flicked again.

Sunday, November 4th, 02:00 (approx.) All of family woken in the night by loud crashing downstairs. MW and RW (that was the older sister, Rachel) *went down to check and found a sofa in the middle of the room, nothing else broken. RW's Audio cassette player and tape missing. Family pack of cards missing. MW's work shoe missing.*

One more.

Wednesday, November 7th into 8th, 2 incidents.

Timeframe unknown – roughly 8-10pm. RW, JF (Jo Finch) & SE (Steph Ellis) report animal apparition on roof of house. 'A very tall hare, thin and standing. Hind legs. Demon?'

*02:00 (approx.) HW (Holly Wasson) woke in the middle of the night. Reported hearing footsteps in the attic above her room. Too scared to go back to sleep. Insisted on light being left on. HW **dead by morning.***

He paused from reading those last three words in bold and looked out of the patio doors. Amelia's bedroom looked out on the garden. He could see her yellow curtains glowing softly, sleeping with her light on just as she'd asked.

Breath skimmed across his lips as he leafed through the pages. He counted sixteen sides of this stuff. He sighed and slid it to the side. He'd check the rest later.

There were cuttings of local newspaper reports too. Local stuff, with punchy titles like 'Poltergeist Havoc for Local Family'. Both stories showed Mary Wasson, looking all sad and emo into the camera, but still pretty glam. In one she held a broken teapot, right into the camera. Thrusting it like they'd told her it was a 3D shoot. The story told him little he didn't already know, except for one little titbit. The house had become something of a local attraction following the reports, with curious residents gathering outside, even knocking on the Wassons' door in the hope of catching sight of the 'evil spirit'. And one particular detail struck him.

Local churchgoers have avoided the house, calling it an 'opening for evil forces'. They have gathered to pray against it.

He thought of those quirky church folk from this morning, out on their prayer walk. Hovering at the school gates. Of that American fella with the goatee, holding his palm out to Matt, in prayer. He pulled out a yellow pad and scribbled a note with his pen.

Stuff to tell Larry.
1) Church connection?

In the other piece, the picture was Mary standing like one of those miserable Victorians in old photographs. Only her hand wasn't on a moustachioed husband. It rested on a hefty leather sofa, which she'd said had been 'tossed over like a kiddie's toy'. He wasn't really sure how she could say that, since she said she hadn't actually seen it being upturned. For all she knew, the poor old spook had spent half the night holding its poor back and puffing out ectoplasm trying to shift the bloody thing.

A smile of self-amusement grew on his face as he set the papers aside and clicked his Glass music off. Then he pressed play on the video player and his smile vanished like the flick of a switch.

Holly Wasson gazed out at him, blinking slowly while wind rattled The Cabin.

He looked over his shoulder and saw a fat moon hanging from the back window.

She was at a dining-room table, hands gently clasped in front of her. Like she'd been told that was how polite girls sit when they are being interviewed about haunted houses. The walls around her were painted green and a dark wooden chest of plates loomed behind her. In the background, he could hear the muffled voice of Bob Hodges chatting. Telling her just to 'sit tight' as he rigged a microphone up. 'Won't take a sec.' The edges of the picture had that fuzzy VHS look, which made him feel nostalgic. Washed-out colours, very little detail. Every now and again a white tape line would ripple up the image, when the tracking went out.

He watched her sitting there, waiting. As *he* was waiting.

She was a skinny nine-year-old, surrounded by pictures of animals on the walls. Pictures she would glance up at, now and again, as she waited. Her long blonde hair curled into little pools on the giant doily that covered the tabletop. Whenever Bob apologised for the delay, she looked off camera at him and smiled. It was crooked, with the typically uneven teeth of a kid. But it seemed genuine and likeable. A tiny dimple marked one cheek and she wore a T-shirt with a cartoon kitten on it, sitting in a ribboned basket. A little babyish for her age, unless she was being ironic – do nine-year-olds even *get* irony?

Despite the occasional smile, Holly would often just look off into the corner without any smile at all. There was a roundness to the shoulders and a body curl inwards that told a story.

She wasn't symmetrical enough to wind up in some catalogue or cutesy calendar – all straight teeth and laughing. Rather, Holly was the sort of little girl you'd see walking home from school, hefting a bag on her back like it was full of bricks. Squinting up into the sun and smiling at the possibilities of the world – just as other kids her age pushed right past her loudly talking, just not to her. He knew this not because he had been one of these types of kids at school, but because he'd seen plenty. Every now and then he'd even stuck up for them, but not always. There were moments that he liked to forget, when he had stood back and let class humour trump basic human rights. But then at the time, being funny seemed so *genuinely* important.

You can tell who gets bullied, sometimes. Who gets forgotten. He'd picked that skill up at school and had professionalised it as a pastor: a sort of grim sixth sense honed by hours of sitting with weeping people. Just a single glance into their eyes could tell you something and this girl was one of those. In that cloak of sadness in her face, he also saw that other emotion, which often bubbled under the surface of the bullied and the hurt. Every now and then, it looked like she had angry eyes.

Just as that thought occurred to him, Holly looked up from the table and stared right into the camera. Which meant right into him. Never looking away.

Bob's muffled voice came off camera. 'Right. Sorted.' He coughed a few times. 'So . . . it's 6:28 pm. Sunday November 4th, 2001 . . .'

He glanced at his sheet . . . Holly killed herself in the early hours of Thursday the 8th.

'. . . we're in number 29 Barley Street, in Menham, South London. Present are myself, Bob Hodges, and my wife, Joyce. And this is . . . can you introduce yourself, please? Full name, please.'

She nodded. Eyes fixed on Matt. 'Hello. I'm Holly Wasson.'

He didn't feel a chill, but rather he just felt something crack in his heart. At the way her eyes looked out at him, personally. Right through the lens, right down through the magnetic tape and across time. Through the phono-to-USB wire and up and out through the pixels of the screen. So that she was looking at Matt in his cosy little sanctuary.

She'd hang herself a few days later.

'Age?' Bob said.

'Nine and three-quarters.'

He let out a long breath and took a longer swig.

'Excellent,' Bob said. 'And can you tell me the first time you knew there might be some sort of presence in the house?'

Silence.

'Holly?'

Silence and slow blinking. She bit her lip.

Matt heard the faint voice of Joyce Hodges, in the background. 'You're doing great, poppet. Now go ahead and answer. When was the first time you knew something was in this house?'

'On Thursday,' she nodded toward the walls. 'When all these got messed up.'

Bob again. 'You mean the animal pictures?'

'Mm-hmm.'

'And how were they messed up, exactly?'

She looked at them and tilted her head as if the walls were turning.

'Holly?'

'Oh, sorry . . .' She sat upright again. 'The pictures were all upside down. That was the first thing I remember. All the animals with their heads down.'

He went to sip a shot of beer as Bob moved onto a new question. Something about small holes dug in the garden. Matt stopped suddenly, glass rim resting on his mouth.

He hit pause.

Rewound a little.

Holly's face rippled with the tracking.

'The pictures were upside down,' Holly said. 'That's the first thing I—'

Pause.

He thought for a moment, then quickly slid the log file back in front of him. He glanced across to Thursday Nov 1st and read the entry.

Dining room pictures (all of animals) removed and hung back on nails, inverted.

He grabbed a pen and his yellow pad.

Things to tell Larry: 2) Upside-down animal pictures in Barley Street AND school???

He unpaused her, and watched some more. Pulling out the final fold of papers as she spoke. Not the originals, but colour photocopies of drawings she'd made, mostly in what looked like crayon, and some in felt tip. There were five pictures, all with the same sort of image. A little girl, which looked like Holly, standing in a summer garden made of slashed lines of green felt tip. Each had a thick tree filled with birds. Each had butterflies floating around flowers. And each had one thing and one thing alone, which had used a black felt tip. A very tall figure, standing on its hind legs, with long thin ears springing up. No features, no face. Just a scribbled storm of black. In most of them, the figure stood by the tree. In one it was up in the branches, crouching. In one, the one he looked at for longest, it was holding her hand.

'Black rabbit,' he said and then the cabin lights went out.

Amelia started screaming in her room.

CHAPTER NINETEEN

Rachel stopped brushing and sloshed the water around her mouth. When she spat it out it slapped into the sink. She noticed some tiny chunks of lasagne mince gathered on the white foam by the plug. Yuk. That was happening more and more these days. Like her teeth were getting gappier with each passing birthday. Maybe when she hit forty she'd be flossing and an entire banana might drop out.

She tried to smile at that, but such things were not in her vocabulary tonight. People could no more smile in Barley Street than they could breathe on the moon. She was standing in her old bathroom, fully dressed. Surrounded by walls of crooked tiles of dark mustard. *Still* lit only by that horrid fluorescent strip above the mirror, that flickered every few minutes with a buzz. The main light had no bulb in it, as usual. She always thought this room looked like the set from a seedy German play. She wasn't sure exactly why she thought it had to be German, but the connection seemed utterly logical as a teenager and it still did now.

She rinsed the sink out and glanced at the bath, with the old moulded soap-holder and its lightning-fork crack across it. And the familiar arches of rust behind the taps. She pictured Holly sitting in there at five years old giggling while Rachel stood pouring water into her little cupped palms. Their cat Pob slinking around until they both sprinkled water at him and he sprang off. Laughter bouncing off the tiles. While weather-girl Mum had her arms folded as she leant against the door frame, smiling and humming out Disney songs.

If this was anybody else's house, she'd have left her toothbrush on the side for the morning. But she didn't like the thought of any of her stuff sitting here by itself. So she slipped it into her washbag, which scraped its metal teeth loudly as she zipped it up.

The only thing in this room that had changed was the shower curtain. Mum had bought a cheap-looking plastic thing. Semi-transparent, but covered with birds, half of which looked like crows and blackbirds swooping down and dive-bombing Tippi Hedren. A totally off-putting shower vibe.

She paused, though, and reached for the curtain. It felt cold and a little damp against her fingertips. She slid it all the way back. The metal rings slowly squeaking on the rail. Then she leant over and put her fingers on the curve of the bath. Just to feel it. Because Holly's bare shoulders had rested against that curve, so many times.

She pictured her in there. The odd little sister who seemed to constantly compliment her. 'You're really pretty, Rach.' 'How come you're so *cool*?' And how Holly had promised that the two of them were going to go to Disneyland together one day, and she would pay for it all. Because she'd be a grown-up and make lots of money as a vet. And how she'd talk about that trip more than any other topic.

A sentence started sliding through the roads and pathways of Rachel's brain. Words that were heavy enough to drop all the way to her heart and leave a stain.

So I'm the sister who got to leave this house, and you're the sister who had to stay.

Bathing forever in this horrid room. Walking these halls on a constant, echoed loop. With not even her big sister for company. Just a zombie mum with bad hair and a house that most locals still crossed the street to avoid.

She stepped back and let the curtain fall back into place. She clicked the mirror light off and headed out onto the dark landing, still in her pumps. She'd been here for a few hours now, but she still hadn't taken her shoes off. She doubted she'd remove them until maybe she was tucked up in the bed. She didn't like the idea of her feet touching the floors of this house. Hated the thought of her socks picking up old, ancient dust, that might have once been part of her, or her mum, or Holly herself.

The light from under Mum's door was spilling out in a golden fan. There was, of course, no light coming from Holly's. In the dim light, the pictures on the door were easy to see. A hundred sisters looking out. For a moment, she considered just going straight in that room and switching the light on. Sitting on her bed and pulling out the old toys they used to play with. Leaning back against the My Little Pony wallpaper and reading some old book out loud, like she used to do to help Holly sleep. Maybe she'd even spend the night in there and close this infernal bloody tragedy loop for all time.

But the images quickly came. Beetles, loose in her brain. Carrying the sights in the precise sequence she saw them. It was always like that. Always well organised.

The power cable pulled tight. The back of Holly's head and her hair lolling to the side. The arms dangling with the fingers curled, but her left little finger jutting. The little feet in yellow socks, with white heels. One slipper still on, one on the floor. Toes pointing inward. The gap between her feet and the floor.

The moment she thought it was a joke.

The moment she knew it wasn't a joke.

The animal roar in the room, which she'd always assumed was

162

her own scream, though she could never be sure in that house.

And here she stood, outside the room that would always define Holly.

And you . . . she thought. *It will always define you, too.*

All those Holly faces looked at her and said a sentence that burst all tender, sisterly memories away. Poisoned them, in fact.

Because when Holly looked out she wasn't saying *hey, sis . . . long time no see.*

She was saying . . . *why, Rachel? Why did you do it? Why?*

She stepped back and quickly closed her eyes, then she rushed along the landing to her room, slamming the door behind her. The echoes of why turning into the ticking sludge of the radiators.

Ironically, and perhaps tellingly, her bedroom was the only one to have been redecorated. Gone were all her movie posters. No more Brad Pitt, circa *Fight Club*, staring out. Now it was a junk room, with mainly old newspapers and magazines, stacked in towers. But the bed was still there.

Still in the same place, up against the wall. She pulled off her clothes, feeling very conscious that the walls would see her bare skin. She pulled some pyjamas on, which felt colder than they ought to. She switched off the light and lay on the mattress, staring at the ceiling, smelling the mildewed carpet. She noticed that the bumps in the dodgy bed springs were now touching different parts of her back, now that she'd grown a little. She could picture herself on a hundred nights, tapping against this wall with her knuckle while Holly tapped back. Their beds together separated only by a few bricks.

If she rapped on the wall tonight, would something happen? Would Holly lift that bent knuckle and knock back? Would a tiny fist break through, grasping for hair?

No. It wouldn't. That's what that professor guy would say. And maybe he was right.

And ironically it was *that* that made the tears come. That's what made thin streams roll sideways down her cheek and seep into the pillow.

Because Holly was dead and Steph was dead, and maybe that really is all there is. Which was way less spooky, but was still the cold, depressing side of realism. As she lay there she almost wished that ghosts were true. And that Holly would tell her that it was okay, and that she could rest and that what happened to her really wasn't Rachel's fault.

And though nothing of the sort happened, Rachel finally turned onto her other side and touched the wall with her fingertip. 'I'm sorry, Holly,' she whispered. 'I'm so, so sorry.'

The silence was too much. Hissing like the sound of a bundle of clothes, sliding across the carpet of the landing toward her room.

So she pulled out her field recorder and slipped her headphones on. She scrolled through some files and settled, as usual, on the sounds of a market in Marrakesh, which she'd recorded last year. A rich soundscape suddenly filled her ears: street chatter, car horns, muffled local music from buildings and the constant sound of unintelligible bartering. And every now and again she'd hear an English voice amongst it all. Debbie. Her ex-girlfriend. Telling her to come and look at something. Handing her a hat and saying, hey, try this on. In the weeks just before she sat Rachel down and said, let's be like grown-ups about this and dumped her for God.

Hearing her voice and the sounds of the market pulled her out of Menham for a moment. Long enough for her to ignore the fact that maybe Rachel was exactly like Holly, after all. Maybe *she* would never leave this place either. Not really. But the sounds played long enough for her to gradually forget where she was, and better still, who she was. Long enough, at least, to tug her into a deep and dreamless sleep.

CHAPTER TWENTY

Amelia was sleeping now, finally. Curled in her giant quilt cloud, with that fluffy tortoise clamped under her chin. He'd bounded across the garden so fast, he'd almost tripped on a little stone tortoise Wren had put out. By the time he got upstairs she was already holding Amelia tight, with the torchlight on her phone giving the room a dull glow.

'It's another power cut,' she said softly, patting Amelia's hair. 'It's no big deal, okay?'

But it had been a big deal. Enough for her to see the shadow in her room again, only this time it was at the bottom of the bed and was climbing up on her feet. She refused to go to sleep in this room even with the light on. Not unless one of them stayed with her. Wren had offered, but she had a presentation first thing. So here he was, sitting on Amelia's window sill, listening to her tiny mouse snore and watching her face crush into her pillow. Ready to reassure her that any figure she was seeing was a hypnagogic illusion. No phantoms here. Her yellow lamp cast a cosy haze across the room. He looked at the corner and couldn't see any shadows to worry about.

As he sat, he nibbled at the corner of a breadstick and gazed out of her window. His beloved cabin sat in darkness in the garden below. He'd switched everything off down there but he had the thought that if this was a movie, this would be the bit when the room suddenly lit up with the flash of that VHS again. And he'd hear the muffled voice of Holly Wasson, talking about black rabbits.

There were no lights, though. So it looked more like a proper shed than ever. He glanced across at the Anglican church just down from them and the corner of the graveyard that was visible from here. Wow, he thought. What the hell did he and Rachel expect? Giving a seven-year-old the room with the best view of an allotment for corpses.

He sighed and stared back down at his phone and the three words he'd thumbed into Google Search.

Demonic. Symbolism. Rabbit.

He tapped the search button and saw stacks of references spring up. He wasn't really surprised to find so many. Animal demons were as common as muck in folk tales and legend. But he was more used to seeing the rabbit symbol in Renaissance art. Like Cosimo's image of a white hare, snuffling Cupid's hand. Or Titian's unusual piece that Matt had once seen in the Louvre. With a cute little white rabbit being stroked by the Virgin Mary, while a delighted baby Jesus looks down at it, smiling. There were carvings of three rabbits on a Swiss cathedral too, who were supposed to represent the Holy Trinity. He knew that much.

But he had to admit he was rusty on his *psycho-evil-rabbit* knowledge.

Turns out, there were plenty of others who weren't.

- *Rabbits and Hares in the Dark Arts.*
- *Rabbits as Demonic Guardians: Ancient Egypt.*
- *The Shadow Demon Rabbit in Mythology and Reality.*

Fascinating.

He swallowed and started tapping.

The Internet, he'd always thought, was ironically a rabbit hole itself and he found himself moving from link to link, winding up in the most unexpected places. At one point he found himself on The British Museum site, scrolling through the funerary papyrus of someone called Bakenmut, an ancient Egyptian priest and scribe. Matt had a fair bit of knowledge of Ancient Egyptian symbolism but he hardly had to be Indiana Jones, or indeed a vet, to spot the figure of a rabbit drawn on the centuries-old papyrus. Described as some sort of demonic guardian, the rabbit appeared to be standing tall on its hind legs, holding a knife.

A few clicks later and he saw photographs of the Notre Dame Cathedral in Chartres, France. He clicked on a link and the screen suddenly filled with a grotesque-looking gargoyle carved from dark-grey stone on the southern portal. It was a tall rabbit on two feet, huge ears dangling. Over its shoulder it was carrying a woman by the ankles and the rabbit looked hungry. Exactly what the rabbit was hungry for was open to discussion, but the fact that the woman was naked made suggestions of its own. Another part of the cathedral showed a soldier running away in panic . . . from a hare.

Then a beautiful, centuries-old building in Dean Street, Newcastle. Overlooking the rear of St Nicholas Cathedral. Over the arch of a door, a mad gargoyle crouched with fangs and claws bared. The good old Geordies had christened it the Vampire Rabbit.

He found a bizarre statue in Dublin, Ireland, which showed three rabbits on their hind legs, holding hands and cavorting at the top of a hill. Close up, their bodies were made of stone, fused with the outlines of scissors and zips and, weirdly, the closed fist of a toddler, trapped in the rabbit's foot.

He swallowed a chunk of breadstick and for the first time he became aware that the hedges in the garden were moving. He stared down there, and cupped his hand against the glass to cut out the lamp light.

– *It's the breeze, stupid. You're getting as bad as Amelia.*

Back on the phone he moved on from the pictures to articles. He found that rabbits had become particularly reviled from the eleventh to thirteenth centuries. This was due to their supposed pagan connections to sexuality and fertility. The pagans embraced them because these animals apparently had the ability to walk between the worlds and commune with the dead. He thought of Holly, sending her animal messenger back and forth between worlds.

This skill of rabbits meant it wasn't a shock that they became so popular with witches, who sometimes kept them as familiars. He saw an old painting of a hook-nosed woman waltzing through a forest at night, as a string of animals paraded in tow behind her, walking on their hind legs, holding candles in their paws. A tall black rabbit led the way.

He clicked on another picture, which turned out to be the frontispiece from the 1647 book, *The Discovery of Witches* by Matthew Hopkins. Ah . . . he knew this one well. The woodcut showed the arch witch-finder Hopkins decked out with his cape and staff, looking Vincent-Price-sharp while he presided over some old lady being forced to name her 'imps'. Toward the bottom left he saw a black rabbit standing on its hind legs, and next to it was the name it had confessed to: Sack and Sugar.

For some reason he tapped the rabbit with his finger. The bushes rustled outside.

He shrugged, moved on, scrolled through more and more of

this stuff, surprised at the sheer amount of it. He glanced up at Amelia, still sleeping, but with her head lost completely under the quilt. Just a lump sitting there in the room, now. He slipped his earphones on when he ventured into YouTube territory.

He started watching the most traumatic clips from *Watership Down* (that had been a '*U*' certificate? Sheesh). Bulgy-eyed rabbits glared as they watched blood spreading in rivulets across fields. And of course the Black Rabbit of Inlé. The grim reaper who lived in a stone warren and announced and delivered death to all other rabbits. Not even a villain as such. He was only doing the bidding of the great god Frith. The rabbit as messenger. The black angel.

He yawned and clicked on a home-made cartoon which turned out to be Bugs Bunny violently sodomising Elmer Fudd while the theme from Benny Hill played. Finally, he laughed at the ridiculousness of everything he had seen and read that night. All that gonzo stuff he'd heard today in the Gazebo took on its right perspective, as the jaunty Yakety Sax rattled his eardrums.

'Bedtime for bonzo,' he said to himself.

He clicked the '*Bugs Does Fudd Gud!*' video off, just in case Wren walked in to discover he had a bizarrely specific taste in Looney Tunes porn. Then he slid off the sill and pulled Amelia's quilt back a touch. He kissed her very gently on the forehead. Looking at her and feeling thankful not to God but that the random chaos of life had got them all out of Hobbs Hill in one piece, this summer. Then a thought came to him. If Amelia had been around in his Christian years, he would have prayed for her right now, just as she slept. He'd have knelt by her bedside and held her hand. Would have asked God to keep the shadows away, regardless of them being in her mind or in the ether. He thought about this for a long moment, then he turned and left her light on, kept her door open and headed off to bed.

It was 1 a.m.

It was only when he crossed the landing that he felt anything approaching real, genuine unease. He glanced out of the large window towards the church. He was getting into the habit of doing that, just in case vandals were up on the roof tearing the lead off to sell.

Tonight though he froze, because he saw a small dark shape springing between the gravestones of the churchyard. On any other night he'd have said, 'bloody foxes,' but he didn't say that because frankly it didn't really look like one of those. He just leant towards the glass, fogged with his breath and watched the little black shadow leap from one grave, then to the next, only to vanish behind the white marble gravestone. The stone was one he recognised, because they'd all walked through there the other day, and Wren had sighed when she saw it. A young kid, dead before he'd even hit his teens. The name escaped him, for now. Though wasn't *he* nine?

He waited for more minutes than were sensible but whatever animal it was never emerged from behind that gravestone again. He was almost tempted to grab his shoes and go out to look but he lay in bed instead, struggling to sleep for a very long time. Funny what darkness can do to perfectly rational minds.

He just kept thinking that the small rabbit (he knew that's what it was) had now burrowed itself deep down into the earth of that little one's grave, and had found itself somewhere warm and dark to hide.

CHAPTER TWENTY-ONE

Jo Finch fluttered her eyes open and looked at the bedside clock. It was just after 2 a.m., though she could barely read the blurred red digits of the display. She pulled her hand from under the quilt and rubbed at her eyes.

Wet.

She'd been crying in her sleep.

The dream had done that. A full-on, smells and sounds memory of her, Kassy, Rachel and Steph singing karaoke in her old bedroom. Warbling Britney Spears hits and strutting up and down her bed. Only in the dream, whenever Steph grabbed the mike she'd open her mouth to sing and she'd snap her head back too hard and her neck would tear open, showing sharp black fur on her insides.

'*No,*' she said.

The image vanished.

She shivered and rubbed the last of the tears away with the corner of her pillow.

'I need a wee,' she said, to nobody. Because Lee had obviously decided he didn't want to come to bed yet, even though she was *clearly* upset. No, he wanted to sit up on his computer and relist his bloody stupid premium golf tees on Gumtree instead of eBay. Like that was a revolutionary business move. He'd normally have caught her vibe and be up here now, holding her and telling her it was okay. He must be getting really desperate now, because he was never this late, normally. He was an idiot, sometimes. A kind one, with a beautiful smile, but an idiot sometimes.

She couldn't even call for Seren, or slip into her room and lie alongside her, like Jo sometimes did at night. Since all this craziness had started, Jo had asked Seren's grandad to look after her for a bit, just until this whole thing died down. He'd love the company.

She clicked on the light and gasped when she saw the black figure out of the corner of her eye.

Her funeral dress, hung from the wardrobe. Already picked out and ironed, ready for Steph's service. They'd announce that any day now, she assumed, so she'd best be ready. She'd bought that dress four months ago for her mum's heart-attack-induced funeral. And now she'd wear it again for one of her best-ever friends, barely into her thirtieth. God, getting older was so, so shit.

She trudged to the bathroom, where her yellow fleecy cleaning uniform was hanging on the dryer, then she dropped her Tartan pyjamas to the floor, hissing at the cold of the toilet seat as it pressed into her legs. She felt embarrassed for some reason, at how loud the flow sounded. Like a hose smashing into a river. She wondered if maybe—

Click.

She frowned at the faint, odd sound coming from downstairs.

Click, click.

It must be Lee, she thought. Tapping his cordless little mouse like a moron.

But this . . . this . . .

Click.

This *wasn't* that, actually.

She sat upright, almost stopping the flow.

She called out, 'Lee? Come up to bed.'

Nothing.

Probably had his headphones on. That flipping Grime music pounding his brain to mush.

She pushed the rest out as fast as she could and stood up, desperate to get her bottoms pulled back up. She skipped washing her hands and crept back to the hallway. Perhaps the clicking was something to do with that energy bulb that she'd just put in the hallway. Maybe the cheap ones took a while to acclimatise? Maybe.

She leant over the banister; downstairs was full of shadows.

'Lee?'

Click, click.

Now the sound was sharp and distinct enough for her to decide something. It probably wasn't clicking after all. In fact, that sounded like *flicking*, not clicking. Yes. Quite right. Full marks Jo, she thought, madly. That's flicking.

A word popped into her head.

Fingernails.

She clutched the front of her pyjamas hard, tartan deforming, and raced across the landing, trying hard not to clomp. She wanted to turn the light on but she chose not to. Maybe whatever was clicking/flicking didn't even know she was there.

Click, click.

It's Lee, idiot. He's doing something you can't figure out.

Then a light-bulb moment.

Ha! He's watching porn and he's getting busy down there. That's what's happening. That's not clicking, or flicking, it's good old-fashioned skin slapping! And that's why he stays up so late. He doesn't even own any golf tees! Ha ha. This is hilarious.

My problems aren't supernatural, they're blissfully norm—
Click.
Click, click.

Louder now. *Closer.*

Her heart hammered against the bones in her chest, and she flung herself back from the banister because she didn't want to see.
Click.
Click, click, click.

It's porn, idiot. And that's okay, even though it's not. Because a porn-hungry mouse click is infinitely preferable to the flicking of long finger—
Click, click, click, click.

Louder. Louder. Coming up the stairs.

'Jesus,' she rushed to her room and pushed the door wide. The door bounced open and she saw her mobile phone lying on the bedside cabinet. Dead as a bloody brick, from all that pointless Facebook browsing of what people had for dinner tonight. She flung the door shut and raced into the room, aware of having not taken a breath for at least one minute.
Click, click.

Muffled through the door, but definitely somewhere near the top of the stairs now.

Don't do this, Jo. Just don't. It's the central heating. It's a dripping tap. It's an adorable hedgehog tapping against the patio doors for a bowl of fruit.

She had a vague sensation of pushing her bedroom window open and looking down at the garden. Of taking it all in, in a single shot. At the white plastic patio chairs and her sad attempt at a vegetable patch. And the old rabbit hutch by the fence where her own pet Six should be sleeping. Only the hutch door was open and it was empty inside.

Her hands were shaking.

She whimpered when she saw something out of the bottom of her eye. A tiny wisp of white directly below that looked like the flash of a girl's dress. A specific little girl rushing into the house, and leading the way for her dark friend. But actually it was the white net curtains from the lounge downstairs. The breeze was blowing them out into the back garden.

The patio doors are open. That's all—

. . . why are the patio doors open?

She turned back to the bedroom door and stared at it.

'Holly?' she whispered, and couldn't believe she'd just said that.

She had the weirdest sensation of itching all over. Like tiny flies had dropped from the ceiling and were sliding all over her with delight. Or actually, no. It felt more like something with hair was passing her by in the dark and was touching her. Fur growing outside of her, at the same time it was sprouting on the inside of her.

She sat on the bed.

Click, click, click.

She thought of something. She could push her chest of drawers against the door. They did that in films all the time. But as she pushed up from the bed she saw that the handle was doing that thing it *always* did but somehow she'd forgotten in all the hullaballoo. That you had to push this door shut hard with the hip, until you heard it click. It was the only way to truly close it. But she hadn't done that. Now it had bounced in and out of the latch again. It was opening slowly. Hinges doing what they wanted to do.

'Lee!' she called out. 'Lee. Lee' But then very soon the word *Lee* changed to the word *God*.

Or rather to the words, *Oh, God. Oh God, Oh God.* A hyperventilation more than anything else.

She slipped clean off the bed in shock and heard how loud the bang was as her bulk hit the floorboards and shook the cabinet.

Even then, in the midst of this, she'd noticed that she had always been horribly bigger than she ever wanted to be.

She spoke in a desperate whisper. 'Holly . . . Holly, I'm sorry.'

But soon all she needed to see was through the gaping, opening door.

click, click, Click, Click, CLICK, CLICK!

A very tall black rabbit, made of pure shadow, was swaying from left to right on its hind legs. And it quickly walked across the landing toward her.

CHAPTER TWENTY-TWO

Couches smell of tears and cider, chocolate wrapper on
the floor.
Drunk man snoring, face a cushion, room lit up with flashing
pictures.
Rabbit nods and opens claws.

Up above them, she is stirring. Splashing water on her face.
Rabbit slides along the shadows, banisters of branch and lace.
Now she shouts so loudly for him. Calls his name, 'come up
to bed'.
She is scared and needs his presence. Rabbit climbs the stair
instead.

Moves across the skinny landing, sniffing carpet, sensing skin.
Sees a light beneath the door. Sucks her scent on everything.
Bedroom door clicks slowly open, now she shouts his
name again.

Rabbit once in deep black corners, sees the world and breathes it in.

Slowly rising, hind legs thriving, front paws spring and don't come down.
Rabbit strides on two legs smiling. Grabs her scream and makes it drown.

click

PART TWO

THERE ARE SUCH THINGS

CHAPTER TWENTY-THREE

It was late afternoon when Matt pulled his car into a rain-pounded Bennington Road in Menham, and he saw a narrow street lined with skinny, pink-bricked houses. Each front garden was just about big enough for a preschool dwarf to sit in, cross-legged, at a push.

It took him a while to park. Mainly because three police cars were hogging the kerb already. All of them were perched outside number 122, which Larry had said was Jo Finch's house. Larry's car was directly outside of it.

He had to head halfway up the street to find a space and pulled up near a bus stop advertising holidays in Butlins. 'It's even better than you think!' it said, which for some reason made him chuckle. He killed the engine. The thunk-thunk heartbeat of the windscreen wipers came to a sudden stop. Then he pulled up his coat collar and stepped out into the rain.

The air had that wet concrete smell that he didn't like and as he headed down the street he heard the low drone of an easyJet plane crossing the sky overhead. There were people up there right now.

Businessmen and families, biting open packets of bread buns on their laps. Oblivious to the mad and macabre world of Menham, South London far below.

There was a cafe just up the street from Jo's house and Matt felt his tongue buzz as he sniffed a burger sizzling on the air. Maybe he could grab one after. The closer he got to the house, the more he noticed the tracksuited locals who had gathered on the pavement opposite. They stood there hollow-cheeked as they sucked on cigarettes, looking bored and cold. Which suggested they'd been standing there for a long time with little to excite them. They perked up when he slowed at Jo's door and he could feel their eyes on him as he turned and tapped his knuckles against 122.

Almost instantly, the door opened. A bald policeman with rosy cheeks leant out. 'Are you selling something?'

'I'm here to see DC Larry Forbes.'

He looked confused and ran his eyes up and down him. '*You're* the vicar?'

'Ex-vicar.' He nodded. 'Very, very *ex*.'

'Bit young to be a priest aren't—'

'It's raining . . . and I'm too young to die of hypothermia.'

'Oh. Two ticks.' The policeman leant back and whispered to somebody unseen then turned back to Matt. 'Wait.' The door closed just as the rain kicked up a gear.

He stepped back to squint up at the top windows, as drops from the heavens whizzed by his face. He used to do that as a kid. Look up at the rain and pretend that the earth was racing through hyperspace. Everything from the outside of the house looked normal enough. Nothing broken or out of place. No creepy rabbit demon striding across, with Jo slung over their shoulders and a dutiful white dog in tow.

No little girl holding the rabbit's hand.

A man's voice came from across the street. 'What's the deal?'

182

Matt turned. 'Pardon?' Rain machine-gunned off his shoulders.

'Three police cars, and now *you* make it four?' The thin man in a hoodie nodded toward the house. 'Who's dead? The woman?'

Another one said, 'It's our street. We have a right to know.'

Thunder started to roll like a distant kettle drum.

'*You'll* all be dead of flu if you don't get inside,' he called back.

The door rattled open again and he turned to see Larry who looked at him and said, 'Nice swim?'

'Move,' Matt pushed past him and pulled off his sodden coat, flicking a little rain Larry's way. But then the door closed and Matt's nervous smile vanished with the click of the lock.

Even before Hobbs Hill, Matt had been to a few investigation scenes before. Mostly suicides, and on one incredibly depressing occasion a domestic-violence case in which a woman from his congregation had been so comprehensively beaten she literally looked like she'd been sprayed with circles of blue and purple paint. That was a hideous moment which haunted him more than most, since his wife Wren had experienced the same thing years back, from her ex. Seeing that lady – the Sunday School teacher – curled up under a lamp in a patch of blood and teeth was one of the many little steps on his journey away from theism.

Jo Finch's place wasn't exactly crime scene central, with swathes of policemen brushing banisters and dropping things into little plastic bags. But there were officers making notes and squinting their eyes while they searched under tables. Looking for Jo or her boyfriend's phone, perhaps.

Or their heads.

Somewhere he could hear the snap of a person taking pictures. The sound that denotes happiness in every context except this one. Larry had Matt by the elbow and guided him into the lounge. So far, he could see no blood, bodies nor smashed-up stuff.

'Is she okay?' Matt said, slapping a hand through his wet hair.

'Thanks for coming,' Larry said.

'Please tell me she's not dead.'

'Well . . .'

'*Is* she?'

'She's missing, basically.'

'Oh,' Matt said. 'And where's the boyfriend?'

'He's missing too. He's called Lee Bradshaw. A mechanic. Well . . . Kwik Fit. Neither of them turned up for work this morning.'

Matt noticed the sofa had about a hundred cushions on it. 'And when were they seen last?'

'Last night, at The Cod Father chip shop, just down the road. That was about 8 p.m. Then this afternoon, a neighbour popped over for something and noticed the front door was hanging open a touch. She popped her head in and called out. She realised the house was empty.'

'Might they have just left the door open by accident?'

'I kind of doubt that . . . follow me.'

'Wait a sec,' Matt said. 'At the park yesterday. I'm sure Jo said she had a little girl.'

'She does. Seren. A pre-schooler. She's been staying with Jo's dad since the dog thing at the school. We checked up and she's fine. Now . . . come and look at this.' Larry headed off into the hall and they both dropped to their haunches, looking at a Day-Glo Post-it note stuck to the hall skirting board. On it was a hand-drawn vine in a crucifix shape, with delicate green leaves and flowers. And in the centre, the clearly crucified stickman figure of Jesus Christ. 'We've found seventeen so far,' Larry said.

Matt stared at the vine and the figure hanging in the centre. He shook his head in surprise. 'This is a Lily Cross. It's used for funerals and Easter services.'

'Yeah, I've seen them. Just tell me what they mean.'

'Well, in Christian art the lily's a sign of purity and chastity.' He looked up at Larry. 'Sometimes in paintings you see the angel Gabriel holding a lily branch when he announces the virgin birth. It's like the opposite of crude. Like it's making sure the sexual element of Jesus birth isn't seen as . . . dirty.'

Larry nodded and jotted something down.

'It's used for the resurrection of Christ too. At funerals, it's supposed to show the dead person's soul's being restored. Made innocent again . . . though to be fair in folklore the meaning is a bit different.'

'Go on.'

'I'm pretty sure people used to plant lilies in the garden to scare off ghosts and evil spirits.'

'Ghosts . . . right.' Larry made another note.

Matt tilted his head a little, looking at the stick figure of Jesus hanging there. Then he nodded. 'Where are the rest?'

'*Everywhere.* There's one on the patio doors, a few up the stairs. We even found one stuck underneath the closed lid of the toilet.'

'Show me, please.'

They wandered through the house in silence. The sort of quietness you slip into, when you feel dread in the pit of your gut, even though it might be unfounded. The crosses were in most rooms and up the stairs. Matt mentally logged each one, looking for variations. There were none to speak of. All of them were just the same simple sketch of a symbol of purity and protection.

He saw the last one in the toilet, stuck beneath the lid. He pushed himself upright with a creak of his knees.

'We found something else too. A picture, stuck on her bedroom door.' Larry led him along the hallway, where a small photocopy was stuck to the white door with a piece of black gaffer tape.

Matt gazed at it. 'This is getting weird.'

It was a woodcut, in the style of early modern European art. Sixteenth, seventeenth century maybe. It showed a furious river, rushing through a forest. Sad-looking villagers walked on the banks, carrying knapsacks and firewood, but they stared over their shoulders in fear of the water. He leant in closer to see the tips of heads, and a hand sticking out, almost swallowed in the waves, with what looked like wooden debris crashing into their backs.

'I've seen this picture before,' Larry said. 'It's in local history books. People think it might be the depiction of a flood that swept through the town, in the 1600s. Though they can't be sure.'

He looked at the image again, frowning at it for a while. 'And what about the pelican?' Matt said. 'Did that show up again?'

Larry nodded. 'You could say that.'

He guided Matt along the landing, the floorboards creaking under their feet. Then he pushed his palm against the bedroom door at the end and it swung open. A man in a suit stopped clicking his camera and turned. 'Oh, I'm almost done, sir.'

Larry waved his hand. 'Don't mind us. Keep clicking.'

The photographer fired off a few more then stepped aside, though he didn't really have to. What he was shooting was big enough to see anyway.

Matt actually stepped back a little and had to grab the banister. 'My god.'

'You okay?'

'Not really.'

The bed sheets were white. Or rather, they *had* been. Now most of them were drenched in the brown-looking blood that had seeped from the animal in the middle. There was a cut right up its middle, and parts of its organs were stretched out in long, slippery threads.

'Closest thing to a pelican round here, I guess,' Larry said. 'We've checked and there's one missing from the park.'

The dead swan lay with its head on the pillow with a white

flower hanging from its beak. Neck broken, wings snapped back and broken wide. Stretched like an angel, feeding the world.

Matt and Larry sat at Jo Finch's kitchen table, while another officer hovered near the kitchen bench, arms folded. Rain pounded the windowpane.

'This is totally insane,' Matt said. 'You do know that?'

'Yeah.' Larry nodded. 'I'd kind of worked that out.'

'And clearly a dog didn't steal a swan and do this.'

'Kind of worked that out, too.'

Matt let out a jittery breath and looked around the kitchen. Jo had hung little box canvases on the walls, with overused sentimental sound bites like *Dance Like No One's Watching* or *Life is a Journey so Travel Well*! It was the type of corny psychology that made him groan whenever he saw them on Facebook profiles. Yet here, in Jo's empty house, they felt horribly poignant. 'Is it just animal blood up there?'

'Yes. We've checked that. In fact, there's very little sign that Jo or Lee have been hurt in any way apart—'

'From the fact that they've *vanished* and there's a swan with its insides strewn across their bed!'

'Let me finish,' Larry said. '*Apart* from an upturned chair at a computer desk, there's no sign of struggle here. Or even forced entry.'

'Which means?'

The officer who was standing cleared his throat and spoke. 'Which means anybody could have killed that bird. Even Jo Finch or Lee Bradshaw themselves. Or both of them together.' He was probably late twenties, with a greasy swoop of ginger hair. His skin was pocked with old acne scars.

'Who are you?'

'This is Keech, and he knows all the details of this, so speak freely,' Larry said. 'He's lived in Menham all his life.'

'And proud of it.'

Matt nodded at him. 'Well, I can't see Jo being involved in what happened at the school, so I doubt she did this either.'

'Why not?'

'Because . . .' Matt shrugged. 'I don't know . . . because I met her. Because she was genuinely upset by her friend's death.'

Larry smiled. It was horribly patronising, made only more infuriating because he was quite correct. What the hell did Matt know about Jo Finch, or *any* of this?

'What do you want from me?' Matt said, finally. 'Why am I back here?'

'Leave Jo and Lee to me. I'm not saying they killed that swan, but hey, let's not rule it out. We'll be looking high and low for them, and figuring out what happened. But for now, I need you to do something for me.'

'Go on.'

'I want you to go to that seance tonight.'

Keech seemed to let out a tiny breath when he heard that.

'*Why?*' Matt said.

'Because Steph Ellis said something was following her before she died. And I want to know *exactly* what that was.'

'So *you* go, then.'

He shook his head. 'They didn't invite me, did they? They invited *you*. Sounds as if they like you.'

'Because they want me to write about them. Raise their profile or something.'

'Fine. Then write about them. Stick 'em in your blog.'

'I don't blog.'

'No? Well, whatever. Just get in there and get me some info.'

He glanced up toward the ceiling. 'And do I tell them about this?'

'Absolutely not. You tell them *nothing*. You just follow the ghost trail and see where it leads.'

'A ghost didn't kill that animal upstairs, Larry,' Matt said. 'And a ghost sure as hell didn't set a skinny dog onto Steph Ellis, then walk it home past the old folk's home.'

'You're right.' Keech said suddenly. 'Maybe it wasn't a ghost. Maybe it was a demon instead.'

Matt almost laughed again, but he saw how fixed and serious the officer's face was. 'Why'd you say that?'

'*Enough*,' Larry slapped a hand on the table and stood up. 'I need to get cracking on this. So for now you need to get in touch with Bob Hodges ASAP and get yourself a seat at that table.'

Matt stood up too and did nothing to hide his sarcasm. 'Okay. I'll sit at said table and ask a long-dead little girl if she knows who killed the swan.'

'Yes, you will.' Larry caught his eye. 'And you'll call me right after and tell me exactly what she says. Got it?'

Larry headed out to make a phone call, while Keech sidled up to him. 'Maybe you shouldn't be so flippant about Holly Wasson.'

'I don't mean to be flippant. It's the ghost stuff I don't care for—'

'Just remember he had to cut her down.'

Matt blinked, 'Pardon?'

'He didn't tell you?'

'Tell me what?'

'Larry, he was an officer here at the time. He was called in and had to cut Holly down from the noose she made.'

'Oh shit.' Matt closed his eyes. 'I had no idea.'

'Yeah, well now you do,' Keech said. 'And stuff like that sticks with you. They never really go away. Maybe that's why they call them ghosts.'

CHAPTER TWENTY-FOUR

Matt stood in Jo's lounge, with his phone pinned to his ear. The low trill of the ringer went on and on. So as he waited for Bob to answer, he listened to it purr and glanced around the room, stomach gurgling with hunger.

Jo had a magazine rack that was bulging with nothing but old copies of *Auto Trader*. The black TV set, which had zero dust on it, had a Pokémon-sounding brand name so obscure it was either incredibly expensive, or incredibly cheap – he could guess which. The mantelpiece had four fancy-looking candles that were still wrapped in their cellophane. He could picture Jo with her boyfriend Lee some nights, looking at those wrappers and wondering if the moment was finally special enough to tear them open and actually light them. Just like he and Wren sometimes did with those pricey candles people bought for them, which remained unspoilt and unused. Evidently, that special night had yet to arrive for Jo as well.

By the radiator, he saw a scatter of framed photographs which hung from the wall. Most were those photo shoots everyone seems to have. Glammed-up family members sitting in pure-white vacuums, heads tilted and beaming, looking like the cover of a magazine that had a generous policy on teeth quality. On one of them, Jo was on her front with her chin resting on her fist. No bones about it, she had a genuinely lovely smile. The type that made you smile back, even though it was just a picture.

He jumped when the phone finally clicked in answer.

'Hello . . . this is Bob and Joyce Hodges.'

'Bob,' he said. 'It's me, Matt Hunter.'

'Oooo, Matthew. Good to hear your voice.'

'And yours, too. Listen, I got your number from the pack you gave me.'

'Great. You read it through?'

'I did.'

'And the video? Were you able to play it? I'd put it on DVD if I had the first clue about—'

'I played it fine, and Bob . . . I found it really quite fascinating. Which is why I'm calling.' Matt turned to the bay window and watched the rain trickling down the pane. 'I'd like to attend the seance after all if the offer's still—'

'Aha! I knew it!'

'Knew what?'

'Joyce only said this morning that you'd call. She had a dream you'd be with us tonight. She said to expect your call.'

'Well . . . she was right on the money. So the offer's still there?'

'Absolutely, we'd love to have you.' He coughed a little awkwardly. 'And what I said about you maybe interviewing Joyce and me, about our work?'

'Yes, I'd be interested in that too. But how about we plug on with the seance first?'

'Of course,' Bob said. 'We'll see you at Barley Street at seven for set-up. Aiming for an 8 p.m. start. Can you get over to Menham for then?'

I'm in Menham now, he thought, *with swan's blood peppering my nostrils*. 'Seven sounds fine, Bob. And thanks for this.'

'Pleasure.'

He clicked the phone off and went to turn but he paused at the mantelpiece. A small photo sat on it, in a silver, swirling frame. A bunch of teenage girls were crammed into a photo booth. Jo Finch, Kassy West, Steph Ellis and Rachel Wasson. They stared out like young people do, with every inch of their faces. Rachel looked strikingly similar, spookily similar some would say, to how Holly looked in the video. Rachel didn't have the short black hair she had now. Back then it was quite long and blonde. He stared at the picture for a long moment as they all stared back at him, brimming with the brightness of hopeful dreams, of summers that lasted for ever.

He glanced back at Jo's smiling picture, but didn't smile back. Where was she? But then he quickly answered himself . . . Larry was sorting that. Meanwhile, he was on ghost duty.

He checked his watch . . . 5 p.m.

Two hours to kill in Menham. Which obviously meant only one thing.

Burger time.

Matt stepped back out into the street. The rain had romped through wild adolescence and matured. From full pelt to a thin, ordered shower. The clouds were cracking overhead, letting the sun loose in Menham. But the air was very cold, and wet things were falling. The locals still hovered too, over the road, but there were fewer of them now. Some had taken his advice and gone home because Jeremy Kyle had far more immediate and tangible tragedy they could feed on.

What surprised him, though, was the other group. Three men standing on the damp pavement, with three separate umbrellas, each of different colours. Black, red and white. Matt squinted and realised their eyes were closed. Then when a wet, pink palm slowly raised itself, from the tall bald guy with the red umbrella, Matt knew exactly who they were.

The church prayer group who were hanging outside the school yesterday.

Interesting.

He pulled up his collar to keep the drips away and hurried across the road, shoes slapping tiny explosions in the puddles as he went.

Matt stepped up to them on the kerb, smiling. 'I reckon Solomon missed a proverb.'

They opened their eyes.

Matt smiled. 'The wise man brings his umbrella with him while the fool leaves it in the hallway at home.'

The tall man laughed. 'Here. You can come under this one.' He leant it forward.

'Better still,' Matt said. 'How about I buy you three a coffee? Get some warmth in us.'

They all frowned at the same time. 'Er . . . but we don't know who you are.'

'I'm Matthew. And I'm interested in prayer.'

The blonde man with glasses and a goatee smiled. He put his hand out and locked Matt's fingers in a take-no-prisoners grip. They shook. 'And I'm Pastor Todd Holloway,' he said, with his American accent. 'And Matthew? Coffee sounds perfect.'

CHAPTER TWENTY-FIVE

Rachel left the engine running. She liked the sound it made. That low rumble that said, as soon as you want to leave you can. You can just push your foot down on this magical spring-loaded lever whenever you want, and you'll space-warp this metal box away from all stress, with you inside it. And guess what? If you want to, you can leave that foot pressed down and never take it off until you see the signs for Manchester. How about that?

Those familiar, default thoughts of escape solidified in her head, but the simultaneous wave of shame came too. She shook her head, looked up at the rear-view mirror and swept her fringe back. 'No more,' she said. She killed the engine.

The door clicked very loudly as she stepped out into the street.

The rain had eased off now but the pavement was still a mosaic of patches and puddles. She leant against the car, liking the reassurance of its touch, and ran her gaze up the council offices next to her. They'd repainted the entire building and clad the front with those panels of various shades of salmon and terracotta. The type you see everywhere these days. At some point in the UK, designers had decided this look was attractive. It wasn't.

The work day was over now, and as the sun gradually jogged on to other countries she could only see a few lights on up there in the offices. A figure was moving in one of them. A tall woman with a mass of permed hair. She was spraying a cupboard door with something and wiping it down with a bright-yellow cloth. She wondered if it was Kassy's cleaning company who'd had that contract. Maybe Jo was up there now lugging a Henry Hoover about and spraying taps with Viakal. Maybe she'd dust a window ledge and spot where Rachel was right now. Down here. *Back* here.

Would that be good if she knew, or bad? She couldn't tell.

All the tallest buildings in Menham were here, making this her very own cut-price Canary Wharf. As well as the council offices, there was Brett House. A gun-grey 80s building that housed a bunch of local businesses. And on the far side of the road she could see the old mill. At one point it made oat-based cereals and bread for the local yokels. Now it was some sort of personal storage facility for the junk people didn't want, but couldn't quite let go of. They'd painted a massive yellow sign across the top of it, with its phone number and website. *Leave it with us!* it said.

If only, she thought.

Because in the centre of it all, enclosed by buildings and a border of road, was a square patch of land about the size of an adult swimming pool. The sign still said CONDEMNED in thick red letters on white. Only these days they'd rigged up a much higher fence of wooden panels that a local school appeared to have painted on, to make it look nicer. In the picture, loads of stick children were playing in a park, flying kites that touched a messy rainbow above them.

It was horribly ironic, seeing all those kids here.

So the big fence was new, but the atmosphere here was very, very old indeed. She felt that familiar churn of the stomach. The slow creep of bumps mutating her skin. Turning her flesh into a frightened reptile.

She glanced at her watch and saw it was 5:30pm. In a few hours' time, she'd be talking to her dead sister. Supposedly.

She stared at the pictures. The colours. The happy scene that had been placed across somewhere that had no colour. That had no light. A community's attempt at therapy, perhaps.

And looking at the picture of those kids, scrawled in busy, bright paint, made her consider something. That maybe it didn't matter if the seance was going to be real or not. Maybe it was just about closing a door, regardless of it being marked natural or supernatural. Psychological or para-psychological, if that was even a word. Maybe her bravery in facing this door, and closing it, would make her a better person. A more attractive human being to be around. Maybe she'd meet someone like Debbie again and they'd not remark on what a 'downer' Rachel always became, when the sun dropped. Maybe she wouldn't have to sit in the middle of a bar with a salsa band playing, leaning over to hear a horrible phrase like 'self-pity isn't attractive, Rachel'. And the real killer, when the night filled up the bedroom with: 'sorry, but melancholy people are a turn-off.' One of the little truth bombs Debbie dropped that still, even now, had its bitter aftershocks.

No. She'd had enough of it.

She wouldn't even have to tell the Hodges the whole deal, because perhaps that was a door she needed to close on her own. Or with the girls, at least. Tonight she could just talk directly to Holly and see what she said. Whether that was from the swirling mists of the ether, or the bubbling soup of her subconscious.

The thought prompted her to stop leaning against the car for safety. No more. Instead she pushed herself off the escape pod and held her breath. She crossed the road, heels of her pumps skimming the concrete. She wasn't a nut. She had no intention of actually touching the fence around the stretch of wild grass. But she had noticed a thin split in the wood that showed her the inside. She *did* stand on the pavement, and walk close enough to look through the gap. Not enough to touch. But enough to see the breeze quiver the thick wild grass and reeds in there. Like the patch of land itself was alive and wriggling.

She could hear her own heart beat too. The squelch-pulse rhythm squeezing around her brain.

She grabbed her phone and checked her messages. Still nothing from Jo, which was odd. Kassy wasn't coming to the seance, but Jo had insisted she be there. The two of them were going to meet up before the seance kick-off and have a glass of wine in town. Have two, maybe. Seven. Her brow crunched again in confusion. No reply to her calls.

So she flicked through the menu to find Kassy's number. Nervous about speaking to her on the phone. She answered almost instantly.

'Yeah?' Kassy had the drawn-out bored tone that perfectly encapsulated the speaker. She could picture Kassy, staring at her nails at the other end. Yawning with tedium, while baby kittens died in flames all around her. 'What do you want?'

'It's Rachel.'

'And . . . what do you want?'

'It's about the seance.'

An unpleasant peal of laughter crackled down the phone. 'I told you. I've got better things to do than talk to a tabletop.'

'I'm not asking that.' Rachel looked down at the pavement. It was still cracked. 'Where's Jo? I haven't heard from her all day and she's not answering her—'

'Don't talk to me about her.'

'Huh?'

'She never turned up for work this morning. I had to shift round half of my other cleaners to sort it out. Caused me a right headache.'

Rachel frowned. 'That doesn't sound like her.'

'Oh, *really?*' Kassy laughed. 'And how in the precious name of fuck would *you* know that? You haven't spoken to her in over a decade. Or me.'

Rachel stared at the swaying grass through the gap, the blades curling up to the wood like fingers, opening. The old urge grew. To cross back over the street and get back into the car. Hit that pedal. Blast off. 'She's not answering her phone.'

'Believe me, I know that. I've tried her a bunch of times.'

'And I can't go round to her house because . . .'

'Because you don't even know where she *lives*, do you . . . Jesus.'

'No. I have no idea,' Rachel said in a sort of shameful whisper. 'But last night she said she'd definitely be at the seance.'

'Then just wait till she turns up at yours. Job done.'

'But what if she's in some sort of troub—?'

'She probably is, cos the police called me this morning.'

'*What?*'

'They're looking for her. And I hear there's been police cars at her house.'

'What?' Rachel breathed in, and it sounded like a wheeze. 'We have to find her. We have to make sure she's—'

'Look,' Kassy's voice sounded a little gentler. 'She's upset by this Steph-wabbit stuff and so she's probably just taking some time out to think. She retreats at this stuff . . . even *you* know that. She might even be hiding in a cupboard somewhere as we speak. Which is all very sad and everything but . . .' Kassy tutted to herself. 'Not turning up for your job is incredibly unprofessional.'

Rachel waited for a moment, staring at the wire fence.

'Is that it, then?' Kassy said. 'I've got stuff to—'

'Kass.'

A pause. 'Yeah?'

'Do you ever think about it?'

'Think about what?'

'About Halloween?'

Another pause. Much longer this time. 'It's a dumb holiday that's fleecing idiots out of cash.'

'That's not what I meant.' She heard a car pass by behind her but she didn't turn to see it.

'Look . . . I've got to go,' Kassy said. Then, after a moment, 'And no . . . I don't think about it and do you want to know why?'

Rachel said, 'Yes,' and was shocked at how pathetic it sounded. *Please please instruct me, Kassy, please please impart your wisdom.*

'Because there's nothing *to* think about because it wasn't our fault.'

Rachel blinked slowly.

'Rach . . .' Kassy said. 'It's going to be okay, alright?'

Rachel closed her eyes.

'You're not a chump. You're one of the few ones who actually have a brain, remember? You and me.'

Kass was a cat. She had this habit of walking over people, but then very, *very* occasionally she'd throw something sweet your way. And when the light flashed out of the dark cave, its rarity always made it appear like precious gold dust you'd run into forever. Rachel listened to Kassy's voice, in soothing, ultra-rare human mode, and was reminded of how much she loved that tone. That rare frequency. And there it was again. Menham shaving off fifteen years of independence and she was like all the others in that school, clamouring for this girl's approval . . . even now.

'So,' Rachel snapped. 'You really find it *that* easy just to—'

She trailed off. Kassy had already hung up.

Rachel opened her eyes wide, like she was waking from a deep, embarrassing dream and slipped the phone back into her pocket. Just as she did that, she noticed the cleaner up in the office window. She'd stopped rubbing the cupboards and now she was taking a break. Or at least Rachel hoped that's what it was. Either way she was standing motionless and staring out through the glass, down at the street where she was standing. Then the street lights clicked themselves on, each in perfect sequence. Click, click, click, up the street and around. The setting of a stage on opening night.

She took one last look at the grass that was pushing at the wood and almost wanted to snag a blade of it to take with her. But instead she turned back to the car.

Which was when she saw a skinny white dog with the eyes of a maniac, over by her rear tyre.

Waiting for her.

CHAPTER TWENTY-SIX

Matt peeled off his damp jacket as he watched the three men flap their umbrellas out at the door. The sound was more like bat wings or a dragon flying overhead, but all he could visualise was a swan making that sound instead. Slapping and flapping in confused panic as a total degenerate snapped its bones and strung its intestines across the bed.

Even if it did turn out that Steph's death was just a freak dog accident, some prick was going to seriously pay for torturing a fine animal like that.

The three churchmen propped their umbrellas by the door, in a neat line, then they shuffled into a booth made of four red plastic chairs, bolted to the table. They all looked roughly the same age. Late forties, probably. The pastor, Todd, was the only American and he stank of coconut aftershave. The other two sounded local. The bald guy was Jerry Marlowe and the other one said his name was Neil White. The last one was easy to remember. His skin was plague-victim pale. One of them had body odour issues. It was pot luck guessing which.

Matt took their orders and loaded up a tray. He also bought a packet of shortcake biscuits for good measure. It was one of the first pastoral lessons he learned in his church years: biscuits were the truth drug for Christians everywhere.

'So, you're prayer walkers?' Matt slid the coffees and teas to the right places. 'For which church?'

'That'd be Menham Evangelical,' Todd said. 'We're the little building on the high street. Right in the centre of town.'

'Good stuff. And how's the prayer going?'

'Why?' Jerry took his mug and warmed his big hands on it. 'Do you believe in the power of prayer?'

He answered carefully. 'I believe prayer can change people, yes.'

The pale guy, Neil, pondered that for a moment with his eyelids down a little. 'You're working with the police, are you?'

'Yes, but I'm not a policeman. I'm a professor. I teach the Sociology of Religion.' He tapped his fingers on the table. 'They've brought me in to advise on the faith angle.'

Todd's eyes rose at that and a bright smile pushed his goatee up. 'Well, isn't that *refreshing*? I always say police and government should be incorporating faith into everything they do. Things would be a whole lot simpler if we didn't insist on separating Church and State.'

'Let me guess . . .' Matt pointed a finger. 'Texan!'

'Ouch. It's Arkansas . . . but close enough, I guess,' Todd laughed. 'You know, I came to the UK on a mission trip way back in 2000. Did a little work at a tiny church in Menham that was ready to close. But do you know what God told me, halfway through that trip?'

Matt shrugged.

'He said, "Todd, my man, I want you to rip that airline ticket into tiny pieces and never, ever go back. You have a new home and a new mission field." And what do you know . . . that self-same week

Menham Evangelical asked me to work as their pastor for a few months. Been doing that ever since. Which was just as well. It's one of the few churches in this messed-up country that stick to the plan.'

'The plan?'

'The Bible.'

''Course,' Matt said. 'And what about Menham itself . . . do the locals stick to the plan? To scripture?'

Todd's face turned grim, and he put an emphasis on each single word. 'Not. At. All.'

Bald head glowing, Jerry set his cup down, seemingly unaware of his new latte moustache. 'What's happened on Bennington Road? Has there been another death?'

'Not that I know of,' Matt said.

'Oh,' Neil looked down at his fingers, almost disappointed.

'We'd heard there might be a death,' Jerry said.

'Nope, so your prayers must be working.'

'Amen,' Todd said.

Matt raised his cup. 'I have a question, though. How did you know there was something going on there anyway?'

'Ah . . .' Neil pulled out a little black gizmo from his pocket. His voice sounded like he'd supped a little helium. 'Best little tool for prayer you've ever seen. Every church should have one.'

He slid the box into the middle of the table.

A police scanner.

Matt whistled. 'Wowee. Pretty hi-tech.'

'Sell 'em in Maplin for twenty pounds a pop.' Todd smiled as Neil slid it back into his pocket. 'But it keeps our prayers real and not just theoretical. Not that the police have any idea why Steph Ellis died, of course.'

Matt tried to keep his eyebrows down, just turned his cup, super casual. 'So why do you think she did?'

'Because she was dabbling in things she didn't understand.'

Todd looked at the other two men for a moment. Each shared an expression somewhere between tragic sadness and eye-rolling anger. 'You see, Matt, we're aware of the local gossip. We know that some are saying that ghosts are back amongst us.'

'*Ghosts?* Who's saying that?'

'People are saying it, but I can assure you that they're not. And contrary to popular opinion round here, ghosts have *never* been in Menham. Because, as you'll know . . . there's no such thing. There's no unquiet dead walking among us. We die once and we face the judgement. Anything supernatural this side of heaven is either good or evil.'

'You mean angels and demons.'

'Exactly.' Todd took a biscuit and idly snapped it in two. A spray of crumbs sprouted like a tiny firework. 'Maybe if poor Miss Ellis had come to our church, she'd've found help. But instead she went to witches and warlocks.'

Neil and Jerry stayed silent.

Matt leant forward. 'Who exactly are we talking about here, Todd?'

He chomped the edge of the shortcake, and chewed as he spoke. 'There's an old couple who lives round here. Name of Bob Hodges and his wife, Joyce. They call themselves something fancy . . .' he did finger quotes, 'demonologists . . . and they say they try and help people fight against evil.' He swallowed. 'But get this . . . the woman's a medium, and she's proud of it. She *flaunts* it. She consults the dead, which as you know full well is outlawed in scripture.'

'They say they fight the devil, but they use the devil's tools to do it,' Neil added. 'Seances, Ouija boards and all that other trash. It's shocking what they're doing. Scary, actually.'

'Those two are light years away from being Christian,' Todd said, nodding. 'And that girl who died, Steph Ellis. She was right in there with them.'

Neil bit his thumbnail, eagerly. 'That's right. She was working with them on something.'

Matt waited, watching all three of them for a moment. 'And how do you know all this?'

Todd leaned forward, and his voice dropped to a whisper. 'Because, she was seen entering the Hodges' house *three* times in the last few weeks. And now, shock horror, that girl is dead.'

Matt frowned. 'Sorry to be frank, but you make it sound like you were following her.'

Todd quickly shook his head. 'Not at all. One of our congregation lives in the same street as the Hodges. They let the church know who comes in and out of there, so we can pray for them. Think of it as the *real* neighbourhood watch.'

'And you know what else . . .' Jerry wiped his big hand across the tabletop. His voice was much softer than Todd's. 'Steph Ellis was connected with the Barley Street Poltergeist. Did you know that?'

'I was aware of it, yes.'

'And did you know the family in that case, the Wassons . . . did you know that when all that bad stuff happened in their house they also *refused* to consult a church? They brought the Hodges in, with their machines and their spells.'

Neil flicked a fingernail as he spoke. 'Seems like the Wassons and the Hodges didn't even believe Christianity would help. Can you believe that?'

'Like too many moderns,' Todd added. 'They went straight to the so-called paranormal community instead. Totally skipped the place that could have actually sorted their demon issues out. And just look where secularism got them, a little girl swinging dead on a beam.' He put his fingers out and swung them back and forth. *Swoop, swoop, swoop, swoop*. Matt hated the gesture and stared at it. It was the closest he'd come so far in dropping his dumb-eyed neutral look and kicking Todd under the table. But he kept his face benign.

'It was a very sad situation.' Jerry sighed and lifted his coffee, only his finger was too crooked for the tiny handle. Matt saw it coming even before it happened. The cup slipped on the tip of his finger and turned a full forty-five degrees. Coffee splurged out across the tabletop. A mini tsunami of froth rushed across the table, waterfalled off the edge, and soaked into Matt's lap.

He couldn't help it.

Matt yelped like a Jack Russell dog and jerked back in his chair, both hands slap-wiping the liquid from his burning crotch.

'Oh, my goodness, I am *so* sorry.' Jerry leapt up and pulled his sleeve into his palm, like he might help to wipe.

'It's fine. Really.' Matt stood, staring at the soaked space between his legs. He laughed. 'It's alright . . . I think I've only lost feeling in one of them.'

'Pardon?'

Matt cringed. Remembered his audience. 'Nothing. It's fine, though, really.'

The other guy Neil had already rushed to the counter and was scurrying back with a stack of napkins. They mopped the table up, and Matt sat back into the damp patch. The three men looked at him for a few moments, with expressions that he found hard to categorise. Were they concerned or were they smirking? Then another thought.

Was that coffee spill *deliberate*?

'Course not. Probably not. Possibly not. He clocked Jerry's fingers again and decided there were probably no cup handles on earth that would fit on such a bent digit.

'Please,' Matt said. 'Let me get you a new one.'

Todd shook his head and silently slid his own coffee to Jerry. 'Have mine.' He looked up at Matt. 'So I'm telling you, the Devil's having a field day in this town. That's why we're on the streets so much. Sooner the police get that in their skulls, the better. A dog didn't kill that girl. It was something *in* the dog. Something truly demonic. Not some malignant spirit . . . it was one of Satan's soldiers, straight from the Bible. That's real demonology.'

Matt waited for a moment, and took a long sip of his Americano. 'And how will you respond if the police conclude that this whole thing isn't spiritual at all? That it's just physical?'

'Oh, we're not dumb,' Todd said. 'We know that's *exactly* what they'll say, but they'd be wrong. There's no such thing as purely physical, anyway. If everything's created by God and sustained by him, then in a sense *everything's* supernatural, don't you think? Like this table. Like your eyebrows. Your tongue.' Todd sat back, looking at Matt's mouth. 'So as long as the police ignore the *real* cause of crime and pain we're gonna keep the prayer pressure up. Especially when everybody around us celebrates this evil, like it's harmless fun. I mean look . . .' He gestured to the crazy-eyed paper skeleton hanging on the wall, ready for Halloween tomorrow. 'I mean, folks are pushing the devil on their kids. So we'll pray that they and the deluded fools like the Hodges'll come to their senses, and stop flapping the doors of hell open and shut. Cos let me tell you this, Matt . . . sooner or later, things are gonna come wriggling on out. And we'll do whatever it takes to stop that.'

'*Whatever* it takes?' Matt said.

'Of course. Because prayer works.'

Matt waited a moment. 'I hear you work with ex-prisoners at the church.'

'We do! It's a counselling group for ex-cons. We're teaching them that their criminal behaviour doesn't have to define them. That they can step out of it and be new men, and it's all based on prayer. You want to know what we're called?'

Matt nodded.

'The Phoenix Club.' Todd sat back, impressed with himself. 'We're renewing the minds of broken guys, and we're smashing down the walls of the enemy. We restore men, Matt. And prayer is the key to it . . .'

Todd trailed off. His gaze dropped to the crackling sound that had suddenly broken out amongst them.

All eyes went to Neil who was tugging at his pocket. He yanked the scanner free and held it up to his ear for a few moments. 'Oh dear.'

'What is it?' Todd said.

'Oh dear . . . a little girl's just admitted she got flashed at in the park this morning . . . sounds like it was that pervert who's doing the rounds.'

Jerry shook his head. 'Never stops, does it?'

'Drink up, guys. We better go and pray over the park. Maybe find where she lives,' Todd took a long, final swig. The others did the same. 'Thanks for the coffee.'

Matt watched them bolt up into action, like one of them might shout *Avengers assemble!* at any minute. Todd swept past him in a cloud of coconut aftershave and dry-cleaned shirts. Then Matt walked them to the door as they grabbed their trusty weapons: the multicoloured sequence of umbrellas. In many ways, it felt like there should be something funny about all of this. Something cute. This little troupe of men being the spiritual superheroes of the town. Only it wasn't that funny at all, seeing them so earnest and passionate about it. Like the Hodges and their devotion to the paranormal, they were all just obsessed with non-entities.

The bald guy, Jerry, flapped his umbrella a few times but paused before opening it fully. The door was now open, so the rain spattered inside. 'You should definitely pass this on to the

208

police,' Jerry said. 'We've tried, but these days God isn't welcome anywhere that's public.'

'Pass on *what* exactly?'

'That crimes and bad things . . . that there's always something bigger going on. That it's not always obvious who's causing it.' His umbrella popped open with a springing slap.

'That demons are not just our enemies,' Todd added. 'They're more like our puppetmasters. Just read your newspaper and you'll see their work.'

'I see.'

'And remember,' Todd added. 'The Devil's not just working in Menham. He's everywhere and he's keepin' busy . . . so keep striving, Matt. Keep God in the public square, my friend.'

Neil and Jerry waited on the street, under their umbrellas. 'Bless you, Matt,' Neil said, with a smile.

Matt could see a white wire trailing from Neil's ear now, vanishing into his jacket and the scanner tucked in there. Pressing a finger into his ear like the president's motorcade was about to pull up.

The sky had darkened overhead and night was coming. Storm grey sinking into a blueberry wash.

He waved the three of them off and watched them climb into a Volvo estate not far from his own car. The Phoenix Club, locked and loaded for prayer.

He checked his watch. There was still time to eat.

Matt ordered a Belly Buster Burger and fries and before it came he went to the toilet and let the hand dryer loose on his crotch, watching the door constantly so that nobody walked in and saw him on his tiptoes, thrusting forward. Still a little damp he sat at the table again, alone now. He grabbed a newspaper and glanced through the pages as he waited for the food to come. The headlines did little to brighten the mood. A law student had been knifed to death outside a local nightclub. The killer was being sentenced this week. The guy who was exposing himself to little girls got a mention, with the catchy title 'Local Pervert'. In another story an overly tired plumber had lost control of his van and ploughed into a charity shop on the high street. A woman and her son were still in critical condition.

Plenty of devil fodder for Todd and his friends.

Matt just shook his head and pushed the depressing newspaper to one side. Instead, he noticed the TV that was bolted to the wall and asked the woman behind the counter to turn the sound up.

He spent the rest of the meal in silence, squeezing out tomato ketchup and waiting for the seance time to come. Watching home videos of bridegrooms fainting and cats falling off window sills, while canned, manic laughter echoed around the empty cafe, like a bunch of giggling ghosts.

CHAPTER TWENTY-SEVEN

She blinked and stared.

Blinked again.

Squinting as if her eyes were being speckled with sudden dust from the street, but all she saw was the four roads intersecting and the big buildings looming above her. As ordinary a place as any except for the dog that was padding slowly across the centre of the empty road, towards her. It had no owner and it was getting closer. She guessed this was some sort of Dobermann, with a skinny xylophone ribcage and weird white and silvery fur. It looked like it was covered in dust. And as it gawped at her she could hear a voice in her head that wasn't her own.

There are such things.

Silly random thoughts. A dog speaking, mind to mind.

Ha, ha, ha . . . this kerazy Menham life is so ridic—

'*There* are *such things.*' The dog blinked. Licked its lips and thought some more, '*And soon you'll get it, Rachel. In fact, it'll be tonight. Tonight, you'll know.*'

She glanced up at the office block again and noticed that the staring cleaner had now gone. The thought occurred to her that this didn't mean she'd gone back to dusting, but rather, she was heading down in the lift now to join them on the street.

Rachel was trembling as the dog slowed to a standstill in the middle of the street looking right at her. Its tail motionless, its eyes slowly closing and opening. At one point it opened its mouth and flashed its fangs, which she kept telling herself was a yawn, because that's what dogs do. That this was just a silly old stray wandering the streets getting bored out of its mind looking at her. Though it still looked more like a hellhound, displaying the weapons it was planning to use on her.

She didn't know what else to do, so she did what people do with dogs. She said, 'Hello, boy.' She spoke in the sort of dim-wit speech patterns people deem appropriate for animals or little kids. Or blind people. 'What are you up to?'

It padded a paw forward and tilted its head. Then it turned very, very slowly toward an alleyway across the street. It kept just staring at it, at the shadowy mouth of the lane. Like it was waiting for something to come striding out of there to join it; its owner maybe or—

—*the rabbit.*

The dog whispering frantically in her ear.

– *Rabbit's coming. And Holly too. 'Cos there are such things. There are, there are, there are, there are.*

– *and tonight you'll know.*

It was barking toward the alley. She wasn't even sure when the dog had started doing that, but she was just suddenly aware that it was. Really loudly. Each snap of sound made her blink and flinch.

She stared at the alleyway as leaves rustled and span out of it, tumbling along the floor. Then she heard someone laughing and realised it was her. A full chuckle that was part madness, part stress and part disbelief at how she was falling for this stuff. The sound made the dog turn back to see her and her brain spoke sensibly at last.

The dog that killed Steph is dead. This is a random stray. Get in the car.

The silvery-white dog stepped forward.

'Can't chat.' She gulped in a breath and held it for the entire speed walk across the road. Never letting that breath out, even as she fumbled for the keys. Even in that heart-thudding few seconds when she pictured that thing racing across the road and springing up onto its hind legs behind her. Sprouting long ears to stride right up to her back, so it could slide its black furry arms around her trembling body.

The car door clicked open and she slipped inside, pulse hammering. Then she cranked the engine and slammed that foot down hard, whacking the door locks down with her elbow. She wheel-spinned up the street not looking back until she got far enough not to resist. Just before she turned the corner she glanced into the rear-view mirror and saw the dog in the distance. It hadn't moved. It was still looking. But as she stared at it, it turned to the right and trotted towards the grass. It nuzzled at the fence, with the rainbow on it, and found the loose section. Then it pulled at it with its teeth and suddenly scraped itself through. The white, unwagging tail vanished inside.

It was about then that she thought she smelt the vague whiff of her dead cat, Pob. Floating in the car, to inform her of impending doom. And she had a full memory of Debbie sitting in this very passenger seat, at the beginning, before it all went sour. That June day when Debbie clunked in her belt and got her summer dress caught. When they untangled it together and she suddenly said, 'I like you, Rach.' The day Rachel had shivered in a good way.

But that seat had been empty for a long time and the sun was now too wet to shine. And she could hear the dog barking, even from here. So she drove on.

Perhaps, she thought, this was a breakdown. Perhaps this is how they start. Or maybe tonight she really would be talking to her sister for real. Whatever the case, she turned the stereo on very loud as she drove back to Barley Street. Just so that she might not have to listen to the sound of herself crying all the way home.

CHAPTER TWENTY-EIGHT

As Menham sat in darkness outside, Matt sat alone with Rachel Wasson in the dining room of 29 Barley Street. Waiting in the designated chairs, as instructed. She looked pale, and her short black hair seemed wet. He whispered to her, 'Are you *sure* you want to do this?'

She tapped her glasses in place. 'It's not really a question of want, is it?'

Just then the dining room door creaked open and Bob and Joyce came through with an air of exaggerated seriousness. There was a regality to their walking, chins up in the air, locked and loaded for a jaunt into the netherworld. If Matt had seen this behaviour under any other circumstances he'd have found it all hilariously pompous, but for now he just sat still in the creaking wooden chair, feeling the tension twist in his chest – not just because of this entire situation, but because according to Larry's latest text message there was *still* no sign of Jo or Lee.

Ominous. That's how he felt about Jo Finch right now. Pretty bloody ominous.

He and Rachel sat around a dark, oval table in the shuffling silence, watching Joyce revolve around it a few times, the lavender reek of her perfume following a second behind. When she finally stopped she folded herself into a seat and looked off at something invisible in the air. Like a cat spotting a piece of its own fur, floating. Finlay, Mary Wasson's *actual* cat, was in the corner of the room, curled up in a ball inside a grubby-looking basket. Its fur rose and fell gently as it snoozed.

Matt looked over at Rachel and gave her one more *escape-if-you-want* nod, but she'd already closed her eyes.

Bob was distracted by something. He was looking at the pot plant in the corner, the leaves of which had browned and dried. He grabbed it and headed out of the room with it under his arm.

'What's wrong with the plant?' Matt asked.

'It's not freshly picked. That's a problem.'

'For who?'

'For the spirits. They seem to like fresh plants and fruit,' Bob said. 'And no, I'm not sure why.'

'Allergies maybe,' Matt said.

'Maybe.' Bob pushed through the door, to ditch the plant.

The plant wasn't the only thing that had been removed from this room. There was a faded space where the mirror used to hang. That had been taken out, along with a glass decanter and some serving glasses. Bob had said they could be dangerous if they shattered during the seance. But for some reason, the animal pictures remained. Spirits seem to *like* them, he said. A regular bunch of David Attenboroughs.

The clock remained. An antique wooden box clock on the sideboard, with a low constant click that felt slower than it should be. Like space between the seconds was a little bit longer here.

Footsteps suddenly rattled on the stairs as Mary Wasson

finally headed down. After an awkward cup of tea with her earlier, she'd told him how ecstatic she was about the impending seance: clapping her hands like a performing seal and bobbing on her feet. She seemed a little swivel-eyed even then. Ever since, she'd been up in her room, 'preparing' for it. Whatever that meant. Now, she finally appeared in the doorway and that question was answered.

It was utterly bizarre.

She was seance-ready, face made up, lank hair curled and pinned. Lips pink and clumsily wiped with lipstick that looked more like marker pen. She was wearing some sort of evening dress, two decades out of fashion, and she had dangling earrings with teddy bears on each ear. Rachel put a hand across her mouth when she saw her mum's outfit but Mary didn't seem to notice. She just sat down in the chair next to Joyce and straightened her necklace.

'Want to look pretty for my girl,' she said.

The girl who had wrapped the stereo cord around her neck and stepped off the window sill – in the bedroom directly above this dining room. That detail, of course, was ever-present and never, *ever* lost on Rachel, who was staring at the ceiling like there were things moving on it.

A thick white candle sat in the middle of the table and, bizarrely, to the right of it was an old school bell made of scratched brass. A slim, frayed loop of leather hung from the handle. Rachel had set up a sound recorder on a side table. It blinked its recording lights.

A decade ago, a sweet, good reverend like Matt Hunter wouldn't have gone anywhere *near* something like this. He'd have avoided it like spiritual scurvy and even campaigned hard against it, because all good Christians know this seance stuff is wrong and treacherous. *A Doorway to Danger!* – so the tracts and leaflets screamed. But now, on the flip side of faith, this felt very much like any church prayer meeting he'd led in the past. The solemn sense of ritual, the quiet approach, the expectation that an unseen presence would fade out of the dark for a moment and change everybody's world.

Of course these days he knew both prayer meetings and seances for what they were – exercises in kidding the self – but that innate sense of breath holding – whenever people sat in quiet circles – was an old habit he'd need to shake, because he noticed that despite himself, he was still doing it now.

Now they were assembled, Bob carefully placed a floor lamp right next to the table and switched it on. Then he killed the main lights so that shadows sprang up from everywhere. It made the room look dark and Gothic. Using the lamp was annoying and manipulative perhaps. But wasn't the swell of a church organ, or the light sprayed from stained-glass windows specifically designed to set the mood and melt the heart? Wasn't it all just suggestion and special effects?

Joyce looked even more gaunt in the low light; disturbingly similar to his own dead mother at certain angles. In the days before a psycho sliced her lips off. Around the walls, the animal pictures hung. Tigers and wolves and birds stared out, the white paint of their eyes catching the light in a way he preferred to ignore.

Bob cleared his throat. 'We're here tonight to speak to Miss Holly Wasson.' This wasn't said to the people around the table as such. This was an announcement to the room, to the forces that might be listening. 'Holly tragically took her own life in this house . . . yet we believe she was *driven* to that act . . . that a great injustice has been done.'

Matt looked across at Rachel. She was pursing her lips, like she was trying to regulate her breathing.

'We believe Holly knows the force that poisoned her heart and we're afraid that force might have returned. So tonight we come here, to this house of power . . . to this place of death.' He opened his hand and called up towards the ceiling. 'And Holly, love . . . we've brought you what you asked for.' Slowly and smiling, he looked down at Rachel and pointed right at her, like she was tonight's sacrifice. It made her shrink into her chair. 'We've brought her. But first . . . music.'

Music? Huh?

Bob didn't whip out a mike and suddenly break into song. If there's something strange, in your neighbourhood . . . Instead, he wheeled a vintage stereo over. It was some ancient thing in a tall wooden cabinet with a glass door and record player on top. He grabbed an album that was leaning against it and with great delicacy placed the record on the turntable, gently hovering the needle above it. Before he put it down he spoke. But this time it was no longer to the room. Now it was to Matt and the other living people around it. 'We're about to get started, folks, so please don't leave, for any reason. I've set up motion detectors in Holly's room, so if the alarm goes off we'll know that something is moving up there. And can you make sure your phones are turned off and please, *please* keep your hands on the table, palms down. The wood will act as a conductor – oh . . . and do *not* touch each other.'

Proto-science babble complete, he dropped the needle.

The crackle of dirt and hair sounded like a fire dying but then classical music filled the room. There was something about the melody that made Rachel visibly stiffen, then she closed her eyes while Mary started laughing, staring at the metal school bell.

He recognised the music instantly.

Peter and the Wolf by Prokofiev. First movement.

'God, Holly loved this music,' Rachel said. 'How did you know?'

When they both looked at Joyce for the answer, she was in no mood to speak. The old woman's eyes were already rolling back into her head and her shoulders were trembling, and she was opening her mouth uncomfortably, painfully wide.

CHAPTER TWENTY-NINE

Rabbit runs with breeze and fur and wind and fire in its
face.
Leaping over logs and branches, beating heart's a ball of
grace.
Bulging eyes
look
back and over,
up
to see what's there.
Veins are flooding up with power.

Still not stopping, rabbit reaches in its stomach for its
soul.
Yanks it out and pets it gently,
Swallows down the power whole.
Scampering toward the light,
fling the fur to heaven's door!

Wild and flying, through the dying,
barely touching paws on floor.

Branches loosen now at last.
Rabbit future, rabbit past.
Free and coming very fast.

CHAPTER THIRTY

Joyce's head started to tremble, not violently, but enough to look like she had a sudden dose of Parkinson's. Yet it was the slack-jawed gape and rolling eyes that really made her look like she needed a straitjacket. It was freakishly similar to a businessman Matt saw on the Tube once, having a fit. He'd frantically tried to stick his jacket under the guy's head as it smacked repeatedly (and musically) against the metal railing. Teeth together, chin pushed out in a grotesque Bruce Forsyth impression.

Joyce looked like she was on the verge of that now. Like saliva was suddenly going to erupt and start spurting down her chin.

After a few minutes of her gurning like this, Bob leant over and switched the record player off, careful to obey his own rules and keep one of his hands on the table. The little red power light faded and Prokofiev's strings dived into a sudden tonal downturn. The music melted in the air and so, perhaps, did sanity.

Bob had a pile of A4 papers and a tub of perfectly sharpened yellow pencils next to him. He gently pushed one of the sheets under Joyce's hand and slid a pencil between her fingers. He squeezed her forearm too, a signal to start or simple affection. Maybe it was both. Almost instantly she gripped the pencil and started to move her hand, her bony wrist slowly sliding from right to left, right to left.

Automatic writing, as it was called. Scrapes and scribbles of a woman in a trance, inviting some other force to guide the pencil into discernible words. So far it just looked like a bunch of soft, slow lines on the paper.

'Rachel,' Bob whispered.

The mention of her name startled her.

'You're sitting closest to Joyce, so you need to read out any words that appear on the sheet, okay?'

'*Me?*'

'Yes, you.'

'Bob, I can read it from here,' Matt whispered. 'How about I—'

'No, no, no.' He shook his head, hairy cheeks wobbling. 'That'd be inappropriate. It needs to be Holly's true connection.'

Rachel frowned, then eventually she nodded. 'Okay.'

'Nice and clear for the recorder. Whatever words come up, you just read them out.'

'Erm . . . right.'

'Good . . . so let's just wait.'

All eyes turned to Joyce, and the paper under her fist.

At first the lead of the pencil glided across the white, making barely any marks at all, just the swish of her arm back and forth. The sound was incredibly similar to the gentle Suffolk coast he heard every day growing up, making him think of his dead mum again, shimmering in the alleys of his brain. Then Joyce's pencil suddenly made stronger contact with the paper, leaving thicker long lines across the sheet. She was like those machines in hospitals that measure brainwaves.

Side to side, side to side, side to side. So many lines appeared under her hand.

This chaotic line drawing went on for a few minutes, and as each paper got filled with random scrapes, Bob pulled it away to slip a clean sheet underneath.

'Holly?' Bob said, projecting and actor-like – a supernatural telephone voice. 'This is Bob and Joyce Hodges. Can you remember us?'

The sound of scratching pencil changed into something less fluid and wide. Now it was short scrapes.

She was writing something down.

Rachel froze when she saw four discernible words there. The fact that it looked so clearly like a child's writing didn't help at all.

'Read it,' Bob said, quite firmly.

Rachel stared at the paper.

'Read it,' Bob said again.

Rachel prised her lips apart. '*My house*,' she read. '*My room.*'

Mary Wasson let out a shuddering, almost orgasmic moan.

'You can see your room, Holly?' Bob said.

The pencil scratching turned to wide scribbles and scrapes again.

'Holly?' Bob said. 'Others are here with us, they're good people. Would you like me to tell you who they are?'

Scratch, scratch, scratch.

Rachel read out a single word. '*Tell.*'

'Excellent. Holly, your mummy's here,' Bob said. 'How about that? She's right here and wants you to know how much she loves you.'

Scratch, scratch, scratch. Words.

Rachel read, '*Poor . . . Mummy.*'

Mary splayed a palm across her chest. 'Oh, I miss you, my baby. I *love* you. I *love* you.'

'And Holly?' Bob went on. 'You asked for your sister. Do you still want to see your sister?'

Scratch, scratch, scratch. All capitals.

'YES.'

'That's wonderful. She's right here with us. Would you like to say hello?'

Scratch, scratch, scratch, scratch.

'Holly? Would you like to say hello to your sister?'

Scratch, scratch, scratch.

'Can you hear me Holly?'

Scratch, scratch, scratch, scratch, word.

'TURN.' Rachel looked up from the paper, confused. '*Turn?*'

'We don't understand, Holly,' Bob said.

Scribble, scratch, scratch, scratch, then sudden, sharp, angry-looking letters.

'*Turn. Out.*' Rachel looked at Bob, a flash of dread in her eyes. '*Light.*'

'Okay. We can do that.' Bob looked towards the lamp. 'I'll switch—'

Darkness and shadows exploded into every corner of the room as the light vanished. Yet everybody's hands were still on the table. Including Bob's.

Blown fuse. Or the lamp must have a floor switch, Matt thought. *Must have.*

The light was now too dim for him or Bob to make the words out. But Rachel was nearer, and there was still just enough glow from the dancing candle to pick out the writing on the paper.

'Did *you* do that, Holly?' Bob said. 'Did you turn out the light just now?'

Scratch, scrape, scrape.

Rachel leant over and read it out. '*I. Did. That.*'

'Well, well done you!' Bob said. 'So would you like to say hello to Rachel now? She's missed you a great deal.'

Joyce must have been pressing too hard, because in response to that question the end of the pencil immediately snapped off. She opened her trembling hand and the pencil fell away. It rolled across the tabletop in a curve, dropping off the edge out of sight. Bob slipped a fresh pencil between her fingers and the violent scraping went on.

Rachel's breath was growing shallow and fretful, so Matt leant towards her. 'Rachel . . . are you oka—'

She hissed at him. 'Shhhhh!'

'Holly?' Bob said. 'Why aren't you saying hello to your sister?'

Scratch, scratch, scratch, word.

'*Holly, is something wrong?*'

Scratch, scratch, scratch. Lines in the dark.

This went on for another minute, and Bob didn't ask anything the entire time. He just frowned at Joyce whose face was twitching. 'Holly,' he said. 'We have another person here. He's called Matthew. He's a friend.'

Scratch, scratch, scratch. Word.

'*Teacher.*'

'That's right! He's a teacher!' Bob beamed at Matt and whispered across the table. '*See?* Now how could that little girl have known your occupation?'

'Because Joyce knows that already . . . and she's the one holding the pencil.'

Bob rolled his eyes and looked away. 'Sorry, Holly. You'll have to forgive Matthew. He doesn't see much magic in the world.'

Scratch, scratch, scratch: '*He will.*'

Bob's smile faded.

'May I ask Holly a question?' Matt said.

Scratch, scratch.

Bob said, 'I don't know if that's—'

'*Yes.*' Rachel read out the word.

Bob looked at the paper, nervously. 'Go ahead.'

Rachel was looking at him, and he wondered if Joyce might be doing the same. What if she was looking at him through a forest of lashes from her supposedly shut eyes?

'Holly . . . ?' Matt said into thin air. 'What's the black rabbit?'

Boom.

Joyce's arm stopped dead. The room plunged into silence.

He waited for a moment. 'Holly? Holly . . . are you still there?'

Bob looked pissed off. 'Yeah, thanks for—'

Joyce was off again, arm scraping. Carving out capitals.

Scratch, scratch, scratch.

Rachel read it out. '*RABBIT'S COMING.*' She muttered to herself, '*Jesus.*'

Scratch, scratch.

Manic, childish-looking words, which she read out, on autopilot.

'*WANT. Rachel. Rachel . . . WANT. Rachel.*'

'She's right here,' Bob said. 'You can speak to her.'

Another word. Then another.

'*WANT. With. ME.*' When Rachel read that part out she looked up from the paper, shaking her head. The pencil marks were growing more intense, angrier, enough to cause tearing and scrunch triangular holes in the paper. Joyce's head swayed left to right, left to right. Stevie Wonder playing a gig in hell, until her neck immediately stopped with an audible, sharp cracking sound. Her head was locked to the left at a vile, inhuman angle.

Scratch, scratch, scratch, word.

Rachel read the word out, confused. It was a name. '*Kassy?*'

'Kassy's not with us, Holly,' Bob said. 'Would you like her to be with us?'

Scratch, scratch, scratch.

'*Want. With. Me.*'

'You'd like Kassy and Rachel to be with you? I see.'

'But where *are* you, Holly?' Matt cleared his throat. 'Where?'

Scratch, scratch, scratch, scratch.

'With Steph.'

Scratch. Scratch.

'With Jo.'

He saw Rachel take one hand and clutch the front of her top.

Joyce's jaw was starting to hang and her shoulders began to shiver and convulse. Like the early stages of that guy's fit, just before he dropped his Starbucks coffee all over the train floor and hunched over in his seat. As Matt's eyes were adjusting to the light he could see a thin film of sweat resting in the deep cracks of Joyce's forehead. She didn't look good at all and Matt started wondering when the point would be when a medium's trance turned into a full-on stroke. To him it felt like . . . right about now.

'Bob?' Matt nodded towards Joyce. 'Look at her. I think we better wrap this up.'

'Holly?' Bob didn't catch his eye. 'Are you saying that Jo and Steph are with you right now?'

Scratch, scratch, scratch, word:

'YES.'

'But *where* are you, love?' Bob asked.

Joyce's wrists weren't just sweeping left and right any more, now they *flew* in wider and wider arcs of pencil. Way, way, way more frantic than before, sliding the whole paper back and forth with it. He noticed suddenly that the pencil was no longer between her fingers. Now it was clamped in her fist like a kid might hold a crayon and as he looked up at her in the dim candlelight he saw the old lady's tongue was poking through the right corner of her lips, concentrating as she scribbled.

The scrapes started to form bigger, furious-looking words, filling the page.

Matt stared down at the paper but didn't speak, and he had the wild notion that if he was to look up at the pictures on the walls, all those animals would be moving in their frames.

Rachel looked at the sheet, and the scraped writing. She *said* nothing.

'Well?' Mary said. 'What does it say?'

Silence.

'We can't see it from here,' Mary snapped, angrily. 'Where *is* she, Rachel? Read it!'

Scrape, scrape.

'Read it,' Bob said, starting to stretch forward so he might see too. 'Come on.'

Joyce suddenly groaned and flung her arms wide. The sheet slid away under her wrist and Matt watched the entire stack float in arcs all across the carpet. Then she started on the next.

Scrape, scrape, scratch, scrape.

'Why are you upset, Holly?' Bob asked. 'Can you calm down a second . . . you're among friends. People who love you.'

Rachel had frozen, so Mary pushed herself up, hands still on the table. She squinted to read. 'It says . . . *Why am I in the dark? In the dark. I'm scared of the dark.*' Her face crumbled and she called out to the ceiling. 'Don't be scared, love. I'm here now.'

Joyce's hand was thrashing wildly across the paper, writing the same thing over and over on multiple sheets as they flew to the floor in a haphazard pile. No wonder Bob had numbered them to keep them in sequence.

Bob slapped his palm hard on the table. 'I said *keep going*, Rachel. *You* read it out.'

'Hey,' Matt shouted. 'Take it easy.'

Rachel shook her head.

Mary suddenly obliged, and no amount of Bob glaring was going to stop her. '*Steph. In the dark. Jo. In the dark. Holly. In the dark. WANT Rachel. Rachel. Rachel. Rachel. Rachel. Rachel and my rabbit. In. The. DARK.*'

A sob erupted out of Rachel and she pushed her chair back. It scraped hard on the floor.

'Wait!' Bob said, angrily. 'Don't you break this circle.'

'I can't do this.'

Matt pushed back too. 'We're done.'

'Just give it a litt—'

'*That's enough*,' Matt shouted back. 'In fact that's *way more than*—'

Something happened.

Something happened and everything changed.

A muffled sound of breaking glass cracked the air and suddenly the piercing bleep of an alarm went off upstairs. The motion detector in Holly's room was going haywire.

Everybody's eyes shot up.

A horrible, heavy thud came from the ceiling, and his brain quickly assembled an explanation for it. That it was a dead little girl up there dropping from her noose to the carpeted floor, so that she could finally come downstairs and greet the ones that had called her. One slipper on, one slipper off. The dark dining room flickered with new light from the detector's LEDs. He saw the cat had roused itself from sleep and was looking up at the ceiling, hissing in fear.

Mary was already on her feet.

'Mrs Wasson!' Bob shouted. 'Stay where you are.'

'She's up there, she's home.' Mary bumped into her shelves and sent the porcelain penguins shattering to the floor because she refused to look anywhere but up. Then she was out of the room and rushing up the staircase. 'Holly, love! I'm coming. I'm coming. Don't be scared.'

Rachel was on her feet too, while Bob protested. She raced from around the table and slipped on the sheets of paper scattered on the floor. She fell on all fours, splayed out on them but quickly pushed herself up again, scrambling through the dining-room door.

231

Matt followed quickly after, calling out for Rachel to wait, but she didn't.

He stumbled on the floor when a piece of penguin snagged into the rubber of his shoe. He could hear it cracking on the steps as he ran up. Wondered if it was pounding in deeper, reaching for the foot through his sock. He had no idea what he expected to see upstairs, and perhaps it was the sheer amount of emotional tension in the air, but the skin of his arms was prickling into visible bumps.

In the dark. Rachel and my rabbit. In the dark.

He heard a new sound, from higher in the house.

Boom, boom, boom.

Footsteps? On the roof? He couldn't tell. It was probably Mary pounding her feet around Holly's room. Maybe.

He paused near the top step and looked through the banisters. Her door was wide open.

Mary was in there frantically opening cupboards, looking under the bed and desperately calling out, 'Don't hide, love. Don't be cruel.'

Rachel ran across the landing and went inside too. She must have accidentally knocked the handle with her hip, because the Holly-covered door was slowly closing, with the two women inside.

The motion detectors were squealing, like car alarms.

He ran up to the door, covered in pictures of Holly, and was almost reluctant to put his finger on one of Holly's smiling, toothy-looking photographs. But he did, and the first thing he saw out of the corner of his eye was a frantic movement. There was white material by the window.

He heard Mary say, 'Holly! It's you!'

Things seemed to slow down, sound itself seemed to suck into silence, and he thought: *this could be the moment . . . the moment where my entire worldview changes.*

Something in his brain told him to brace himself. That he was about to see Holly swinging, swinging wild and chaotic from the beam, just like Pastor Todd's frantic little finger dance, but instead he saw a long white curtain blowing into the room from a sharp wind that was sweeping through a jagged, freshly made hole in the glass. And when he looked at the floor he saw shards of the shattered pane, hundreds of pieces of it.

Amongst it all Rachel sat on her knees, cradling something in her hand.

He dropped next to her.

'Matt?' She looked up at him and opened her hands, tears flooding her eyes. 'What's happening here?'

The hefty wooden cross that had ruined the window slid from her grip and landed with a thump on the glass-strewn carpet, while the little painted Jesus nailed to it gazed up at him with bright, eager eyes.

'What's happening?' she said again.

While downstairs, the school bell was ringing madly.

CHAPTER THIRTY-ONE

'And you really saw nothing . . .' Larry stepped across the bedroom carpet, trying to avoid the glass shards but still causing cracking sounds. 'Nothing at all?'

'I looked out of the window, I ran downstairs. I ran up the street both ways and saw *nothing*.' Matt was sitting on Holly's bed, with crumpled My Little Pony faces looking warped and deformed as his weight pressed into the mattress. 'You need to ask the neighbours if they saw anything.'

'Really? Do you think?' Larry snapped, then frowned at the cross on the floor. He tilted his head to look at it. 'I've got people doing that right now.'

'Sorry, I didn't mean to—'

He held up an apologetic palm. 'Don't apologise. Long day, that's all. And you really think it's the prayer group that did this? Like, *really*?'

'Well, I don't *know* it was them but . . .'

'And they knew a seance was going on here, *how* exactly?'

'They're pretty clued up on local affairs . . .' He rubbed one of his eyes with the knuckle of his thumb. 'All I'm saying is, if you're looking for Menham people who might want to shut seances down, then those guys are at the very top of the tree. Heck, they call themselves the Phoenix Club. How gung-ho do you want?'

'So they'd throw a cross as a protest?'

'I don't know. Maybe the evangelicals were getting a little symbolic in their spiritual warfare.' He shifted on the bed. 'It worked, anyway.'

'The cross broke the spell then . . .'

'No. The cross coming through the window scared the crap out of everyone, before we even got to anything really interesting. But if it *was* them that threw it, then it's reasonable to consider they might have put those lily crosses up in Jo's—'

'Hey.' Larry waved a finger. 'You just be cautious, throwing around accusations, okay?'

'These guys were pretty rabid about their faith.'

Larry slipped what looked like an oversized sandwich bag over the cross, overturned it and sealed it shut with a jerk and swish of his thick fingers. The plastic billowed out, catching the air. Now it was upside down and hanging by Larry's side Matt had this silly echo of a minister's voice. Some twitch of the superstitious nerve that said: Um . . . maybe it'd be better if you turned the cross upright and didn't walk around with it looking so bloody Satanic. Jesus is going to get a nosebleed.

'And there's no sign of Jo or Lee?'

'No.' Larry checked his watch, an old digital thing. He wandered to the door, cross in hand, where Matt had propped up a broom, bucket, dustpan and brush, which he'd found in a cupboard downstairs. Larry stopped suddenly. 'Do you need a hand cleaning this up?'

'I can sort it, thanks. Besides, you'll be busy. I guess you'll head up to the church next? Talk to these Phoenix guys?'

'No, Matthew.' He had that parental, cautionary tone again. 'I'm going to the Hodges' house. I want to hear their angle on all this.'

'Hmmm. Good luck with that,' Matt said. 'Bob reckons when you cut a seance off mid flow it causes some sort of psychic wrenching. So don't expect Joyce to be in a chatty mood. I think that's why he whisked her off. To get her some rest.'

'I see.' Larry paused in Holly's doorway and looked back up at the wooden beam silently. *Holly's* beam. He did that for a long moment, enough for Matt to hear the breeze through the window and the tapping of the curtain rail.

'Larry,' Matt said. 'Are you okay?'

He didn't say anything.

'You know, Keech told me . . .'

'Told you what?'

'That you were one of the officers who helped get her down. How come you didn't mention that?'

He shrugged.

'I can't imagine what that's like.'

After a long pause he said, 'Holly was the first dead child I ever saw. Managed to avoid clocking something like that for years, until I came here that morning, back in the day.' He pulled his eyes away from the beam and started to slowly scan the room. '. . . All that stuff you said happened in the seance. The alarms going off, the writing . . .'

'What about it?'

'You say Bob's convinced that was Holly Wasson . . . breaking through?' He glanced at the open door, and at the hundreds of Hollys staring out. Faces that seemed a little psychotic before were now sweet and innocuous, disturbing only because of their

236

angling, and the sheer amount. One of them, a shot of her as a toddler pushing a wheeled horse down a path, was peeling off, so Larry pressed his finger against it, setting it carefully back into place. 'In your . . . professional opinion, I mean – how do you explain this stuff? Don't you reckon the Hodges might be onto *something*?'

'No, I don't.'

'And why's that?'

'If I'd seen someone levitate, or saw Holly herself appear on the doorstep, well, then I might be thinking differently. But all that so-called evidence tonight . . . a busted bulb, an old woman writing out what popped into her head. That was all circumstantial.' He said it gently. 'I'm sorry, but to me this is all just . . . just chasing after the wind.'

For the first time, Larry took his eyes from scanning Holly's room and locked them on Matt. 'You know something? You're a mate, and no offence, but I don't think I'd like a mind as black and white as yours.'

'Just check the churches, Larry. Check all the churches.'

He nodded silently and headed out, and Matt stood on the landing to watch the front door of Barley Street click shut. Larry gone, Matt stood at the top of the stairs with his hand on the banister and had one of those silly, momentary lapses of self-awareness that sometimes follow times of high tension. Maybe he was just tired. Maybe he was finally admitting to himself that the seance, as silly as it was in theory, was actually quite stressful and upsetting in practice.

And as he pondered finishing the cleaning and then grabbing his stuff to head back to Chesham, he had the silly sensation that he didn't live in Chesham at all. He lived here in Barley Street. That there was actually no such thing as Wren Hunter and his two girls. They had only been some exquisite dream he'd had through the night, but that *this* was his reality. That he was Rachel Wasson's dad, and Mary Wasson was his mad, bony wife, and that he lived and paid the mortgage in a house filled with ghosts.

As if to press the point home, he heard a dim muffled scream coming from Rachel's bedroom.

He tapped on the door and it opened slowly. She was exactly where she'd been for the last thirty minutes, where Larry had questioned her. Legs crossed under her, in the centre of her bed. Hands clasped around her retro pumps, the type basketball players wear. But now she had a pair of headphones clamped to her head.

She was listening back to her recording of the seance, and the sound of wails and squeals meant she'd gotten to the chaotic bit when everybody scrambled out of the room. He could hear his own voice booming out, telling Bob to shut it all down. She must have had it incredibly loud, because Mary's screeches were bleeding out into the room.

She looked very pale and fiercely focused, pushing the headphones hard against her ears, like she was doing backing vocals on a very grim charity single. But soon she felt his presence, blinked and looked up. She jabbed the recording off quickly.

'Rachel?'

She dragged the headphones off her head, like a teenager caught with contraband. 'Yeah?'

'Can we talk?'

CHAPTER THIRTY-TWO

He'd already offered to clean up the glass in Holly's room yet as Rachel came out of hers and leant her head into next door, she shook her head.

'Oh, you can't do all this yourself,' she said. 'I'm going to help.'

She stepped inside, then stared at the glass on the floor. Went a little pale again.

He moved forward and reached out his hand. 'Then, I bagsy the broom.'

His voice broke her trance because she shook her head and made a weak attempt at a smile. 'What a mess.'

He grabbed the broom and started to sweep the glass into piles, while she was on her haunches with the dustpan and brush. For the most part they did it without speaking, the silence punctuated only by the sharp snap of glass dropping in the bucket. That and the constant scrape and jingle of the metal rings of the window rail. That white curtain *still* danced and *still* reached into the room. He could feel the cool breeze against his shoulder.

Finally, as they got the majority of glass cleaned up, she spoke. 'Where's my mum?'

'She's in the dining room.'

'*Still?* What's she doing?'

'Just sitting there in the dark. Still waiting, I guess.'

They caught each other's eye. He tugged at his lip nervously.

She turned. 'I'll get some cardboard and tape.'

'No. Wait a sec.'

She paused and walked over to the gaping, breezy window. Pulling her cardigan across her as she gazed out at the dark street below. He stood alongside her and for a while, they said nothing.

Menham Park was over the other side of the street but the wide expanse of grass and trees, lake and gazebo, were thoroughly lost in inky-black shadows, which the orange street lights here could barely penetrate. The wind made the trees shimmer and hiss, so for a while they both just stood there, listening to it. He knew from his pastoral days that you don't rush a traumatised person. And he could see by the stare in her eye and scrape of the wrist that Rachel was very close to the edge right now. So they watched a glowing cloud slide silently across a ringed, grubby moon.

Finally, he spoke. 'She had a really good view of the park, didn't she?'

Rachel tucked some hair behind her ear. Her fingers were trembling. 'She'd sit here after school and watch the trees and count the birds. She always said she was the luckiest in the family since she got the best view in the house.' Her mouth faltered. She dropped her hand to her side. 'Which is why she did it here. I've always known that. Even that morning, I knew. That she wanted to be looking at something pretty, at the end. She'd kept the curtains open, by the way. Just a touch. Not too much that she'd be seen and scare anybody. But enough so *she* could see.'

A few seconds ticked by; neither of them moved from the

carpet, which felt more worn than anywhere else in the room. He looked at his shoes.

'Can I ask you a question?' Matt said.

She nodded.

'From what I understand, apart from the figure on the roof . . . you didn't personally witness the poltergeist in this house?'

'I saw the leftovers. I saw furniture pushed over, the pictures upside down, the taps going on at night. I knew some stuff was missing from the house.'

'What stuff?'

'Ornaments. A few pictures. An old tape recorder I had was taken which really cheesed me off. One of Mum's shoes. Random stuff. Bob reckons they might never be found.'

'But you never witnessed anything supernatural happen in front of you?'

'No.'

'So, didn't you doubt it at first?'

''Course I did . . . but then I saw that shadow thing on the roof and I wasn't so sure any more.' She turned to him. 'There really *was* something there, you know. A creature.'

'Forget the shadow for a second.'

'That's easier said than done, Matt.'

'Before that . . . did you ever think the poltergeist was just somebody making it up?'

'I used to think it was Holly . . .' She turned back to the window. 'I thought that she'd invented it all.'

Somewhere way up the street he could hear a group of women suddenly cackle.

'And why do you think she'd do that?'

'Because she was lonely. Because she didn't have any friends.' She blinked slowly; her eyes kept looking for the unseen women. 'I read that some kids make this stuff up to get noticed. Which

241

certainly happened here. God, Holly's become a *legend* in this town. You know, after she killed herself I'd sometimes spot kids down there in the park.' She nodded at it. Filled with so many shadows it looked like a hole in the world. 'They'd gather in little groups under the trees down there and look right up here. Hoping for a sight of her. I went down to chase them off once and do you know what I found? They'd made a Ouija board out of cardboard and a cap from a deodorant bottle. They had a newspaper picture of Holly pinned to it with a branch . . .'

'People are drawn to mystery,' he said. 'And to the beyond. The afterlife helps them make sense of the world . . . it helps them make sense of death.'

'Well, Joyce tells me the local kids still do that. They come looking for the infamous Holly Wasson because . . . because they think she *still* lives here.' She shuddered then turned away from the window and looked directly at him. 'And after what happened downstairs . . . I think they might be right.'

'Well, respectfully, even after the seance, I'm not convinced. But for the sake of argument . . .' He put a palm out. 'Let's say ghosts really *do* exist. That the dead might have the ability to communicate with the living.'

She nodded. 'Okay.'

'Well, if that was actually true . . . that Holly could talk to you again . . .' He saw the shift in her jaw, the loss of focus in her eye. He was speaking as gently as he could. 'Would you even *want* her to?'

She blinked a few times, like her brain was computing something. 'If you're trying to say something. Just say it.'

He nodded. 'Okay, you loved your sister, I think that's clear. But Rachel, I saw you at the gazebo the other day, when Joyce mentioned Holly was calling out to you. Then tonight at the dining table. I saw your eyes when Joyce started scratching out those words . . . when she wrote your name.'

242

'And?'

'And I'm getting the distinct impression that you really *don't* want to hear from Holly, even if you could.'

Rachel suddenly spun back towards the window.

'And I want to know why.'

She took a step towards the frame.

'Did you and she not get on?'

He heard her breathing. It sounded shallow.

'Did something happ—'

'Wait,' she said. 'Did you *hear* that?'

He followed her gaze through the gap where the window was supposed to be. If this was a musical, this would be the part when they'd both sing out a lament to the empty street below.

'It's the wind,' he said. 'Now *focus*. I noticed you didn't read one of the sheets out during the seance. What did it say—'

'Dammit . . . *listen*! Something's,' she said it in a shuddering whisper, '*squealing*.'

The wind slid against his face and riding on it he could hear a weird, muffled sound coming from somewhere outside.

'Just an animal . . .' Then he frowned. 'Maybe it's just one of the swans?' *Being torn to pieces, from the sounds of it*. He leaned forward and pushed his face through the hole in the window.

She clutched the front of her top and with a quick glance toward the ceiling, she jerked back into the room. 'Matt. Pull your head back in.'

He whispered. 'It's not coming from the roof, it's coming from the park.'

She grabbed his elbow. '*Pull your head back in*.'

'Shhhh!' He gazed out through the shimmering branches at the black void beyond. 'I think it's getting louder—'

It happened. Just then.

A sudden small light flashed through the twisted branches.

Then the squealing started again. Only now it was more frantic and pained, yet still distant.

He squinted his eyes, leant forward even more, then said all he could think of. 'Holy shit.'

'What?' She stared over his shoulder at the little light. 'What is it?'

But he was already running towards the door, Holly's furniture warped in the corners of his vision as he ran. He scrambled down the stairs, skidding off the bottom few, then he raced past the dining room, fast enough to almost fall, but not so fast that he didn't notice a snapshot diorama of Mary Wasson in the dining room, still in her evening dress. One side of her hair had unpinned itself and was hanging like some mad fright wig. Her cheeks were now streaked black with running eyeliner while she laughed and danced around the table holding what looked like a child's nightie to her chest. *Peter and the Wolf* drifted gently through the air. A bottle of vodka sat on the table with a missing cap. Next to it was a white mug. It said 'World's No.1 Mummy.'

He rushed outside.

'Matt!' Rachel called down to him from Holly's open window. 'What the hell's going on?'

'Call the police,' he shouted, racing madly down the concrete path and across the street. 'And the fire brigade. Call everybody now.'

CHAPTER THIRTY-THREE

He'd been a pretty fast runner in his time. Did the London Marathon once for charity. Admittedly it nearly killed him and he almost vomited twice (on miles fourteen and twenty) but he still did it in just over four hours. Enough for him to paw at his little medal every night for two weeks after: his one triumph in an otherwise abysmal sporting career.

But now his legs felt bulky and stiff, especially in his trousers and smart, flat shoes. Clumsy knees locked into place as he pounded desperately across the Barley Street road. Then he grabbed the iron railing and pulled himself up and over it, gasping. From this distance it was difficult to tell what was on fire exactly, only that whatever it was, it was screeching. It also didn't help that in this part of the park there were no real street lights to speak of, only the ones from Barley Street. They faded with every step. Yet as he scrambled across the grass he could see the edge of the tree trunks slowly starting to flicker as the flames grew larger. He saw faces shimmering in the glow, which startled him at first, until he realised they were figures running towards the same sight he was. Drawn by the spectacle of it and the awful inhuman wailing that was growing louder with every hammering step.

It was disorientating, because the closer he got, the more it looked like the flames were hovering above the floor. Then gradually as the light grew larger he started to get his bearings. Over to the left, the silhouette of the gazebo was slowly flashing into life and to the right of it, that long thick branch of the heavy oak tree stretched towards it. The fire was literally floating under the branch and the flames made the tree, and the ones near it, look like they were alive. It was a common optical illusion. Still, though, he had no care for the way those branches seemed to writhe and dance as the screams went on. Nature itself rejoicing at pain.

For a while all he could hear was the wailing sound along with his own wheezing breath, but then laughter came from behind him. Without slowing he quickly jerked his head to see a row of teenage boys chasing him. Or rather, they were just running like he was. Snorting and saying stuff like, 'Bet you any money, it's a tyre. Bet you that's the rubber screaming.'

It wasn't a tyre.

Just as the breath in Matt's lungs began to ignite, he was able to make out the shape now. It was a roughly cylindrical object, engulfed in flames. An oddly clear bright line – like a sharp finger – had started to grow from it toward the overhanging tree above, too straight and perfect to be a branch. It took him a good few steps to realise that the line wasn't part of the tree. It was rope.

Ironically, the squealing sound had started to die down the closer he got but it was now replaced by the whoops and witch-like cackles of four girls nearby. They looked like they'd been walking back through the park from a pub. Laughter fell into sharp screams and hands clutched kebabs in fright. Two of them toppled to the floor in heels not designed for backing away. Mouths hung open on hinges.

'That's . . .' one of the boys said behind him. 'Bloody hell.'

Matt didn't stop running. Not even when his cheeks began to burn. It was only when wisps of material or ash – he couldn't tell which – went dancing towards his eyes that his legs stopped churning and he gasped out breath. He stared up in dread at the flashing shape, which wasn't moving at all save for a slight twist to the rope with flames running up it. Something was creaking. Either the rope or the branch it was tied around. The wrench of neck bone, maybe.

God.

There was so much smoke and fire that he wondered if this might be an animal, strung up. But then, with a sensation that felt very close to a stomach punch, his brain assembled the shapes and colours together. He saw something clearly discernible in the haze, suspended a metre from the grass. He was looking at bare human feet, dangling and motionless apart from the sizzling and popping of the skin. Every toe was curled.

'They're still alive!' one of the boys jabbed a finger. 'Check out the head!'

There *was* movement, he was right. Because in amongst the flames Matt could see the oddly misshapen outline of the head, with some sort of bag or sack over it. It was twitching left and right. The squealing came again, only now it was very quiet. A sort of low moan that made his gums tingle.

A throb of insane hope exploded in his gut in a flicker of Channel Five TV shows he'd idly watched, when he was supposed to be writing lectures. Of people who'd suffered horrendous burns but had been given plastic surgery. They'd sort of turned out okay. They lived a life.

He had to get them down.

He looked across at the gazebo. Two homeless guys were lying in there, covered in blankets, surrounded by crushed cans of cheap lager. One of them was sitting upright and looking at the fire like this was his version of TV, mouth gawping at a particularly absorbing show tonight. The other one was snoring in a heap.

Matt blundered up the steps. Grabbed the blankets. 'Move!'

'We've as much right to be here as—'

He yanked the man's blanket hard and rolled him completely out of it. The guy thumped a shoulder against the wood.

'You bloody, cheeky bugger.'

'Move!' Matt barked again and pulled both stinking blankets from the men. The sleeping one started shouting abuse, loudly.

They say that in moments of extreme pressure the brain reverts to tunnel thinking, and Matt had no idea if this would work, but all he could think of was the simplest of physics. Fire hates water, fire hates water. So heaving exhausted breath through his body, he ran to the edge of the small lake where he'd spotted that family of swans yesterday. Then he plunged the foul-smelling blankets into the ice-cold water. He hauled them back out and rushed back to the dangling shape. Amazed at how heavy the material felt, like a body itself.

Somewhere in the distance, sirens were howling.

'It's going, it's going,' someone said and immediately the rope snapped with an audible crack. So loud he thought the entire, fiery tree was going to come crashing down onto their heads, and spark up the entire gazebo. But only the fire-lump plunged to the floor. It collapsed into a mad, flashing heap.

Matt ran towards it and opened up one of the wet, heavy blankets. Just as he went to fling it over he called out to the others. 'Somebody! Grab the other one!'

Nobody did and that was the first time he noticed the smell of petrol in his nostrils. It was also the moment that he was fully aware that the lump on the grass was a woman. A large, burning woman with her blackened skin on fire. The misshapen, now unmoving sack on her head still covered her face, but as soon as he saw the shape of her body, single shots of memory flashed across his mind, in a swift flickering parade: of Jo Finch hugging Rachel on the steps of the gazebo station, of her resting her chin in her hand, beaming out smiles at a photoshoot.

He couldn't see her face, but he could see that her arms weren't arms any more.

– *No.*

'Help me!' he called out. 'Someone.'

They ignored him. Totally oblivious to the concept of involvement.

'What is wrong with you people?'

He threw the sodden blanket across the top half of the body and yelped when a tongue of white light flicked out of her belly. It slashed across his wrist. His eyes flooded with instant water and he pulled his hand to his chest, the extreme heat bubbling into the flesh of his thumb. He took a breath and grabbed the other towel, throwing it across her legs. He noticed, just then, that her head, still covered, had finally stopped moving.

The blankets were so thick and wet that they managed to put most of the fire out. Now masses of smoke and steam swept past him in huge billowing plumes. His first, foolish hope was this: that Jo Finch's soul was real and was rushing past him right now, through him and up into the tangled branches of the tree. Then there was silence, apart from the sound of rain. Though he quickly realised it wasn't really rain at all. It was the sound of her skin, still cracking, still snapping.

Somehow the smoke stole all the moisture from his eyes and he felt the inside of his chest filling with wasps and bees and anything else that stings. The grass under his feet began to pulsate, the grass no longer bright orange now, but a shadowy, smokey black. He sank to his knees by the steaming girl.

Retching out a bone-shaking cough he looked back up at the boys and the homeless men and at the young women with kebabs. The homeless ones were the only ones watching all of this happening with their eyes. The rest of them were holding up their phones, filming it all, their faces lit by an electronic glow, expressions somewhere between horror and mouth-watering delight. More, he feared, the latter.

Amongst them, like any other local, he saw Rachel Wasson emerging, holding her side and out of breath. Only she staggered forward, further than the others, straight into the cloud of billowing smoke that wrapped itself around her like tentacles. She was staring at the steaming lump on the grass and had clearly understood it, because she was holding both hands at each side of her head like her skull was about to explode. He watched her scream with a horrible, animal ferocity that was shocking in its power. Frightening, even. And somewhere among the mad wail, he was sure he'd heard words lodged in his brain. It sounded like apologies, fired up to the sky.

She roared so loudly that some of the kids were now starting to turn their camera phones on her.

And for a short, scary second as he looked back at Jo and the kids filming her, Matt was a full and unadulterated believer. Not in ghosts or demons, not in God, or the Devil. But in something more abstract and terrifying, something horribly mundane. That maybe evil – actual objective, personified evil – really did exist, after all. But that it didn't hang out in hell. It preferred to stroll the parks and streets of places like Menham, slipping through the screaming air and climbing inside people and houses and dogs and psychologies, looking through their eyes and seeking out whatever there was to devalue and devour.

He coughed harder again, only this time he threw up. He wiped his mouth and looked up at the moon, shaking.

And Rachel screamed on.

CHAPTER THIRTY-FOUR

Chaos.

That was the word. It was utter chaos as the fire crew pushed through the mushrooming crowd, no doubt summoned by eager text messages and status updates of those first witnesses.

Watching a woman burn to death. Lol!

The police were here now, barking at people to stay back. But he spotted plenty of them crane their own heads so they could look at the monster on the grass. The thing that had what looked like a small farmer's apple sack tied to its head. Tied tight with metal wire. Matt was sitting on the back step of an ambulance with the rear doors wide open, legs dangling off the edge like Huck Finn fishing in a pond. In the flashing emergency lights, he could see the parkland grass churned up with tyre marks.

'Breathe,' the paramedic said. 'Breathe.'

He closed his eyes and let out some air as they pressed the oxygen mask close to his face. Someone was wrapping his wrist in a bandage.

The paramedic spoke again. 'I said, are you feeling okay?'

'I told you, I'm fine. Now let me talk to the woman.'

'Are you a relation?'

'Yes.'

The paramedic thrust a bottle as the bandage was finished. 'Okay. You're fine to go but, drink this first.'

He sloshed the water down and it felt exquisite. Then he twisted around to see Rachel, lying on the stretcher in the back. Her face was covered in another oxygen mask.

The paramedic nodded at him. 'Be quick.'

He pushed himself up and knelt next to her. Her eyes were shut and he hoped she was asleep, dreaming of something distant and unreal and complet—

Her hand shot out from the blanket.

He jumped as she grabbed his arm. Her eyelids flicked open, and she stared at him with red eyes, raw from tears.

'Rachel, it's me, Matt.'

She groaned.

'You're going to be okay. They're taking you to hospital—'

She started to speak, her voice muffled under the mask. She reached up quickly and pulled it to the side of her face.

'Better keep that—'

'My mum.' Her voice sounded like it had gravel in it. 'Is she okay?'

'I guess she's still back at your house.'

'Check. Go to my . . .' she coughed hard, 'house and check if she's okay.'

'I will.'

She squeezed his wrist, harder than ever. 'And get my recorder. Bring it to me.'

'Okay . . .'

'Hey,' the paramedic called out from behind him. 'Get that mask back on her.'

She rasped out some words. 'Did you see it?'

'See what?'

A bundle of sound from behind him, 'I said get it on her.'

'The rabbit?'

He shook his head. 'Did *you* see it?'

She started to laugh, madly, nodding as the paramedic barged past Matt and leant over.

'Where?'

'Up on the hill,' she said, as the mask started to slide back into place. 'Watching it all. It was up there looking and dancing on the hill.'

Her voice warped into muffled sobs and laughter, while the paramedic grabbed Matt's forearm. 'She's in shock, now give her some space.'

He did. He crawled out of the van and stood on the grass as the doors slammed shut. Then he wheezed out a breath and scanned the park for the only hill he could find. There was one on the other side of the lake.

'Hey,' he called to a policeman, still coughing. 'Whoever did this was spotted up on the hill.'

A few officers hurried over and they all trotted toward the lake.

But with the remnants of his energy he climbed the hill to find nothing but grass and white flowers, whose petals throbbed with colour from the emergency lights. The police shrugged, and looked around, and their faces grew hard and less accommodating when Matt hit the ground and felt inside a hole in the soil saying, 'It's a warren.'

Only it wasn't even that. It was a recess for some sort of sprinkler.

The rabbit hunt might have been funny in some parallel universe. But in this one, Matt just pulled his arm back, fingers caked with soil, dumbstruck by the last two hours of his life. He sat on the grass, head pounding and looked across at the lights. Through the trees at the very far edge, he could make out the strange hole of light that was Holly's window, and in it stood a small figure, which must have been Mary. Yes. Of course it was. It was Mary Wasson at the window, on her knees for some reason. Not Holly on her feet staring out and admiring her view. 'Course not. 'Course not.

'Are you okay?' an officer said. 'You know we'll need a statement.'

He had no words to reply with because the bubbling hellfire flesh of Jo Finch was still in his nostrils, making his brain pulse and contract. A soiled breeze swept up the hill, fast and full of death. He slid a hand through his hair, soil and all, and waited with the flowers, trembling in the sudden cold.

CHAPTER THIRTY-FIVE

Matt stood on the doorstep of Barley Street, reeking of bonfire night. 'They're taking her to hospital.'

Mary sipped from her mug and winced. She put a hand on the doorframe, painted fingernails pressing into the wood.

'Mary, did you hear me? I said she's in the ambulance now.'

'You know she never told me about you.' She blinked slowly and looked at him. 'She kept you a *biiiiiig* secret. Now why is that?'

'There's nothing to tell. I'm just a friend of Bob and Joyce. So do you need a lift to the hospital?'

She nodded. 'Can I get my jacket?'

'Of course, and I need to get her recorder. She says it's in her room.'

'Fine. Fine.' She stepped aside and started tugging a black jacket from a coat hook, struggling to yank it free. She shuffled her feet to stop herself from stumbling. He'd found some gaffer tape and cardboard earlier and it still sat to the side. He quickly grabbed it and rushed into Holly's room. Sliding the tape against the pane he secured it as best he could, except he nicked his finger on a shard of glass.

'Dammit.' He sucked the red bead that mushroomed from it and noticed his fingernail was black with soot. Then he looked at Holly's room for a few moments, before switching off the light.

Rachel's recorder was still on the bed. It reminded him of a Star Trek tricorder. He bundled it and the headphones up, grabbing the charger just in case she needed it. Then he paused.

'I'll just be a minute,' he called down. 'I have to check if it's working.'

He pulled the headphones on and tapped the power button. When he hit play, the sound of the seance exploded in his ears and he frantically turned it down. He rewound it a touch and listened for about thirty seconds to the part she seemed so engrossed in. But he heard nothing new, nothing that he didn't hear at the time.

It was just after he was slipping it into its case that he bent down to grab the headphone wire. He saw the paper out of the corner of his eye. The corner of the folded sheet stuck out from under her mattress, like a shark's tooth.

'Just packing up now,' he called out as he tugged the tooth free.

He knew what it was. Knew it instantly even as it folded itself open as he brought it into the light. Unfurling like it was eager for air and keen to be read.

The scrapes of Joyce's mad, spirit-driven pencil had marked deep, jerky lines across the sheet. This was during the pencil's angry, intense phase. In the top corner, he could see one of Bob Hodge's numbers that he'd handwritten in neat blue ink.

#44.

Around the outside, he could see the scrawled words that he remembered Rachel reading out. In fact, it was the exact part she'd been listening to in the recording, over and over.

In the dark. In the dark. With Me. In the dark.

Fine, but he wasn't interested in those.

He pulled the paper closer and read the other two words in the centre. Words that he knew for a fact Rachel had skipped reading. Words that nobody else had seen and that weren't even on the recording. He frowned and gazed at them for a second, tracing out the scraped lead with his finger.

He left a tiny scrape of dried blood on the sheet. 'Shit.' He pulled his hand back then folded the paper back up. He slipped it into his pocket, confused at why she'd hide this. And as he trotted down the stairs to get Mary, the two words swam and dived into his memory, even though he had no idea what they meant.

The vaults.

CHAPTER THIRTY-SIX

Where fields are open and the sky is warm,
And the smells are precious.
Rabbit was.

Trickle-sound of rivers running,
Time is kept.
So rabbit leapt.

Then

Clouds fell from the mountain,
They dried the sea and snapped the door,
Broke the lock upon the fountain.
Left old rabbit scared and shouting,

Whore, whore, evermore.
Who took my hand and danced the floor.

Whore, whore, witch and bitch.
Who took my life, my all.

Let me stop, and catch a breath.
And do your will no more.
And do your will no more.

CHAPTER THIRTY-SEVEN

Morgues, Matt discovered, are very bright.

They're not mood-lit techno caverns or chambers, like the movies tell you. They're crisp and clean and looked to him surprisingly similar to a peanut factory he worked in when he was a student. Glaring fluorescent bulbs glowed through frosted plastic squares set into the roof and shone off stainless steel sinks and slabs bolted to the washable, white-tiled floor. But a closer look brought out the strange little features that he didn't fully understand. He could make a grim guess at their function, though. Suspended over each metal body-table was what looked like sleek white hoovers, emerging from industrial, dentist-style arms and brackets. And on the metal slabs themselves were little white rollers where the bodies would lie. It must have been a lot easier to slide the cadavers on and off that way.

There was one other detail too, which was perhaps the first truly significant step in setting his teeth on edge. Up on the wall, near the ceiling, he could see two rings, glowing blue behind a metal grille with the brand name *Insect-o-cutor* written across it. A sort of meticulously clean version of those industrial fly- and wasp-killers you see up in the corner of a fish and chip shop, buzzing now and then as they spark out another life. The sight of those two glowing rings did no favours to his imagination, and he wondered what things might creep or even fly out of the seams of the silent guests they had in here.

No wonder, then, that even Larry looked a little pale. He certainly kept tugging at his tie, loosening its grip on his neck.

The latent smell of the Jo Finch smoke had pretty much tattooed itself on his nostrils last night. It had been present all the way to the hospital as he dropped Mary off. All the time he'd sat with her watching Rachel sleeping, and all the way back to Barley Street. Thankfully, the smell had gradually reduced on his drive home to Chesham at one in the morning. But he'd still showered like a madman to try and ditch it, from his hair particularly. He wondered if he might always smell this way.

Now it was first thing in the morning and he'd returned to Menham. Meaning the smell of dead flesh was fully back since the original source of that smell was somewhere in this room, still emanating.

There was no delay, no build up. A pathologist called Bochenski, who looked like a male model – and creepily symmetrical too – took him and Larry to the centre of the room. Then he rolled a metal trolley which was covered with a sheet and he grabbed the edges of the material. Then with his gloved fingertips he yanked it completely off her, wafting it up like some hideous *Voilà!*

oh . . .

oh shit . . .

Larry tutted and shook his head while disgust instantly raced from the table and ran at Matt, full peg. It punched him hard in the heart, making him want to gag. He hid the retch and just groaned. But he refused to look away, despite every nerve ending in his brain insisting he do exactly that.

When you see a building that's burnt to the ground, you can still see smoke rising from it the next day, or even the day after next. This wasn't quite like that. After all, there were obviously no flames on her any more. No fire burning deep in the embers of her body, but Matt was sure he saw a certain amount of steam rise from her as the sheet rose in the air and he thought if he was to put his hand on her (though he would never do that in a thousand years), his fingertips would feel a horrible, latent warmth.

At least her eyes were closed.

Last night, when Matt had knelt on the grass by Jo's side there had been way too much smoke to see her properly. Too much pumping residual heat to fuzz his vision, and all that glare in his eyes made her little more than a blurred meteorite fresh through the atmosphere. But under the fluorescents, without the heat and smoke, she was a high-definition monstrosity.

'She looks even *worse*,' Matt said, convinced the room felt hotter now the sheet was off.

Bochenski started tucking the sheet into the end bar of the metal table. 'They often look worse in here. It's the lights.'

There was no sack across her head now, no clothes at all, in fact, though there were parts where it was hard to tell if material had fused with skin. Either way, Matt could now see her fully naked and complete. The hair, which had hung so pretty across Jo's shoulders, was almost all gone, save for a random clump of short frayed strands up above her right ear. Otherwise she was bald. Mostly the skin was black, with areas of furious-looking red and pink near the top of her body. On the curve of her shoulder, he saw a rare patch that was untouched by the flames. It still showed half a small tattoo that she'd had in life. The head of a blue sparrow, tail lost in black, like the bird was desperately trying to peel itself away and escape her.

Running his rapidly depressed gaze across the top of her chest, breasts, groin and legs brought Matt his most honest and accurate thought. That in places she looked almost identical to a sausage left on the barbecue for far too long, caked with hard black crust which, if you were to peel it away, would tear the skin off and leave something glistening underneath.

Jo Finch: a husk.

'Why is her stance so . . . odd?' Matt drew out a slow breath. 'She looks . . . bow-legged.'

Bochenski nodded. 'That's normal. The extreme temperature sometimes makes the body form what's called a pugilist position. Basically, the heat plays havoc with the muscles and the protein, so they dehydrate and contract. Makes the cadavers look like boxers, starting a fight. Pretty kooky, really.'

Matt rubbed his eyes, like a man desperate for sleep.

'So there's general fire damage, as you'd expect,' Bochenski said. 'Some of it's caused holes to break out around the fattier tissue. Like the left breast.'

'Holes?'

'Well . . . it *looks* like holes. But I'm putting that down to the start of skin splits. That's where the heat makes the soft tissue contract, so it starts to rupture.' Bochenski popped his lips. 'Anyway, the neck's broken, obviously. From the noose.'

He was right. It *was* obvious. Jo's neck was bent at an almost jaunty angle, which had an unnerving ring of familiarity about it. He thought of Joyce at the dining table last night, with her head cocked horribly to the side during the weird throes of the seance. Thankfully, Jo's eyes and a large part of her left cheek seemed untouched by the flames, except for one horrible fact. There was a ragged hole in it. A tattered little circle revealed a partial line of grey teeth inside. It looked like she was cackling to the side. A private joke that only the dead understood. He had the absurd notion that if he was to lean in close, those teeth would still be chattering together.

'She was a cleaner,' Matt suddenly said randomly. 'Her house was tidy and she liked candles.'

'Er . . .' Bochenski shrugged. 'Okay.'

'This is horrible.'

'Yeah . . . gotta admit . . .' Bochenski said. 'This is one of the grottier ones.'

Matt looked up at Larry, the acids in his gut rejoicing at the new view. 'So what about the boyfriend, Lee? Have you tracked him down yet?'

'No sign of him at all, which obviously doesn't put him in a very good light.' Larry cleared his throat. 'Anyway . . . hanging's usually enough to kill a person, which means this fire business must be something else. Cruelty, most likely. Bravado.'

Bochenski waved a palm across the air. 'A sadist's flourish.'

'Exactly. We have a very twisted person on the—' Larry paused for a moment, eyeing Matt. 'Why are you shaking your head?'

'I've been thinking about this. In fact, I haven't thought of anything else . . . what if the fire *wasn't* about cruelty,' Matt said. 'Whoever did this is the very opposite of discreet. He chooses a public park at night. He lights her up even though the noose had probably already killed her . . . why would he do that?'

'Um . . .' Bochenski said, half smiling. 'Because he's a psychopath?'

'Or because he . . . or she . . .' Matt corrected himself, '*wanted* people to come. This wasn't just a hanging; this was a *public* hanging . . . with a fire to summon the community to see it.'

'You mean . . . he hangs her and snaps her neck to make an *example* of her?' Larry said.

'Something like that, yes.'

Larry was looking increasingly uneasy. 'But why? What did she do that was so bad?'

'Hang on,' Matt turned to Bochenski. 'Are you *sure* she died from a broken neck before she burnt?'

He curled a lip. 'Of course I'm sure. Her trachea, her bronchi, all her airways were pretty much free of soot. If she'd been breathing during the fire she'd have sucked all that in.'

'Well . . . I'm sorry, but that can't be right.'

'Oh, *really*?'

'Yes. Because Jo was screaming while she was burning. We all heard it. I even saw her head moving inside the bag, like she was struggling to—'

'Ah . . .' Bochenski said.

'Slow down, Matt.' Larry put his hand up. 'She was dead alright. The screaming was something else.' He sniffed and turned to Bochenski. 'Show him.'

Bochenski nodded and moved toward a bank of metal doors, which Matt had thought were lockers.

He turned to Larry. 'What's going on?'

But by then, Bochenski had already unlocked one of the doors and was sliding out a metal shelf. What was inside was covered in the same titanium-white sheet that was over Jo. 'You probably *did* see movement.' He pulled the shelf out all the way and yanked the sheet away. He watched the wave of confusion spread across Matt's face. 'But it wasn't her.'

'What the hell is that?' Matt said.

'That's what was inside the sack around her head,' Larry said. 'It's Jo Finch's pet rabbit.'

'Matt?' Larry's voice sounded muffled in the air. 'You okay, Matt?'

He blinked, and eventually looked up from the mad, frozen eyes of the rabbit. 'I'm fine, sorry.'

'Animal lover, I take it?' Bochenski said.

He actually laughed at that. 'Not particularly.'

They stood gazing at the fuzzy black lump, which looked like it was made of two halves. As Matt stepped to the side he could see that it still had its head and face intact, scorched in soot. A silver disc on a collar shone brightly around its neck, shining where Bochenski must have cleaned it. It said the rabbit's name was Six, and the address below was Jo's place on Bennington Road.

It was a surreal experience, looking at a burnt rabbit corpse alongside its equivalent human.

Something like panic, desperation or basic agony had forced the animal's eyeballs to bulge horribly proud from the sockets. A little nudge might make them pop out and roll onto the floor. Animals have minimal expressions at the best of times, so he'd never really imagined what terror would look like in a creature's face. Now he didn't have to. It was plain, and not up for debate. One of the long (very long) floppy ears had burnt away and was now just a tattered black rag. Yet just like Jo, the real damage was to the bottom half of it. Part of the front paws and most of the hind legs and tail looked like bundles of brittle black sticks or twigs sticking out from its body. A horrid joke rabbit with black pencil legs, twisted and burnt, ready to snap if it ever tried to run.

God, how freaky to see this thing running, Matt thought. 'So let me get this right, she was dead and *this* was alive.'

'Yes, though obviously it can't have been alive for long.'

'So that hole in her cheek . . .' Matt barely hid the shock on his face. 'It wasn't caused by the fire was it . . .'

'Nope. Looks like our little friend here panicked and was trying to hide from the flames. Couldn't burrow out so he burrowed . . .'

Matt closed his eyes.

'Well, you get the idea.'

'So putting the rabbit up at the top of her, in a bag, kept it alive and screeching for longer, like a siren . . .' Matt said. 'It got people coming out. That's how *I* noticed it. It was the noise.'

Larry said nothing. He was too busy scratching at the wiry grey hairs of his neck, hard like it might hurt. 'Are you still going up to visit Rachel Wasson?'

Matt nodded.

'Then I'm your plus one.' He looked to Bochenski. 'And get rid of that awful little thing, will you?'

He nodded and threw the sheet back over it. Bochenski said 'Sweet dreams,' to the white lump. Then he pushed the shelf hard and slammed the black rabbit deep into its hole.

CHAPTER THIRTY-EIGHT

Larry pushed the morgue door open and they both stepped into the quiet corridor, where the walls were decked with black and orange streamers. The patients from the children's ward had put up a Halloween display of ghosts and pumpkins.

'Before we go up.' Matt touched Larry's arm. 'Grab a seat.' He gestured to a couple of soft chairs.

'I've got a lot to do on this, Matt. I'd rather get on wi—'

'What are the vaults?'

Larry frowned. 'Where did you hear that?' He sank into one of the chairs and a crepe paper werewolf wafted against the wall above him.

'This came out at the seance last night.' He rummaged in his pocket and pulled out the paper, handing it over as he sat. 'But Rachel Wasson refused to read those two words out. She tried to hide the paper . . . so I want to know what it means.'

Larry let out a breath. 'Wow, we're talking vintage here. The vaults are on the other side of the park, down Kirchin Road.

There's a bunch of old bomb shelters from the war, which are still there today. A few tunnels and old stone rooms. Up until the late 70s there was an old children's home next door to them.'

'Something happened there?'

'A big scandal in '78 or '79. Can't recall the year, exactly. Anyway, it turns out that a few of the staff were using the vaults to abuse little kids.' He finally looked up from the sheet. 'They'd invite rings from uptown to come over and watch it all. It made the national press but I guess you'd have been a little kid then.'

'I wasn't even born then.'

His lips flapped a breath. 'Yeah, thanks for that. Anyway. It happened ages ago. The home was shut down soon after and was turned into the council offices. But the vaults are still there. It's just a patch of grass now, to be honest. There's a major issue with subsidence, so nobody dares build on it. But then, nobody *wants* to build on it. 'Course, the locals say the place is haunted with all the ghosts of the children.'

'Kids died down there?' Matt said. 'It wasn't just abuse?'

'Just abuse? You really just said that?'

'You know what I mean.'

'Nobody died, officially,' Bob said. 'But of course there's always rumours. Suspicions.'

Matt sat, thinking quietly.

'So has Rachel told you why the vaults are mentioned on this sheet?'

He shook his head, 'She didn't mention this at all.'

'Well, the abuse case happened way before any of those girls were born, so I don't see how—'

Matt was on his feet and walking toward the lift already.

'We're going?' Larry pushed himself up.

'She's on Ward 12.' He reached the lift and started jabbing at the button.

* * *

The hospital had given her a private room, but when Matt and Larry arrived they found she wasn't alone. In fact, they were all there. All the big names.

Bob and Joyce Hodges were sitting closest. They were right by Rachel's bedside, holding her hand and talking to her about something. Mary Wasson was in the corner, sitting in a tub chair and quietly stroking the arm of it, like a cat. And Kassy West was up at the window, leaning against the frame and gazing out. They all turned their heads when Matt and Larry tapped on the door.

He saw Rachel attempt a smile as they came inside. 'Hi. Thanks for bringing my mum last night.'

'No problem.'

Mary Wasson put her hand up. 'If you don't mind, I'd like some air.'

Larry looked at Matt. They both nodded at the same time.

'That'd be fine, Mrs Wasson. Go ahead.' Larry waited till she toddled out, then he turned back to Rachel. 'So how are you feeling?'

'My throat hurts, but they're letting me out this afternoon.'

'Well, I'm glad to hear—'

'Rachel?' Matt cut him off completely.

'Yes?'

'What did you do to Holly?'

A shocked whisper, a long pause. '. . . *what do you mean?*'

He glanced up at Kassy. She'd lost colour. The Hodges were looking at one another, confused. Larry said nothing, just waited.

'You and the girls . . .' He pulled out the seance sheet and dropped it on her lap. 'What happened at the vaults?'

She stared at it for a very long time and when she looked at Bob and Joyce, her eyes glistened with tears. 'Please don't hate me.'

CHAPTER THIRTY-NINE

'Holly didn't really fit in. She wasn't like us . . .' Rachel finally said, as Larry sat into Mary's tub chair and Matt sat onto the end of the bed. 'She wasn't just nine but she was like a young nine. She still talked about Disney and angels and fairies . . .'

'Holly was a space cadet,' Kassy said, her back pressed against the window. 'But me and the girls were fourteen and already getting drunk and smoking in the park at that stage. But Holly was still obsessed with *The Faraway Tree* and shit like that.'

Bob frowned at her. At the swearing, but Kassy went on.

'She actually believed that magic stuff, so she was gullible too,' Kassy said. 'We told her there was an angel at the bottom of her garden once and we said that it loved Britney Spears songs, so Holly sat there warbling "Lucky" for an hour, waiting for it to come. An *hour*. I'm not even making that up.'

'While we watched her from my bedroom, laughing . . .' Rachel pulled her gaze from Kassy. 'Though when it was just me and Holly it was fine. I mean really good. I played games with her, we talked. We went on walks in the park and sat under . . .' she paused. 'The tree that Jo . . .' The sudden memory of that burning hanging corpse turned the fear in her face to something closer to shock. She gripped her elbow. 'Jesus. Holly always said that tree was special to her. That particular tree.'

Bob made a note of that. 'Interesting.'

'So, hang on, Rachel,' Kassy said. 'You were nice to her when she was alone, but as soon as *we* all turn up you treat her like a little dweeb? Great sister you are,' she tutted to herself. 'Were.'

'Dammit, Kassy!' Matt glared at her. 'Do you have any sort of filter?'

A tear rolled down Rachel's cheek.

Larry pulled out a small blue notebook and pencil. He cracked the spine back. 'Carry on, please.'

'No. Kassy's right. She's absolutely right cos that's how it was.'

'Listen.' Matt leant forward. 'Siblings get at each other, that's what they do. I've got a sister and we used to give each other hassle all the time. It's not great but it's not weird either.'

'You don't get it . . .' Her lips turned a little thinner, shoulders creeping higher. She was opening up like a door and letting the light in. But he could tell that with this opening came an old, bitter cold. She looked at Kassy for a few seconds, as if for confirmation, and he was sure he saw Kassy shiver. Convinced of it. Even if it was for a second. No smiles, no wisecracks.

'It's good to say it,' Joyce suddenly said. 'It's better.'

So Rachel turned back to Matt.

'I think you need to get this out,' he said.

She swallowed, then an entire minute later, she spoke.

'It was Halloween. 2001. September the 11th had just happened the month before so people kept talking like the world was going to end. We still went out trick-or-treating and we let Holly come with us. To be honest we were all being really nice to her for a

273

change. Me and the girls had this talk about how crappy we were being. People in the world were crashing aeroplanes into buildings and for some reason it was making everyone a bit nicer. Including us. And back then, if you were a kid on Halloween, you'd go to the vaults on Kirchin Road.'

Joyce gave a little gasp.

'Matthew might not know exactly what the vaults are,' Bob said.

Larry flicked his hand. 'He knows. Carry on.'

She nodded. 'So we took Holly to the vaults. She'd never been there before.'

'Why did you take her?' Matt said. 'To scare her?'

'Yes, but not in a bad way. Like, it was to help her grow up a bit. We were all planning on scaring *ourselves*, not just her. That's what Halloween's about. We just wanted to include Holly for a change.'

'We invited her,' Kassy said. 'Told her it was a night of being afraid and she was up for it.'

'She was nervous, but I think she was more excited we let her in on something. We were all dressed up in these tacky witches' hats and plastic brooms that we bought from the market. Apart from Holly—'

'Who of course wanted to be an angel,' Kassy added, with a tut.

'She wore this little white dress and some white wings she'd made from some feathers she'd picked up in the park. Took her all week – cost her money too. It was the prettiest thing I'd ever seen . . .' Rachel looked down at her lap. 'That night was a big deal to her, because we let her into the group.'

Kassy turned and stared out of the window.

'Anyway, we all had torches and chocolate and we were laughing. We had drink too: cider, mostly. Holly even tried a bit but she almost choked on it. She seemed really happy that night. Happiest I remember seeing her. God we were all laughing *a lot*.'

Kassy nodded, silently.

'Those vaults . . .' Rachel said. 'They're fenced off now, but back then it was just chicken wire, so people got through. But they're still all locked up with metal hatches. They look like manhole covers in the ground. You can't actually get inside and climb down so most kids just hover around the top, listening out for ghosts, looking through the cracks in the hatches and doing Ouija boards till the police move you on. Stuff like that. When we got there nobody was around, but we went late, like ten or something. Only we noticed one of the hatches actually looked loose . . .' Rachel stopped talking suddenly, as if the air was growing thinner and she didn't have enough to get her words out. She started scratching the inside of her arm.

Kassy turned back from the window. 'Some kids must have prised it open earlier and ran off. So we thought what the hell, and we all yanked it open. It took some doing but there were a bunch of us. When we flipped it up we saw this metal ladder going down, bolted to the wall.'

'Tell me you didn't go down . . .' Bob suddenly said.

Kassy frowned. ''Course we did.'

'On a powerful night like that? To a place like that?' Joyce started shaking her head. 'This is madness.'

'Yeah, anyway . . .' Kassy brushed Joyce away with her hand. 'We were having a laugh. Holly was too. But when we all clambered down to the bottom it was like pitch-black, and to be honest, even *I* got freaked out. We had a look around the place but it's pretty much just a hole in the ground, with old brick walls that don't look safe.'

'The vaults are condemned,' Bob said. 'For Pete's sake, there are signs all over them.'

'I *know* that,' Kassy said. 'Place looks like you could kick it and it'd crumble. It's bigger than we thought but there's sod all to see down there. A few locked metal doors, which we tried but not much else. Great for a ghost story, though. We had our lighters out but to be honest it didn't take long before we all started to spaz out a bit. Like it wasn't that fun any more, once we were down the ladder. People started talking about what happened there, in the past.'

Matt said, 'And Holly?'

'Oh, she was fine. She loved being down there, which is pretty weird when you—'

'God, Kassy, it wasn't the place. You *know* it wasn't the place. She was happy cos she was with us . . .' Rachel almost smiled. 'She was just playing along with the Halloween vibe. She started slapping a few of us on the back, to scare us, which wasn't funny at all, but she thought she was doing the right thing. Only it was just *too* scary down there, knowing the history. I think she thought we were pretending to be scared, like it was all part of the fun. Anyway, she started making ghost noises and stuff. Said some strange things.'

'Such as?' Larry asked.

'She said animals spoke to her sometimes. Said they told her things that were going to happen, before they happened.'

'The mood sort of changed,' Rachel said.

'Steph climbed up the ladder first,' Kassy said. 'She was going to wet her pants, she was so petrified. To be honest, I wasn't as bothered about it but then Jo climbed up so I did too.'

Rachel was sitting up in her bed, looking beyond the room, through the wall, like the entire scene was playing out in the air around her. 'I told Holly to stop trying to be scary, that it wasn't funny any more, but she kept waving her hands about. So I told her to grow up and I crawled up the ladder.'

'Didn't she follow you up?' Matt asked.

'She was still down there in the dark. She made odd noises like grunts and . . . when I looked back down, she was on all fours.'

'She knew what she was doing,' Kassy said. 'She was trying to get back at us for treating her like crap. Either that or she was totally insane, which is possible, considering how she ended up . . .' She trailed off when Matt stared at her again.

Rachel shook her head. 'She *wasn't* insane. She was just doing what we wanted. A night of laughs and scares. That's exactly how we'd sold it to her. We were all at the top of the ladder, looking at each other, feeling freaked out, while Holly was whooping and whispering down there. I went to call her back up but . . . well . . . I don't know what happened . . .' Rachel was leaning forward in her bed, arms hugging her knees. 'I don't talk about this.'

'Rachel,' Joyce said, 'it's time.'

She squeezed her knees a little tighter and said, 'Everyone just looked at each other and someone said let's close the hatch. Kassy, I think.'

'Excuse me?' Kassy tilted her head. 'Babe, that was you.'

Rachel's eyes sank to the floor, whispering, 'I thought it was you.'

'It doesn't matter who said it, just . . . did you?' Matt said. 'Did you close it?'

'We kept looking at each other, me and Kass and the others and I don't know why, maybe because we were all in fancy dress and looked so bloody ridiculous with the hats and stuff, but we started laughing and cackling and swigging the cider down, faster than we'd ever drunk it before. I was pretty drunk anyway, but it was a tension release, I think. Like it was us being us again, just the four of us. Holly was still doing new freaky noises down there. So we just wanted to do something that might be funny and not scary. Someone threw one of the plastic brooms down at her and it hit her in the shoulder . . .'

'Yeah, we shut it,' Kassy said, her voice far softer than before. 'Then we ran away—'

'. . . and we just kept on running.'

'You *left* her down there?' Bob said. 'A nine-year-old in that place, in the dark?'

In. The. Dark.

Matt assembled his face. 'How long?'

'I don't remember,' Rachel said.

'*How long?*'

'Take it easy, Matt,' Bob said.

'I was so drunk, I'm not sure. Twenty minutes maybe . . . half an hour?'

'Oh, an hour at least,' Kassy said.

Rachel stiffened. Larry jotted something down in his book.

'Look, Rachel was drunk and could barely walk, so we took her home. Then eventually me and the others went back and got Holly out. We walked her back to Barley Street. She was fine, just quiet. Just very, very quiet . . .' Kassy trailed off, and bit her lip nervously. 'But, hey, every kid has a moment like that. It's a rite of passage.'

'No it fucking isn't!' Rachel slammed her palm down on the mattress. Particles of dust danced in the air. Her eyes were brimming. 'Think! She hung herself a week after us turning on her, Kassy. One week later she was dead.'

Silence.

'And the poltergeist?' Matt said, quietly.

'I thought she might have staged it. Like it was some sort of cry for help . . . but even then . . . even then nobody really listened to her . . .' Rachel put her face into her hands.

Kassy shook her head. 'That wasn't our fault. I've told you that.'

'Wasn't it?' She glared at Kassy, then turned to Matt. '*Wasn't* it?'

She seemed to be asking him for the correct answer. So after a moment, he found his most honest thought and laid it out. 'If someone did that to my daughter, I'd come down on them like a ton of bricks.'

'See?' Rachel looked at Kassy. 'We might as well have strung her up our—'

'*But* . . .' Matt said, 'Are you to blame for her death? Of course you aren't. You don't even know if that was the reason. Or at least the *main* reason. You didn't plan on this.'

She stared at him.

'And you've all kept this secret, for all these years?'

'Yes,' Kassy said. 'But that doesn't mean it's our fault she killed herself.'

Rachel said nothing. She just stared at the window and the clouds that were gathering outside.

'Rachel,' Matt said. 'Maybe you telling us this . . . might be the first step in letting this go. Somehow.'

Her eyes flickered, like she was zoning in and out of the room. 'You can't tell my mum. You can't, you just *can't*.'

There was silence for a while and Matt turned to see if Mary might be pressed against the glass window, taking it all in. She wasn't.

'You need a hug.' Joyce pushed herself up and moved towards Rachel. She slipped her arms around her and pushed her lips close to Rachel's ear. 'You're not to blame, poppet. You're not to blame.'

Now her resistance broke fully. Rachel crumbled against her as the wrinkled, vein-strewn hand patted and stroked the back of her head. He saw Joyce pucker her thin lips and kiss Rachel on the scalp, holding her mouth there for long seconds, eyes closed. And when Rachel spoke again it was through the sobs into Joyce's neck. 'The last thing I remember that night . . . was waking up to find Holly right by my bed, but,' she sniffed, 'she wasn't looking at me. She didn't even look angry, though I know she must have been furious. She was just sitting on the floor of my room.' She wiped her eyes with the heel of her hand, but her cheeks grew instantly wet again. 'And she was drawing all these pictures with crayons. Loads and loads of pictures. Sheets scattered all around the carpet . . .'

'Pictures of what?' Matt asked.

'Stick figures, really childish, even though I knew she could draw better than that. But I could tell who they were supposed to be. They were us; me and the girls and . . .' a tremble ran through her. 'In every picture, twenty of them, maybe thirty, she'd drawn a tall black shape next to it. A black shape with long ears in all of them, holding her hand. And then she finally spoke . . .'

Matt waited. 'What did she say?'

Rachel suddenly stopped crying and her voice sounded measured and clear. Like this was the only conclusion that made sense. 'Holly just said . . . *rabbit's coming . . . rabbit's coming.*' She looked at Matt, but this time her eyes were saying – *are you getting this now, Matt? Are you starting to believe?*

'I thought we'd driven her crazy,' she said, 'and the poltergeist was some mad, lonely thing she did herself. But after all that's happened . . . I think she must have picked something up in the vaults.' She looked at Joyce. 'Some entity?'

'I think that's very, very likely,' Joyce whispered. 'In fact, this makes a lot of sense.'

'Does it, now?' Larry said, closing his book.

'Yes . . . I believe Holly's anger at what happened that night is fuelling the negative energy and the chaos that's reigning all around us. Sometimes pain, hurt and anger can manifest into a living spirit.'

'Oh, come on,' Matt said. 'A ghost or demon or malignant bloody whatever didn't set fire to Jo Finch last night. But somebody did. Somebody dangerous.'

'Or something . . .' Rachel said.

He gawped and stared at her. 'You cannot still . . .'

Of all the emotions he could have shared with Rachel at that moment, snarling disappointment shouldn't have been one of them. He couldn't help it, though. He stared at her like a fish he'd caught that wasn't up to standard. He quickly changed his expression: went all pastoral again. 'Look, I understand that you're upset. Who wouldn't be, but—'

Too late.

She looked away from him, shaking her head.

'Miss Wasson. Matt's quite right,' Larry said. 'It's sensible to deal with the practical matters first. And the fact is we have a real-life crime on our—'

'And completely ignore the fact that something happened in that seance?' Rachel glared at him. '*Something* set the alarms off.'

Matt threw up his hands. 'That was the cross coming through the window!'

'So what made the school bell ring?'

'Someone must have grabbed it.'

'And what spoke through Joyce?'

'These can all be explained naturally.'

'Oh, can they? And how do I explain the fact that I saw some sort of monster on my roof when I was a kid? And how do I explain what I feel?'

He waited. 'And what do you feel?'

'I feel . . .' Her anger slid away for a moment. Now she looked at him with a look of such dread, it made the room feel instantly cold and horribly small. 'I feel this darkness. This thick, thick darkness . . . and it's been with me ever since that night. But now it's creeping around me every single second I walk in this town. I think Holly wants to hurt me,' she looked at Kassy, 'and hurt us. Maybe what's happening is . . . payback.'

Matt looked, and spoke as softly as he could. 'That darkness you feel . . . it's shame, Rachel. It's regret. And it's normal.'

'Yeah? And how normal is the timing?' Rachel said. 'Because it's Halloween tonight, Matt. *Tonight.*'

Kassy leant forward. 'You should listen to him.'

'Look . . . even if a person did do that to Jo . . . that's not even the point,' Joyce suddenly said. 'It's what's *fuelling* them. Something spiritual, something negative is driving whoever it is to—'

'Aw, come off it Joyce . . . you didn't even figure out what happened to Holly until Rachel told us.'

'Didn't I?' Joyce pulled Rachel closer to her chest. Patting her like a mother would.

Kassy, who'd been quiet for a while, saw the gesture and shook her head.

Larry checked his watch and caught Matt's gaze. Not quite an eye roll, but enough to say that the info unfurling here was a little too spectral to matter much.

'I know what must be done,' Joyce said. 'We need to contact Holly again and let Rachel express her sorrow. Her regret.'

Larry was on his feet. 'You want to finish the seance?'

'Yes. Only, this time Rachel can finally be honest about all of this. She can ask for forgiveness and stop the cycle. I'm sure it will help.' Joyce looked up at Kassy. 'You should be there, too. To apologise.'

'Hey, no way, I'm done,' Kassy said. 'We told the truth, so how about we just leave it at that?'

Bob walked towards Kassy at the window. 'Don't you think you should be supporting your friend right—'

'Get away from me,' Kassy shouted. 'Don't you dare tell me what to do.'

Bob's jaw dropped. He stopped walking. Everybody stared.

'Spend a lot of time with Holly, did you?' Kassy said.

'I beg your pardon?'

'The two of you,' she nodded at Joyce. 'Spend a lot of time with Holly . . . by herself? And now you can hug her sister too.'

'What the hell is that supposed to mean?' Bob stepped forward.

'Don't even think about touching me, you old man.'

'Calm down, Miss West,' Larry said, frowning. 'Just sit down and we'll—'

'We've told the truth.' Kassy turned and hurried to the door. 'End of.'

'Wait . . .' Rachel called after her. 'What about what happened to Steph? And Jo?'

Kassy paused with her fingers on the handle, then she turned to Larry. 'Just some random psycho who's cruising through town. Who the police should be chasing right now, rather than sitting around listening to campfire tales.' She pushed the door open. 'I'm done, Rach. See you at the funerals.' She vanished into the corridor, calling out behind her, 'Assuming you bother to turn up.'

'Let her go,' Joyce said. 'Let her go.'

Larry got up. 'I'll go after her.'

The door closed, and Matt turned back to see Rachel's face. Now it was a white skull, washed out with stress. He was seeing in action the rationale behind her never wanting to come back to Menham again. Because guilt isn't just a ghost. It's a vampire. One that feeds eagerly and deeply. The longer she stayed away from this town, the longer she could pretend it wasn't there. But it was.

'How soon can we get a seance together?' she said, quietly.

What Matt said next made the others stare at him. 'No.'

Joyce frowned. 'I beg your pardon?'

'It's too risky. Whoever threw that cross at your house might be the same person who killed Jo.'

'But . . . we made contact—'

'Look, I don't know what's going on here, but I think you and Kassy need to get out of Menham.'

'And that's the solution to everything, is it Matthew? To run?' Joyce held his gaze for a long moment. Like she was pulling out a file in his mind.

He looked away from her.

'A door has been opened, and it needs to be closed.'

When he turned back, Rachel was pulling her recorder from her bedside. 'And how do you explain this?'

Bob coughed. 'You're familiar with electronic voice phenomenon?'

Matt nodded, but didn't add the fact that he often used examples of EVP as an opener to his lecture on gullibility and confirmation bias.

She clicked play, and voices of the seance filled the room. She kept playing the same part over and over. The bit with her saying, in the dark, in the dark.

'Can't you hear it, in the background? That little whisper?'

'Saying what?'

'Saying the vault, the vault, the vault,' she said. 'It's Holly. Listen again.'

She played it a few more times. He heard nothing but movement in the background, maybe a casual sniff or breath in and out. It was a typical EVP, the paranormal poster child for apophenia. A random noise, being shoehorned into saying something spookily coherent. Even the Hodges didn't seem quick to defend it.

Exasperated, Matt finally said the sentence he'd been sitting on. 'This is madness.'

She looked at Matt for a few seconds with an expression he couldn't quite understand: a drawing together of her eyebrows and a baffled little gasp. 'You haven't heard a single thing I've said, have you? I've just shared my worst moment and . . . you haven't even listened.'

Bob was on his feet. 'I think you better leave, Matt.'

'Can't you people see the danger? Don't you have a duty of care?'

'You people?' Joyce chuckled. 'Why do you even fear us mediums and psychics if you don't believe?'

'Oh, it isn't fear, it's—'

'The same thing that fuelled centuries of persecution of gifted people,' Joyce was shouting now. 'A few hundred years ago, people like you would have thrown people like me in a river to see if they float. They'd have searched me for the Devil's mark, wouldn't they? Got a history of that round here, you know. But nobody seems to realise that it wasn't the churches that did that sort of thing. The main persecutors were the scientists. The *clever* men. They feared people like me and wanted us gone, because we didn't fit into their frameworks. As you no doubt want us gone.'

'You are totally missing the point.'

Bob was already seizing Matt's elbow and dragging him out to the corridor, while Rachel was leaning into Joyce, who was kissing her hair again.

Joyce caught his eye and mouthed the words, *Go away.*

'Sorry it turned out this way,' Bob opened the door, 'but we'll keep her safe.'

Matt went to say something but didn't bother, because he realised how pointless it all was. Instead he stomped out, slamming the door shut with exasperation. He heard a clicking sound, but didn't bother looking back. He knew it was the blinds being shut with a snap.

He found Larry halfway down the corridor, on the phone.

Larry nodded up to Rachel's room. 'Those cruel little shits. Throwing a little girl down there of all places.'

Matt said, 'Did you catch Kassy?'

'No, she slipped into the crowd. Not much of a fan of the Hodges, is she?'

'Neither am I. They think they're helping but they're programming that girl and they don't even know it. She isn't mentally stable enough for this.'

'I spoke to her doctor. He's about to discharge her. She'll be back in Barley Street within the hour . . .'

Matt tutted and shook his head. 'So . . . what happens now?'

'I'll get some officers to keep an eye out over there. But, now we try a little real-world stuff,' he said. 'I'm going back to Jo's house.'

'Why?'

'I've had Keech go back in there, to dig a bit deeper. He just called.'

'And?'

'He's found a bottle of her piss.'

'Pardon?'

'A plastic bottle, half-filled with urine. He just got word back that it was Jo's. It was in her rabbit hutch.'

For the first time all morning, Matt allowed himself a laugh, because his psyche desperately craved one. 'Well, this is just the gift that keeps on giving, isn't it?'

Larry wasn't laughing. 'Found a knitting needle too. Any ideas?'

Matt started buttoning up his jacket, slowly. Thinking. 'Not yet . . . but I should like to see that bottle of urine.'

Larry sniffed as they walked to their cars. 'You always were a weirdo.'

CHAPTER FORTY

There was something under the wiper of his car.

Matt frowned as he crossed the hospital car park. He looked up for Larry, but he'd parked up at the maternity bay, closer to the building. He'd already climbed in and was pulling away with a squeak of tyres.

He turned back to his car where a slip of paper was flapping against the screen, like a trapped fish. Yay, he thought, a parking ticket, that's all he needed. Any other time he'd have muttered some expletive under his breath, but as he grew closer he was confused by the shape of it. It was folded many times into a long thin strip. Perhaps it was one of those adverts about making a small fortune at home, stuffing envelopes. Maybe he should read it. Preparation in case that book of his didn't sell.

He teased it out carefully and spotted it was printer paper. He leant against the bonnet, looking back over at the hospital as he scrolled the sheet open. The printed writing was small, in the world's most demonic font: Comic Sans. He paused.

What the hell is this?

He flicked his eyes up immediately, looking to see if anybody shifty was lurking nearby; someone who might have been creeping near his car. A spindly marionette of an old woman, a patient, stood outside one of the entrances. She was wearing an obvious wig and was gripping onto an IV drip with one skeletal hand while puffing in cancer smoke with the other. Two hospital porters were giggling and panting as they lugged huge bags of toilet rolls out of a van. But there was nobody really dodgy looking, near the car.

Dear 'Reverend', it said.

'Reverend' being in inverted commas.

Last night in Barley Street, certain enemies of God were summoning the forces of Satan. A man with your history should be well aware that arousing Black Magic power is nothing short of heresy, and it has been noted, with disappointment, that you seem to be a co-conspirator with these witches and wizards. Not just observing, but desiring. While the battle rages for the soul of this town, you are courting the High Priests of Set who have a Satanic agenda to trick the holy, poison the heart and corrupt children. Please understand that such people will not go unchallenged by the Lord.

And so, with all this in mind, a prayer . . .

'Lucifer, we order you, we instruct you, we compel you to go, and in the authoritative name of the Lord Jesus Christ . . . leave this town for good.'

He read it over four times. He flipped the sheet, looked over the edges and even sniffed it because that's what detectives in movies probably did, to check for a clue. Perhaps he'd get a whiff of the coconut aftershave that Pastor Todd was wearing the other day.

There was nothing to smell or see. No scrawled sign-off saying Yours Truly: The Phoenix Club.

He ran his eyes down it, one more time.

Last night, in Barley Street, certain enemies of God were summoning the forces of Satan . . . witches and wizards!

Okay. So these witches and wizards were the Hodges and the Wassons. He'd worked that out. He ran his fingers down the sheet.

While the battle rages for the soul of this town, you are courting the High Priests of Set who have a Satanic agenda to trick the holy, poison the heart and corrupt children.

He tapped his finger on it again.

To corrupt children . . .

The sudden footfall of shoes on gravel crackled out from behind him. He flicked his head back to an alley leading off down a slope. Footsteps, running away.

He sprang off the bonnet, racing past the skinny old lady, but when he got to the mouth of the alley it looked long, but it was very empty, except for some wheelie bins and a lamp post that seemed to be making a buzzing, crackling sound. He presumed it was dodgy electrics until he spotted the dead sparrow at the bottom of it, open ribcage quaking and rippling with slowly moving flies.

What . . . so was the bird a message too? Another dead animal to add to the list?

He looked at the carcass for longer than he needed and glanced back up at the hospital. He wanted to waltz up to that ward again, push open Rachel's door and shake the note in their faces: *See? See what you're up against?*

But instead he just popped open one of the wheelie bins and fished out an empty Tesco Metro carrier bag. He knelt down and plucked the bird from the ground. Wincing, he shook the flies out of it as they darted toward his face and hair. He spat, spluttered his lips and wafted them away. Then he walked toward the car, carrying the bird in the bag, like he'd bought small groceries. The entire time, the old lady in the wig had watched it all. She was so shocked that she'd stopped sucking on her cigarette and was staring at him open-mouthed.

'How about I buy you a sarnie, son? From the machine.'

'Huh?'

Her eyes were full of heartbroken concern as she gazed at the bag with the dead bird in it. 'Man loses his pride, what's he got left? So don't reduce yourself to this.'

CHAPTER FORTY-ONE

Officer Keech led him through the hallway and kitchen. Jo's old familiar photographs gazed down at Matt, but he made a conscious choice not to look at them. He'd only see a burnt face and a gaping burrowed cheek staring out.

'This way,' Keech said, raking his ginger fringe away from his barely visible eyebrows.

He stepped out of the back door and walked directly into the wind. It had brewed up over lunchtime and was now swaying the trees, bushes and hairdos of Menham with mischievous abandon. Larry had arrived a few minutes earlier, so was already standing at the bottom of the path, and his tie seemed to be having a blast in the weather. It would sometimes swing and rise, like someone with a reed pipe was sitting cross-legged in the garden, charming it.

The garden was overgrown and scattered with angel ornaments. Jo's daughter, Seren, was still staying with her grandfather, but Matt noticed her twitching pink Frisbee lying in the grass and a set of Velcro pads with a ball stuck to them lying next to it. He could picture Jo and Lee sitting out here after work, supping a beer and playing lawn games, talking about their day. And Lee would be doing dad-type things with a little girl that wasn't his. Memories flashed of Matt doing the exact same with Lucy. Scenes of it filled his mind that felt like minutes ago, not years.

Keech led him to the bottom of the path and Larry glanced at the plastic bag dangling from Matt's fingers. 'You brought takeaway?'

'It's a dead bird.'

'A what?'

'I appreciate guests usually bring wine.'

Larry and Keech waited for a moment while Matt told his story. Larry read the note quickly and groaned as he did it. He called one of the officers over. A policewoman with freckles on one cheek, but not the other. 'Check this animal out, will you?'

'Will do,' she nodded.

'And use gloves.'

'Er . . . of course.' She hooked her fingers under the bag and toddled off, dead bird swinging.

'Right,' Larry turned to Keech. '*You* . . . fire away.'

'Okay, since Jo's body was found we've been back over this house, like you asked.'

'Good. Did you find any more fingerprints?' Larry patted his tie down.

'It's mainly just Jo, Lee and the kid's prints all over the house.'

'Show us this bottle, then.'

'Come to the hutch.'

They walked to the end of the garden, where a rickety-looking wooden hutch sat.

'You didn't search this last time?' Matt asked.

Keech said nothing, looking awkward.

'When Jo was just missing we didn't think much of her having an empty hutch,' Larry said. 'We figured she used to have a rabbit, or was planning on getting one. But ever since hers wound up a co-victim' – he said that with no hint of sarcasm – 'I asked them to have a closer look.'

'And?'

The hutch was old and flimsy, with some caked bird crap crusting on the side. Larry leant over and tapped the stiff little peg lock. The door sprang open like something invisible was leaping out of it. The breeze made the straw of the hutch tremble.

'We found these two things buried under the straw.' Keech nodded to one of the other officers, who brought over a chrome flight case. He popped the catches and opened it up. Inside, wrapped in a transparent bag, was a small bottle of Evian. Only what was in it didn't look much like spring water. It was yellow.

'This was in the hutch. I could tell straight away what it was. Like I said, turns out it was hers.'

Larry turned to Matt. 'So, Professor. Explain that, would you?'

Matt waited for a few moments, then nodded at the case. 'Is that the knitting needle?'

'Yeah,' Keech pulled out a long transparent evidence bag, sealed at the top. He lifted it and shook the bag. 'It had blood on it, sir. We got the results back along with the bottle.' Keech was looking pleased with himself. 'It is, without a doubt, Jo Finch's blood. They clocked a perfect DNA match with her corpse.'

Larry frowned for a second and took the bag. Staring at the pointed end of the needle.

'What is it?' Matt said.

He lifted the bag and turned it.

'Larry? What *is* it?'

'Bochenski said there were holes in her.'

'What?'

'Remember? He logged it as just fire damage.' Larry shifted his step a moment. 'He said there were holes in her body.'

'Where exactly?' Keech said.

'You're right . . .' Matt blinked as his brain started to whir and buzz. 'Around the left nipple.'

'Urgh.' Keech pulled a face and pointed his finger at the end of the needle. 'Well, the blood only covered the tip really, boss. So if *this* made those holes it wasn't pushed in that far. Just a little jab.'

Matt chewed the corner of his thumb. Something he'd done since he was a kid, whenever he needed thinking time. There was an idea in him, bubbling slowly to the surface.

'So basically,' Larry said, 'someone stabbed her with this thing?'

'Looks that way,' Keech nodded.

Matt looked off into the air pondering it, feeling his thoughts shimmering out of the shadows. In fact, he did that for a long moment. Long enough for the other two to stare at each other and shrug.

'Matt?' Larry said.

'You mean they pricked her with it?' He started pacing across the garden. 'That's what you mean. They *pricked* her.'

Keech shrugged. 'Pricked, stabbed, whatever . . .'

'With a needle . . .' Matt stared at the hutch, thinking. Something brewing in the chambers of his brain, turning it over as the chilly breeze swept across Jo's garden. The trees around them swayed gently and he looked up into the sky at the fast-moving clouds. In another garden somewhere, a dog had started barking angrily into the wind.

'Well?' Larry said.

'The picture,' Matt said. 'The woodcut from her bedroom door. The one of the flood. Do you have it?'

Larry nodded at another officer who came over with a plastic file. 'There's a copy in there.'

Matt pulled the sheet out. The paper flapped against his hand. 'And kill their animals . . .' he finally said, and stared at the woodcut on the front. At heads drowning in the water. At what he'd assumed was wooden debris, cracking over their heads.

That wasn't debris.

He counted four heads . . . all women.

'What are you thinking?' Larry said.

'This . . .' He tapped on the paper. 'This wasn't a flood. This picture isn't a flood.'

'What are you talking about?'

'This isn't a flood . . .' Matt let his hand fall to his side. 'Holy shit.'

'What?'

A second dog joined the other, and as the barks grew, another.

'Pricking the skin. Killing the pets.'

'English, Matt. *English*.'

'Then hanging her on a bloody gallows tree? Burning her? I'm an idiot . . . it's so blatant . . .' Matt scraped a hand through his hair and gave out an exasperated groan. 'The urine.'

'Just bloody well speak, will you?'

'This town . . .' Matt said, as the dogs howled. 'Joyce said it used to kill witches.'

CHAPTER FORTY-TWO

Girls and rabbit run together.
That's the way it's always been.
Never been a one for men,
It's
Female hands and female friends,
That
Rub the rabbit,
Make him run
Make him swift and
Make him fast.

Paws are aching, snapping back
Sack and sugar, tall and black.
Even when he weeps to scurry.
He shouts Stop!
But they scream,
hurry.

CHAPTER FORTY-THREE

It felt surreal, sinking into Jo Finch's white leather couch, around a coffee table displaying needles, urine and a mondo piece of centuries-old art.

Matt glanced down at the picture again and the drowning women. The objects behind their heads were *not* debris from a flood, but the solid wooden planks of the ducking stool. Alongside it, the note from his car sat unfurled.

Larry pulled his notepad open. 'So . . . I'm listening.'

'Okay. This is pretty wild, but bear with me,' Matt said. 'People have been killing suspected witches for thousands of years, but it exploded across Europe and America in the sixteenth, seventeenth century. Now you have to understand that this was a legally sanctioned, religiously justified series of trials, tests and executions.'

Larry was listening and breathing slowly.

'People used to think a way to find a witch was by pricking her skin with a pin or a needle. They had these special tools to do it called . . . erm . . .' He looked up to the left . . . searched the files, '*Bodkins*, that was it. Bodkins. It was a pretty common method. Also witches were thought to use all sorts of animals back then. Not just black cats but dogs, foxes, toads . . . and of course, rabbits.' He had a sudden flash of that old picture he saw the other night in his cabin. Of witch-finder Matthew Hopkins and the black rabbit walking on its hind legs as an accused witch confessed its name: Sack and Sugar. 'These animals were thought to be gifts from the Devil. Helpers. They called them familiars.'

'I've heard of that,' Larry said. 'They were like little demons. Didn't the witches supposedly breastfeed them?'

Keech screwed up his face. 'You knew *that*, sir?'

'Shoot me. I get the History Channel.'

'You're right. People thought witches' breast milk was a source of power for these demon animals. Suckling familiars, they were called. That's why the witch-finders would often prick the nipples . . . It was a bizarre test they came up with.'

Larry blinked.

'Anyway. Sometimes communities wanted to destroy the familiar and not just the witch. And here we are with a dead rabbit and a dead swan.'

'And a dead dog,' Larry said.

'Er . . . hang on fellas,' Keech said. 'Steph Ellis's dog was beaten to death by a bunch of parents.'

'Precisely,' Matt said. 'But whoever left her dog in there *knew* it'd get the blame and be destroyed. Even though it might have been this other white dog that actually did it. Either way, Steph was dead, and her dog was dead. Witch and familiar . . .' he opened the fingers on one hand, '*gone.*'

Larry twisted his mouth. 'This is pretty out there, Matt.'

Matt smiled through his teeth. 'I appreciate that. But what we do have is two dead women and a needle for pricking. We have medieval symbols of Christian protection against evil, plastered on the crimes scenes. Plus, we have something we didn't pay enough attention to before . . . two dead pets.'

'Explain the bottle of whizz, then,' Keech said.

Matt sat forward, palms together. 'Okay . . . these witch-finders, they had a lot of weird tests, not just pricking. But I think when you hear this you'll start seeing where I'm coming from. They used to collect the urine of girls that were under trial. They'd mix the urine with rye meal and they'd make a cake.'

Keech burst out laughing. 'Try that on *MasterChef*!'

'Dammit, Keech,' Larry snapped. 'Let the man speak.'

Matt waited for a few awkward seconds. 'It was a bizarre mix of almost voodoo and Cartesian medical theory.' He spotted their blank faces. 'You don't need to know what that means, but look, I know Church history. I teach it. Bottom line is they felt like the particles of the witch would still be in her fluids. I think they called it "effluvia". So they'd make a cake with her urine and let a dog eat it. If she felt pain when the dog ate the cake they'd have proof of effluvia, that she was somehow *in* the cake, which was proof she was a witch. Job done . . .' He trailed off when he saw Larry sitting up. 'What is it?'

'You know something? We found Steph Ellis's urine all over the floor of that music cupboard, mixed in with her blood.' Larry scribbled something down. 'We all just figured the shock made her . . . well, you know.'

Keech waited for a moment and when he spoke he was as serious as he could manage. 'I'm sorry but with respect this is the stupidest thing I've ever heard. I bet these girls just had weak bladders. And as for the killing of animals, well loads of serial killers do that. It's kind of their thing. The needle prick on her . . .' he trailed off. 'Well, she could have been one of those self-harmers.' He turned to Larry. 'I'm not saying we shouldn't look into this, sir, but I reckon you need to be extremely cautious about leaping onto this Hammer Horror thing. I mean I know it's Halloween and everything, but . . .'

'I do hear you,' Matt said. 'Plus this theory still doesn't explain what makes these particular girls so . . .'

'Punishable?' Larry said.

The word made Matt blink. 'Exactly. Look, these days, witches are just another faith group. They have conventions, specialist shops, they meet freely. No one tries to kill them, on the whole. Heck, they don't even believe in the Devil. But if you're looking for the witches' worst enemy, then you check the churches. Mainstream Christianity says it's a sin. Deuteronomy even says "you shall not suffer a witch to live".' He shifted in his seat. 'And what do you know, someone in Menham clearly has an issue with the occult because we had a ruddy great crucifix thrown through a window. And this weird note.'

'We check the churches, then,' Larry said.

Matt resisted the urge to say *just like I said last night*. Instead he said, 'Good idea, Larry.'

'We'll go together. And we can talk to these Phoenix blokes.' Larry slipped the note into his pocket. 'Me and you. But first, we tell the Hodges to call this seance off. We don't want to anger this nutter any more than he is already.'

'And Kassy? And Jo's boyfriend Lee?'

'Oh, I haven't forgotten about them. My guys will keep searching. We're not sure where Kassy is right now, but we'll find her and warn her.'

They walked toward the door, and paused only to turn back to Keech.

'Did people *really* piss in cakes, back in the day?'

Larry tutted.

Suddenly the other policewoman from before popped her head through the door. 'Sir? The bird?'

'Go ahead.'

'I had a look and I really don't see anything worrying. Looks like a cat got it. Or a rat.'

'Oh,' Matt said.

'You can tell. My little Tinker does that all the time. Brings them in and drops them on—'

'Fine,' Larry said. 'Bag it up properly and we'll confirm it later.'

Larry walked quickly to the front door, and Matt rushed to catch up. He clicked it open, and they both headed out onto the pavement outside, into the wild wind once again.

'Matt, this is a pretty whacky theory.'

'Not nearly as whacky as a dead girl and her demonic black rabbit killing everybody.'

'Let's just hope you're not just reading patterns into stuff that isn't there . . .'

Matt smiled. 'Touché.'

It was moving into late afternoon but this was the last night of October. And even though the sun was still up, Matt could see the early evening starting its sly creep over the buildings. It was moving slow, seeping through the street like a fine, black, barely visible gas. Shadows from the lamp post grew long and spindly in the dwindling, pink light as they both sank into Larry's car outside Jo's house. Other dogs were barking now, but were unseen. Larry turned the ignition and immediately Matt saw the street lights flicker into life, one after the other, in a weird domino effect down the long street. Some wild part of his brain was saying that the world was settling itself into place for something to happen. Which he knew was just his brain attaching dramatic significance to unrelated signifiers. The coming darkness, the lights, the howling wind, the shining eyes of pumpkins lit in windows, the fact that tonight was

Halloween. There was nothing inherently ominous in these things, and therefore his placing any narrative power on them was pure conjecture and pointless pattern finding.

Still though, despite himself, it felt like something bad was coming.

CHAPTER FORTY-FOUR

Larry nudged the car up onto the Barley Street kerb, right outside number 29, where Bob and Joyce were standing at the open boot of their car. The sound of Larry's engine made the two of them swivel around to look; Bob had some ancient-looking gizmo with dials and meters stuffed under his arm. Like he'd just burgled the BBC Radiophonic Workshop.

Matt and Larry clicked the doors open and stepped out at the same time.

'Oh, I see . . . I see how it is,' Bob said. 'We're under surveillance, now?'

'Where's Rachel?' Matt asked.

'Where do you think she is? She's right up there . . . getting things ready.' Bob nodded at Holly's window, still covered in cardboard from last night.

'Mr Hodges,' Larry said. 'There's been a development and it may be nothing, but I think it'd be a sensible idea to postpone your work tonight.'

'A development?' Bob raised an eyebrow. 'Well, we're all ears . . . aren't we, darling?'

Joyce nodded but she didn't say a word. She was too busy pawing at the dangling talisman round her neck, looking back at the house nervously.

Matt didn't like the look in her eye, and it sparked his feet to move. 'Rachel needs to hear it too.' He pushed through the gate and hurried up toward the door.

'Hey,' Bob called after him. 'What happened to respecting a lady's privacy?'

Matt ignored him and didn't bother knocking either. He pushed the door to Barley Street wide open and saw nothing but the empty hall, with its small windows and dull gloom. He thought he heard a soft voice coming from upstairs. He walked up, quietly.

Through the banisters he could see that Holly's door was shut tight and he wondered if Rachel might be in there. Maybe she'd be kneeling at her sister's little bed and begging for forgiveness. But as he moved across the landing he heard a gasp from behind him and he quickly spun around. The door to the bathroom was now wide open. Mary Wasson was in there, with what looked like a set of hairpins sticking out from her grey lips which were pressed hard together, and behind her he saw Rachel, her fringe swept back and tied up in two small, infantile bunches. The top she was wearing was an old-looking T-Shirt which looked a few sizes too small for her. It dug into the flesh of her arms. The front had the logo of an old band he remembered called Blink-182. Yet the weirdest part of all was clutched in her hands. A pointed black hat, the type you'd get in a fancy-dress shop, or in the Halloween aisle in a supermarket.

A witch's hat.

'Who let you in?' Rachel quickly grabbed a towel and pressed it against herself, like she was naked, even though she wasn't. Her face looked wrong too. He'd spotted she usually wore a little

304

make-up, but never as thick as this, never as juvenile-looking.

He frowned. 'What on earth are you doing?'

Mary beamed at him, and turned back to wedge another hairpin into Rachel's scalp. 'Might as well be fourteen again, don't you think?'

Just to make it clear that Matt and Larry were *not* invited to stay, they had the entire discussion in the downstairs hallway. Bob and Joyce stood by the banister, leaning elbows against it, while Mary and Rachel sat on the lower steps of the staircase, hands on their knees. It looked like the Wassons were the children and the Hodges were the parents, posing for a bizarre Christmas card shot.

Rachel had pulled a purple dressing gown on to hide her outfit, but she couldn't cover her hair and make-up, which even Larry frowned at. It turned out that the Hodges had insisted she dress in her old clothes, to recreate the feel of that Halloween night. The night – Joyce had insisted – that had brought 'the blackness' on Holly which would lead to her death a week later. Apparently making these kinds of connections would help create a 'true psychic bond' tonight. If Rachel looked like she did on the night of the vaults it would make it easier for Holly to seek her out 'in the spectral fog'. Such pseudo-scientific bullshit phrases made Matt want to throw up his hands and roar, but the fact that she was sitting on that step, doing what they'd told her, was tempering his anger with a sort of glum, depressed resignation. She looked bewildered.

So they all stood like that in the hall, while Larry and Matt laid out their witch theory. He mentioned that the hat she was holding might be an obvious link and he kept an eye on Rachel at regular intervals, her face moving between confusion and dread and back again, like a horrid dance was taking place in her psyche. The note he'd found on his windscreen seemed especially to put her on edge.

It took a long time before Bob said anything. 'Well, that's a fascinating hypothesis.'

Matt tried not to sound as jumpy as he actually was. 'And of course we might be wrong, but the evidence is pointing that way.'

'At least at the moment,' Larry added. 'And we need to find Kassy West too, to make sure she's okay. Do you know her whereabouts?'

He said it to Rachel but she shook her head.

'And you really think the seance might put these girls in danger?' Bob said.

'Don't *you*? Bob, the first time I saw you . . . outside the school that first morning,' Matt said. 'The Phoenix Club were there, remember?'

'*What a name . . .*' Bob laughed and shook his head. 'You mean the church group? Those prayer fellas?'

'Yes . . . and do you remember what they shouted at you? They shouted *witch* at you, right across the street. I mean, come *on*.'

Joyce waved veiny fingers in the air. 'Bob and I have had to put up with that sort of medieval prejudice for years, but it's a side issue. We can deal with it.'

'Oh, you reckon?'

Bob suddenly clapped his hands together, and he saw Rachel blink at the sudden snap. 'You've got to appreciate the irony here,' he said. 'You're so convinced that the cause of this is not paranormal and yet the theory you come up with is waaaay wilder and – if you don't mind me saying – not a little preposterous. So I'm sorry, but I can't call the seance off.'

'Oh, for crying out loud, Bob. Be reasonable.'

Larry raised a cautious hand. 'Matt . . .'

'Just give the police a few days at least—'

Bob took a step forward. 'I've been married to Joyce for forty years and I trust her judgment completely. Do you understand the word *completely*? She's convinced there's negative energies at work here – architects behind human agents, perhaps – but only she and I can stop it.'

'By apologising to Holly Wasson? By telling her to call off her big black bunny rabbit. So . . . do you think *Holly's* a malignant spirit now?'

'How dare you!' Rachel's voice.

He looked at her, apologetically. 'Just think about this. Use your logic.'

'Matt?' Joyce said.

He ignored her. 'You're a rational person, so don't fall for this stuff.'

'Matt?' Joyce again.

'*What?*'

Her voice was a nanny putting a silly child to bed. It made him want to strangle her. 'Holly's an innocent little girl who's become the fixation of a dark energy. I think her forgiveness of these girls is going to unlock us from all of this. It'll help her spirit move into peace and bring this—'

'Stop the seance, Rachel.' He took a step toward the stairs. 'We don't want to provoke whoever's—'

'Spirits walk among us,' Joyce said, stepping between him and the stairs. Not angry, just maddeningly calm. 'Don't you even hear her calling to you at night? To your family?'

'Who? Holly?'

She shook her head. 'Your mother.'

Silence followed that. A tense, ticking quiet.

Joyce tilted her head. 'She's called Elizabeth. Isn't she?'

'How do you know her name?'

'She died horribly, didn't she? Don't you see her reaching out to you? To your daughters?'

'How do you know her *name?*'

'Don't you see her standing in the corner of your room?'

'No, I do not.'

'And why is she so angry?'

He snapped, right into her face. 'Did you just *Google* her, you fucking charlatan?'

'Whoa,' Larry stepped in. 'We're leaving.'

'I'm genuinely sorry you feel this way. But your mother wants to communicate but there's something wrong with her mouth—'

Fffffft – crack.

A picture frame fell from the wall.

It slid down the wallpaper and snapped itself on the skirting board, tipping onto the carpet face down. Just a loose nail, *obviously*, but in the hysteria of this place everybody stared at it, even Larry took a worried step toward it.

Joyce glanced at it once then smiled before she carried on. 'There are living, thinking shadows in this world, Matt, behind every evil deed. Call them demons, call them negative energies, it doesn't really matter in the end. And that horrendous vault's created a sea of them. All violence does. And sometimes when these entities smell a troubled person like Holly . . .'

'You're an actual insane person.'

'. . . or when they smell even you, Matt . . .'

'*I'm* not troubled.'

Larry's hand on his shoulder. 'I think we'll head off.'

'. . . they're drawn to that soul. Like a shark gets drawn through the ocean by a trail of blood. The demons long for people like you. But when we show love and forgiveness, the negative spirits lose power and so you ought to let us end this.'

'People are being killed, Joyce. They're being murdered.'

Larry dropped to his haunches, lifting the broken picture up and turning it. It wasn't a photograph of Holly looking strange or malevolent, it was a print of a tree in the middle of a field filled with birds. A single crack from one corner ran to the other. Larry got to his feet, and checked the nail.

'Then let me attend, like before,' Matt said.

'No way, Josè,' Bob said.

'I'll sit in the corner. I'll just observe.'

'Your pessimism is going to poison it. It'll give the rabbit power,' Joyce said.

– A mad sudden image of the Duracell bunny marching in the dark.

'Then *you* make them stop it,' Matt said to Larry.

'What they're doing isn't a crime.' He turned to Bob. 'But you can't stop us from watching the house from outside. From being out on the street while it happens.'

Joyce started complaining about that as well. Spouting some bilge about it messing up the spectral vibes, but then Rachel suddenly spoke and said, 'Why can't we just let him watch the house? Just to be safe.'

'Fine,' Bob said. 'Fine. Stand outside, but you leave us alone to do our work, speaking of which . . . we need to get a wriggle on getting the equipment upstairs.'

'Upstairs? You're not doing it in the dining room again?'

Bob shook his head, 'We're doing it in her room, right where she died.'

'We follow the heartache,' Joyce said.

'Rachel?' Matt put his hand on the bannister. 'You could come with us right now. And be safe. We'll find Kassy.'

She shook her head, and her odd, tiny hair bunches bounced and swung. She had a look in her eye like resistance was beyond her now, that his asking her to leave was a luxury she couldn't afford, so that all that was left was participation and fear. Looking at her face, all made-up and weird, troubled him no end. She had climbed on a ghost train, but couldn't lift the security barrier up any more; and she'd never be able to get off until it reached the deepest rooms, the darkest corners.

'Just watch the house, will you?' she said, trying to smile at him. 'Keep an eye on us, from outside?'

He nodded, 'I'll be a shout away.'

'Just you wait.' Bob walked forward, ushering them both away with his hairy hands. 'After tonight things are going to be much, much better.' Bob stood on the doorstep, making sure they were leaving.

Halfway down the path, as Barley Street was turning fully dark, he looked across the street at a gaggle of children who were walking with plastic buckets, dressed as pirates and monsters.

Larry whispered, 'Bit spooky that. Knowing your mum's name.'

'I mention it in my book. She probably just read that part,' Matt said angrily, a little breathless. 'Big wow.'

'Then why are you so upset?'

'I'm not . . .'

Larry raised an eyebrow.

'It's just this sort of thinking . . . it's dangerous. It twists people's minds and gets their hopes up.' He shook his head. 'It's bullshit, Larry. It's cruel bullshit.'

Matt stared at the park, as the kids headed off. He could just about make out the curve of the hill where Rachel said the rabbit had danced, and beneath it was the thick spread of night shadow that contained the gallows tree. His mum was standing under it, her mouth just a hole of blood, and at her shoulder what looked like a tall shadow standing behind her, father-shaped, slinking its arms around her belly.

He looked away and turned back to look at the house, just in time to see something beyond Bob's folded arms in the doorway. Rachel's ancient white trainers and tight yellow ankle socks disappeared up into the gloom of the landing. Then Bob stepped back and the door to Barley Street slammed itself shut.

'Trick or treat!'

A squeaky little girl's voice came suddenly from his right. He turned to see a skinny white shape standing under a white sheet, shaking out her bucket. Her fingers looked black and dirty, nails packed with soil. There was nobody with her. She said it again, and her eyes flashed beneath the torn holes. 'Trick or treeeaaaat, mister?'

He turned away and walked to the car.

Matt and Larry didn't talk much as they drove. His mind was too jumbled to know what to say anyway. So he pulled out his phone and tapped some words into Google.

Menham Vaults Child Abuse Scandal

A rack of results flipped up and he scrolled through a few. Clicking on one from a local history website. An article appeared, with pictures.

Menham: Town of Tears by David Locke

The phone felt heavy in his hand.

He scanned the pages, filled with grim photographs of the 'scandal-ridden' children's home. He scan-read a few paragraphs and confirmed that yes, these historic cases of abuse did indeed happen down in those vaults.

Into which Rachel and her friends dumped her little sister, remember. For a laugh.

The thought of that, of Holly locked down there, was one of those things that made him look up from the phone now and again just to see the shops go by. It was all those photos of the kids' faces that did it. Morbid and hollow ghouls, barely into their teens and a few even younger ones too. There were shots of them showcasing the neglect side of the abuse. Kids with hefty cheekbones and sunken sockets. They didn't look world famine level, but it was enough to make it clear to any social worker or passing milkman that these kids had barely eaten. But it was the several grainy black-and-white shots in what seemed like an endless scroll that really turned his stomach. Of naked boys lying in pools of their own filth, some curled up, embryonic in a corner, hugging stick knees to stick ribs.

Genitals blurred out. Dusty concrete floors, and crumbling brick walls, curved into arches all around them. Scraping their shoulders as they huddled against them.

There was a shadowing around the edges of the pictures too, which told a story in itself. These shots were taken in full dark. The only light in the vault was from the flash. Eyes squinted painfully at the light. They were all turning into Morlocks down there.

He shook his head and let his thumb bring him perhaps the grimmest image of them all. He brought the phone close to his face, squinted at a detail on a metal door, then noticed in the next shot Locke had blown that part up because he'd noticed it too.

Fig 1. Fingernail scratches on the north door.

Hundreds of them.

Matt looked away and whispered, 'Jesus' and was surprised at how it sounded less like a swear word, and more like some old prayer he used to say. He flicked past the section on 'Neglect' and the next heading said 'Sexual Abuse'. He shook his head and hovered his finger over the off switch.

'I wouldn't look at those for too long, if I were you,' Larry suddenly said. He'd been watching out the corner of his eye. 'Pictures like that have a way of burrowing in and not going away.'

'I think you might be right.' Matt switched the phone off and buzzed his windows down to look out. The first thing he saw was a family who were eating in the front window of a Burger King. A little boy and girl, in paper crowns, were laughing very hard. He looked away from that, too.

CHAPTER FORTY-FIVE

It was 6 p.m. when Larry and Matt rapped their knuckles against the front door of the Evangelical Church, which sat slap bang in the middle of the high street, wedged between an off-licence and a laundrette. Shops were closing, shutters were being pulled down. The chip shop had a queue out the door and into the street.

The sun had finally slid off the edge of the earth's rim, so Menham had descended into its most fitting state. Night. The haze of the streetlights turned the underside of the clouds orange. A thin canopy, a tent roof. Though Matt knew that way above that glow was silent, infinite darkness.

Larry had just checked his phone and to Matt's relief he confirmed that Keech and a few other officers were en route to Barley Street right now. They'd set up both in front and behind the house to keep an eye on the seance. Larry said that he and Matt would join them back there soon.

Larry hammered his knuckles on the church door a second time. Much louder.

As they waited Matt slipped his hands into his pockets, kicked a stone on the pavement and looked up and down the street. A harsh clash of music was coming from a pub a few doors up. The chalkboard outside said a Bon Jovi tribute act, called Jon Bovi, was playing later at 7 p.m. They were halfway through a sound check and the music was spilling into the street.

'Oh dear,' Matt winced, eager to break the tension in his gut. 'So that's an hour they've got to learn the guitar.'

Larry went to smile, but then the door suddenly rattled as locks and bolts slid back. There were lots of them, like this was the front gate of a dingy prison, not a church porch.

The door opened a tiny way and standing in it was the bald guy from yesterday. Jim . . . no, Jerry. That was it. Jerry. The one with the bent fingers, who'd almost nuked Matt's gonads with spilt coffee.

'Hi, Jerry,' Matt said.

'Oh . . .' He smiled nervously. 'It's you.'

'It's me . . . and this is Detective Inspector Forbes.'

Larry stepped forward. 'I'd like a quick word with your pastor. Is he in there?'

'I'm . . . er . . . I'm afraid Todd's busy right now.'

'This'll only take a minute.'

'He's in a meeting, you'll have—'

Larry put a hand on the door. 'This isn't going to wait.'

Jerry ran a nervous tongue across his lips, looking at Matt now and again.

'Jerry?' Matt said. 'I think *you* better just let us inside, okay?'

He sucked in lips that looked chapped, squirmed a little, then finally he nodded. 'Suppose.'

Once they were inside, the first thing Matt noticed was that all the church lights were off, and Jerry made no attempt to switch any of them on. He just led them through the dark, dusty foyer and into the main sanctuary where rows of rickety wooden chairs were swamped in inky shadow. There were no pews here. No stone arches. Just mildewed carpets and decades-old paint jobs. It reminded him of the Scout hut Matt tried out as a kid. The one his mum took him out of because he found the badges too stressful. Anyone getting married here would either have to be blind or not having a photographer.

He glanced above the pulpit and froze.

'Relax.' Jerry chuckled. 'It's just Jesus.'

A pair of dull but huge eyes stared out of the shadows. Each was licked with a slightly reflective paint so they almost glowed. It was a large, fibreglass Christ. Hanging on his cross and leaning forward. Staring down at Matt with that familiar look of forehead-slapping disappointment.

'Where are you taking us?' Matt asked.

'Are you nervous being in a church?'

'Just wondering how long it'll take.'

'One minute. They're all down in the cellar.'

Larry and Matt glanced at each other. *The cellar?*

Jerry put both of his palms up. 'Both of you wait here and I'll get him. Grab a seat. Pray if you like.'

Fibreglass Jesus creaked.

'Nah,' Larry said. 'We'll tag along with you, thanks.'

Jerry mulled this over. His cheek bulged with a pondering tongue.

'Then we'll find him ourselves.'

Jerry sighed. 'This way.'

He unlocked another door, which led to a long dreary corridor with a floor of sticky lino, torn in places. Matt could hear the soles of their shoes peeling off it like sellotape. At the end, a flight of stone steps led down to a metal door at the bottom. A bare bulb on a very long chain dangled from the ceiling, throwing an insipid, depressing glow across the stone steps. Matt could see the faint wisps of a spider's web swaying in threads, wisping and reaching from the chain.

Jerry looked down the stairs and seemed startled to see that the door was slightly ajar. Enough so they could all suddenly hear low voices.

'Stay here,' Jerry said quickly. 'I'll get him.'

'Wait,' Matt whispered. 'What are they doing down there?'

'It's a private meeting. I don't like pulling him out of it.'

Matt moved his foot down one of the steps. 'Sounds like . . .' he turned to Larry. 'That's a man crying down there.'

'It's private. Step aside.'

Larry reached out and grabbed Jerry's arm. 'Just give it a sec.'

Jerry strained his face, but Matt noticed he still did exactly as he was told. Not much of a rebel, this one.

Matt heard the faintest sound of Todd's American accent drifting up from the gap in the door.

'You say it's a natural feeling,' he sounded soothing and pastoral, 'but, guys let me tell you, it's *not* natural. It's an ungodly urge, see? And if you follow it down that rabbit hole, you're all gonna wind up back inside. Back in *your* hole. And who the heck wants to spend time in that sort of hole?'

Laughter.

Matt leant into Jerry. 'This is the Phoenix Club?'

Jerry nodded. 'We're helping ex-offenders get their—'

'You two,' Larry whispered. 'Shush.'

'. . . the Devil's whispering in your ear that it's okay,' Todd went on, 'but that's just him getting his hooks in. Gets you rationalising sin until you skip right into it. Till you start seeking out some poor—'

'Enough.' Jerry yanked himself free from Matt's grip and headed down the stairs, loudly calling Todd's name so that he knew full well they had visitors. There was a sudden murmur of nervous voices down there, the scraping of chairs.

Matt glanced at Larry with an uneasy shrug.

The door was opening slowly and Todd emerged in a flicker of light. It looked like they had candles burning down there. Goatee beards have a tendency of making their wearers look like Vegas magicians. Matt trialled one for a month and couldn't cope with his reflection. He felt like waving his hands in mysterious ways whenever he saw himself staring back. Todd's goatee flickered in the light and looked a little more sinister than that. Actually, a lot more. Like he might twiddle it while he tied young women to a train track. He was wearing a baggy white shirt tucked haphazardly into jet-black trousers. Quite the Gothic dandy, apart from the bottle of Dr Pepper in his hand. He screwed the lid off and took a long glugging swallow before gasping out a satisfied sigh. He wiped the back of his wrist across his wet mouth and said, 'Maybe you two could do with a group like this. Couple of full-blooded fellas like you.'

The pale guy Neil, – who carried the police scanner yesterday – came creeping out too. He looked up and frowned, with a wet looking cheek. He wiped it quickly with his sleeve.

'We're coming down,' Larry said. 'We need to talk.'

'Nah . . .' Todd said, closing the door behind him. 'We're coming up.'

CHAPTER FORTY-SIX

Rachel stood in front of Holly's wardrobe with small clumps of hair sprouting from her head, gazing at the imitation wooden doors that hung slightly crooked. They'd bought this from MFI, she recalled, on a very rainy day. Building it had been a team effort and had taken most of that afternoon. Mum and Rachel did most of it, while Holly sat on the floor, excited and giddy to see it take shape. Holly's job had been to count out the screws and she handed them over like a surgeon's assistant. Funny how it's the cheap furniture that often has the most memories. Because you have to build them at home and you need others' help and you don't always get it right.

Maybe there was a lesson in that, she thought.

On the left door, a poster of a fairy was stuck to the wood. A drawing ripped from a kids magazine. She could see the date in the top right-hand corner. August 2001. A couple of months before the vault and the haunting, the hanging. Rachel had a vivid memory of this. Of she and the girls striding into the room, spotting the poster and laughing in Holly's face. Not just metaphorically, either, but a spluttering big guffaw which was their way of saying that she was hilariously immature. That fairies and wizards and talking animals were for babies. But she recalled that the loudest phrase about this image was something Kassy had said.

Or was it Rachel?

Lame, lame, lame!

Rachel looked at the fairy. It was hovering over a white rose and scattering glitter from a basket that turned half of the white flower into red. She'd always assumed this was supposed to depict how roses were made. But the 'lame' little fairy looked a lot less babyish now. She had hopelessly underestimated Holly, and also, it seemed, this fairy. In this light those little eyes looked like pinpricks of rage and hatred. She wasn't building this white flower into a rose. She was destroying it with acid. She was turning the world into blood.

'*How angry* are *you, Holly?*' she whispered to the fairy, and to herself. '*Angry enough to kill us?*'

'How are you getting on, love?'

Rachel jumped.

Joyce pushed through the creaking door of Holly's room and came up behind Rachel, placing a leathery hand on her shoulder. 'Would you like me to help you get it?'

Rachel shook her head. 'No, I'm fine. Thank you.'

She swallowed and pulled both doors open. She sucked in a shivering breath at all of Holly's clothes still hanging there. Mum had kept it neat and ordered. In general colour sequence, because that's how Holly used to do it. Lots of white and creams, moving into yellow and occasional browns. No pinks, no reds, no blues. Never, ever black. Just one long bright meadow of a fashion sense. Rachel reached out and touched one of them. An orange summer dress that Mum had made Holly wear for a barbecue.

Holly had said she felt 'scratchy' in it, but she did as she was told because she was always such a good girl. Always Mum's favourite, as a result. Rachel remembered thinking her little sister looked impossibly beautiful in this dress. She also remembered choosing not to tell her that day, because it felt 'embarrassing' and 'corny' to say such things.

An idiot. That's what Rachel had been. An idiot.

And still was.

'She was a pretty girl,' Rachel said, softly. 'Prettier than me.' Not so much to Joyce as to the clothes themselves and the spirit that might, on some nights, touch them too.

'Is it in there?' The low masculine slash of Bob's voice felt intrusive and clumsy in a room of delicate tension.

Rachel took a long breath then nodded as she reached over and touched the hanger with the white flowing top. Gently and with nothing less than reverence (fear actually, it was fear) she pulled it from the wardrobe and Joyce looked down at it. A white, flowing top with long sleeves and stitched white-flower patterns on it. Little tassels around the hem. The bent coat hanger wings on the back.

The base clothes for her Halloween angel outfit.

Joyce's voice was soft and gentle. 'Are you sure this is what she was wearing?'

'Yes,' Rachel said. 'It got dirty in the vault so Mum washed it. Is that a problem . . . if it's been washed?'

'No.' Joyce reached for the top and lifted it up. 'That's not a problem at all.' She put it to her face and sniffed it, eyes locked on Rachel.

'This is going to help us connect,' Bob said.

Rachel looked at the two of them, standing there. Oddballs, they were, quite frankly, with the sort of strong convictions that scared her no end, if she really thought about them. But through all this they had at least been constant. They'd been two sturdy concrete posts in a sea of shifting ideas and theories. And they had the sweetest faces. The kindest eyes.

But still, as Joyce leant forward and held the top up again, as if to set it against Rachel's chest to see if it might fit, Rachel took a step back from it.

Joyce said. 'Is something wrong?'

Rachel looked at the carpet.

'Do you want to stop the seance?'

Silence.

'Rachel . . . speak to—'

'What if Matthew's right? That this isn't real.'

'Do you think he's right?'

'I'm not sure. Sometimes, maybe.'

'He isn't on this occasion. But Rachel . . . there's something else.' She took a tiny step closer.

'What?'

'You've been looking at me strangely,' Joyce whispered. 'Ever since we got back from the hospital. Better say it now, girl. It'd be best.'

Rachel looked back up. 'It's Kassy.'

'What about her?'

'She doesn't believe in this. She says I shouldn't do the seance.'

'I know this.'

'She doesn't believe in you.'

'I know that too.'

'No,' Rachel shook her head. 'She . . . she said some things about you. Things I've never heard before. She's asking people questions about something that happened at our school. When you were teachers.'

Joyce closed her eyes and with a push of the lips she said, 'What things?'

'Bad things.' Rachel looked down at her hands and noticed how old they were looking. 'About why you left teaching early . . .'

'Ahhhh,' Joyce said, drawing the sound out for a weirdly long time.

Bob groaned and walked away shaking his head. 'Never ends, does it, love?'

'So was she lying? About what they found in your bags?'

She noticed that Bob had closed the door, then walked back to his wife.

Joyce ran a tooth across her bottom lip, and shook her head. 'She wasn't lying.'

PART THREE

EFFLUVIA

CHAPTER FORTY-SEVEN

Todd creaked back into his pastor's chair in a church office filled with wet-looking cardboard boxes. They were stuffed full of cartoony religious pamphlets saying *This Was Your Life* and *Q: Are Catholics Really Christians? A: Nope!* A dying pot plant sat on his desk and behind him hung a ridiculously large poster of Jesus Christ in a white robe and sandals, stepping off the clouds and coming for a second time into the world. The words underneath declared: *Perhaps Tomorrow, Perhaps Today!*

Perhaps never.

The letter from Matt's car windscreen lay flat on the desk, though the tight folds were making it slowly coil back into itself, like a dying insect scared of the light. Neil and Jerry stood near one of the bigger cardboard box piles, looking edgy. At one point, Matt saw Neil close his eyes and pray.

Todd started rhythmically pressing his back into his chair. 'Well I'm offended, gentlemen. I'm offended.'

'What's the problem?' Larry said.

'That your first thought is to march in here and accuse us.'

'Did you write it?' Matt stood next to Larry in front of the heavy desk. There were no other chairs.

'If I said no, would you believe me?'

'That's not an answer,' Larry said. 'Did you write it? Or someone you know?'

'Sorry, but no. I have no idea.'

Matt leant onto the desk. 'All we're asking for is your help, Todd. A woman was *brutally* killed last night.'

'Well, we hardly need reminding of that. The whole town ain't talking of anything else.'

'Police scanner went into meltdown during that,' Neil added.

'You were listening in?'

He nodded, ''Course.'

'And did you all go over there? To the park?'

'Me and Jerry did. Just to pray for the dead woman. We couldn't get very close because of the crowds, but we still prayed.'

'I see . . . well like I said,' Matt turned back to Todd, 'the evidence points to someone with a thing about witches. And to be fair, your little Phoenix Club . . . has a thing about witches.'

'See, guys. What did I tell you?' He opened up his palms. 'Accusations.'

Jerry and Neil looked at each other, but said nothing.

'Look.' Larry took a step forward, voice calm. 'Maybe someone just heard one of your sermons and took it a bit far. You say you didn't write the note. Fine. But now we're asking if you know anybody in your group that might be unstable or have a history of violence. Someone who might not have the right sort of parameters.'

Todd put both hands on the desk, checking his fingernails. He actually looked bored.

'Well?' Matt snapped. 'Is there anyone?'

Jerry shuffled forwards. 'If you're looking for someone who thinks witches, demons and new age religion might well be the source of evil in this world then, yes, I do know somebody.' He tapped a hand against his chest. 'Me.'

'And me,' Neil added.

Todd looked at them both and smiled.

Jerry went on. 'And if you're asking if dabbling in the occult is punching holes in the light and the demons are spilling back in, I say absolutely. But if you reckon the good people of this church are gonna take God's law into their own hands and actually kill a person. Not a chance.'

'And I resent the fact you thought there even could be,' Todd added. 'We keep ourselves pure here. Clean hands, clean hearts. Isn't that true, boys?'

'Yes, but—'

'But what?' Todd glared at him.

Jerry tugged nervously at a button on his shirt. 'But since we do have a strong stand on the occult maybe somebody could warp the message? The least we could do is pray and think hard if there might be anybody here who could . . . take things too far. As horrible as it sounds.'

'Good,' Larry said. 'Then I'll take the names and addresses of all your congregation. You can write yours out now.' He tore off a Post-it note from Todd's desk and handed them his pen, clicking it on. As they scrawled their details out he added, 'And I want details on all the other members of the Phoenix Club. Plus, I'm going to send some more officers up to search this building.'

Todd closed his eyes. 'Unbelievable.'

'Are you saying we can't?' Larry said.

'We don't have anything to hide,' Jerry said.

'If that's the case,' Matt spoke softly, 'tell us what the Phoenix Club were doing, just then? Why were you crying, Neil?'

Neil shifted from one foot to the next and looked to Todd for guidance.

Todd just shrugged, 'I told you, we help offenders settle back into society. Admirable work and effective too. Sometimes that can be painful. For us as well as them.'

'And you're both involved in that too?' Larry asked.

Jerry and Neil nodded, then Neil quickly added, 'As counsellors, though. We're not on the programme ourselves, obviously.'

'And I take it you all tell them it's the Devil that makes them do it?'

'Quite right.' Todd nodded. 'Which isn't only true, it helps them stop hating themselves. Helps them know they're not the ones to blame, in the end. Prisons obviously appreciate what we're doing, cos guess what . . . the chaplains keep sending them our way. You should be impressed. Men and women are rising up from the wreckage of their lives. And being renewed. That's why we call it the—'

'There are women in the group?'

'A few,' Todd blinked, then suddenly gave Matt an odd look. 'So fine, search the place, because you won't find anything. Menham's got nothing to fear from this church, in fact it's quite the opposite. We keep the Devil at bay down here, cos that's our job.'

'Go to the cellar and tell this support group to sit tight down there,' Larry said. 'I want to speak with them.'

Todd chuckled. 'You'll be lucky . . . they heard you coming and slipped out the back way. The group sessions are anonymous, for heaven's sake, it's an important part of the programme.'

'Well, I still want their addresses,' Larry said. 'You can print them out now.'

Todd rolled his eyes. 'Go ahead, Neil. Get him what he wants.' Neil vanished into another room.

They hovered for a few moments, in a very thick silence.

'Well,' Todd said. 'How about we use the time to pray for the Hodges and especially for their little protégée, Rachel Wasson?' He screwed up his face like he'd swallowed a wasp. 'That godforsaken Barley witch.'

It happened before Matt was even fully conscious of it. He clenched his fist and pounded it hard on the top of Todd's desk, making a pen roll off the edge. He felt his muscles filling with blood and power. Ready to let the coil go and plough decades of religious disillusionment into Todd's grinning face. But Larry's arm was quickly on his shoulder and Matt let the fist uncurl by his side.

'You're dangerous, Todd.'

'Don't fear me, Matt. But be watchful,' Todd said, quietly. 'That the Devil doesn't climb into you one of these nights. And make you do something hideous that *you* never forget.'

Neil came back, holding an A4 sheet. He looked confused by everybody's expression.

Larry pulled Matt back and grabbed the sheet. 'We're leaving.'

'We're going to figure all this out, Todd,' Matt narrowed his eyes. 'Do you hear me?'

Todd was all out of shits to give. He shrugged.

Larry glared at Matt and was already off through the door and marching down the long corridor toward the cellar. Matt jogged after him. He could feel the tingle of adrenaline and stress firing through his arms and body, but when he trotted down the cellar steps and found Larry in there, neither of them spoke. Larry was putting his phone away and looking around the room. It was abandoned, with just a circle of empty metal chairs, some of them on their sides. Another doorway led out the back.

He heard Larry grab his radio and call in the names of Todd Holloway, Jerry Marlowe and Neil White. He read out their addresses and asked for a background check. But other than that, he and Larry did all this room-scanning in complete silence. It was while they were walking back through the dark church that Matt finally looked at Larry, expecting him to be shaking his head at the stupidity of it.

'I'm sorry. I shouldn't have lost my temper.'

Larry didn't say anything.

'It wasn't very professional.'

'No shit? If you'd punched him, we'd have been done, you know. I couldn't have you out with me any more.' He moved down the shadowy aisle of the church sanctuary. 'So don't you ever do that again; do you hear me? *Always* do the right thing.'

Matt nodded. 'I'm sorry.' But of course, he wasn't.

That godforsaken Barley Street witch.

Wow. He wanted to stomp back into that office and finish what he'd hardly even started.

Larry was already out the door, meeting some officers pulling up in a car. Matt felt the urge to turn around instead. To look at a church one last time and maybe even to scream at it: *There is no framework – There are no patterns – I can do whatever the hell I want! I can punch a weirdo who's threatening an innocent woman and it's neither right nor wrong.*

When he finally *did* turn there was nobody there. Nobody, that is, except the fibreglass Jesus hanging heavy from the cross. The doll-eyes looked hungry and judging. The mouth, eager and fierce. Matt stepped backwards, startled. The fibreglass groaned again, though it sounded more like the statue itself, expressing an emotion. Like this was the exact second Christ was going to lose all patience, and rip himself down from those nails so he could stride up the aisle and strangle his latest betrayer.

CHAPTER FORTY-EIGHT

Matt, Larry and Keech were leaning against the police car, three of them in a row, with feet locked against the kerb directly outside 29 Barley Street.

Matt hitched himself up on the bonnet and gazed up at the night clouds, which were glowing as they slouched across Menham. A few houses up the street, more midget vampires and werewolves were rapping on doors, demanding sugar. Whenever they trotted up to number 29, Larry moved them on. But Matt rummaged in his jacket pocket and pulled out a small bag of Haribo he'd bought earlier. He tossed it into a skeletons bucket.

'Great night for ghosts this,' Keech said. 'If you believe in that sort of thing.'

'And do you?' Matt asked.

'I'm an undecided. A fifty-fifty guy.'

Larry said nothing, just took another swig of his water bottle before glancing up and down the street for signs of people. So far, it had all been exceptionally quiet. Which felt both reassuring and worrying, all at the same time.

Matt kept staring at Holly's old room and the roof above it, where the black rabbit supposedly first stood tall. Directly underneath, Holly's window still had the cardboard taped across it and the curtains were shut tight. He thought of himself and Rachel standing there together and talking last night. Just before she'd fallen into the final spiral that was turning her into the fourteen-year-old hysteric the Hodges were morphing her into. The glass was glowing a little from the light inside and every now and then he'd see shadows moving as they set up their equipment.

Larry's radio was strapped to his shoulder and it kept squelching and buzzing as the other officers periodically checked in. He'd stationed another two watching the back while a further two were up at the church right now, keeping an eye out there.

Quite the operation, Keech had said earlier, in a tone that in reality said: *is this really a good use of police time?*

They sat there, waiting in silence for many minutes, until Keech said, 'Sir, what was it like?'

'What was what like?'

'You know . . . seeing Holly Wasson, all hung up like that.'

Matt quickly looked at Larry. Tried to gauge the face. Morose was the closest word he could think of.

'I just helped out in the morning . . . All we did was take her down.'

'That can't have been easy,' Matt said, quietly.

'Well . . . bakers bake, postmen post . . . and police do what they do.' He gave an unconvincing it's-no-big-deal shrug. 'Got called in to help out one morning. Then moved on.'

'Which means you actually touched Holly Wasson.' Keech was wide-eyed.

'The girl wasn't toxic, you know . . . and despite what people round here think, she wasn't a monster. She was just this normal, pretty little girl . . .' He decided not to finish. He shook his head then kicked a pine cone that had somehow made its way to the pavement. It bounced angrily at the wall.

Keech waited for a second. 'One little question . . . I heard the sister tried to saw through the flex with a bread knife, but she wasn't strong enough to—'

Larry slapped Keech on the arm. 'Enough talk.'

It was too late. An image of Rachel hacking away at the cable, while her sister hung there swinging, started flooding Matt's mind like a swift cancer.

'Look, fellas,' Larry said, 'I think I'll have a quick wander up and down the street. So Keech, you look after the front for a few minutes. I'll be five minutes, tops.'

'No problemo.'

'And Matt, why don't you walk with me?'

'Actually, I'll stay.' He nodded toward the house. 'I'll keep an eye out.'

'Fine.' Larry headed off, talking into his radio again.

He wandered off. He and Keech watched the house in silence, until Matt felt his phone chirp in this pocket. He pulled it out and saw a message from Wren.

Hey M. When you home? Amelia really freaking out about her room tonight. Worse than ever. xxw

He sighed and jabbed a quick message back. Apologising that it might be a late one.

Keech leaned over and said, 'Uh-oh. Having a few issues at home, ey?'

'Er . . . do you mind?' Matt clicked send and dropped the phone back.

They watched the house some more.

Matt didn't like this, the waiting around. The not knowing what on earth was happening in there. The assumption that everything was alright. And the curiosity. The ravenous curiosity he had to break into that room to listen and watch what the Hodges were doing with Rachel, even if it was just more mumbo jumbo around a table.

Just as he thought that, he suddenly spotted something in the house. The lights were off downstairs, but Matt saw a black shape flicker in the glass of the front door. He pushed himself from the car.

'What?' Keech said.

'I saw something.' Matt took a step towards the gate. 'Someone's moving downstairs.'

Keech shrugged. 'So what? Maybe one of them's gone to the kitchen to get a Coke.'

'It's a good time to check if they're okay.'

'But you can't go in.'

'I *won't* go in. I'll stand at the door and I'll check on progress, alright?'

Keech strained his neck to see where Larry was.

'It'll be fine.'

Keech looked over at the door. 'Just don't go in, okay?'

With a nod Matt headed up, pushing the iron gate, quickening his pace up the path. As he hurried up there, he noticed that the dandelions and wild nettles were swaying in tiny little circles. All of them. He slowed, and watched them move.

The breeze isn't doing that, you know.

– Focus.

Round and round the flowers went, leaning toward him.

Round and round.

– *Holly in her room, slowly revolving, slowly revolving.*

A small metallic squeak caught his attention and when he looked back at the door he saw the frosted glass suddenly filled with a light inside, half of it instantly vanished as a black figure rose to fill the space.

He looked back at Keech.

But then the door opened and Mary Wasson shuffled into view, looking spaced out. Her wild hair was a galaxy of kinks and curls. Swaying on her feet, she had a glass of milk in her hand, tilting it so that she was very close to spilling it. She saw him and blinked slowly, cocking her head towards her shoulder and clicking her spine into place. He realised she was trying to figure out who he was.

'It's me, Matt.'

'Ah! You again . . .' She raised a finger. '*You* can't come in.'

'I know that. I just wanted to check to see if you were all okay.' He sniffed. 'Have you been drinking?'

She gave a dumb-looking smile. 'We're aaaalllll okay.'

'How's the seance going?' He glanced up the stairs.

'Mr Hodges said I can't let you in or you'll muck it up. He said they both had to be with Rachel alone. No interruptions. They're just about to start so . . .' she stumbled a little. 'You need to get back in your car.'

She went to shut the door but he put his foot half-inside. 'Are you sure this is a good idea?' He smiled at her, conscious he sounded like he was talking to a four-year-old. 'What do you reckon, Mary? You think Rachel should give this one a miss?'

'Oh, why don't you just faaaaaaade away.' She wiped her unsteady fingers across the space between them. 'Just fade away and leave my kids alone.'

He could hear voices upstairs. Bob and Joyce were making some sort of announcements. The ritualistic opening of the seance no doubt, and though Matt wanted to push Mary aside and rush up there, he knew it was pointless. 'Fine.' He turned to head back to Keech.

'And why don't you tell those policemen to do something useful?' Mary nodded towards the street. 'Like finding our cat.'

He froze, mid step. Turned. 'What was that?'

'Finlay's gone. Haven't seen him since this morning. So get that lot—' she lifted her glass toward the police, and a bunch of milk swilled over the side, soaking her thumb. She didn't seem to care. 'Get that lot to bring our cat back. He's old, you know, and he gets very, very scared on his own.'

Matt stepped back from the door as it slammed shut, while his phone started buzzing in his pocket.

He grabbed it quickly, wondering if it might be Rachel, but it was an incoming call from a number he didn't recognise.

'Hello. Matt Hunter.'

'Yeah, is that the professor guy?'

'Who's this?'

'It's me. Kassy West. Rachel gave me your number.'

'Kassy. Are you okay? We've been looking for you. You might be in danger.'

She laughed. 'I'm fine. In fact, I'm great. Cos I've got some info for you on the Hodges you'll probably want to know. Been doing a bit of digging.'

'What info?'

'Come and meet me, and I'll tell you.'

'Just tell me on the—'

'Come and meet me. You'll be glad you did.'

He waited. 'Where are you?'

'Where do you think? I'm at the vaults. Meet you up top.'

'Why on earth are you at the vau—'

'See ya soon.'

'Kassy, just get yourself . . .'

336

She hung up and when he dialled back, it went straight to voicemail.

He rushed back to Keech and spotted Larry trotting back down the pavement.

'What's going on?' he said.

'The seance is starting, but listen . . .' Matt turned to Larry. 'The pet cat's missing, which yes, sounds pretty bloody worrying to me.'

Larry immediately leant his head to speak into his radio, lips close enough to touch the plastic grille. 'Butterfield? Come in?'

'This is Butterfield.'

'Everything alright back there?'

There was a beep and a sharp hiss, then a voice said, 'All good. Couple of teenagers necking in the alley, but nothing to worry about.' He checked in with the officers at the church too. Nothing unusual there either. Good old Pastor Todd was doing as he was told. Walking the police around the building, letting them see everything. They were just about finished apparently, with nothing odd found.

'There's something else. Kassy West just called. She's got some information on the Hodges, and she wants me to go to the vaults to get it.'

'Tell her to get her backside over here and tell—'

'She's not answering her phone.'

Larry blew out a breath. Checked his watch. 'Fine. Keech. Go and pick her up. Make sure she's safe.'

'She specifically asked for me.'

'Then go with Keech and for God's sake bring her back so we can keep an eye on her, too.'

'What about you?'

'I'll watch the house.'

'Well . . .' Matt waited. 'Be careful.'

Keech was already up the street, popping the police car open. 'You coming, or what?'

Matt hurried into the passenger seat and was pulling his seatbelt on when he paused midway. 'Who the heck are they?'

A crowd of four or five teenagers were walking up to Larry, staring up at Barley Street and giggling. One of them even tried to climb over the wall and into the garden but Larry hauled him back.

'Just kids. They come round every Halloween,' he turned the key and the engine growled. 'They want to see Holly's ghost.'

'Oh, right,' Matt said.

'It's kind of a tradition round here.'

They pulled away just as Matt saw Larry flash his ID and angrily yell at the kids to clear off.

CHAPTER FORTY-NINE

Obviously, there was no table this time. Instead Bob, Joyce and Rachel sat in a circle of three creaky camping chairs. Joyce had her hands on her lap, upturned. Her eyes were closed, lips quivering with silent conversation to the dead.

Bob was sitting in his chair, looking at Joyce and back at Rachel, tapping nervous fingers on his knees. Whenever he caught Rachel's eye he'd give one of his pat-you-on-the-back smiles. A sort of grandad's reassurance that *it'll be alright, young'un*, yet there was something in his eyes that looked off kilter. Like he wasn't entirely sure if it would be alright, after all.

There was only candlelight this time, which they'd stood on any surface they could find. Teardrop flames and little tea lights danced. Joyce had even bundled in one of those expensive Yankee Candles from the garden centre. 'Sycamore Dreams' it was called. It made the cold air in here sickly sweet.

If she was in another person's life – like, a normal person who worked at Jessops selling cameras – who came home at night to grumpy kids and miserable husbands. If that was her right now, she might launch her own personal investigation into why candlelight and shadows put a person on edge. Was there something inherently wrong when the shadow of somebody's nose sways and grows and leaps up to cover the eyes? Perhaps there was some sort of science behind why certain physical properties made you feel fear.

But right now she was just sitting here, terrified of the way the flames moved, close to tears.

They'll put that on your gravestone, Rach.

Rachel Wasson, sound designer, daughter and very bad sister. Who was always and consistently, for her entire lonely life . . . close to tears.

She swallowed just as Joyce started to speak. 'I can feel her coming through.'

Rachel started to close her eyes and stared down at the white flowery top, lying on the floor. It looked tiny and impossibly childish. Like it was for a baby and not a nine-year-old. Already Rachel's lips were moving and hot frequent whispers were warming up her icy-cold mouth. The words I'm sorry, I'm so sorry tumbled from her psyche like lava.

And it was cold. Incredibly cold. Enough for her to be shivering under the cardigan they'd let her wear over the top of her late-90s T-shirt. By now, though, she knew it was impossible to tell what was cold and what was terror. She had passed the point of differentiation on such topics.

Bob reached over and tapped a button on one of his gizmos. In his hand he held up an EMF meter. He waved it about, like it was a mobile phone trying to get a signal. Not that many signals worked down here.

The candles lit up a quivering oval of dirty bricks arching above them, but they didn't reach all the way to the other end of this particular vault.

This was the special vault, of course. *Holly's* special vault. The one they left her in on a cruel, drink-fuelled lark.

We'll have the seance *here*, Joyce had said. In calm, soothing tones. We'll be closer to Holly and that moment. We'll be away from the negativity of the police. She thought of all that quick bundling up of equipment into Bob's car, so they could be gone from Barley Street before the police arrived. At one point the two old fogeys even giggled, like this was an adventure. A mischievous romantic romp for them both. Until they actually got down here and their faces turned pale. Rachel figured their washed-out skin was just a classic pensioner reaction to climbing a ladder. But now she could tell it was something deeper. They looked scared.

And Rachel had said yes, of course. Because it all made a sad and perfect sense to be here. And not only that, just as she couldn't tell the difference between cold and terror any more, she'd equally lost understanding of madness and sanity. There was little awareness of such demarcations any more. Frameworks had vanished. A few days ago she'd have never, ever allowed herself to be in this position, but that was her false self. The projection of who she thought she was. The new self she was trying to concoct was just an avatar. A computer game character. Who she *really* was, deep inside herself, was right *here*, finally facing the danger and not running from it. Wearing old, ill-fitting jeans. Was she brave, stupid, gullible or wise? She hadn't the first clue how to answer that question. Rachel looked over Joyce's shoulder into the vast ink of blackness. Like the three of them were floating in starless space. Satellites built and designed to constantly revolve around 'Holly's heartache'. . . as Joyce so frequently liked to put it. At one point Rachel considered that these weren't shadows around them at all. They were swarms of unnameable insects, scuttling as easily as the rabbit danced . . . closer and closer on the command of her sister.

'She's calling out to you, Rachel,' Joyce said. 'She's started.'

Rachel could feel her heart literally vibrating in her chest. She thought of her only girlfriend, Debbie, stroking her thumb against her wrist. The soft, gliding caress that always calmed her down.

'I'm sorry,' she said it out loud this time. 'I'm so sorry, Holly. For making you do what you did . . .'

'Say it again. Open your heart.'

'Holly . . .' Rachel sniffed. 'It was the worst thing I have ever done in my life. And if it helps . . . it's ruined me. It's coiled me up. I'm a bitch and I'm sorry.'

'Shhh,' Joyce put her hand up.

Bob frowned, and Joyce was frowning too, her eyes were so tightly shut her face looked like it was cracking.

'Something isn't right,' Joyce said. The thin mounds of her chest rose up and down in quick, worrying movements.

Rachel looked at Bob. 'What's happening?'

'Quiet.' He moved closer to Joyce. Leant in and whispered, 'Talk to me, love.'

Joyce opened her eyes, candlelight flickering in the old pupils. She locked her gaze on Rachel. 'She doesn't want an apology.'

'What?'

'Don't say sorry . . . that's not . . .'

'What are you talking about?'

'She isn't angry she's . . . she's scared for you . . .'

'What?'

'It's not anger . . . God no . . . it's fear . . . Something's not right.'

Rachel looked down at Holly's white dress, because now it was quivering and moving. Her heart, which was already pounding, felt like it might crank so fast it could reach the fluttering rate of a baby's she once recorded for a client, during her false life.

Holly's top. Was it moving?

Was it growing?

Filling out?

'Oh my God,' Rachel said. 'Oh my God, she's coming.'

'Something's not right,' Joyce said again.

Bob was on his feet.

She stared at the material. Even if it was a breeze, where was the breeze coming from? And what if it *wasn't*? What if it was Holly rising up through the ground with a cracked neck and blue lips. Ready to slip her cold little hand in Rachel's, so they might play in the concrete cracks down here for ever.

She shouted it out, so that her voice echoed at the far end of the vault. 'Holly, what do you need me to—'

Something scraped in the corner of the room.

Her head snapped hard to the left. Bob's did too

'What was that?' she whispered.

'Rachel, whatever you do, do *not* let go of Joyce's hand.'

She stared into the corner, the corner nearest to her, trembling. But when she looked over it was silent and pitch-black. The camping light they were using was far too insipid to pick out any—

Click.

'Oh, God,' Rachel said. 'Something's here.'

'It's starting,' Joyce said. 'Don't let go.'

Rachel called out to the shadows, 'Holly?'

And what came back was, *click, click*.

Things prickled across her skin, then she realised that she couldn't see Bob's other hand. Was *he* making that sound, in the darkness? Scraping something on the floor to scare her?

Click. Scratch, scratch. Click.

'Bob?' she said. 'Are *you* doing that?'

He shook his head. She couldn't understand his expression. The candlelight made his eyes look mad.

'Bob?'

'It's *not* me, I swear to—'

Scratch, scratch.

Less gaps now. Growing more constant. The scrape of all those pencils on the paper the other night in Barley Street.

Scratch, scratch, scratch. Click.

No . . . that wasn't pencils . . .

It was the echo of those children, locked down here and trying to escape the staff. From all those true Halloween tales this town loved to tell one other. Of traumatised little kids scraping their fingernails against the metal to get out of this grave. Like Holly may well have had to have done.

Jesus, she thought.

This really sounded like that.

That sound was fingernails, scrabbling against metal. Quick and desperate. Like Holly was bringing out all her new friends. The long-dead vault kids, who were the only ones who let her play.

Bob looked at Joyce. 'Petal, are you okay?'

Scratch, scratch. Scratch, scratch.

'Holly?' Rachel called out into the dark. 'What do you want? What should we do?'

Click. Scratch, scratch. Click.

Then a simple thought: not fingernails.

Claws.

Joyce flicked her eyes open, and she let out a shrill, heart-stopping screech that filled the vault with sound.

Bob gasped. 'I'll check it. Okay, love?'

'Where are you going?' Rachel said. A desperate hiss of a whisper.

'I need to check what it is.' He lifted his EMF meter-reader like the world's most feeble pistol and started walking toward the darkness, vanishing into it.

'Joyce?' Rachel said. 'Is it Holly? Is she here? What is she saying?'

'She's screaming. She's screaming your name.' Joyce's eyes closed again and her silent lips were moving now at a frantic, crazy pace. All Rachel could do was close her eyes too and think of being in Marrakesh with Debbie and holding her arm and hearing her heartbeat in the hotel room. Hearing all those sounds of happy chatter and bells and goats and music and banter and wishing to God she could stay in that moment for the rest of her entire life because—

Thud, thud, thud, thud.

The sound of footsteps forced her eyes open and she saw something that finally made sense. That finally locked the shifting sands of belief back into something that was at least understandable. As dreadful as it was. At least now she knew.

Under the stone arched ceiling of the vault, the black rabbit stood, swaying. Tall on its hind legs. Like a man. One black arm held out toward her as it gathered pace. Shimmering from the shadows and pounding toward her.

She tried to scream, but even sound, her oldest friend, had abandoned her now.

CHAPTER FIFTY

'*Sir?*'

Larry felt his belt buzz and he quickly jerked to grab his radio from it. He could instantly tell that Butterfield was out of breath.

'What's going on?'

'Sir. You need to get in there, quick. We just saw a man climb over the back wall.'

Larry sprang off the bonnet of the car, his eyes frantically scanning 29 Barley Street.

'He's in the back garden.'

He kicked the gate open and ran up the path toward the house, radio pressed against his lips as the garden flowers danced. 'You get after him, Butterfield. Do you hear me?'

'Climbing the wall, as we speak,' he was gasping.

He was halfway up the path when something filled the air. Something that made him stumble. He slowed and turned to see a group of men, about ten of them. They were walking down the street, with candles in their hands and they were singing 'How Great Thou Art'.

He craned his neck to see them. They weren't teenagers. They weren't kidding around. *What the hell?*

No time.

Larry turned and ran toward the house. He clenched his fist and hammered it against the door three times. 'Mrs Wasson? Bob?'

Bang, bang, bang.

His radio crackled. 'Suspect's trying to get in the back door, sir.'

He cupped his hand around his mouth and shouted up to Holly's window. 'Rachel!'

No answer.

'Rachel, this is the police. Open this door up now!'

Bang, bang.

Male voices grew louder. They were singing 'How Great Thou Art'.

'Rachel!'

Movement.

A click of the lock, a slide of a bolt. Mary Wasson's gaunt-looking face peeked out from the crack in the door looking like she was about to complain 'What's going—' The sound of singing quickly reached into her ears. Her face lit up with a child's smile. 'What's that? What's that beautiful—'

He slammed his hand into the door, almost toppling her as he blundered into the house. He looked at the hallway, and the closed door to the kitchen out to the back. There was no man coming in.

Yet.

He grabbed Mary's hand and dragged her up with him. 'You need to get upstairs.'

Mary Wasson dangled like a doll on his arm. 'I want to hear the music.'

He kept shouting, 'Bob, I *have* to come in right now, okay?'

347

When he reached the top of the steps he felt his feet slowing. Despite himself and the clear madness of the situation there was still enough time for that old fear to come back. That same dread that had sunk into him every time he passed this house, whenever he used to regularly patrol this part of London. It was that same fear he'd kept hidden from Matt the other night, because he was embarrassed to be so superstitious around him. Like most other people in Menham, Larry feared Barley Street. And him with more reason than most, because after all he'd cut her down, and she'd fallen into his arms and flooded him with cold. He stepped towards Holly's door, hearing voices from the inside. Calling out and saying Holly's name over and over.

He took a breath and pushed through the door, one hand gripped into Mary's. He opened his mouth, 'Is everybody alri . . .' He closed his mouth again. Bob Hodges was saying something and there was the sound of loud scratching like an angry pencil on paper. But it was coming from an expensive-looking audio player with speakers in the centre of the room.

Other than that, the room was empty.

He grabbed the recorder's plug and yanked it out. Rachel's voice vanished and another one replaced it.

'We've got him sir, in the back garden,' the radio crackled again. 'All under control. He's got some sort of liquid with him.'

Somewhere downstairs, he could hear shouting.

Mary's hand slid out of his and she rushed to the window where she grabbed the cardboard. She ripped it away in delight because it was the opening of a gift. The men's voices drifted in and she closed her eyes. She twirled and hugged herself, dancing along the waves of harmony.

When through the woods and forest glades I wander
and hear the birds sing sweetly in the trees;

He moved toward the window without thinking.

When I look down from lofty mountain grandeur,

He pulled back the curtain.

And hear the brook, and feel the gentle breeze;

He leant toward the glass to see who was down there and saw what he now knew was the Phoenix Club, carrying candles and holding tiny crosses toward the house, like it was one big, pebble-dashed vampire. And when they looked up at the window some of them gasped to see a figure there, even though it was just him. Like he was the Barley Street ghost.

He stepped back from their gasping gaze and that same old floorboard creaked beneath his feet. The one he remembered when he stood here, when he reached up to cut her down. And Holly was in his ear again, which froze him to the spot. Something stroked the back of his neck, and he wondered if it was her long hair, dangling from the beam and touching him, like it did that morning. Her toes, brushing his stomach, like they did. Her curled, blue hands, bumping against his shoulders. Her feeling so light.

'Sir,' Butterfield said through the radio. 'Did you hear me? We've got him.'

He blinked once. Twice. Told himself to get a grip. There was work to be done.

He rushed from the room, pushing past Mary, and not looking back. Refusing to look at the window again, just in case she was there.

They always told him that the first dead body of a child never really leaves you. And they were right.

CHAPTER FIFTY-ONE

Keech curved his police car around the corner of Barley Street
and into Perry Road, letting the tyres drift a little into a skid. He
caught Matt's eyes at the screeching squeak of rubber on tarmac.
'One of the little perks of the job,' he said, then slammed the car
back into fifth.

Around him, Matt watched the shops and homes of Menham
flick by. Urban, into suburban. Retail park into industrial estate.
MOT garage into plumbing suppliers, and then what looked like a
scrapyard of old cars.

Keech snuck one last skid out, around an empty roundabout
and then they were pulling into Ashburn Drive. It quickly led to
a square of connecting roads, surrounded by tall, empty-looking
buildings.

He jerked the car to a quick, shoulder-wrenching stop and killed
the engine. 'Behold,' he yanked the handbrake. 'The outer rims of
infinity.'

They both stepped out and Matt was surprised at how desolate this part of Menham was. It was close to the bypass and far from any shops, houses or pubs. All around were industrial buildings and council offices and a storage place with a few lights on. Most of the buildings were dark and empty now. He saw one with a sign saying Council Offices. As he recalled, *that* was the former, infamous children's home.

And in the centre of the buildings was a square of land, about the size of a petrol forecourt with a fence around it and a painted mural of happy children. A sign hung from the wood.

Danger: Subsidence

The vaults.

It was odd, but he didn't feel like he was standing in London any more. Other than Keech, he couldn't see a single other person walking these streets. But more than that, the city sounds were extremely quiet. Which struck him as very strange. It was as if the rest of Menham was many miles away and not just down a few streets and turns. This was a sound stage, where the buildings had nothing behind them, so that all life here had a sense of unreality about it.

But then he saw the *one* other car parked. A BMW.

Just as he clocked it, the driver's door popped open and two long legs slid out. High heels landed with a click on the pavement.

'Well, hello . . .' Keech said, under his breath.

She didn't walk towards them both. She *strode*. 'Who's this?'

'I'm Police Constable Keech, madam.'

She looked down at his earnest, cap-doffing style, the hinge at the hip, and just snorted out laughter. Keech looked instantly crushed.

'What do you have on the Hodges?' Matt said. 'And make it quick, please.'

She flicked a thumb against her chin. 'Let's just say that I've been wondering if their interest in Holly Wasson wasn't a little more than . . . scientific.'

'It'd be helpful if you could be less vague.' Keech pulled out a notepad.

'All I know,' her voice was low and raspy, 'is that Joyce and Bob Hodges taught science at our school.'

'That's common knowledge,' Matt said.

'And I always remember they retired early. Not long before their official retirement was due. Anyway, I've been digging into that and it turns out there was a very good *reason* why they stepped down.' She pulled out her vapour pipe and gave it a quick suck. 'Rumour was that they were found with kiddy porn in their work bags.'

Matt waited to compute this. Keech scribbled a note.

'Were they charged?' Matt said.

'No. But that doesn't mean much, does it?'

'But if the school found out something like that, they'd prosecute. They'd tell someone.' He turned to Keech. 'Do you know anything of this?'

'News to me.' He shook his head. 'Who *told* you this?'

'The lab assistant at school told me tonight. He fancied me at the time. He'd have asked me out back then if I wasn't a student but, hey . . . I'm not a student now . . .' she trailed off with a smirk. 'I tracked him down and asked him outright. He said they found a picture of naked boys in their bag. They said it was just a prank. Someone planted it on them . . . The school fell for it and let them off, but he's not so sure. And neither am I. Plus . . . *guess* when all this happened?' Her eyes sparkled, relishing the drama. 'Just after Halloween, 2001. When they were . . .' she put up her fingers to make air quotes, 'helping poor little Holly out with her ghost problem.'

'If the police didn't prosecute, maybe it *was* just a prank.'

She shook her head. 'Think it through. A couple of teachers with busy hands leave school cos they get caught with their filth. So they can't get their rocks off by spying on pupils any more, so what do they do? They find a kid they can sit alone with for hours on end. They can sit with her in her bedroom with her mum's complete permission, just so they can,' she used air quotes again, 'talk about spooks and video her and God knows what else.' She blew out another cloud of vapour, on a roll now. 'Haven't you ever noticed what the symptoms are?'

'Symptoms?'

'Of kids who are supposedly haunted? They're withdrawn, they're distant, some of them rush off into fantasy worlds. And some of them even,' she whispered the words, drawing out each one, 'kill themselves.'

Keech shook his head, unconvinced, but Matt just waited in the silence. Considering it.

'Think about it, Matt.' Kassy leant over, in a cloud of sickly perfume. 'Aren't those the exact same symptoms of a kid that's getting fiddled with?'

He winced and stepped away from her. 'Do you always have to put things in the starkest way possible?'

'It saves time, but I've got a point, though, haven't I?'

He thought about it and decided that yeah, the symptoms were very similar indeed. 'So what are you proposing here?'

'Proposing?' she laughed. 'I'm saying we barge into that seance and tell Rachel she's got a couple of pervs for friends. And heck, who knows what they're doing to *her* right now.'

'Fine,' Keech said. 'Then get in the car.'

'Huh?'

'I said get in the car. We'll go back to Barley Street and ask the Hodges abou—'

'Barley Street?' She screwed up her face. 'They're down *there*, dimwit.' She flicked a thumb back to the fence. 'Rachel filled me in.'

'They're in the *vaults*?' Matt flicked his gaze past her.

She was already kicking off her high heels and was pulling out a pair of pumps from her bag. ''Course they are. There's a crack in the fence. So now I've you and a copper with me, we can head down and get some answers. Because despite what Rachel thinks, I know it wasn't the vault that drove Holly to top herself. That's a complete dead end. I reckon it was those two old buggers. And the state Rachel's in and the guilt she feels . . . well. I mean she and Holly were sisters; what if they're as fragile as each other – know what I mean?' Kassy pointed at her brain, tapping her temple. 'What if she's liable to follow her sister and hang herself, you can see how guilty she—'

'Enough!' Matt narrowed his eyes at her. 'We need to check if they're okay . . .'

Keech's radio suddenly crackled into life.

'This is DS Forbes. Sergeant Keech? Come in?'

He grabbed his shoulder and spoke into the black box strapped to it. 'This is Keech, come in.'

'We need you back at Barley Street. Suspect has been apprehended. Repeat, suspect is apprehended and in custody.'

Matt's jaw dropped and he rushed over. 'How? Who?'

'Matt? Is that you?'

'Yes. Who was it?'

'We've just arrested Pastor Todd Holloway from Menham Evangelical. We got him climbing over the back wall of Number 29 and attempting entry to the house.'

'Bloody hell.'

'Suspect's admitted he threw the cross the other night. Tonight he was carrying a smaller cross and a bottle of liquid. Might be acid or something for the urine. We're getting it checked out.' He paused. 'Was acid used against witches?'

'No,' Matt frowned and stared down at his shoes, thinking.

'Oh, and one thing. It looks like the Hodges shifted venues on us. They've been playing a recording up there the whole—'

'We know. The seance is here,' Keech said. 'At the vaults.'

'Is it? Oh. Right. Well . . .' Larry thought for a second. 'Well, drag them all out of there, they're trespassing. And report back to Barley Street straight after. Over and out.'

The radio crackled into silence, and Keech looked up, smiling. 'Typical. We dick off just when all the action happens.' He caught Matt's eyes, and frowned. 'What's up with you?'

Matt shrugged, and shook his head. 'I'm not sure.' Then he turned to Kassy. 'Listen, we'd better get—'

The pavement behind them was empty.

'Where'd she—'

'*There*,' Keech pointed to the opened crack in the fence. 'She's heading down there already.'

He watched the curve of her blonde hair lowering into the grass, like she was being swallowed by the world. But then she put out her hand. She curled a beckoning finger towards them.

Come on . . . come down here. It'll be fun.

Words she had no doubt said to Holly.

She pulled the hatch shut.

Keech was already jogging toward the gap. 'Let's get after her.'

Matt winced. 'Maybe we should wait.'

'What for? The guy's been arrested and I'll only be a sec.'

He watched Keech scrape himself through the gap on his own. He shook his head.

'Hold up,' he ran up behind him and stooped through the fence. Splintered wood scraped the back of his head. Inside, the vaults were just a patch of knee-high grass. They waded through it as it swayed in the night's constant breeze, and a few huge nettle bushes that looked like mad alien creatures tried to reach out and grab them both. On the ground he kept noticing gaps in the grass that hid grey discs sitting at the bottom. These were the sealed metal hatches to the vaults. Though in this light they looked, naturally, like rabbit holes, burrowing into the ground.

He kept moving, confused at how it seemed to be taking them such a long time to cross such a small space, and he could see – near the far corner – the faintest glow coming from a slit in the ground. They hurried toward it and discovered the only hatch that was open, just a crack. So was this the one Holly was dumped in, one cruel Halloween night? With a bunch of cackling harpies in fancy dress slamming the lid shut?

Keech grabbed the rusty handle and yanked at it like it was the door of a tank. It opened pretty easily and popped further back than he expected. When they looked down Matt saw a row of three candles ten foot down in the dirt, flickering at the base of a warped-looking metal ladder.

He got an instant flash of anger. Picturing Holly thrown down here and shut in. And he figured that Holly really did deserve an apology, even if she couldn't possibly hear one. He was about to head down when he heard his phone was ringing. He was surprised when it was the ringtone he'd assigned to his house, which Amelia had insisted he install. 'Calling Occupants of Interplanetary Craft' crackled out. Amelia liked that song because it was about space. It sounded tinny and slim now, echoing off the tall black buildings. Karen Carpenter sounded like some wistful ghost, dancing through the long grass behind him.

Keech stared at the phone in confused disgust. 'I'm going down.'

'Just give me a minute,' he fumbled with the phone.

'I'll meet you down there.'

'Wren?' Matt said, as Keech put his foot on the first rung.

'It's Amelia.'

'Hey, Midget,' he whispered. 'I'm busy and it's really late. I'll have to call you ba—'

'Come down to me.' Her voice was quiet and gravelly.

'Pardon?'

'The shadow in my room . . . it says come down here and give your mum a hug.'

He frowned at the phone, 'Amelia?'

'Nana's opening her arms . . .'

'Amelia, you're dreaming. Put Mummy on.'

'It's cold here, Matt. It's cold in the dark.'

'Put Mummy on.'

'Soon, she says. She's going to see you soon. And you're gonna *like* it.'

Keech called up to him, still waiting at the bottom of the ladder. 'Call them back! Kassy's long gone.'

Matt heard a ruffled sound, and then a new voice answered. 'Matt?'

'Wren.' His shoulders sank in relief. 'Is she asleep?'

'Yeah. She's walked into my room. Found her standing by my bed, which was freaky. Listen, when are you coming home because we all—'

'I'll call you back, okay?'

Wren let out a breath into the phone.

'Sorry. Just tell her I love her and I'll be home as soon as I'm—'

'Fiiine,' she said. The phone clicked off.

'Are you done?' Keech was at the bottom.

'Coming.'

Matt looked down the rusty metal ladder, bolted into the stone. The light from the three candles shimmered off Keech's shiny shoes. God, it looked like a grave down here; they'd locked her in a tomb. Just before he headed down he glanced back at the gap in

357

the fence and the police car beyond it. Then up at the black spread of the sky above him.

Back in Dunwich, where he grew up by the sea, he and his mum would often sit on the beach at midnight, watching for falling stars. The skies were far, far clearer than they were here. Whenever one of them streaked across the sky, she'd say that the night was so full of stars that every now and again God would flick one away to make room for the others. But as he looked up now, he saw nothing but cloud, smog and dust-covered moths in the air, and he felt a biting coldness moving through his chest that he was struggling to explain because right now the breeze had gone.

He put his foot on the ladder.

Don't jump off, son.

He started heading down.

CHAPTER FIFTY-TWO

Rabbit tumbling down the hill,
in grass and flowers, filled with plenty
pleasures growing, singing gently,
channelling the power of twenty,
thousand, million days and seconds,
Sad for those that never ran,
Never stopped the girls
Who climb inside the riddled mind of man.
who
Smash the heart of worlds and planets.
Devils hopping through the wood,
Calling up the seed and soil.
So gentle grass might turn to blood.
But not for rabbit,
Time to tear a
Light in shadows,
Almost there.

Almost there.
To cut her down.
Snap the twig,
To save the town.
Snap the twig,
And slit her open,
Guzzle
all her power down.

Turn the bad to light.
Petals back to white.
Shout it from the hill and dance,
That rabbit made it right.

CHAPTER FIFTY-THREE

So, Rachel thought, as the images swam. Hell is a warren.

Hell is a rabbit warren deep inside the earth with barely any light, with dusty brick corridors and the strangest-looking beetles you ever saw. While the King Black Rabbit drags you by the hair through it all, for eternity because you had the balls-out audacity to think making your friends laugh was more important than another human being's sanity.

She rolled her eyes up, though she didn't want to, and saw the rabbit pressing on ahead. Her trendy quiff, the one she'd specifically told the hairdresser to keep long with the rest of it short because she felt that was *next* not now, was revealing its true purpose. Bunched together and pulled straight and tight. Terminating into a single point that was somewhere inside the rabbit's hand.

When it first slashed its claws at Joyce and Bob it had reached over and yanked Rachel's hair, dragged her right off the chair and spun her round. Even as the Hodges cried out and stumbled after her. At first the pain in the scalp was immense. As if her entire front fringe would loudly tear away like a badly glued wig and her Joan of Arc head would crash to the floor.

But it didn't tear away because even in hell good genes remain good genes. And after a while the pain slipped across the threshold of hurt, over the peaks of agony and settled itself into a numb shutting down of the nerves in that part of her body. She could barely feel it now, even as the rabbit dragged her over the loose bricks that were scattered in the dirt.

Every now and again the rabbit would look back down at her and tilt its head a little. And at one point, through the bubble of her tears, she saw a flash of its eyes locked on hers. She wondered if that was hunger she was seeing there. And quickly decided yes, it was definitely, certainly, undoubtedly *hunger*. Maybe that's all hell is, after all. Just an elaborate tube and tunnel system to get people to Satan's kitchen. To his oven. His plate.

She felt the rabbit slow down. She heard the sound of tinkling metal.

Keys.

The rabbit was rattling keys into a rusted iron door that said 'Recreation Room' above it.

I don't really feel like ping-pong right now, she thought – screaming or laughing, it didn't matter which. Down here, such expressions were essentially the same thing.

Then the door creaked open, catching on some rubble on the floor so that the rabbit had to grapple with it and drag it open. Then she was in a room that had actual light in it. Not candlelight but electric light. Dull and buzzing in the corner, turning this part of the vault into a deep, photographer's-studio red. *Hell* red. Over in the corner she saw a huge pile of heavy bricks and breeze blocks, like that rabbit had been knocking walls down as it burrowed its way down here.

She felt that clump of fringe sliding through the rabbit's hand

362

and a second later her right shoulder crashed into the floor. The side of her skull clocked off the concrete with a comedy-sounding pop. A cricket ball cracking off wood. The impact set tiny fireworks exploding in the corners of her vision. Then the rabbit was crouching, yanking at her arms and tying her to what looked like metal pegs wedged into the floor. Her arms stretched wide and the rabbit kicked her legs open and tied the ankles.

She was a star shape. She was a snow angel, bathed in red light.

She could hear the rabbit's breath heavy in its mouth and every time it breathed its face seemed to suck in and out, like it was puckering up for a kiss.

No . . . not an *it* . . . she thought. A *he*. The Black Rabbit is a *he*. And he is preparing his:

Snow Angel.

His rape victim.

She heard herself say. *Oh, God.*

He kicked her ankles apart.

It was while he was tying up the last ankle that she first started to pay attention to the walls. To what looked like hundreds of pictures stuck there with gaffer tape. Pictures that were ragged and torn at the edge. Ripped from newspapers and magazines. Even in the midst of hell, she found it hard to resist that habit she'd always had when she was alive. Of always wanting to lean over on the Tube or in the street to see what book a passer-by was weeping or yawning through.

She lifted her head a little and blinked. Lots of pictures, lots of faces on the wall.

That was when the rabbit started to talk. Standing up above her, sucking his face in and out. And he said, 'Say the Lord's Prayer. *Say* it.'

'What . . .' she said, 'what?'

Then she heard a noise coming from beyond the wall. The Rabbit flicked his head to the side.

Some sort of scrape.

The rabbit gasped.

'The prayer. Try and remember it,' he said. Then he suddenly scurried off into a dark corner. Gone.

She stared at the red glowing bricks above her while her baffled brain flicked through the files of desperate fears, of teeth chatters, of heartbeats close enough to the chest to hurt. Searching like a madwoman for sanity and courage but most of all . . . for long-forgotten prayers.

CHAPTER FIFTY-FOUR

He skipped the final rung of the ladder and dropped soundlessly into the dirt, just behind Keech. The impact wafted a tiny cloud of dust around his ankles that fluttered the three candles at the base. One of them blew out and he saw its ghost twist into the air, then vanish.

The candles must have been there to mark out the exit and he was pretty convinced the Hodges had put them there. The biggest clue they were down here was one of those expensive Yankee Candle jobs called Sycamore Dreams – and everybody knows that only English old ladies and American cat-fans buy those from garden centres. Try as it might, the thin flame did nothing to overcome the intense odour of dust and wet stone.

Frankly he was amazed the old coots had managed it down this ladder without snapping a hip. They were dedicated, he had to give them that.

They were in a surprisingly long, very narrow arched corridor, sloping downwards into claustrophobia. It was made of rotting, crumbling bricks. He could hear trickling water coming from somewhere.

Matt could visualise the patch of grassland directly above him and realised that this tunnel that he was looking at stretched beyond that. It meant the vaults didn't just sit under that modest square above, but ran deep beneath at least the street, and maybe under some of the buildings too. Presumably to the council offices, where the children's home staff utilised every inch of this place.

They started heading down the dusty slope, but slowly. Trying not to slip.

'It used to be a bomb shelter back in the 40s,' Keech whispered, flicking on his torch. The beam revealed glistening, black-looking bricks, close enough to scrape each shoulder. 'The council kept it like that till the early 90s just in case another war kicked off. Anyway, nobody knows what to do with it. Companies have tried to redevelop, but there's something up with the ground round here. It's too wet. History groups keep trying to get it listed. For the war part. Them sorry buggers like to list anything as old as they are. Pretty spooky though, eh?'

The corridor started getting even more narrow so Matt kept sliding his elbows against the stone. They passed a green metal door to the side, but when Matt pushed it, it didn't budge.

'That's been locked for decades. Seance must be through the bottom one, in the main vault.' Keech swung his beam to it and got moving again. Still chatty. 'Turfed a homeless couple out of here once, and, you know, I *almost* left them. Least it was out of the rain.' They trudged through the filthy sloping floor. 'Almost there.'

It was cold down here. Really, really cold. Enough for Matt to start shivering under the thin blazer jacket he was wearing. He pulled out his phone for a little extra light. He shone it behind him. The corridor must have turned on a curve, because he couldn't see the candles by the ladder any more.

Unless someone had put them out.

The light of his phone didn't reach far, which meant that theoretically there could be someone creeping behind them in the blackness back there and they wouldn't know.

He looked away and saw a mass of rubbish strewn along the floor. Crisp packets and coke cans and what might have been condom packets. There were tiny bits of white too, which at first he thought were cigarette butts but when he kicked some by accident they turned out to be bones from mice. Or maybe birds.

They reached the door, and it looked like something from a World War II submarine. 'I come down here every couple of months, you know,' Keech said, as he put his hand on it. 'To break up parties. Some kids brought a whole sound system—'

He froze.

A murmur came from beyond the door.

They looked at each other.

Keech pushed but it didn't seem to move much. So he heaved a little harder and Matt pushed too with both hands splayed. It screeched itself open, dragging on gravel into a stone room filled with pitch-darkness.

Matt scanned the room with his phone light while Keech flicked his torch beam.

'*There*.' Matt immediately picked out a metal folding chair sitting near the centre. Two more were nearby but they were tipped on their side.

Keech shrugged. 'Where are they? Have we missed—'

'*Bob?*' Matt darted to the shape on the floor. 'Oh shit.'

He was lying on his right side, with an arm stretched out in the dust. There was a reek of metal in the air. Iron. Matt knew that wasn't the door smell. It was blood.

'Keech,' Matt called out. 'Radio for help. Now.'

'I doubt there's any signal . . .' The cold room echoed with the squelch of static as he tried to call it in. 'Bastard,' he snapped. 'Nothing.' He flicked the torch beam at Bob. 'Oh . . . oh, that's not good.'

Bob's beard was spattered with blood and it glistened in the light. His glasses were misted.

'Bob? Can you hear me?'

Nothing.

'Bob. It's me. It's Matthew Hunter. Where's—'

Slam.

Matt jumped. Keech jumped. Bob lay still.

The metal door they'd just pushed through had slammed back into place. Keech raced over to it.

'Some joker's locked us in! Dammit.'

'Bob?' Matt shook his shoulder. 'Can you hear me? Where *is* everyone?' He quickly tugged Bob's glasses off. 'Bob?'

His eyes were blinking slowly.

'What the hell happ—'

'Turn . . .' Bob groaned, '. . . it . . . off.'

'What?'

'Turn it off . . . the light.'

'We need to see. Bob, where are the others?'

'Took them . . . white door.' His voice was like dry leather, twisted. He moved his head a little and wheezed horribly. Matt shifted his phone light down and groaned. A fist-sized chunk of Bob's thigh was hanging off.

'Oh, crap,' Matt said.

'Turn off the light . . .' Bob whispered.

'Keech, he's really hurt.'

But Keech was already rushing to the far corner, snapping out a combat stick like he thought he was a ninja, stepping into battle. The torch beam picked out a white door. Keech slammed his foot into it. It swung inward with a horrible metallic wailing.

'Wait,' Matt shouted but Keech was already through. He vanished inside.

Seconds. It was literally a handful of seconds before it happened.

First, Matt saw the torchlight vanish. Then he heard Keech scream from the shadows. Loud and panicked. And then – and this was the detail that made Matt stumble back – the scream sounded *wet*. Matt quickly set his phone on the floor, so its pathetic glow might light up the room.

The dull glow was nothing like the torch had been. It made the place look like a dream.

A black figure came tumbling out of the door.

Matt frantically looked around for a weapon. A brick. A metal bar. There was nothing.

A chair. He grabbed one of the chairs and raised it up high.

'Keech?'

The figure stumbled into the glow of the phone and started to speak. 'Something grabbed me in the dark . . . they got my torch and my baton,' Keech spat something out. Retching.

'What's on your face?' Matt gripped the chair, chest heaving. 'What the hell is on your face?'

'Bugger smeared me with something,' Keech touched his mouth, then he leant over and instantly started to vomit. In the dim light, Matt could just about make out an odd shape at the bottom of the door. A circle, rolling. Wait . . . he stepped forward. The rim of a metal bucket, tipped on its side. Mary Wasson's dead cat slid out in a pool of its own fluids.

Matt heard a bizarre voice snap out from the darkness, shouting a word.

The word was 'Eat!'

Bob's groan. 'Turn the fucking light off.'

Then a bigger shadow moved above the cat in the bucket. A

shadow strode over it, pushing the bucket aside. Not a man. Not a hellish rabbit creature.

But an animal, none the less.

Something on all fours. Springing from the door and bolting for Keech.

That voice again. 'Eat.' Then the door slammed shut.

The white dog raced across the dust and leapt through the air at Keech.

And Matt knew in the bullet time moment that this wasn't just the creature that had ripped a chunk from Bob's leg. It was the one that tore the throat from Steph Ellis. And the one that peered in at a frightened old lady in the dark. Muzzle caked with blood.

His phone toppled over. The light went out.

And the world turned black with male screams and tears and ravenous growling.

CHAPTER FIFTY-FIVE

Rachel blinked.

Rabbit was back.

Hope, dumb as it was, died.

'I'd like you to recite the Lord's Prayer, please.'

It was an unexpectedly gentle voice. Echoed and muffled, but soft.

'Why do you—'

'From the beginning and say it all the way to the end, with no mistakes. You have three chances.' The rabbit scraped up a wooden stool and sat on it. Perched. His fingertips now looked wet and sticky-looking. He was holding something black. 'Now, please.'

She frowned at him and looked back at all the newspaper clippings on the wall, and the door next to it. For the first time she thought, maybe this *wasn't* hell after all. Maybe Jo and Steph and Kassy and Holly were going to burst through the door with a camera crew and say, 'Ha ha, our epic, years-long prank is complete! We got you good, didn't we?'

And maybe the rabbit would pull off its mask as well and it'd be Debbie saying, 'Hey, hey! You have passed the test! You are way tougher than I thought you were. Let's get married!' Applause. High fives all round.

Is that what it was? A mask?

As she thought about all this, the rabbit stared at her through the holes in his face. 'You can't even *start* The Lord's Prayer?' he said. Not angry, but pleased.

When she spoke, it was through a long, fretful groan, 'Our Father . . .'

'Yes?'

'Who art in heaven . . . hallowed be . . . hallowed be thy name.'

The rabbit dragged his seat forward a little, scratching the floor. 'Yes . . . yes?'

'Thy Kingdom come, thy will be done. On earth as it is in heaven . . .'

'Heaven, yes . . .'

'. . . er . . .'

He sat suddenly upright, head twitching to attention. 'Stuck?'

'. . . is in heaven . . .'

'Yes,' he nodded. 'On earth as it is in heaven . . .'

Wait . . . What was next? On earth as it is in heaven . . .

– forgive.

– Forgive?

– Give!

'Give us this day . . . our daily bread.'

The rabbit sighed and wiped his sticky fingers on his knee. Then he lifted the black thing in his hand. She heard a click. A hefty beam of light shot out of his hand. Dust, hair and flies danced in it. The glow shone up his face and Rachel could see that despite his calm, pleasant tone, his eyes were wild and bulging behind the small latex holes. He turned his head and followed the

372

torch beam. He took one of his long fingers and pointed it in the direction of the light.

'Carry on . . .' he said. 'Our daily bread.'

She turned to see what he was pointing at, 'As we forgive those—'

The words froze in her throat. Literally froze, sharp enough to cut her.

'Yes?'

No sound came out. How could it?

'You can't finish it?'

'*Kassy?*' she said into the beam of light.

'Finish it now or you'll have failed the test.'

'*Kassy?*'

'Please, I'm serious. Finish the test.'

'*Kassy!*'

The rabbit was on his feet, shaking his head. Leaving the torch on the floor so he could freely wander along its beam of light toward Kassy. She was unconscious and tied to a chair.

Rachel called out her name again while he started slapping his palm hard across Kassy's cheek, trying to wake her up.

Is this in my mind? Is this a breakdown? Am I sitting in a doctor's surgery right now, back in Salford, while nurses shake and prod me awake . . .

'Well, it looks like you've both failed the test,' he said into her ear.

'Did Holly send you?' Rachel said to the rabbit, crying now.

It was the only thing she had said so far that slowed him down. Rabbit paused, and looked up at the red ceiling. 'In a way, yes.'

'But I've told her I'm sorry. For what we did to her.'

'Oh really? And what about them?' He pointed over at the wall with the newspaper cuttings plastered on it. 'And what about all the other children you've corrupted?'

'What children?'

'You've forgotten their names? They're nothing to you, I bet.'

'*What* children?'

'Well, how about I remind you? Penny Mendelson, Stephanie Billing. Rachel Tovey. What about Helen Bexley or Louisa Ford?' He shook his head. 'And what about that little girl in the park the other day? What about her?'

'What? Who are you talking about?'

'Your victims!' He shouted it so loud, so sharp, that it felt like the bricks might instantly loosen from one another and the vaults would bury them all.

Rachel was bewildered but she noticed Kassy's eyes were fluttering open. One of them looked black from some sort of impact.

Rachel called out, 'Kass?'

The rabbit was walking towards Rachel and she could tell he wasn't so much angry. He was wringing his wet, bloodied hands and was whimpering. Heartbroken. That behind that mask—

– *it was a mask. She knew that now.*

—he was distraught. And he dropped to his knees and curled a wet finger toward himself. Tapping on his chest with it, and then with the flat of his hand, which somehow told her that she really *was* here. And that he was really here as well.

'And what about me, Rachel?' He was weeping against rubber now. Openly, with huge, quaking shoulders. 'What about me and the life you all sent me on? Are you girls ever going to apologise for that?'

CHAPTER FIFTY-SIX

A silver-looking Dobermann with a collar made of thick string dangled off Keech's shoulder. Hanging with nothing more than the power of its jaw.

Matt raced at Keech, with the chair held high. The polite professor voice in his head said, *Ermmm, Matthew, old chap. Is this wise? Mightn't you hit the policeman?*

Keech's eyes were bulging.

Matt wound his arm back, coiled the spring and let rip, canvas and metal slashing through the air.

Crack.

His arms shook with the impact. The dog instantly yelped and opened its mouth. It dropped to the floor. He watched it scamper into a shadow and vanish. Keech slapped a hand against his shoulder, grabbing at the gap where the dog had been. The pink skin of his fingers flooded instantly red.

Keech groaned, 'Shit, shit, shit.'

'Get your jacket off. We can tie—'

Claws. Scraping into a run.

Matt spun and lifted the chair for another smack but the animal slammed into his legs, way sooner than he expected. He noticed the sensation of needles being plunged into his foot. He yelped and dropped the chair, falling to the floor. Something warm flooded across his ankle.

The dog was clamped on his shoe, dragging him.

Short of breath, Matt clenched his fist. He couldn't think of anything else. He just accessed a fact logged from a documentary he'd watched about sharks. He made a fist and slammed into the dog's eye. Sharp hair spiked into his knuckle. Then he did it again. And again. Smack. Smack.

Every punch and the vice grew tighter.

Agonised, and gasping in panic—

There's a woman screaming, he suddenly realised. *There's a woman down here screaming, and I can hear it.*

—he punched again.

He had a brainwave and pushed the wedding ring finger out a little. He punched one more time, as hard as he could manage. The golden band that Wren had given him on the best day of his life sunk into the dog's eye. It suddenly squeaked and eased off his foot. It staggered to the side. Went to turn on him.

Matt jumped right on top of it and it rolled onto its back, paws kicking the air. He grabbed a paw in each hand. Hairy joysticks controlling the most repellent moment that now hurtled toward his life experience.

'Snap the fucker,' Keech said. Slumped on the floor and weeping with the pain. 'Go on.'

His brain slipped into instant schizophrenia.

'Snap the dog,' Keech winced. 'Snap him.'

Matt thought, *I'm a university professor. I don't do that. Our campus has a very strict policy on animal welfa—*

376

Furious barking.

'Snap him. Snap the fucking dog!'

A sudden, random image of him with his angry father in a pet shop.

But I don't want a dog, Dad.

Furious barking.

How could you not want a dog, son? What's wrong with you?

The hot gush of canine breath. All this in the dark.

It happened so quick that it was almost impossible to understand it. Matt gripped both paws and quickly pushed them outwards, away from each other.

Wider.

Wider.

Maybe it'll get tired, he thought. *Maybe its fight's all gone.*

He liked that option. Loved it, in fact. Threw his psyche with wild enthusiasm all over it. But the dog started snapping even louder at his face. So he pushed. Pushed as hard as he could.

'*Do it!*' Keech screamed.

Matt smelt his dad somewhere in the room, scurrying up to him on all fours in the dark—

what's the matter with this kid, Elizabeth, what's the matter with him? All boys want a dog, for Christ's sake—

He leant forward with all his body weight. The dog's paws raced away from each other, far past their normal arc. He closed his eyes, tight, and heard the sound of wet popping. A moist, loud crack in the dog's chest.

He retched right there and spat out a globule of bile. He somehow had the presence of mind to aim it away from the dog – like such a courtesy would balance out what he'd just done to it. But by then the dog's death nerves were twitching and Matt was climbing off.

Finished.

He pushed himself backwards. Chest heaving, hands shaking. Then he flipped into autopilot.

'Get your jacket off,' he hobbled to Keech, yanked the black policeman's jacket and tied it tight around his gushing shoulder. Then he ripped off his own jacket and did the same for Bob. Only for him, he had to pick up the small chunk of flesh and muscle that hung by threads. He popped it back into place. Almost puked.

Then as he tightened the knot he heard it again. The low muffled sound coming through the walls.

Somewhere in the vaults, a woman *was* screaming.

He stood up and glanced back at the metal door.

'I told you, it's locked.' Keech tried to hitch himself up but he didn't have the strength to stand.

So Matt turned back to the white door, knowing it was either that or sit in here while Rachel or Kassy or whoever it was that was screaming came to a stop. He looked down at his throbbing foot. There was some blood, but not a lot. The sole had protected him, mostly. He could limp through, at least.

'You better stay here,' Keech said, wincing. 'Help might come.'

Matt stared at the door.

'You should stay here.'

Matt shook his head. 'She's screaming.'

The stories you hear are how people leap in, despite all wisdom, despite all advice. They can't help themselves. It isn't stupidity, it isn't even bravery. It's just how the human brain works. Because leaving people to die when you can save them may well be a morally neutral act, philosophically speaking, but that didn't matter much, down here. Christians would call this divinely programmed altruism. He would call it evolutionary programmed herd survival. Save the others in your tribe, ensure longevity. Neither pointed to any overarching objective morality pattern. So he stood by everything in his book. Yet still, he knew, that in his world, to stand here and wait would be wrong. That he'd never, ever forget it.

He grabbed his phone, spattered with blood and dog hair. He smeared it on his jeans, one side then the other. He quickly hobbled to the door.

Another scream came, muffled and desperate. He had no weapon.

Somewhere in the vaults of his own heart, the ghost of the vicar he once was had already dropped to his knees, pleading with God for this to turn out okay. But when he reached out into the void, desperate for a rare second to be that man, it shimmered away and other voices, more gleeful and cruel, started whispering right into his ear.

Teenagers in witches' outfits, supping cider and laughing into the night. 'Let's leave her in there. Yeah, let's shut the hatch and run off.'

'No,' he said to them. 'Not me.'

No time left, no more moments in the jar.

Phone light. *Click*.

He pushed the door open.

CHAPTER FIFTY-SEVEN

It was an empty stone room, with a mattress in the corner. The place stank of oil and what seemed like . . . he sniffed the air . . . rubber.

He spotted another door on the other side of the room and was about to go through it when the screaming stopped. At the same time his phone light fell across a small desk that had been pushed against the wall. A metal chair was underneath it. A pile of history books sat neatly on the side. The top one was on medieval history, the one underneath was something on the Salem Witch Trials. The local paper lay on the desk, neatly folded, with its headline about the masturbating man at the school gates. But the page had been scribbled over with a few pens' worth of ink. The Menham Evangelical notice sheet sat next to it too and a flyer for the Phoenix Club.

Get your life back! it said.

He found a grubby notepad too, filled with strange poetry in blue ink.

But underneath that were a few articles, neatly cut from

newspapers. A five-second glance showed they had the same theme. They were reports about indecent assaults on girls. All of them were under ten. There were no pictures, no victims were named.

Which was why it was so odd that above each block of text, a name was neatly written.

Louisa Ford, 9, Penny Mendelson, 9, Ella Hudson, 9 and others. He leant forward and saw an article that looked different from the rest. This one had a photograph and a name.

Haunted House Mystery Ends in Suicide. Girl, 9, Dead

Holly Wasson stared up from the table, in a shot he hadn't seen before. Smiling on a swing, both hands holding the chains. Her head was cocked to the side with some sort of daisy clip in her hair, eyes squinting in the sunlight.

And then one final sheet, underneath them all. Not a newspaper cutting but a photocopied page from some old report. He slid the Holly picture to one side – with the phone rather than his fingers – and saw a series of young boys, naked. They stood in a line in front of a bare brick wall. Some had their hands over their eyes to block out the light from the flash. Instantly he knew what they were, because he felt that familiar loping, acidic turn in his stomach. The children's home abuse scandal. The pictures he'd seen on his phone.

This clipping was decades older than all the others on the desk, but it did share one thing with the rest. Directly above the head of one of the naked boys was a name, written with care though perhaps not pride. A very tall, skinny kid with a bulk to his shoulders and a haunt in his eye. He was looking at the camera as if the Devil himself was holding it, and Matt could tell who the boy was. It was the bald guy from the Phoenix Club, the one who had prayed at him the other morning, the one who spilled the coffee. The one with the gentle smile.

Matt stared at the picture of the boy on the table, and the name pencilled across.

Jeremy Phillip Marlowe, Aged 9.

He looked away at the bricks on the wall next to him, and then back at the ones in the picture. The same place.

The rubber smell was setting his teeth on edge, and he noticed an old cardboard box under the desk. He quickly dragged it out, looking for a weapon. He found something else instead.

Rubber masks.

Lots of them. Shaped like animals with string threaded through the back, all tattered. They had peeling labels inside, which looked very old indeed, thick with dust.

The box lid said *Christmas Show. 1979.* In red felt tip.

He glanced back at the picture of the boys. The date, January 12th 1980, was typed in the corner. He wondered . . . who had used these masks last? The children?

Something shivered across his back.

The staff.

The *staff* had used these. For anonymity.

He wanted to burn them. Nuke this repellent box into oblivion. But instead he quickly grabbed two, which turned out to be a white goat and a black owl. He quickly stretched the rubber around his foot and looped the masks together, threading each through warped eye and mouth holes. Animals in every sense, gripped him tight. It seemed to stay threaded. Seemed to keep the gash on his foot together. At least for now.

He heaved his leg to the other door and went to push it, but it was locked.

'Dammit,' he said, and wasn't surprised at how desperate and shaky he sounded.

His phone light picked up a hefty padlock with a large keyhole. It looked brand new. He grabbed the metal chair and started smashing the padlock as hard as he could. The sound clattering into sharp, awful echoes. All the while he fought against the images in his mind, of what these walls might have seen.

And as he pounded the door, a memory crept back. One of the chilling paragraphs from the Internet article. An interview with a local social worker in the late 90s. The essence of it had lodged in his brain and efficiently replayed itself, just like Larry said it would. Just like he'd said it would stick and never really leave.

Some of the boys used to come back . . .

After the home and the vaults were shut down and everything was locked, Menham people tried to forget, at first. And the abused kids got transferred to other institutions; or they left altogether and went out into the real world. And some of them did alright, you know? Some of them got jobs and got wives and broke free from all that darkness. But there were others who just couldn't. They wound up in prison. Now, I'm not saying all of them ended up doing what was done to them . . . but . . . there were some that did. And even after all that pain, some of the boys . . . the men . . . some of the men would come back. Sometimes even years later. Decades, even. Men in their thirties and forties who'd lost everything down here but we'd find them here at night. Heck, you know something . . . we still do. We still find a few of those men trying to get back in the vaults. And when we ask them why they'd want to be anywhere near this place they always tell us the same thing. They cry a lot and they say what's the harm, they say the vaults are empty anyway. And you can tell, and you want to know something? It breaks your heart every single time. You can tell it in the way they look at the place. They think they belong down here.

Matt glanced back at the sheet on the desk. The naked boy with large hands looking up and the name written in pencil above his head.

Jeremy Phillip Marlowe.

And in a circle, words that said: *ME . . . aged 9.*

'Jerry . . .' Matt closed his eyes. 'My God . . .'

He gripped the chair and pounded the lock with every ounce of strength that he had.

CHAPTER FIFTY-EIGHT

Rachel, still splayed out on the cold concrete, looked up at him. 'We'll apologise. Just tell us what we did and we'll—'

'It's just way too late for that.' The rabbit's voice was very low now. The melancholy tone had stepped aside, so that anger could come instead. 'Because you can't change what you are.'

'And what *are* we?' Kassy spluttered, finally. Struggling at the plastic cable ties trapping her to the chair. 'Come on, you weirdo. What are we?'

He flicked his head toward her and the rubber ears slapped against his face. He stood up. 'Now pay attention . . . both of you . . . thou shalt not suffer a witch to live.'

'Huh?' Kassy said, coughing.

The rabbit reached his hand up to scratch his neck. For the first time Rachel saw the fingers disappear under the latex flap of the mask. Because this was a human. This was reality, not hell.

Maybe he could be reasoned with.

'Can you please tell us what we did wrong?' Rachel said. Subservient. Polite. 'How did we hurt you?'

'You didn't just hurt me . . .' he said. 'You hurt all those girls. And Holly . . . the first. You know all this.'

'I don't understand.'

'You gave her to me,' he said. 'You threw her down here and you offered her up.'

'What are you talking about?'

'On your special night. On Halloween. You gave Holly to me.'

'. . . I don't under—' Clarity. Bursting like a bubble of vomit in her throat. A low explosion on the horizon of her mind, growing into a giant, terrible mushroom. 'You were *down* here? You were down here that night?'

'You *knew* I was down here. That's why you came.'

There was a scream deep in her heart, one which had been assembling itself for half of her life, that now started to fight its way up her throat for light. She started swallowing hard to keep it down, just a minute longer.

'You came here,' he said. 'With your pointy hats and your witches' capes and you threw her down. And you *knew* what I was fighting down here. You knew that I didn't want to do that sort of thing. But you pushed her right under my nose and you made me go over to her.'

Rachel's eyes were closing and she could feel her jaw starting to tighten. She started to shake her head from left to right, ears scraping the dirt floor.

No. No. No. No.

'And at first I tried to be good. I tried to turn it all around. You'd left her and she was crying so I held her hand and I told her it'd be okay. Told her I'd get her out of here and take her back to her parents . . . I . . . I told her I was lonely like she was and that maybe we could be friends.' He let out this long groan of regret. The latex hole across his mouth stretched into a gaping ellipse. 'But then I could hear you up there. The four of you. Laughing and egging me on. And you were putting that spirit in me. The one you've been pumping down here for years. Into any man who's ever set foot in here. And you were making me *want* to . . . even though I didn't want to. I was holding her hand and you made me . . .'

'Don't say it,' Rachel gasped. 'Don't say it, don't say it, don't say it.'

Kassy was silent.

The rabbit was crying into his mask again. 'And I was scared she'd tell after . . . so I had to find her house and scare her, that's all. I had to tell her the rabbit would get her if she told anybody . . .' A gulping sob. 'But I never wanted her to hurt herself. My God. Not *ever*.' The sorrow fell back into fury again. These, she could tell, must have been the constant rhythms of his life. 'But *you* did, didn't you? The four of you. She told me how much you hated her.'

'I didn't . . . I didn't hate her . . .' Rachel's face crumbled into despair.

'Because that's what you people love, isn't it? That's why you exist. To steal, kill and destroy.' He flung his hands toward the wall.

'You're insane,' Kassy said and for the first time in her life Rachel could hear tears in that voice.

'And you've been there, every time,' he went on. 'In the shadows of my room. All four of you. Telling me to find someone. And I've seen you in Menham Park by your tree. You stand by the swings in the afternoons. Calling me over and showing me what you have for me . . .' He snapped his words out. 'But it's got to stop, do you hear me? It's got to stop right now. Because I'm not your familiar and you can't do this to me any more. I'm getting my life back, and you can't hurt those little angels any more because it's just wrong. Witchcraft is a sin and the four of you . . . you've bewitched me.'

'What if we repented?' Rachel said. Even as the walls dropped silently away and she fell backwards through the concrete under her spine and down into the Abyss. Didn't Joyce say that forgiveness could unlock any prison?

'But you'll never repent! You've been ruining men for centuries. So I won't stop this until it's over. I swear to God, I'll kill the last of the Menham witches.' He turned to Kassy and hissed, 'Especially you.'

Rachel's crying halted for a minute. She swallowed. 'What do you mean, "especially her"?'

Silence.

'What do you mean, "especially her"?'

'I mean . . . she's the one . . .'

'What?'

Kassy's voice. 'Stop it.'

'The one that told me.'

'*Told you what?*'

'Don't listen to him, Rach. He's mad—'

'To wait down here. That night.'

Kassy started moaning. Yanking hard at the plastic cables. 'He's . . . he's . . .' She couldn't get her words out.

'She said I should wait down here.'

Rachel flicked her head to the side so fast it scraped lines in her cheek.

Kassy was staring over at her, mouth moving but nothing was coming out. Her swollen, purple eye was trying to peel open.

'She said wait in the dark and a little girl would come.'

Kassy started flailing her hands and feet but they were locked tight to the chair at the ankles and wrist. And then suddenly her gasps turned into desperate, guilty sobs. 'It was a joke. It was just a stupid joke. I just wanted to scare her.'

The rabbit started walking towards Kassy. He pulled

something from his pocket. A pile of bright papers. Post-it notes.

'You *knew* he was down here?' Rachel said.

'I thought he was some homeless guy. I thought it'd scare her.'

'We left her down here and you *knew*?'

'I didn't mean . . .' Kassy suddenly erupted into tears. A shattering display of someone who wasn't Kassy and yet was. 'It was a stupid fucking joke. I didn't know he'd actually do anything to her, I swear to God we didn't.'

'*We?*' Rachel said.

Kassy nodded. 'Me and Steph. And Jo.'

She felt a tiny flutter of breath shake her chest. '*You all knew?*'

The rabbit was round the back of Kassy's chair now. He started peeling off Post-it notes and thumbed them carefully against the chair, against her legs. Her shoulders, her hair. Lots of odd drawings that looked like flowers but were shaped like crosses. And birds feeding their young. Many of them peeled away and floated to the floor. But some of them stuck fast. 'These might save you. Give you a chance on the other side.'

'Please,' Kassy said.

He peeled off the last one and stuck it to her forehead. Then he dug into his other pocket and pulled something bigger out. He flicked his hand, and shook something out. A thick, transparent, plastic bag.

He leant across to a wooden table that had an old tape recorder on it. One that she instantly recognised, because it was hers. Her Alba DR-160. This was the machine she first used to tape and log the sounds of her life, building up her first ever audio library. She'd filled C-90 tapes with the noise of doors closing, taps running, birds in the trees of the park, and of course . . . voices.

The recorder that went missing during the poltergeist.

He pushed his fat finger into a button and she heard that familiar, exquisite plastic click.

One of her old tapes started whirring, she heard a hiss, then Holly's voice filled the room singing an old song from primary school. 'My Grandfather's Clock'.

Rachel closed her eyes. Her voice so thin, so delicate.

Happy.

My grandfather's clock was too large for the shelf, so it stood ninety years on the floor.

Kassy was shaking her head from side to side, immaculate hair now grimy with sweat and tears.

It was taller by half than the old man himself, though it weighed not a pennyweight more.

The rabbit walked up behind Kassy, opening the plastic bag.

Kassy begged, 'Stop it, please, stop it. Stop it.'

It was bought on the morn of the day that he was born,

'. . . for God's sake . . .'

and was always his treasure and pride.

'Rabbit does . . . what rabbit should,' it said. Stretched the bag.

But, it stopped, short, never to go again, when the old man died.

And all Rachel could do was look away.

'I didn't mean it. It was a joke.'

Somehow Rachel felt nothing as it happened. Nothing as the shouts turned to screaming. And finally to a hideous begging. As Kassy called out, 'I'm sorry, I'm sorry. I didn't mean it. God forgive me, I didn't mean it. Holly, I'm sorry.' Rachel heard a crunch of plastic and then Kassy's voice sounded muffled and very far away. Saying the same thing over and over. 'I'm sorry. Holly. I'm sorry. I'm sorry.'

The words quickly moved into rhythmic, screaming roars and Rachel closed her eyes and filtered all sounds out except Holly's sweet singing. And she sang too, lips in the dirt.

Ninety years without slumbering, (tick, tock, tick, tock).

Perhaps if she simply kept her eyes shut, and kept singing, she would die too. Maybe she'd sink into the floor and drift into the deep darkness that lives at the heart of the world. And maybe she'd find Holly there. She hoped so. More than anything in the world she hoped for that. Then they could hold hands and talk and laugh and sing. And walk on cold stone floors for ever. And all would be well.

CHAPTER FIFTY-NINE

A woman was screaming. Muffled and quiet but unmistakable.

Matt hammered the chair harder and harder, wincing with the pain in his arm. And on the second blow the cheap metal padlock finally snapped open. He shoved his shoulder against the door and it opened halfway. Then it stopped with a soft thud. He squeezed through the gap, and found Joyce Hodges shivering in the corner. Her hair was a wild fright wig and her fingernails were snapped from clawing at the door.

'Joyce?'

She stared through him.

'Are you hurt?'

She shook her head. 'There's a body down there.'

He flashed the phone light down and he felt his heart plummet. He saw a heap at the far end of the corridor.

'Who is it?'

'A man . . .' she said, in a voice that was little more than a long drone. 'A dead man.'

He tugged her away from the wall and helped her to her feet. 'Joyce, the door's open. Bob's through there and he needs you, okay?'

She stared again, nodding slowly. He had to physically turn her to guide her through the door.

Then he let go of her arm and skidded his feet along the dusty floor of the corridor. This one was wider than the first, with bits of rubbish strewn about. There were loose bricks too. But these things were shimmering in the corner of his vision because he was bounding toward a doorway and the lump, with one of the bricks in his hand.

It looked like a bundle of clothes. A bundle of clothes with a person inside them.

A young man, about Jo Finch's age.

He lay in the dirt, with cable ties tight around his wrists and his ankles, with doll's eyes staring wide and dead into the gloom. His stomach had been hollowed out into a ragged hole, filled with things that were not connected any more. The sharp teeth of his ribcage jutted through the gristle.

Jo's boyfriend, Lee.

Matt gagged into his hand and he knew the rabbit hadn't done this. This was the dog's work. Any guilt about snapping it in two vanished at once.

He couldn't look at it.

So he pushed on the door instead. He was dreading it being locked while simultaneously hoping like hell that it *would* be locked. That this steady stream of trauma was done. But when he pushed it softly, it swung completely open and he was flooded in red, glowing light.

What he saw stopped him dead.

Directly in front of him someone was tied to a chair, with a plastic bag over her head. He knew it was Kassy by the mass of blonde hair that was trapped and splayed under there. She was jerking and twitching. The toes of her bare feet were curling. And at the other side of the room, a tall figure in a mask was dragging bricks and breeze blocks toward Rachel who was tied to pegs on the floor.

Tiny pieces of paper were scattered around them both. Some stuck to their heads and arms. Lily crosses and pelicans. Symbols of salvation and restoration that said God could make even the worst of sinners righteous again.

Matt silently stepped up behind Kassy and grabbed each side of the bag. He tore a ragged, gaping hole across her mouth.

Her terrible, wheezing gasp filled the room.

The figure snapped its head around and stood up tall.

He ripped the plastic away from Kassy's head but his eyes were locked on the six foot rabbit dressed in black. Before Matt could even compute what he was seeing, the thing was pulling something from a strap on his back.

A Stanley knife.

Oh, shit.

The rabbit man started looking around. He jerked his latex face down at the hefty blade in his hand, then to Rachel on the floor. Then he sprang off, walking slowly towards Matt.

'Jerry?'

The rabbit froze.

'It's me, Matt. Remember? From the coffee shop? You spilt a drink on me?'

The rabbit tilted its head.

'Jerry, listen . . . this isn't the way.'

Jerry stood motionless for a few seconds, other than the subtle blade swinging from his hanging left hand. His eyes drifted to Kassy, and the plastic bag that now hung around her neck like a ragged scarf.

'Don't,' Jerry said. 'Don't remove that. Please.'

'This isn't right.' Matt gripped the brick.

Then Jerry took a step forward. 'You can't mess with this.'

Next to Rachel was a pile of bricks and rocks. Jerry had been stacking them on her, trying to crush her chest and asphyxiate her. A classic method of execution for witches. But so far he'd only put a few of them in place meaning she wasn't in massive danger. So Matt wasn't going to risk the Stanley knife by rushing over, like he wanted.

'He's a child molester,' Kassy said suddenly, through wincing coughs. She wheezed with the pain of breath and speech but was desperate to get her point across. 'He thinks we're witches who make him touch kids but he's mental. I came down into this hole to get Rachel then he pounced on me and dragged me down here.'

'Take off your mask, Jerry.' Matt said it gently. 'Would you do that for me?'

He shook his head.

'Please?'

'Do I have to?'

Matt frowned at that and waited for a moment. Surprised at how submissive Jerry was being. Why wasn't he just flinging himself forward and breaking Matt's neck in those blood covered hands of his?

He wasn't quite sure where the idea came from, though in the thick of stress who knows where such things are generated. Perhaps in madness, perhaps in wisdom. Often in panic. But wherever it came from, his hands and body had begun to obey the idea. Because the rabbit was nearly on him and he knew full well that the crumbling brick in his hand would do nothing against this beast and his knife.

So Matt reached down and yanked at the masks around his ankle. They sprang free instantly. A deflated goat face lay on the floor, staring at Kassy. While an owl dangled from his hand.

Jerry slowed to a stop. Watching all of this curiously.

Matt lifted the owl mask and slid it over his head.

* * *

395

'Jerry Marlowe!' Matt shouted. 'What the devil do you think you're doing?'

Jerry took a single step backwards, knife in hand.

'What's all this?' Matt the Owl took a step forward. His voice was pumped with low, cold authority. He saw Rachel turn her head and look at him. Baffled and horrified, but wise enough to stay silent. 'Well?'

'I . . .' Jerry said. 'I want it to end.'

'Then put that knife away.'

Jerry looked down at his hand then jumped when Matt shouted again.

'Do it *now*! And take your mask off.'

He shook his head. 'Do I have to?'

'Yes, you do have to. Take it off. Take it all off.' There was something vile about the tone Matt was using. Something that made his stomach ache with nausea, but he couldn't think of what else to do. So he kept on stoking those memories of subservience, barking out instructions from behind the rubber. 'Take it off.'

Just do what they tell you, mate. Get it over with, it's the best way.

Jerry's shoulders shrank as he dropped the knife into his pocket.

'And the mask,' Matt said, more gently this time. 'Take it off, son.'

'I'm not like the rest of you,' Jerry said, then he actually did what he was told. He peeled the mask back to reveal a bald head drenched in sweat beads trickling down his temples and streaking his cheeks. Though there were tears there too, Matt could tell that. It all glowed deep red in the light. 'I need them to stop doing this to me.'

'But they aren't the ones to blame. You have to let them go.'

'Pastor says the Devil's behind every bad thing, and these are *definitely* the girls who threw Holly dow—'

Matt frowned. 'Blame the people from this place, not them. It started with them.'

He was blinking repeatedly, looking at the floor. 'Blame *you*, you mean?'

'That's right.' He drew in a breath of the rubber owl mask and the thick air. 'We're the ones to hate. Not these girls. Hate us.'

'I don't want to hate you . . .' He started to chew his thumb. 'I'm scared to hate you.'

'Then, I'll get you help. Do you understand?'

'You mean *prison*? You want me to go back to prison?' Jerry staggered a few steps back, mask dangling from his chunk of a hand. 'It's as bad as it was down here.' A fresh horror riddled his face now, with an awful implication of what he'd experienced inside. Eyes flooded with panic and sorrow, veins pulsed in his neck, and Matt saw that little lonely boy again. The one in the photograph of all those naked kids.

Kassy suddenly broke the silence. 'You *are* going to prison, Jerry, but this time it's going to be a thousand times worse.'

Matt looked at her and shook his owl head.

'And even if you kill us,' Kassy went on, 'you're still going to go there and live there, and probably die there. Aaaaaall alone.'

Matt put a hand out. 'Kassy.'

'You are going to prison, Jerry. The police are coming and they're almost here.' Kassy's chest was heaving and her eyes were flashing full of life. Her voice sounded different. Lower. 'And you absolutely are going to be pounded up the arse for the rest of your pathetic life. So listen to me—'

Matt took a step, pulling off his mask. 'Kassy, shut up.'

'So if you want this to end, Jerry, then why don't you get that knife of yours and shove it in your neck.'

Jerry slowly – very slowly – stepped towards her.

'Ignore her,' Matt said. 'Just hang tight and we'll get you

397

help. There are ways to deal with this.' The sentiment seemed phenomenally naïve. 'Just put it down.'

'Nah, Rabbit, you hold on to it,' Kassy said; and then in a seductive whisper she said, 'Down the hill for suicide, a thousand times, to end your ride.'

Jerry was walking toward Kassy, transfixed by her voice, like it was the sweetest music he'd ever heard. Rachel said nothing. Just stared at it all, like a slowly blinking corpse on the floor.

'My poem,' Jerry whispered.

'Shut up, Kassy,' Matt said. 'Shut up.'

'Time to tear a light in shadows, almost there, almost there. Rabbit does . . .'

'. . . what rabbit should,' Jerry said. 'Will I be free?'

'Like a bird,' Kassy said. 'One last task for us, Rabbit, because we really *are* witches and we always will be. Just like I told you we were. So one final act of misery and then we'll be full up and we'll leave you alone. And you can rest in heaven for ever and we'll find someone else. Maybe Matthew, here. And Holly's up there too, you know? In heaven. She wants to see you. She wants to forgive you. They're all there.'

'Stop!' Matt couldn't believe what he was hearing. What was Kassy – *was it Kassy?* – thinking? He turned to Jerry. 'Give me the knife. This is ending right now.'

'Get that thing and shove it deep into your little neck, before the police get here. Then all the sadness is going to stop. But Rabbit, I swear to you, that if you don't . . .' She flashed her teeth, and for a second her face grew weirdly dark, her cheeks thin, and her eyes bulging. 'We'll have them gut you in prison. Do you hear me, boy? They will gut you.'

Matt glared at her. At those narrowing eyes and the push of her lips: that low scuttle of a voice that made him half-expect a lizard's tongue to come darting out. As if he wasn't hearing the voice of a thirty-year-old woman but some ancient, striding thing that had made its home down here long ago, giddy at the hope of new blood.

But he noticed Rachel was silent, not encouraging Kassy, but not stopping her either.

'Do it for Holly, and I promise we will never ever ask you to do it again.' Kassy smiled at him. 'Listen, Rabbit . . . jailer's coming.'

Jerry was now swaying on his huge feet, like he'd heard those words a million times in his life, but perhaps now they made sense. When he finally *did* speak it was one tiny word that felt small and obedient, as if he was nine years old. 'Okay,' he said. 'Okay.'

'Wait,' Matt called out. 'Jerry.'

But he was already pulling the rabbit mask back on and he rushed for the door. Then just like that, he was gone, and it was just the three of them in a horrible, red cave.

Matt looked at Kassy and for a dangerous second he considered leaving her down here for ever. But the malice that was in her just a moment ago had gone completely. Now she wept bitterly, sobbing onto her chest like a little girl. A different person entirely.

'Why?' Matt said to her. 'Why did you say all that?'

And all she could say was, 'I don't know . . . I don't know.'

Rachel wasn't crying, she was staring at the ceiling, unable to speak or look in Kassy's direction. Then she turned her head to him and noticed the look in his eye. She shook her head.

He turned for the door.

'What do you think you're doing?' Rachel called out. 'Just leave him.'

Kassy wept.

'Leave him,' she shouted. Pleaded. '*Let* him.'

But Matt ran.

CHAPTER SIXTY

He raced out of the room, refusing to look at Lee's open carcass lying in the dirt. Then, with ankle-stabbing footsteps he pounded and hobbled back up the rubbish-strewn corridor. He was shocked at the amount of insects he could now see swarming across the floors. He was also suddenly aware that the vaults were probably not as big as he'd imagined. They were just packed in with tunnels turning back onto themselves so that it was like those hedge mazes where you feel like you're stumbling for ages until you see it from higher up and it looks embarrassingly small. But right now he was *in* it, not above it, and he was starting to lose his bearings. He couldn't quite work out where he crawled into this pit in the first place.

When he got to the end he slammed his good shoulder into the door where he'd found Joyce, calling out through the pain. He tried to holler out to Keech and the rest to brace themselves while the now lockless door swung open and cracked against the wall.

But Jerry Phillip Marlowe hadn't rushed through the other door to where the others were. He was still in his little room that stank of rubber, on his bed, mask still on. He was curled in the corner, clutching the sheets of newspaper to his chest. Matt stepped forward to speak but felt a spasm of shock.

The papers were already rapidly turning wet with blood. All those girls' names and Jerry's too, now in the stream of what was flowing out of him. And somewhere in those papers was that strange little book of his poems, and Holly smiling on the swing. Her darkening smile joining with his blood and becoming a part of him. Fluids joining. Souls entwining. Becoming one.

Effluvia, Matt thought, and shivered.

Jerry's arm lolled out to the side and the sodden Stanley knife clattered out of his hand. Matt leapt down to grab the newspapers. He started stuffing them back around Jerry's throat to force the slit back together.

Blood gushed hot against his hand and Matt could feel the rhythmic pulse of the flow. All the while Matt kept wondering what he was doing here and why his own heart was cracking. If he shouldn't just throw himself back and let this murdering child molester die. Maybe it was because Jerry was wearing that damn rabbit mask so that all Matt could visualise was somebody else inside it. Not Jerry the man, but a terrified, lonely little boy. As if *that* was who really lived under there, even after all these years, and not the monstrosity he would become.

He heard a new sudden sound. The metal door from the adjoining dog room must have been heaving open, and a flurry of frantic voices filled the space, echoing everywhere. And Jerry said something, just as the pulse of blood was starting to slow. He said, 'They'll leave me alone now. Won't they, sir?'

Sir, like Matt was his teacher. Like he was staff.

'Won't they? They'll keep their promise?'

He went to reply but the door behind him burst inwards and two officers scrambled towards the bed. 'Step aside,' they shouted.

Matt let go of the papers and fell hard against the desk, though he felt no pain as his shoulder cracked into the wooden frame. And he saw Larry hurry into the room, heaving breath and holding his back. Mouth dropping open in shock. 'Jesus Christ.'

Matt could barely speak. He just pointed his wet, trembling hand toward the other door and said, 'Rachel . . . Kassy . . .'

Larry looked at the door and shouted for the others to come running. The room filled with the buzz of radio static, the scramble of echoed feet.

Matt couldn't remember the exact point when Jerry Marlowe died. He just heard a long, bubbling groan come from his throat, then Jerry was still. But he did remember one of the officers asking Matt if he was alright, because he'd noticed that Matt had started shivering and hugging his knees. Right there in front of those policemen, right in front of Larry. And it was almost impossible to work out what exact horror it was that was making that happen. There really were so many to choose from. But he could somehow hear a breeze in the room now. Unmistakable and real. Holly in the shadows, sitting with him. And perhaps that was what really did it, when Matt felt a little hand lacing into his, telling him that he was safe now. That despite what he had begun to think, that he would see his wife and kids again.

But still, Matt couldn't remember exactly when Jerry died. He just remembered hiding his own face, right into hands that were drenched in animal and human blood, and he was unable to speak or look on anything else. And Larry and the other policemen stood there patiently, not rushing it. Just looking at the floor in silence, waiting for Matt to open his eyes again.

It took a while.

CHAPTER SIXTY-ONE

Matt looked up. Larry was walking into the hospital cafeteria to join him. He nodded to a night nurse with a doff of some invisible cap, like some 1940s gentleman. He had a Tesco Express carrier bag dangling from his hand. He'd taken off his tie.

Matt spun the wheelchair in his direction, but Larry hurried toward him, palms up. 'Don't strain yourself.'

'Nah, I'm fine. I'm pretty good on this thing.' Matt nodded to a high-backed chair. It was pushing midnight, so they'd stopped serving drinks from the counter. He had an insipid tea from the machine instead. 'Pull up a pew.'

Larry laughed and slid into the chair next to Matt, sinking into it with a groan.

'How's the foot?'

'Throbbing like hell, but it seems like I've avoided rabies. Which is a bonus.'

For a moment they said nothing. They just looked out of the large glass windows of the cafe that stretched from ceiling to floor, with black and orange streamers hanging. The lounge overlooked a hill swooping down to a stretch of grass and a crop of trees. The branches swayed silently in the darkness. In the corner a TV screen was playing some late night Halloween movie. It looked like *Night of the Living Dead* from here.

'So, do you reckon you'll actually get home tonight?' Matt said.

'It's hectic. Lots going on downstairs, but I'm okay. I'm *really* okay, actually.'

'You want a coffee?'

'I got you a present.' He lifted up his plastic bag.

'You know I didn't really want that dead bird back. You can keep it.'

'Shhh.' Larry looked left and right, then opened the bag up and pulled out two mini bottles of Jack Daniel's. 'Bit small, I know. And you're probably on medicat—'

'I'd lick whisky off the floor right now.'

'That's the ticket.' Larry spun the tops off. For a few moments they just sipped and breathed, sipped and breathed. Smiling at the occasional staff member who wandered up to the vending machines. Whenever that happened they'd both clasp their hands completely around the contraband mini bottles and give solemn nods, as if in prayer.

'Are the Hodges still okay?' Matt said. 'And Keech?'

'Keech is going to be fine. And at least they're going to be able to save Bob's leg. He appreciates what you did for him. Oh, and he says he'll wash your jacket and get it—'

'I don't want the jacket.'

He laughed. 'I told him you'd say that.'

'And Kassy?'

'Physically speaking, fine. Mentally, though? God knows.' Larry waited for a few moments and took another sip. 'She wants to see Rachel; says she wants to talk about Holly.'

Matt looked down at his hands. 'Rachel was in here a couple of hours ago, sitting with her mum. They were talking for ages. Both of them were sitting upstairs with the Hodges.' He nodded to the wards above. 'Joyce says Holly wasn't angry with Rachel – or any of them, in fact. She was just trying to warn them.' He sniffed and shook his head. 'It's just all so miserable, isn't it? Little boy gets warped by a bunch of perverts with full access. I'm not excusing what he did, but . . .'

'At some point you've got to take the blame.'

'True, and I guess Jerry never could.' Matt flexed his fingers. They were still stiff from holding that bloody brick.

'They do stuff like that, sometimes. Killers. They act like they never *really* did the things they did. Like it was someone else's fault. Sometimes they blame God or the devil . . .'

'And sometimes they blame witches.'

'. . . and sometimes they blame witches.'

Larry blew out a long, sad breath. 'He must have snagged some vault keys when he was a kid and held on to them all his life. Probably hid them locally while he was in prison so when he got out he could go back.' Larry stopped speaking and took a quick drink. 'To where he felt safe, I guess. Weird.'

'Did you save any of the newspapers he had? The list of names?'

'Most of them, and the photocopies of the naked boys.' Larry cleared his throat. 'You realise he slipped a copy of that into the Hodges' bag at school.'

'I was starting to wonder that.'

'I guess he thought Holly might tell Bob or Joyce what he'd done to her. Maybe he told Holly that he'd hurt them, and so he did, in his way. Got them in the shit at school, at least.' Larry ran his hand through his hair. 'As for those reports of other girls . . . we're working through them, but they're scattered all over the country. He must have travelled. Tried to get away from here, though he couldn't really get away. Not in the end. Obviously we'll contact the families and follow them all up. And just hope to God that none of them spiralled down like Holly Wasson did.' Matt spotted Larry throw most of his drink down his throat at the mention of her name. 'At least we have a pretty good idea that the perv hanging around the local schools won't be coming back. Seems that was Jerry.' He looked down at his shoes, and kept his gaze there.

'Are you okay?'

'You know what, Matt? I think you're wrong about this spirit stuff. This demonology thing. I'm thinking there's something to it.'

'Even when the poltergeist was faked? He turned up in the mask, climbed up on her roof. Got into the house and stole stuff, turned sofas over. Said if she told anybody she'd be in trouble. There's nothing supernatural about—'

'Don't you get this feeling, though?' He was looking at one of the strip lights above them. It was flickering. He put his fingertips against his chest. 'In here, I mean. That Holly's at peace now. Does that sound ridiculous? That I feel like she's . . . like she's resting now? That she got him to stop?'

Matt kept quiet.

'We informed Steph's husband, Greg, of what happened tonight . . . which reminds me. Josh Ellis gave me a message for you.'

Matt sat up. Pictured himself with the kid sitting in front of Scooby Doo. 'Yeah?'

'He says . . .' Larry dug into his inside pocket and pulled out a sliver of torn paper, about the size of a train ticket. A note was scrawled in kid's pencil. Larry squinted to read it out. 'Thank you for killing the bad thing.'

Matt still said nothing.

'Well . . .' Larry said, spotting Matt's discomfort, and raised the tiny dregs of his bottle. 'To Steph Ellis and Jo Finch and to Holly Wasson. Rest for ever in peace, girls.'

'And to Lee . . . . what was his second name?'

'Bradshaw.'

They held up their bottles and clinked them together. 'To Lee Bradshaw.' Then they swigged and winced.

'By the way, that bottle Pastor Todd was carrying . . . it was holy water.'

Matt closed his eyes and chuckled for some reason.

'He still thinks he and his clan were furthering the cause of the church. The cross, the note under your wiper. Anyway . . .' He shifted in his chair. 'And Matt, I want to thank you. I mean really thank you. If you hadn't gone down there tonight and found them . . .' He went to stand. 'Are you going to be okay, on your own?'

'I'll be fine.'

'Matt, I'm serious.' He felt Larry's hand on his shoulder. 'Are you okay, mate? Do you need anything?'

'Wren's on her way,' he smiled at him. 'It's gonna be a long night explaining all of this.'

'Maybe that's because some things are unexplainable,' he said. 'See you later, Matt. And thanks again.'

He nodded and watched Larry walk down the corridor; he slowed only to look back at the flickering light for a few moments. Then he buttoned his jacket and vanished through the door.

The doors slid shut and Matt was alone in the cafe. Tea steaming while silent zombies scratched at a farmhouse on the silent screen. He wished he could find the remote.

He checked his phone again, and read the text from Wren that he'd been reading over and over since he got it an hour back.

Amelia's sleeping in her own room with the light off! Says the shadow's finally gone. Result! xxw

He stared at that for a long moment, wondering if Amelia's bad thing was the same as Josh's bad thing. The black rabbit demon that Joyce had said fuelled Jerry. He felt a prickle of cold and heard the echo of Larry's voice.

Don't you get this feeling . . . that Holly's resting now? That she got him to stop?

Then Joyce in his ear . . . Matthew . . . what if there are such things?

'Yeah, right,' he said to the empty room, then looked up at the TV on the wall. He could call a nurse in to change the channel. Sit in here and watch mindless chat shows until Wren turned up to whisk him away to normality. But just as he turned his wheelchair, the lights of the cafe flickered more frantically than before. Then after a click, they went out. All of them. The TV too.

The windows lost all their reflections.

The cafe was suddenly black.

Now he just saw darkness outside and the much clearer strip of trees and bushes, and the hill swooping down. He saw a gravel path winding near a tree. And standing in the treeline, he saw a black figure emerge. Thin and spindly. He slapped his hands on his wheels instantly and went to back away.

But he frowned. Despite himself, he pushed himself forward towards the window. Because he knew it couldn't be *Jerry* again.

Joyce's voice again: *It's not Jerry. It's what was* in *Jerry. And is now* out *of Jerry.* The black rabbit needs a new home.

Trick of the light. Trick of the dark. Whatever it was, the shadows fell in a very particular way. He knew that in essence they were random patterns of light and shade. Shapes that if Joyce or Bob or Rachel had been here, would have had them squealing rabbit and running for the door.

His heart started to pound. God, that did look like a tall rabbit. Which made him shake his head.

It's nothing. It's you reading order into chaos.

It was moving. Swaying from side to side. A tall black figure.

You skipped rabies and got apophenia instead.

It took a step forward and he thought he might be trembling.

A cloud crossed the moon, and the shadow moved a little. Like an arm rising up and pointing across the grass at him. He felt the blood in his veins turn slowly to sludge.

The breeze threw leaves against the window, and the breeze said his name.

Maaaaaaatttttthew. His mother's voice. Or rather something trying to sound like her. *Mama neeeeeeed.*

He lost a breath.

There are such things.

Then he heard an electric buzz and a mechanical click, and the lights flickered back into life. A nurse with John Lennon glasses suddenly popped her head in.

'Sorry about that,' she said. 'Got someone fixing it now. You okay?'

He didn't speak. Just nodded.

'Call me if you need me,' she said, 'and happy Halloween!'

He looked back out and saw nothing but trees and shapes and shadows that were shadows and nothing more. There was a thick signpost that could have been the shape. *Could* have been.

Not could have been, his mind shouted, was!

Still though, he wheeled himself back to grab his tea. He wanted to laugh at his moment of weakness, because that's what he felt it was. A weakness. An ironic dose of belief.

But he didn't laugh. And he didn't grab the tea either. Or the empty bottles of whisky.

In fact, he didn't even stop to do anything, because he would prefer to be away from that window and was wheeling himself fast from the cafe and into the reception. He'd wait for Wren there, and when she turned up they'd talk about Amelia and Lucy and he'd find out what they'd been up to today. He'd ask her how work was. They'd plan a meal for all four of them. A restaurant. Ice cream. Bowling. All things normal. All things good.

And until Wren and the real world returned he'd wait in this bright reception near the nurse and her goofy smile. Where his brain wouldn't scramble around for meaningless data. Where there was sound and there were people. Heels on floor. Words in the air. And where the lights would stay on and do what light did best. Keep the lying shadows away.

For now.

CHAPTER SIXTY-TWO

Rabbit resting in the soil,
Turning over, crumbling in.
Letting out its veins and sinews.
Growing flowers in its skin.
Folding in its limbs and fingers,
Hiding every stick and pin.
Making shadows dance and spin.
Weeping is its violin.
Till he climbs back up again.
to
Wake

ACKNOWLEDGEMENTS

I'm filled with thanks to the trusty team who unhooked this novel from my head and installed it into yours. To my agent, Joanna Swainson, whose bright-eyed wisdom brought the story life and definition, and to my fine publisher, Allison & Busby, who gave *Unleashed* a home, particularly Lesley Crooks, Susie Dunlop and Daniel Scott. It's been fantastic to have genuine, proper 'book people' champion Matt Hunter and his quirky tales of fright and crime. I also thank my editors Kelly Smith and Fliss and Simon Bage, who were amazing at spotting my mistakes, both large and small (such as the fact that Sugar Puffs changed its name to Honey Monster Puffs in 2014. I had no idea! In the end I made the Hodges eat Coco-Pops for breakfast instead). Thanks also go to Christina Griffiths, who not only designed the cool cover image, but has also given this series such a striking visual identity on the shelf. I want to thank Emma Finnigan too. She's a PR whizz with a terrific superpower, she can open all sorts of media doors. Thanks go to all the magazines, newspapers and book bloggers who reviewed my first novel, *Purged*. Seeing such widespread praise was quite the tonic, after years of getting publishers' rejection slips.

The next one on the list isn't really a thanks . . . it's more of a businesslike acknowledgement of the demon black rabbit that a vicar claimed was standing next to me one Sunday evening. Yeah, that's right . . . in the early years of my Christianity, a church minister insisted he'd seen a tall black shape following me around and that it was standing at my shoulder in a Lancaster church. Imagine my shock when I even saw it myself a few weeks later, walking toward me in a hotel room in Blackpool. Perhaps I shouldn't have been so surprised by its arrival. After all, it looked so very similar to the frightening black figure my friends and I saw crouching on a roof one night, back when we were teenagers. We'd hopped the fence of a former hospital for miners and were looking for ghosts. We saw a black humanoid shape standing on the roof, and when it turned its head to stand, we ran too, just like Rachel Wasson and her friends. 'Course, whether all these appearances of a tall black rabbit were real or just the product of collective apophenia, who's to say? But hey . . . I got a book out of it, at least, along with images that I'll never, ever forget.

Thanks go to Mikayla Shuttleworth, a lovely dog behaviourist I met on the 'parent and toddler circuit'. After much coaxing in a playgroup, she finally explained to me an effective way to kill a dog barehanded. I've always wondered if any of the other parents overheard that conversation, but the RSPCA are thankfully yet to call. I want to thank some of the folk who read *Unleashed* in its early form, too (when its working title was *Black Rabbit*), and my gratitude goes once again to Jan Evans, who looked after my young son a few days a week so I could actually get out and write this thing. She's one of life's gems.

Heartfelt thanks goes to that extra special treasure, my mam, to whom this entire book is dedicated. Even in the thickest darkness she manages to find something to joke about, a skill I hope you see reflected in Matt Hunter sometimes too. To my sister Julie and my brother Norman, I say thank you. They've shared and reshared my book stuff so much, they're like a little PR team in themselves. They rock, and I'm blessed to have them in my life.

And of course my thanks go to you, the reader, who has tugged this off a shelf be it digital or real. Writing novels is a team effort, a joint journey, as you've seen above. But let's face it . . . you're the one that truly matters, because you were always the destination of this story. Even before I knew it myself, it had your name written on it. It was written for your brain, your bag, your shelf, your device, your heart, and I just hope it threw a few shadows into your world, at least for a little while.

In many ways *Unleashed* is about the human desire to find patterns in the jumble of life's experience. So it seems fitting to offer my deepest thanks to God, my wonderful wife Joy and my children Emma and Adam, because I've noticed that whenever they breathe, they seem to bring order and meaning to the chaos.

So there you have it. The proverbial second album, which tells a story that really matters to me. But then I tend to find, it's the oddest ones that often do.

Peter Laws, a Bedfordshire coffee shop, March 2017.